MR. BOARDWALK

Louis Greenstein

MR. BOARDWALK

a novel

NEW DOOR BOOKS
Philadelphia   2014

NEW DOOR BOOKS
An imprint of P. M. Gordon Associates, Inc.
2115 Wallace Street
Philadelphia, Pennsylvania 19130
U.S.A.

This is a work of fiction. Any resemblance herein to actual persons, living or
dead, or to actual events or locales is purely coincidental.

Library of Congress Control Number: 2014932100
ISBN 978-0-9788636-7-8

Cover design by Miriam Seidel

To Catherine, Barry, Hannah and Sam

If you want to know the true nature of a hero,
ask his children.

—*Chinese Proverb*

Prologue

Atlantic City, New Jersey
March 1999

THE CASINOS ARE more ostentatious than I expected, but the souvenir shops and frozen custard stands look the same as when I was a kid: reliably, comfortably tacky.

The air is so blustery my ears prickle. I hitch my jacket collar to staunch the chill. Gripping the boardwalk railing, I study the beach. Four shaggy teenage boys toss a football. A middle-aged couple walks a shepherd-collie, straining on its leash, barking into the wind. Beyond the shoreline the water's choppy, the tide's low. A hundred yards out, whitecaps flash like static. In the distance an ocean liner glides across the horizon.

This is where I got my start as a soft-pretzel baker, boardwalk shill and juggler—all before I was ten years old. Later, in the early 1980s, I juggled in college theaters and rock-and-roll clubs, opening for groups like Pure Prairie League and the Nitty Gritty Dirt Band. For a while I traveled with a New Vaudeville revue—magicians, sword swallowers, contortionists and a punkish brass band that played Balkan waltzes. I got my higher education on road trips from New Orleans to Boulder to San Francisco, in midnight diners and public libraries, in moldy youth hostels and flickering Motel 6's.

Now, fourteen years into marriage, I am the father of a teenage daughter who disdains me. A year ago my wife Eileen called me "detached." Three months ago she changed her assessment to "disaffected." She is seriously considering leaving me. She says I've built a wall that separates me from the people I love. Other than her and our daughter, everyone I loved is gone. First they lied to me, and then they disappeared.

I feel a rustle. Eileen is at my side, squinting at the ocean. I can guess what she's thinking: *You really blew it this time, Jason. I don't know if I can forgive you, but you have today to explain yourself.* She studies boards and beach as if everything I recognized were a fresh betrayal.

Like the veteran street performer I am, I tell myself: *Tough crowd.* But I can't shake the jitters like I used to.

Beyond the breakers there's a sudden swell, a natural pull and drift. I watch the water swirl. I think about the calm below the surface.

A question hovers like a purple cloud: Why didn't I tell Eileen until three days ago that I have owned a house here for the past twenty-two years? I want to ignore that issue. It's not a big deal, right? On the vast scale of marital duplicities, not telling your wife you own a rental property is on the low end.

No, I hear her unspoken answer. *When you share your life with someone, you don't omit something as big as a house. If you do, there's an even bigger reason.*

I left this place when I was eighteen, and rarely thought about it until last December, when, coincidentally, I learned two things the same week: that a marketing analyst I work with grew up here, and that my cholesterol was off the charts. The analyst, Jennifer, was the first person from Atlantic City I've met in all these years. I knew better than to talk with her about it; I knew the trouble it could create. In retrospect, that's why I blundered into her cubicle to talk about Atlantic City. I was ready to tell Eileen, but afraid to approach her directly. So I forced my own hand. And the more Jennifer and I talked, the more I recalled the smell of crabs and funnel cake, the shuffle of sandy feet, the cling of salt water.

I returned today because I promised the therapist I would tell Eileen and our daughter Ruth about the house and my childhood here. Over the past few weeks, he has pressed me for details about my boardwalk summers. He thought it unusual that despite my colorful memories—not to mention my real estate holding—I haven't set foot here since 1978.

"I haven't been back to Atlantic City," I finally told him, "because it isn't there. It changed. I moved on." The therapist nodded. I added, "I don't know why I never told them. They know about my years out west. That counts, right?"

He shifted in his chair and jutted his wide, doughy jaw. "So you haven't gone back because it's changed? I'm a little surprised you're not curious about what it's like these days."

"I'm not sure what you mean." I felt a headache coming. Therapy had not been my idea but Eileen's, and my employer's—their recommendations coming, improbably, within twenty-four hours of each other. "Why would I be curious about that?"

The therapist raised his hands, supplicating me. "I'm just saying, most of the year, you were an unhappy kid, and with good reason. But every summer you were on top of the world. You've told Eileen and Ruth about growing up and juggling on the streets in Philadelphia, but nothing of Atlantic City—even though you have this connection, this *real* connection? That's unusual, wouldn't you say? And I'm surprised you're not curious about what's happening there."

"But there's no *there* there," I said. "It's all casinos. All the old places are gone. I don't gamble or drink, I don't like oldies acts. I don't patronize prostitutes. Why would I go there?"

I watched his lungs fill up and deflate. "Why'd you keep the house?" he asked.

"Well, if I sell, Eileen will, you know, find out. . . . And, I guess, the longer I go without telling her, the more impossible it gets."

At last, sitting in the therapist's office that day, I saw two possibilities: Either I drop dead of a heart attack and Eileen learns about the house, in which case she'll divorce me even though I'm dead and then she'll hate me for the rest of her life; or I don't drop dead, and she meets Jennifer at the firm's spring gala next month. Jennifer will mention my childhood in Atlantic City, and then I'll wish I'd had my heart attack.

The therapist didn't come out and say it; he didn't have to. There was a third, less dramatic possibility, which did not involve a myocardial infarction: This morning the three of us piled into the minivan and took the Garden State Parkway from Yonkers, across the bay, then down Pacific Avenue, past motels and casinos, liquor stores and pawn shops. We turned right on Virginia Avenue, a residential block of mustard-colored cottages. I parked and pointed at one.

Eileen rolled down her window. Until last Thursday she thought I'd inherited a share of an industrial investment property from my father, who'd inherited it from his uncle. I told that lie to explain the rental income we had to report to the IRS. In truth, the only thing I inherited from my father and his uncle was arteriosclerosis.

"That's it?" she asked, surveying the sagging front porch. Her first words to me in more than two hours—and one of her few comments since I came clean three nights ago. "Anyone inside?"

I shook my head. "Summer rental only."

"Can we go in?"

"Sorry. No key. I called the property manager yesterday but haven't heard back yet." Eileen fiddled with the zipper on her parka. "We can look through the windows," I said. She tightened her zipper and shrugged me off.

Ruth, in the back seat of the minivan, leaned forward. "Dad, wait, like we *own* that house? For real?"

"It doesn't even have a mortgage," I said.

"Good, 'cause it looks shabby," she snorted, drooping back against her seat, her honey-colored eyes fixed on the cottage. She's barely spoken to me for six weeks, since the night I lost my temper and humiliated her in front of her friends.

"All right," I said, opening my door and stretching my legs toward the street. "Let's hit the boardwalk." We climbed out of the minivan. "But first . . ." I trotted up the cracked cement path to the house. Eileen and Ruth followed hesitantly. "I'm just gonna take a quick look." I put the heel of each hand on the east-side window and peered inside. The living room was dim and sparsely furnished: a flimsy plaid sofa, a TV with rabbit ears, a card table and an oak hutch filled with cheap plates and snow globes. I puffed my cheeks and exhaled, fogging the windowpane. "I'll call again. Maybe we can get inside after we walk."

Though Eileen hadn't voiced it, she must have feared the house bore secrets. A woman. A hidden life to which I've retreated when I told her I was out of town on business. None of that's true. Yet how can I convince her? The plan is to tell my story as we hike the boardwalk past my old haunts, or what's left of them. If it's not too cold and Eileen and Ruth are willing, we'll make it to the inlet at the northern end where the ocean meets the bay. The walk should take two or three hours, enough time for them to see and hear and, just maybe, understand. Forgiveness will be a longer haul. But today could be a start.

So, now we've trudged up Virginia Avenue, hunched like a mime troop walking against the wind. Up a splintered wooden ramp, along the boardwalk, past Victorian homes and reedy dunes, to the bling of casinos, restaurants and amusement piers. I'm watching Ruth tromp ahead, past the Tropicana's pillared, sandstone facade, defiant as a picketer, my little Goth girl with her raven-black hair and lipstick and raccoon-like mascara. Eileen and I hang back. We lean against the railing. I inhale through my nose. "You smell that?" I ask.

Her nostrils tic like miniature sensors. "Salt," she says, "the ocean."

"No, it's more than that."

She adjusts her floppy knit hat, tucks in her hair. She nods, her quick eyes puzzled but urging me to continue.

1

"THE BEARDED LADY's a big fat fake."

On a balmy afternoon under a cotton candy sky, Million Dollar Pier smelled like seaweed and French fries. The only money among the three of us was what Bobby had gotten from Mom and Dad, and from Norman and Betty, in exchange for keeping an eye on Lita and me for the afternoon; and Bobby had no intention of blowing his babysitting pay on a freak show. "I got a date tonight with an Irene's Fudge girl," he said. "I'm holding on to my money, and so should you. That Bearded Lady's phony."

The barker in front of the Bearded Lady's tent must have heard Bobby. The hulky redheaded man stopped mid-pitch—"*Step right up, ladies and gent . . .*" He glared at us. Bobby, sixteen and street-wise from years on the boardwalk and in gypsy camps in Florida, stuck his tongue out at the man. The three of us turned to go back to the boardwalk.

"What's a Bearded Lady?" asked Lita. She was only five—two years younger than I. She had mud-colored, curly hair, like mine, but hers was long, cascading in ringlets past her shoulders. And, like me, she was reed-thin and suntanned. Some people thought we were siblings, even though we'd met only a week earlier.

The barker hollered, "Step right up, ladies and gentlemen! Come see the In*cred*ible *Beard*ed *La*dy! Only a quarter—one thin quat-*ah*!" Lita stopped; she dug in her heels, grabbed our wrists and tugged us back toward the tent.

"It's dumb, it's fake!" Bobby said. He stooped and looked Lita in the eye. She pouted. Suddenly Bobby's face lit up. "All right, you want to see the Bearded Lady? Follow me. Be cool." He led us around to the back of the tent, by the edge of the pier, then checked both ways to make sure no one was watching. He got down on his belly, lifted a tent flap and peeked underneath. "Quick, you guys," he whispered. "There she is!"

Lita and I dropped to our bellies and slipped our heads under the flap. Inside the tent a skinny, bare-chested man sat in an easy chair, drinking a bottle of beer and reading a newspaper. He wore a thick black beard, a long green skirt and a pair of white socks. His chest was hairier than Dad's.

"That's the Bearded Lady?" I asked.

Bobby chuckled. "What'd I tell ya?"

"What's he doing?" asked Lita.

"He's taking it easy between shows." Bobby knew all about show business. His dad Jimmy ran the marionette theater next door to Dad's soft-pretzel bakery.

"But it's just a man in a dress," I said.

"Shh!" said Bobby. But it was too late; the Bearded Lady heard. When he saw us spying through the tent flaps he dropped his beer bottle. We scrambled to our feet. Lita's eyes were open wide, like she'd seen a ghost. Bobby was still grinning.

At that instant the redheaded barker appeared from around the corner of the tent, only a few feet away. "Hey! Hold it right there!" he shouted, waving his beefy sunburned arms. "I'm calling the cops!" He was so close I could see his yellow-stained teeth.

"*Run!*" cried Bobby, yanking Lita and me by our wrists and dragging us toward the midway. We wove in and out of the crowd, dodging through lines of people waiting to board rides and buy snow cones, till we stopped at the base of the Ferris wheel. No barker or Bearded Lady in sight. We were safe. "Let's beat it," said Bobby. "And you better not tell your folks!"

RUTH SEEMS TO have realized that storming ahead of Eileen and me won't push our buttons. She's free to roam the boards; we know she won't get lost. But she's circled back to join us. I think she actually wants to hear about my mysterious childhood summers. She's not looking at me; she's studying a strand of small shops on our left—polyester sweatshirts bearing vulgar slogans, a Burger King, a tattoo parlor. But I'm pretty sure she's listening.

Dad would have called the Bearded Lady incident *a matter of principle.* You don't interfere with somebody's livelihood. Bearded ladies and the guys who pitch them deserve to turn a buck like everybody else.

"Did you ever tell your dad about the Bearded Lady?" asks Ruth. As I suspected, she's listening.

"Not for a few years."

"Did he yell a lot? Was he mad all the time?"

"Not really," I say. "He was pretty happy for a while once he opened his own business. But he had his principles, and when he defended them he could get loud and sound angry."

Ruth watches a group of college-age kids emerging from Trump Plaza's triangle-shaped front entrance. Two giggling, leggy girls in little black dresses walk arm in arm, while the boys—in Gap sweaters and khakis—pump their fists in the air under the casino's wave-crested facade. They roar like young lions, like drunks at a football game.

Down here, the summer seasons played counterpoint to my dreary career in public school. Eleven years, give or take, till my abrupt departure—all of which I've trained myself not to think about. Like how we arrived here in the first place; how one night when I was in first grade, Dad came home from work and told Mom and me that he had a surprise: He was quitting Westinghouse and signing a lease on a boardwalk storefront. He was going to be a pretzel baker.

He must have had another fight with his boss. Practically every night before that, he came home mad at his boss, *that goddamn*

idiot with his goddamn small-minded office politics that stifle orig-
inal thinking! He'd sit at the dinner table, mashing his peas and
carrots with the back of his fork, grumping about how he was
born to be self-employed.

Mom set her fork on her plate. She dabbed at her mouth with
her napkin and cleared her throat. She looked across the table at
Dad and raised one eyebrow. He made a placating smile. "Judy,
trust me. I'm a Wharton School graduate. I have a business plan,
I can do this and I'm never going to work for anybody else again."

Mom twisted her napkin between her thumb and forefinger.
"Will you make enough?"

Dad looked her in the eye. "I guarantee you there's nothing to
worry about."

"What about your job security?" Mom asked.

Dad shook his head. "That's an illusion. I could get fired tomorrow. And then what? I'd have no source of income. But if I own
my own business, no corporate jackass can fire me. If I don't make
enough money, I'll sell more pretzels or cut my expenses. *That's*
job security!"

It was like the Seder at the Jewish Y a couple weeks earlier, where
we asked the Four Questions. Why was this night different from
all other nights? Because on this night Dad was joking about
bureaucratic stupidity, not complaining about *stupid bastards.*

"Atlantic City's where Mom and I fell in love," Dad said. "On
Steel Pier." He'd already told me how he'd first gone to Atlantic
City when he was a teenager to visit his great-uncle Joe, a doctor
who took care of the boardwalk merchants and workers—immigrants from Italy and Russia, gypsies and barkers from the amusement piers. "Someone had to help those people," Dad had said. "It
was the Great Depression. Nobody had money, so Uncle Joe put
it on their tab, or they'd pay him with a chicken." When Dad was
in college he worked the boardwalk as a soda jerk every summer,
scooping ice cream and mixing fountain flavors.

Now he set down his knife and fork. "I don't want to go to the
shore just on weekends." He rose from his seat and held his hand

out to Mom. He took her in his arms and waltzed her around the kitchen.

Mom was reluctant at first, but soon she gave in. "This is going to be quite an adventure!" she chirped.

My parents had their own dance. They looked like two chickens strutting and pecking, wrists on hips, necks jutted out, circling each other and whirling their waists, grinding toe to floor. They'd made up their jazzy routine when they couldn't afford Arthur Murray lessons. Our kitchen was their ballroom. Mom, dark-eyed and reedy, waggled her slender fingers while Dad, thick-framed and balding, cavorted pigeon-toed in his stocking feet, wiggling his ears, his broad lips stretched into a grin.

"You're going to love Atlantic City," Dad promised me. "You'll never want to leave!"

SEE THEM TWISTED SEE THEM BAKED!

THE SIGN EXTENDED from a pole on the bakery's roof: five feet wide by nine feet long, with a glossy white background, a red border and hand-drawn, pretzel-colored letters. Dad made up the slogan, and Mom painted the sign in the little studio Dad had built in the attic of our house. In between "TWISTED" and "SEE" she'd painted a pretzel, oven-browned and speckled with salt.

On our first day in Atlantic City, after Dad hung the sign and returned the ladder to the marionette theater, the three of us stood in the middle of the boardwalk, admiring Mom's handiwork. I liked the boardwalk's smell: Grease and sugar wafting from the takeout stands. Cigar smoke. Roasted peanuts.

Dad took off his glasses and wiped them with the tail of his Hawaiian shirt. Squinting in the sunlight, he mopped sweat from his forehead with the heel of his hand, pushing back a thin strand from his receding hairline.

Mom knew how to paint more than just signs. She painted sailboats and fruit baskets in her attic studio back home in Philadelphia. After she finished a painting, she'd carry it downstairs draped in a white sheet. She and Dad would hang it on the wall and make a big fuss about "unveiling" it.

Now Dad looked up and down the boardwalk. He smiled like he knew where a secret treasure was buried. He put his arm around Mom's shoulders and kissed her cheek. Mom put her arm around me. The three of us lingered on the boardwalk and gazed at Dad's bakery, tucked in between the marionette theater and the Two for One Arcade.

Inside the bakery, Dad and the college boys he'd hired for the summer had arranged all the equipment that he'd been storing in our garage back in Philadelphia since he announced his plan. First he bought two black Blodgett ovens, the kind you see in pizza joints. Next he found an industrial-size dough mixer and a rolling machine—a wide, canvas conveyor belt with a white iron hopper at one end where you stuff the dough. The dough in the hopper gets sliced into fist-sized chunks and then rolled into strips for hand twisting at the other end of the conveyor belt. He bought a metal vat and a wire mesh basket for dipping the pretzels in a solution made from lye and water. He bought wooden paddles for sliding the pretzels into the oven, and a dough retarder, which is like a refrigerator but not as cold. Inside it were slots for the wooden boards filled with twisted, unbaked pretzels and compartments for the bricks of springy-smelling yeast. He bought an old cash register with a bell that rang when the drawer sprung open, and a crate of yellow, plastic mustard dispensers.

"There's dough to mix and pretzels to twist," Dad said now. "Time to put on our aprons and get to work!"

After my first week in Atlantic City, the boardwalk was the center of my life. Thousands of people, young and old, swarming the custard stands and shooting galleries; bare-chested muscle boys dashing across the sand, plunging headfirst into the foamy ocean and swaggering out like James Bond. There was noise everywhere, all the time. Carnival sounds. Carousel music. Flags rippling. Gulls squawking. Waves rumbling. Fast-talking pitchmen outside

Madame Tussaud's. Wheels of Fortune clicking like ticker tapes. The clattering, rattling roller coaster at Million Dollar Pier. The clomp-clomp shuffle of a hundred thousand feet.

On one side of our bakery stood the Two for One Arcade, a humid, army-green cavern of pinball machines with names like "Zoltan" and "Mad Dogs," skeeball ramps, a photo booth and an "iron claw" that dug for prizes. Inside, the lights were dim and the games flashed and chimed like cranky robots. The air swelled with bells and whistles, sirens and mechanical voices, and clouds of cigarette smoke from the teenagers who played there. Sometimes when it rained and sales were slow, Dad gave me a handful of quarters and sent me to the Two for One. Norman and Betty, the owners, patrolled the aisles—policing fights, coaxing stalled games back to life and making change from coin dispensers clipped to their waists. Norman and Betty had no children, but they were raising Lita, who was either Betty's niece or a family friend. Dad had told me they came from "the old country"—Poland—after the war, and now they stayed year-round in Atlantic City.

I had two jobs that season. One was standing on a metal milk crate behind the counter in the bakery, ringing up sales and stuffing steaming hot pretzels into brown paper lunch bags for the customers who lined up on the boardwalk, sometimes for half a block. Behind me, Mom and Dad and the college boys—lanky, crew-cut college students—stood by the rolling machine's conveyor belt in their white tee shirts and khaki pants, snatching strips of rolled dough, twisting them into pretzels, pinching them together into neat rows of a half-dozen on wooden boards and sliding the boards into the dough retarder. In the back of the bakery, beside the mixing machine, sat the two ovens, the dipping vats and the salt tray.

My second job was shilling for the marionette theater next door. The owner, Jimmy—Bobby's dad—was a dark, wiry man with a bulbous nose, wavy black hair slicked into an enormous pompadour, and a tiny gold earring. Some days he smelled like garlic, other days like beer. Jimmy and Dad knew each other from Dad's college days when he worked the boardwalk every summer. Bobby told me I was lucky our families were friends. "Gypsies stay away from *gadjos*," he said. *Gadjo* was the gypsy word for "outsider." "But you guys ain't *gadjos*."

"What are we?" I asked.

"You're honorary gypsies."

"Norman and Betty and Lita too?"

Bobby shrugged. "Sure, why not."

One rainy day, instead of going to the arcade, I visited the marionette theater and found my second job. That day, Bobby built a marionette out of one of my toy animals—a raggedy stuffed dog named Floppy. While sheets of water pounded the tin roof, Bobby and I sat backstage, side by side on a wooden bench. Bobby worked diligently with a big needle, attaching thin strings to Floppy's head and limbs. He showed me how to work the wooden handle: level to keep Floppy still; palm down to sit; index and pinky up and down to move the legs; middle finger up and down to make his head bob. He showed me hand exercises, stretches to help isolate each finger. And he told me to practice. "Every chance you get," he said. "You can do anything if you practice."

I promised to practice every day.

"Even that dumb old Bearded Lady's gotta practice, practice, practice so he can go out and trick people," said Bobby. "And the auctioneers," he said, handing Floppy over to me so I could work the handle, "that's how they talk so fast. Practice. And that's all you got to do to get good at something. Ya do it over and over until ya can't do it no more. And then ya make yourself do some more. And then, when ya really can't do it no more, ya do some more anyways. And when you ain't practicing, you're *still* practicing in your head. Don't think about nothin' except what you're workin' on. Pretty soon you're so good everybody's going 'how the hell's he do that?' Easy answer: Practice."

Five times a day, Bobby and I stood on the boardwalk, him with his big dancing bear marionette and me with my Floppy marionette, with James Brown or Diana Ross and the Supremes blaring from a tinny speaker hanging from the awning outside the marionette theater. People on the boardwalk stopped to buy soft pretzels and watch the dancing marionettes. Everyone laughed and clapped and took our picture. When the music stopped, we'd dance our marionettes into the theater, luring the crowd to the "Big Show" that Bobby and his family put on. They came up with a new show every season. My first year, it was a circus theme with clown marionettes dancing out into the audience and tickling people's heads. Jimmy and Bobby and Bobby's two older sisters worked the life-sized creatures. The puppeteers wore black costumes. They were on stage, but they faded into the background. When a marionette acrobat did a tightrope walk over three marionette lions, no one in the audience made a sound. It was like they couldn't see the gypsy puppeteers yanking the strings and waving the sticks.

"You guys are invisible when you're working the big marionettes," I told Bobby after I saw the Big Show for the first time.

"Right," he said with a grin. "Not to you, 'cause you're an honorary gypsy. But to the *gadjos*, forget about it."

"How do you get invisible?" I asked.

"Just like I told ya. Practice."

Another time when Mom and Dad paid Bobby to babysit me for a couple hours, he took me to meet Madam Diane the fortune-teller. Her shop was across the boardwalk from Million Dollar Pier, about six blocks from the bakery. The sandwich-board sign out front said:

FORTUNES TOLD DAILY BY MADAM DIANE

Inside, it was shadowy as a spook house and smelled like spices. Purple silk curtains hung on the walls.

"Jason," said Bobby, "this is my Aunt Diane."

"I know about you, Jason," said Madam Diane, rising from a small round table in the center of the room where she'd been shuffling a big deck of cards. She took my hand in hers and bent down to my level. She wore a long purple dress, and she was barefoot, with gold rings on her toes. Raven-colored hair crept out from under an orange scarf tied to her head. "Your partner here tells me you're quite the showman," she said.

"Yep, and my dad makes the best soft pretzels in the world!"

"When I visit, will I get a free pretzel?"

I paused, breathing in Madam Diane's dusky, earthy scent. "I don't know," I teased. "I'm not the fortune-teller, you are."

Madam Diane and Bobby laughed. "Sit down," said Madam Diane, guiding me to her table. "Your uncle brought me into the world. Did you know that? Now, let me see your palm." I climbed up on the folding metal chair across from the gypsy woman and watched as she studied the inside of my hand, squinting and wrinkling her nose. "Hmmm," she said, tracing the lines on my palm with the tips of her bright red fingernails.

I giggled. "That tickles."

"Sit still." She sounded like a teacher at school.

"What do you see, Diane?" asked Bobby, arched over Madam Diane's shoulder for a look.

Madam Diane studied my palm. Then she clasped my hand in both of hers. She stared into my eyes. I stared back like we were having a contest. "What do I see?" she smiled. "Cherry is your favorite flavor. Right?"

"I don't know," I said.

"Trust me, it is. You will know magic. And loyalty. Love greater than the ocean." Bobby inched closer. "I see . . ." Madam Diane studied my palm like a road map. "I see the best soft pretzels in the world." She reached into the folds of her dress and handed me a cherry lollipop, the same color as her nails.

"Thank you," I said, unwrapping the treat and popping it into my mouth. Madam Diane stood up and mussed my hair. She led Bobby and me to the door. Momentarily blinded by the sun, I shielded myself with my forearm, squeezed my eyes shut and then opened them slowly, fixing them on the boardwalk. When I looked up, Madam Diane was watching me. I couldn't read her expression. Half her mouth was smiling, and the other half looked forbidding. Was she about to laugh or cry? I blinked.

"You're a good boy." Madam Diane bent down and kissed me on the cheek. I got another whiff of her perfume. Spicy. Pungent.

On our way home, Bobby and I stopped at Irene's Fudge. Bobby told me to wait out front. The sweet, thick aroma of fresh fudge floated out the open doors. Inside the shop, Bobby talked with a girl behind the counter. She wore a red and white checkered Irene's Fudge shirt and had a long brown ponytail. I twirled the cherry lollipop in my mouth. The girl scooped peanuts into a little white bag and handed it to Bobby. I chomped on the remains of my lollipop, swallowed it as quickly as I could and gobbled down free samples of peanut butter and chocolate fudge from a sample tray that another teenage girl held at the shop's entrance. Bobby came back out and we started walking again. A few stores down, a bunch of seagulls swooped and cawed above our heads.

"Where do you guys live all winter?" Bobby asked. He glanced up at the birds, shielding his eyes from the sun with one hand and opening the bag of peanuts with the other. "Philly?"

"Yeah," I said. For the first time in weeks I thought about the red brick house where we lived during the "off-season." Our neighborhood, aptly known as Rolling Hills, comprised four square blocks of steep hills lined with three-story houses separated by stone walls and dense hedges. On our front lawn were two dogwood trees and a Japanese maple. A bed of rhododendron rimmed the house. A flagstone path snaked from the sidewalk to the black shellacked front door. It was all so boring.

Bobby held the bag of peanuts out to me; I grabbed a handful. "We go down to Miami all winter," he said.

A blue wicker rolling-chair with two white-haired old ladies in it glided up behind us, and we stepped out of its way. The old black man pushing the chair winked at me and wiped his head with a yellow handkerchief. "Pretzel Boy!" he called to me.

Bobby reached into his bag, tossed a peanut into the air and caught it in his mouth. I tried to copy him, but my peanut bounced off my forehead and landed on the boardwalk, near a pigeon. The bird skittered away, then hopped back, pecking timidly at the nut.

"Is that where you go to school?" I asked. "In Miami?"

Bobby tossed another peanut into the air. He stopped, put out his arms like a tightrope walker and caught it in his mouth. "Nah. I bus tables all winter down Miami and then we see the Gypsy King in May, so who has time for school."

"Who's the Gypsy King?" I asked.

"He's an old fat guy. Lives in a trailer in Florida. We go every year. Bring him gold. All the gypsies do it."

"Neat-o." I imagined a fat king sitting on a throne in a trailer, with bus boys, puppeteers and barefoot fortune-tellers lined up outside the way customers waited for Dad's soft pretzels.

BEFORE LONG, the boardwalk was my favorite place on earth. Strolling with Bobby or Jimmy during the day, and sometimes with Mom at night, my senses exploded like fireworks on July Fourth: the scent of Belgian waffles in the cool night air; strains of carousel music; the clanking roller coaster at Million Dollar Pier and its riders screaming in free fall; freak shows and bellowing barkers; peals of laughter from sun-bronzed teenagers, licking their frozen custard, groping and kissing against the boardwalk's railing.

One wavy-hot afternoon in August, a tall man with combed-back silver hair and a pencil-thin mustache appeared at the counter. He wore a cream-colored suit. "Ten cents apiece, three for a quarter," I told him. He pointed at me and laughed. In a moment he was joined by a heavyset woman with hair the color of coal pulled back tightly over her head. When she saw me she put her hands to her chalky cheeks and her mouth formed an "O" like she was surprised. The man laughed again. "Hey!" I said. "You're holding up the line!"

"I'll bet you're Jason Benson," said the man.

"How'd you know?" I asked. "Are you a friend of Madam Diane?"

Before he could answer, Mom hurried out from the back of the bakery where Dad had been teaching her how to dip and bake. Brushing flour off her apron and adjusting her hair, she raised the counter on its hinge, rushed out to the boardwalk and gave the man and woman each a big hug. "Jason," Mom said, "come out here and give your grandparents a hug and a kiss!"

"And leave the counter unattended?" I asked as I bagged a half-dozen for a throng of teenaged girls who'd come up from the beach.

My grandfather put his hands on his hips and shook with laughter. "Such language from a little *pisher*?"

"It's okay, son, I'll take over," said Dad, coming up behind me, guiding me under the counter to the boardwalk.

When my grandfather saw Dad he stopped laughing and cleared his throat. "Good to see you, Ed." He shook Dad's hand over the counter. "How's business?"

"Fantastic," said Dad. "Better than I expected."

"Seriously?" asked my grandfather. He reached over the counter and pumped Dad's hand again. "Glad to hear it!"

Dad rested his elbows on the counter and looked out at the boardwalk. "This time of day's always slow. But from seven, eight o'clock until midnight, you won't believe it. We can hardly keep up."

Mom beamed at Dad like he was her hero. "Isn't that dandy!" said my grandfather, turning to my grandmother, who smiled stiffly and raised one eyebrow like a marionette villain.

Another group of teenagers in sandy bathing suits approached the counter; each one bought a bag of three for a quarter. My grandfather watched the money change hands, wriggling his mustache against the bottom of his nose and nodding his approval to Dad.

Dad offered my grandparents a bag of soft pretzels. "We already ate," said my grandmother, holding her hands out in front of her like she was warning Dad to step back.

"Later," said my grandfather, his hands over his belly. "We ate at the hotel. Big smorgasbord."

It was a surprise visit—my grandparents' first that I could re-member. They'd retired to California the year before I was born. Now here they were on the boardwalk, on a sweltering afternoon— my grandfather squeezing my face in his manicured hands, my grandmother fussing over the specks of flour in Mom's hair and the dough under her fingernails. "He makes you *work*?" she asked under her breath.

Mom turned to me, put her hand on my shoulder. "Honey, go to the back room for a few minutes, would you?" I hesitated. She cast a stern eye toward the storage room filled with sacks of flour, paper bags, napkins, crates of mustard and spare parts for the oven, the mixer and the rolling machine. Reluctantly I scuttled past the ovens and the dipping vat. Even before I got to the back room, I heard them arguing.

"You had a good job at Westinghouse!" said my grandfather.

"That's not what you told me a year ago," said Dad. "You said I wasn't executive material. You said I lacked ambition. You called me a glorified accountant. But look at me now. I'm running my own business and making twice what I made at Westinghouse!"

"Twice as much for ten weeks!" said my grandfather, his voice rising. "And then what?"

Dad corrected him. "Twelve weeks."

"How you gonna pay your mortgage?"

I peeked out the back room's door and saw Mom. Her jaw was quivering. "I told you," Dad said brusquely, "I'm opening a bakery in Pennsauken, and another at the Downingtown Farmers Market. Next year, I'll open at the Montgomeryville Mart. I'll hire managers. I'll be the GM. Three, four bakeries year-round and we'll come down here for the summer."

My grandfather put his hands on his hips and shook his head. "A Wharton School graduate hawking crap like a carnie!"

"I'm an entrepreneur!" Dad said, his voice growing louder too.

"An entrepreneur don't put his wife and kid to work! What kind of life for the kid? I know this shabby town! I know these dirty gypsies!"

"Stop!" cried Mom.

Dad stormed to the cash register, where he began stuffing money into a brown bag, ignoring the bewildered customers.

"What the hell are you doing?" said my grandfather.

"Paying you back!" Dad barked. After Dad emptied the register, he cleaned out the metal cash box under the counter. "Here's seven hundred. You'll get the rest tomorrow." He thrust the bag at my grandfather, who looked around helplessly, lifted his hands in resignation and accepted it.

"Now get out!" Dad yelled so loud everyone on the boardwalk could hear. Bathers up from the beach. Moms with their sandy-footed kids wrapped in beach towels and staring gape-mouthed while Dad hollered, "I don't want your goddamned help!" Groups of teenagers, ice cream men—everyone was watching.

My grandfather turned to my grandmother. "What did I tell you? He's a hothead!"

"Get out of here!" Dad shouted. He stomped his foot on the floor. "Who do you think you are, embarrassing a man in front of his family? What gives you the right?"

My grandfather poked his finger at Dad. "Hothead!"

"Get your goddamned finger out of my face," Dad yelled, "or I'll break it off and shove it up your ass!"

Mom gasped. "Ed! No!"

Lita came over from the pinball arcade and joined the crowd. Bobby came from the marionette theater. I hoped he hadn't heard my grandfather's "dirty gypsies" remark.

Mom turned and saw me spying. She glared at me and I shut the door. Pretty soon the yelling stopped; all I could make out were tense, muffled voices. Before long, Dad came and got me while Mom washed her face at the metal sink in the back of the bakery.

"Would you keep your eye on the counter, son?" Dad asked tenderly. "I've fallen behind with the baking."

I didn't feel like working. I felt like crawling under the counter and being invisible. I pulled my metal crate out from under the counter, stepped up and began stuffing pretzels into bags. "Soft pretzels," I said, my voice cracking at first but gradually gaining strength. "Fresh, hot, soft pretzels. . . . See them twisted, see them baked." I took a deep breath like Bobby had taught me for concentrating before a marionette show. "Soft pretzels!" I hollered. "See them twisted, see them baked! Ten cents apiece, just one thin dime! Three for a quarter! Yes, sir-*ee*, boy! Get 'em while they're hot!"

During the dinner-hour lull, Mom took me back to our hotel and we shared an Italian sub from the mini-fridge. Her eyes were red and swollen.

"Why'd Dad give your dad a pretzel bag full of money?" I asked her.

Mom sawed the sub in half with a white plastic knife. She surveyed our tiny, wood-paneled room, heaved a gentle sigh and picked up her half of the sub. "Because they loaned him money to start the bakery," she said, "and now he's giving them their money back."

"They don't like our pretzel bakery, do they?"

Mom rubbed her eyes with the back of her hand. "My father was an executive. He was a big businessman until his sinuses got so bad he had to move to California. And he wanted your daddy to be a big businessman too."

"Why'd they buy Dad the bakery?"

"They *helped* him buy it because I asked them to, and I'm their daughter. And a mommy and daddy are always there for their child, no matter what. Do you understand?"

"Mm-hmm, I guess."

"Remember that. Dad and I will always be behind you. No matter what you do or where you go in life. We'll always be there." She put her arm around my shoulder and drew me close to her. "When my mother was just a couple years older than you," Mom said, "she had to quit school and go to work for a man who made hats. And she had to walk three miles each way to and from work. One day there was a blizzard with big snowdrifts that buried all the cars. The subway was running, but she didn't have money for the fare, so she walked through the blizzard. By the time she got to the store, she was half-frozen. Her boots had soaked through. Her feet were so cold she was limping. She was an hour and a half late for work. Her boss lived in an apartment above the shop, so he didn't have to walk anywhere except for downstairs. But when she arrived, he told her she was late and he fired her. And she had to turn around and walk home in the snow."

"But that was the olden days," I said.

"That's true," said Mom. "It will never happen to you. But it still makes your grandmother afraid, and we should try to respect that." She put down her sandwich and looked out the window. Our hotel was on the boardwalk. One window offered an ocean view; another framed St. James Place with its white brick boarding houses and what Mom and Dad called "an Irish bar" on the corner. Mom and Dad had decided on a smaller room in a boardwalk hotel instead of a bigger room off the boards. All three of us slept in one room—me on a cot in the corner, Mom and Dad in a queen-sized bed behind a white, lacy curtain that Mom had hung from the ceiling.

A wisp of ocean air blew in through the open window above St. James Place. Mom turned her face toward the breeze. She closed her eyes. Out on the street, a car horn pierced the lavender night. Mom sat as still as a statue.

"Will you and Dad help me buy a fudge shop?" I asked.

Mom smiled. "Maybe when you're older." She put her arm around me and pulled me toward her. Outside our window, mosquitoes and moths buzzed the lamppost on St. James.

"How much older? When I'm ten?"

"We'll see. Eat your sub, honey." I scrunched the crusty roll between my fingers and took a bite of the meaty, garlicky sandwich.

"Eleven?"

"Jason, eat."

RUTH CREASES her brow. "They were my great-grandparents, right?" she asks me. We're walking past a shop with a bright yellow and green sign advertising bicycle rentals from 6 a.m. until 10 a.m. and "Lucky Souvenirs" the rest of the day.

"Mm-hmm. I barely knew them. After I left here, I visited them in California one time."

"Did they buy you the house?" Ruth guesses.

"No. I bought it with my own money."

Eileen shakes her head so slightly it looks more like a twitch. Her jaw's locked tight as a deadbolt.

"How old were you?" asks Ruth.

"Seventeen."

"Where'd you get the money?"

"Saved it up. Juggling, mostly. And working for my dad."

Now that I've begun my tale, I know I'll have to complete it. As my life story plays out in my head, I share mostly the Atlantic City chapters with Eileen and Ruth. They hang on my words, absorbing this new and strange aspect of their husband and father.

I've always admired Eileen's stride. Long-legged and sure-footed. A half-inch taller than I, with a strong chin and cheekbones like mounds, she's aging well, with barely traceable crow's-feet emerging at the corners of her almond eyes. A librarian by profession, well-read and demure, she's more comfortable among stacks of books than crowds of people. Her beauty is natural, her posture superb. Eileen eschews makeup and fashion in favor of her own personal style of muted colors and clean lines. She cuts a nice figure, clasping my arm like a proper lady, not leaning on me or hanging from me, but holding me, proclaiming to the world that we come as a unit. At least for now.

Ruth looks at me like all of a sudden I'm interesting. But it's a long story, and she might not feel this way by the time she's heard everything.

Labor Day weekend marked the end of the summer season. On Saturday night we watched the Miss America Parade from behind the pretzel bakery counter. "Best seats in the house!" Dad boasted.

The boardwalk was a mob scene with all the parade watchers cordoned off to the side to make room for the fleet of fifty Cadillac convertibles gliding down the boardwalk, each bearing a leggy girl perched on the back of the passenger's seat, her hair done up, in a sparkly gown, with a ribbon over her shoulder that said *"Miss Alabama, Miss Alaska, Miss Arizona, Miss Arkansas . . ."* Flash bulbs popped and sizzled; the crowd cheered every passing Cadillac. "They look like princesses," Mom whispered in awe.

Mom and Dad stood on milk crates to see over the heads of the crowd. Dad hoisted me up on the counter for a good view. "Wave to Miss Pennsylvania. Here she comes!" Miss Pennsylvania wore an emerald-green gown and had long brown hair that dipped into large curls below her shoulders. When her car passed us, Dad put his fingers in his mouth and whistled. Miss Pennsylvania turned her head and waved.

"Oh, Jason," Mom said, her fingers fluttering as she waved to Miss Pennsylvania. "Isn't she beautiful?" Outside, the car engines thrummed. A gust of air wafted through the bakery, carrying scents of sweet perfume, gasoline vapors and cigarette smoke.

I looked up at Mom. "Yeah, but you're more." She kissed my head and clutched my shoulder.

The college boys twisted and baked nonstop, pulling rack after rack of steaming hot pretzels from the oven and sliding them into a metal basket at the front counter where Dad stuffed them into paper bags. Between batches, one of the college boys, Doug, grabbed a bag of pretzels, ducked under the counter and bounded onto the boardwalk. He worked his lanky frame through the crowd, caught up with one of the Cadillacs and handed the bag to Miss Tennessee. She took the pretzels and blew him a kiss. The crowd went wild. Doug raised his fists like a prizefighter. Two guys with cameras took his picture, their flashbulbs popping like summer lightning. "Hot soft pretzels!" Dad shouted. "A Miss America favorite!"

The day after Labor Day, Dad told the college boys to clean the ovens one final time. They poured the pretzel-dipping solution down the metal sink in the back of the bakery. They scraped the wooden pretzel trays and dough mixers, then disassembled the rolling machine and dabbed at every piece with scrapers, screwdrivers and damp towels. Mom and I spent most of the last couple days on the beach, she in her pink one-piece bathing suit, lying on a navy-blue blanket; me, squatting in the wet sand by the ocean, splashing in the shallow water, entertaining passersby with impromptu Floppy the Marionette shows.

On our last day, Dad came down to the beach for the first time all summer. He sat on the blanket next to Mom. He put his glasses inside Mom's white cotton beach bag, slipped out of his moccasins and drove his toes into the sand. He wore a pair of baggy red and white swim trunks and had the whitest chest on the beach. He stretched out on his back next to Mom, shut his eyes and groaned contentedly as the sun warmed his pale trunk. Somewhere up the beach I heard the flat clang of a cowbell and a muffled call: "Fudge bars! Italian ice!" I snatched a dollar bill from Mom's beach bag and trotted off to find the ice cream man.

That night we ate dinner with Bobby and his family and Norman and Betty and Lita in a noisy Italian restaurant on Atlantic Avenue. Jimmy was loud, and his bright purple shirt was soaked with sweat and stained with tomato sauce. Madam Diane was there. Bobby's mom was there too: a frail, tight-lipped woman, with drabber clothing than the other gypsies. She rarely emerged from the marionette theater where she spent her days backstage, quietly sewing colorful marionette costumes. Jimmy called his wife "My Edna," so I thought her name was *My Edna*.

Bobby's sisters whispered to each other, flicking glances at the tall, dark busboys. Donna was eighteen and Julia nineteen. When they weren't performing in the family shows, they made up their faces and hung out on the boardwalk, leaning against the railing, smoking cigarettes and laughing with the college boys from Mr. French Fry.

Jimmy raised his glass. The red wine sloshed around and spilled down his wrist. "A toast!" he cried, slurping wine off his cuff. "Pour for the kids, a little wine won't hurt 'em. Jason, hold out your glass for My Edna." My Edna filled the glasses. Jimmy stood up and everyone grew quiet.

"Some magic you can't explain," he said. "Some you can. It starts with a dream. You add a little faith, a lot of hard work . . ." He raised his glass. "A toast to my good friend and honorary gypsy, Ed Benson. An American Dream come true in twelve weeks!"

We all clapped our hands. Jimmy yelled, "Speech! Speech!"

Dad stood up. "Twelve one-hundred-and-twenty-hour weeks," he said, raising his wine glass. "Thank you all for being here to celebrate my family's success." Jimmy, My Edna, Madam Diane, Norman and Betty nodded approvingly. "To my Uncle Joe, may he rest in peace, who introduced me to Atlantic City . . ."

"Uncle Doctor Joe!" Jimmy cried gleefully. "Rest in peace . . ."

Dad looked at Mom and me. "And to Judy and Jason, the two hardest-working first-timers on the boardwalk! Until next season!"

We all responded, *Till next season!* and drank our wine.

After dinner, the three of us walked down Atlantic Avenue to our car. All summer long I'd hardly been off the boardwalk. Before we got in the car, we lingered for a couple minutes, looking up and down the busy avenue as the blood-orange sun smoldered over the bay. A sudden squall clipped the moist air—a gentle nudge from Mother Nature. Autumn was coming. "We should go," Dad said softly.

We squeezed into the front seat of our Chevy station wagon and pulled onto Atlantic Avenue. This was a part of Atlantic City I barely saw all summer: streets lined with four-story boarding houses; broad whitewashed front porches; motels with flashing neon "Vacancy" signs; squat twelve-seat "jitney" buses tooting their horns on the Avenue; men and boys lugging crab traps along side streets, headed to the bay.

After a couple blocks we turned right, away from the board-walk and the ocean. Before I knew it, I must have fallen asleep with my head on Mom's shoulder, images of boardwalk life dancing in my head.

2

"**That was the** shitty part of every season," I tell Eileen and Ruth. "The last days. I didn't want to leave."

Eileen mulls that over, trying to fathom what I was like as a kid. Moody and disaffected?

Secretly, I've always been jealous of my wife's childhood. She grew up in a Norman Rockwell painting outside of Minneapolis. Her parents are still living. She has more aunts and uncles and second cousins than you can shake a family tree at. We visit every summer. They don't like New York, but they accepted me right off the bat—a short, swarthy East Coaster who didn't go to college and talks like a carnival barker.

Growing up, Eileen idled away her summers reading, catching fireflies and canoeing on a placid lake. Nothing mysterious. No gypsies or roustabouts, no hawking to tourists. Her life's an open book. Mine's a secret code.

Now I dread that if I cannot explain myself today or if she doesn't believe me, she'll leave me and take Ruth with her back to Minneapolis.

At least she's listening. She says, "But your family was living in a hotel, you said. This was just a summer break from Philly, right?"

"Yeah, but I wanted to move down here year-round, especially after my second summer."

"What happened that summer?"

"Bobby taught me how to juggle."

"HOW WAS YOUR school year?" asked Bobby. It was late in the afternoon, our first week back.

"Worse than prison," I said over the thrumming, clattering pretzel-rolling machine. "Because when they let you out of prison at least you're out for good."

Bobby grinned at my remark. He stood on the boardwalk, leaned over our counter and poked his head into the bakery. His curly black hair was longer this summer, about half an inch over his ears.

School was in fact a terrible place for me. I hated sitting still, my grades were poor and the teachers told my parents I "failed to pay attention."

Mom and Dad had encouraged me to try and make some friends during the long, dull school year. "But I already have friends," I'd told them. "Bobby, Lita, Jimmy . . ."

I didn't like the kids at school. On the first day, the teacher had made us stand in front of the class and talk about our summers. The other kids didn't believe me when I told them about the boardwalk. They didn't believe I was an honorary gypsy or that I could make a marionette dance. They smirked and chuckled like goddamned idiots.

Miss McCue stood up. "My, my," she said. "We certainly have one imaginative young man in our class, don't we?"

Imaginative?

"Jason, you may take your seat now." Indignant, I tromped down the aisle to my desk, ignoring my fellow students' stares and giggles.

I made one friend over that winter. Skip Schwartz was my age and lived two blocks away—down our hill and over one block—with his mom and dad and his two older brothers. One Saturday afternoon in autumn, after Mom nagged me to "go outside, make some friends and play," I began knocking on doors asking if there were any kids my age there. "I'm Jason and I'm seven. Got any kids my age here?" Mostly, the moms and dads scowled and closed their doors, which is what I had expected. I'd already told Mom that the neighborhood kids were either too old or too young. No one in my homeroom class even lived in our neighborhood.

Ultimately, though, one of the moms pointed out Skip's house four doors down. I walked up the driveway and knocked on the door. "I'm Jason," I told Skip's mom. "A lady up the street said there's a kid my age here. Does he want to play?" I half-hoped she'd brush me off so I could prove my point to Mom. But she invited me in.

Skip's mom had red hair piled up high like a Miss America contestant. She wore a white bathrobe, even though it was the middle of the day, and a pair of fuzzy slippers the color of grape Kool-Aid. She took my hand and led me down a hallway with thick green carpet, into a gleaming kitchen with big windows on two of the four walls. Skip sat at the table with a glass of milk in front of him. His real name was Lionel, but everyone called him Skip, even his teachers.

Skip's mom poured me a glass of milk too.

"Guess what," I said. "I'm an honorary gypsy."

"Know any tricks?" he asked. "Can you pick pockets?"

"I can almost be invisible."

"Neat!" Skip drained half his milk in one long gulp. "Where do you go to school?" He set his glass on the table and belched.

"Chapman Park," I said, recalling the red brick minimum-security facility where the school bus dropped me off every weekday morning.

"I go to private school," said Skip. I'd never heard of private school. At first I thought he attended his own school where no one else went. That sounded better than mine. I imagined Skip at recess, standing alone in a windy playground next to an empty swing arcing back and forth.

Next thing I knew, we were on our bellies on his kitchen floor, pretending we were swimming in an ocean of muddled green tiles. While we scissor-kicked and breast-stroked, Skip's mom talked on the telephone. We were frogmen, exploring the green ocean's murky depths. His mom's legs were a coral reef, the phone cord dangling like a squid's tentacles.

Skip was my height and a little chubby, with wavy brown hair, a broad, pale face and thick tortoise-shell glasses. His brothers, seven and eight years older, were already in high school. Skip hated reading. His mom and dad made him go to a special reading teacher twice a week after school. His brothers called him "stupid."

One nippy Saturday morning in November, Skip invited me to play in the woods at the edge of the neighborhood a few blocks from my house. "There's a creek and an old fort down there," he said. "It's from, like, the Civil War. I think it's the Alamo." He led me down a steep dirt path lined with shrubs and mossy rocks. We passed oak trees and a stand of white birches. Soon we came to a dilapidated shell of a sandstone building that was not the Alamo— which I'd read about in a comic book about Davy Crockett and knew was in Texas, not Pennsylvania—but an old mill. At the base of the path a brook trickled over a bed of smooth white rocks. Water bugs skittered across the green surface. Skip and I sat side by side on the pebbly bank, watching the creek flow. He grabbed a handful of stones and flicked them into the water, one by one.

"This is nice," I said. Sunlight pressed through the treetops.

Skip stood up. "Watch this." He scrambled over to the water's edge, reached in and retrieved a coke bottle from the bottom of the creek. Then he wound up and threw the bottle across the stream. It hit a rock and shattered into pieces.

"Why'd you do that?" I asked. "Somebody could cut their feet."

"Uh-uh. Nobody walks there." He returned to our spot, his knees muddy and his arms dripping wet.

I lay on my back, closed my eyes and felt the crunch of pebbles pressing the back of my neck. The flowing water sounded like rain.

EILEEN, RUTH AND I walk past a pavilion of bright blue park benches jutting out over the beach. Old men and women sit bundled in winter coats, some chatting with each other, others just watching the ocean.

"Skip got drunk at your bar mitzvah!" says Ruth, recalling one of my Philadelphia childhood stories.

I chuckle and shake my head at the memory. But I'd rather talk about our second season down here, and the day Bobby taught me how to juggle.

On that day, while Bobby and I talked, I twisted strip after strip of dough that rolled down the conveyor belt, adding each twisted, unbaked pretzel to the neat rows on a wooden board on a metal rack to my right. When the board filled up, I hit the red button to stop the belt, put the board of unbaked pretzels into the dough retarder, hit the green button and filled up another board.

Bobby watched me from across the counter. "What grade you going into next year?" he asked.

"Third," I said, contemptuously. "They make you sit at your desk all day. They make you do dumb homework every night. And the kids at my school—none of them even work in the summer! They all go to camp."

"What kind of camp?" Bobby asked.

I pressed the red button, grabbed a sticky hunk of dough from the mixer and stuffed it into the hopper at the end of the rolling machine. "The kind where the grownups make you have fun and play baseball, and swim and make crafts."

"What crafts? You mean like boats?" he asked, uncomprehending.

"More like wallets."

Bobby narrowed his brow and changed the subject. "You want me to show ya how to juggle?"

That summer, 1968, juggling was a boardwalk fad. The best was Henry the Juggler, a hippie who performed for crowds in front of Steel Pier.

On my first night that season, I'd walked up to Steel Pier and watched Henry the Juggler's show. He began by doffing his bowler hat, shaking out his dirty-blond shoulder-length hair and announcing, "Right on, ladies and gentlemen, right on, boys and girls! I am Henry the Juggler . . . and these are my balls." I didn't get the joke, but I knew it was funny because the grownups and teenagers laughed like crazy.

In the mornings, three or four other hippies juggled on the beach in front of the bakery. None were as good as Henry the Juggler. Mostly, they just hung out while burly lifeguards and other kids' dads yelled at them. "*Get a haircut!*" "*Take a bath!*" "*Get a job!*"

Over the winter, Bobby had learned how to juggle. But he wouldn't juggle with the hippies. "They're dirty and lazy," he warned me. "Stay away from them."

Dad didn't think they were so bad. "They're just college kids looking for attention," he said.

"Bobby says they're lazy." It was an overcast Thursday. Dad and I were taking a break from mixing dough for the night, looking over the counter and up the boards, watching the hippies juggle on the beach.

Dad scraped a patch of dough off his wrist with his fingernails. "I don't know if they're lazy," he said, "but I'm not going to find out by hiring one."

"How come?" I asked, craning my neck to watch the hippies juggle.

"Their hair's too long," said Dad. "If it gets caught in the rolling machine they'll sue me."

"But you let Mom work here and she has long hair," I said. Mom tied her hair into a ponytail when she worked a shift.

"That's different," Dad said. "Mom's a girl."

"I think they should get jobs," I said, jutting my chin toward the beach where the hippies were tossing bright yellow tennis balls up and down. "They're so poor, yesterday I saw three of them under the boardwalk sharing one cigarette."

Dad flinched. "Bobby's right," he said. "Keep away from them."

Just then, Mr. Peanut, the Planters mascot, pranced along the boards, jaunty and lithe, swinging his cane, a top hat and monocle on his yellow peanut head. A couple of kids called his name. He turned and waved his yellow-gloved hand. When the hippies on the beach saw him, they dropped their juggling balls and jostled up the steps to the boardwalk, where they followed Mr. Peanut, aping his jolly strut. When Mr. Peanut and his hippie mockers came within earshot of the bakery, I heard them making fun of him. "He's not allowed to say shit back," one said, sidling up to Mr. Peanut. "He's like the guards at Buckingham Palace."

Suddenly Dad ducked underneath the counter and stormed out onto the boardwalk, waving his arms at the hippies. "Leave him alone!" he shouted. "Go on, get!" He shooed them like houseflies. "Don't interfere with a man's livelihood! What the hell did your parents teach you?"

The hippies scampered back to the beach and resumed their juggling. Dad returned to the bakery, red in the face. "Never interfere with a man's livelihood," he told me, a purple vein throbbing on his neck. "Don't waste somebody's time when he's working. It's a principle."

Now, on day three of the season, having watched Henry the Juggler's show in front of Steel Pier on the two previous nights, I was ready to learn. "Soon as I finish twisting this batch," I told Bobby. I pressed the green button and the machine clanked into gear. While I twisted, Bobby ran next door to grab a couple cans of tennis balls. A minute later, he was back. I slid the last board of pretzels into its rack in the dough retarder, rubbed the bits of flour off my palms and knuckles, and ducked under the counter.

Bobby and I took off our sneakers and raced across the boardwalk to the beach. We jogged about halfway to the ocean and dropped our sneaks in the sand not far from where three of the hippies were juggling.

Bobby opened a can and took out three yellow, woolly tennis balls. "Watch," he said. He juggled for about a minute, making only one drop. "Sand's the best place for beginners. You drop 'em, they don't bounce nowhere."

He handed me a ball. "Watch me," he said, tossing his ball into the air from one hand to the other. "Up and down. Ya see how it curves? The ball goes up. And then it comes down. But you see that split second where it ain't going up and it ain't going down? That's called the *peak*." He tossed the ball gently, in an even arc, from his left hand to his right. "That's where the magic happens— at the peak. See?"

He tossed the ball another time. "Right . . . *there*! That's when you throw. If it ain't going up and it ain't coming down, for just that millionth of a second, it's like the sun in the sky." He showed me again, tossing a tennis ball high into the air, tracking its flight and saying "Now!" at the moment it hit its peak.

Next it was my turn. I tossed my ball from one hand to the other, missing it once in a while but getting the hang pretty quickly. Then Bobby pulled two more balls out of the can. "All right, now start with one in each hand. Good. You throw one, just like before—from left to right. Okay? Then, when the ball hits its peak, you throw the other, from right to left."

I tossed one, then the other—over and over. Usually I'd catch the first and drop the second. Sometimes I caught them both, but my throws were uneven. "Easy," said Bobby. "You flick your wrist, gentle, like this. Easy up. Easy down." He tossed a ball with his left hand and caught it effortlessly with his right. "See? One and two— and one and two—and one . . ."

An hour later I could juggle three balls, usually a half-dozen throws before dropping them. "Magnificent!" said Bobby. "Took me like three days to get that good. Just practice, buddy. You practice every day, I swear to God you'll be better than Henry the Dirty Hippie by next summer."

I tossed the balls into the air, *one-two-three*. Caught and tossed, *one-two-three*, kept it going, my neck craning, legs spread, feet shuffling back and forth in the sand, straining to make each catch, grimacing with every throw.

Bobby watched me. "Get control. Gentle throws. Easy. Good. You're not breathing. Don't forget to breathe."

Meanwhile, there was a commotion down the beach: three policemen in dark blue uniforms and stiff white hats tromped unsteadily across the soft sand in their shiny black shoes. Bobby and I stopped juggling and watched the police make their way to the circle of hippies. They talked for a minute before the policemen put handcuffs on one of the hippies—a tall, skinny guy with blond hair down to his shoulders—and led him toward the boardwalk.

"What happened?" I asked.

Bobby watched the policemen walk the handcuffed hippie up the steps to the boardwalk and out of sight. For the longest time, Bobby didn't say anything; he just twirled two tennis balls round and round in his hand. At last he shook his head. "No idea. But like I told ya, stay away from hippies."

I happened to glance up at the boardwalk and saw Dad leaning over the railing, waving at me. "I gotta go work the counter," I said, handing Bobby the tennis balls. Bobby slipped the balls into their can and then gave it to me. "Keep 'em so you can practice," he said. We grabbed our sneakers and trudged across the sand toward the boardwalk.

Halfway there, Bobby slowed his pace and turned to me. "I have an idea. I'm gonna practice being invisible, and guess what? I'm gonna start by making myself invisible to cops."

"Why?" I asked.

"So they can't see me jaywalking or littering and stuff."

"What's jaywalking?"

"It's against the law. So, when you see the cops, let me know and then I'll be invisible."

"Okay, but why?"

"You ask a lot of questions for a pipsqueak. You gonna help me or not?"

"Okay."

"It's a secret," Bobby whispered. "Just between us. Don't tell your old man, all right? And don't tell mine, neither." We arrived at the splintered, sand-covered wooden steps leading to the boardwalk where Dad was waiting.

"What was the racket?" Dad asked.

"The cops caught one of the hippies," said Bobby, shaking sand out of his sneakers.

"Doing what?"

Bobby shook his head again, mystified. "Cops will be cops and hippies will be hippies."

I showed Dad the can of tennis balls Bobby had given me. "I'm going to practice until I'm as good as Henry the Juggler."

"Did you say 'thank you'?" asked Dad.

"Thank you," I said to Bobby. "Hey, what time's our pre-show?"

Bobby picked at his chin and twisted his mouth as I waited for his answer. "Look, buddy," he said, "I can't do no more pre-shows for a while." He bent down toward me and he winked. I knew it had to do with being invisible. Bobby held up a finger as if to shush me. Then he trotted across the boards and disappeared into the marionette theater.

Dad put his arm over my shoulder. "Let's get to work before you and Mom break for dinner."

The next day, I asked Jimmy about doing the pre-show solo, to draw people in to see the new Big Show, an ocean theme this season, with marionettes in sailors' costumes fighting pirates and sailing off to Hawaii at the end. Jimmy shook his head consolingly. "You did a good job last summer, but I can't let you do no solo act yet."

I asked why Bobby had to quit the pre-show. Jimmy didn't answer. "Kids . . ." was all he said. He lit a cigarette and shook his head grimly. "Just practice your juggling. Practice, practice, practice."

"I will, I will, I will," I said. "But why can't Bobby . . ."

Jimmy put a finger to his lips. "Bobby's funny like that. You let him be."

I practiced on the beach every morning from six-thirty until eight-thirty, before the crowds arrived. "Ladies and gentlemen," I'd announce to the assorted gulls and pigeons and the occasional horseshoe crab that had straggled up from the ocean, "let's give a big Atlantic City welcome to the one and only Jason the Magnificent!" And I'd begin: *One-two-three . . . one-two-three*—striving for smooth tosses that arced up and down, landing cleanly in my hands. I'd draw a circle in the sand with my big toe, stand in the middle of it and will myself not to step outside of it to make a catch. Then I'd erase it and draw a smaller one. Sometimes Norman, Betty and Lita came out and watched me practice, applauding and shouting encouragement through cupped hands. And sometimes people on the boardwalk stopped to watch, but I didn't pay attention. According to Jimmy, I had to learn the basics— "make it look easy"—before performing for a real audience.

The more I practiced, the more people said, "Hey, you're good!" as I walked up and down the boardwalk juggling. When it rained, I practiced in a big, empty room in the basement of our hotel. This season we had a bigger room—"a suite," as Mom called it—with a sliding wooden door between my bed and Mom's and Dad's.

All summer long, Bobby hardly ever came out of the marionette theater. When he did—once a week or so—it was at night when the boardwalk was mobbed. He wore a baseball hat pulled down so you couldn't see his face. He did the Big Show with Jimmy and two college kids Jimmy had hired to replace Bobby's sisters, who didn't come at all that summer. But Bobby never came out to juggle or just hang out in front of the bakery.

The first time he came out at night to walk with me, he told me that Mom and Dad weren't even paying him to watch me this season. "We're buddies," he said as we passed a shooting gallery where a line of men shot .22 caliber rifles—*pop-pop-pop*—at tin cans and plastic ducks. "Buddies don't get paid to hang out. Now you keep an eye out for cops and let me know."

I scanned the crowd for telltale traces of blue uniforms, shiny black shoes and white hats. When I spotted a cop on foot patrol, I'd tap Bobby's leg. He'd push his cap brim down, slink his shoulders and take hold of my hand like he was my dad. Sometimes he'd duck into a shop or an arcade, leaving me outside to stand guard.

Almost every night I walked to Steel Pier to watch Henry the Juggler's show. Sometimes I brought Lita, sometimes Mom and once in a while Dad, when he could take a break from twisting and baking. *I'm going to be as good as him*, I promised myself, standing among the rapt crowd, craning my neck for a better view. I watched how he tossed behind his back and under his legs; how he caught some catches overhand and bounced balls off his knees, head and feet; and how, when he missed a catch from time to time, he'd make a joke ("I will drop a ball from time to time so that you know how difficult this is").

After a few weeks, the hippie beach jugglers disappeared; so did Henry the Juggler, who announced one night after his show that he was headed for a music festival in Wisconsin. Jimmy and I watched Henry the Juggler snake through the crowd, derby in hand, tips flowing into it. "You master juggling," Jimmy told me, "you can make a living anywhere you go." I didn't want to go anywhere but Atlantic City, but it was good to know.

By the end of the summer, I could juggle a basic cascade pattern for ten minutes at a time; and when I made a drop, I could usually catch it on a bounce and get back in the rhythm. I could toss behind my back and under my legs. And as Bobby had taught me, when I wasn't practicing juggling, I was thinking about juggling.

On the last night of the season, when we went out to dinner, My Edna started the occasion by giving me a gift—a black felt derby with a short brim and a round top.

I held my new hat with my fingertips, slowly turned it around, inspected its smooth curves, teeny-tiny stitching and spiffy brim.

"Did you make this?" Mom asked My Edna.

My Edna's lips curled into a bashful smile. She lowered her eyes.

"Try it on!" said Jimmy. I raised the derby above my head. A hush fell over the table. A waiter and a busboy stopped to watch, trays of food suspended in their hands. I lowered the derby little by little until it landed on my head. A perfect fit. It felt like we'd all been holding our breath, and now came a collective exhale.

"It's gorgeous," Mom whispered in awe.

Everyone applauded and whistled, even people from the other tables.

"My Edna's a genius," Jimmy boasted. "What she can do with a little extra fabric, you know, it's absolutely unbelievable."

"And when you outgrow it," said My Edna, "don't even worry, because you'll get another."

I got up and darted around the table to My Edna. "Thank you, My Edna." I kissed her on her cheek.

"It's a gift for life," she said.

Returning to my seat, I looked around the restaurant. "Hey, when's Bobby coming?"

Jimmy waved his hands. "He's gone. Cleared out this morning."

"Why didn't he come say goodbye?" I asked, stung by the news.

"He did, but he couldn't find you and his bus was leaving."

It wasn't fair that Bobby had taken off without saying goodbye. He'd spent all summer perfecting his invisibility, and I'd helped him, and now he disappeared on me.

Madam Diane distracted me from my agitation. Sitting across from me at the table, she reached over and lifted the hat off my head. She inspected its inside and raised her eyebrows approvingly. "What are ya gonna call your act?"

"Jason the Magnificent," I said. Everyone laughed and clapped.

Jimmy raised his glass of wine. "Oh, yeah!" he said, gushing. "I like that! To Jason the Magnificent!"

"*To Jason the Magnificent!*"

Madam Diane leaned across the table. She put the derby back on my head and pinched my chin.

"You gonna practice all winter?" asked Jimmy. "Every day, right?"

"After he finishes his homework," Mom told him.

Jimmy winked at me. "Nothing wrong with that." He raised his glass again. "To homework!"

"*To homework!*" everyone hollered.

Madam Diane leaned in like she was about to share a secret. "Next season, people are gonna throw a lot of money in that hat."

Dad asked, "Is that your professional opinion?"

Madam Diane pinched my cheek. Then she held my face in both of her hands. And once again, just as she'd done on the day we met and she read my palm, she stared into my eyes. Everyone grew quiet. After what seemed a long time, Mom cleared her throat and Madam Diane released me. She leaned back in her chair. "No, Ed dear. That ain't my professional opinion. Just a feeling."

Later, when we were getting ready to leave the restaurant, Lita presented me with a conch shell. "Thanks. It's pretty," I said, inspecting the chalky pink spiral.

"You can hear the ocean inside," Lita said.

I put the tip of the shell to my ear and listened to the soft whoosh.

Lita stretched to her tiptoes and kissed me on the cheek. "You're even better than Henry the Juggler," she whispered. My face prickled like I'd been hit with a sandblast.

Lita scooted off, disappearing into the back of the restaurant, all skinny legs and curls. Everyone hugged and shook hands. When I looked at Mom she pointed her chin at the exit and took hold of Dad's arm. It was time to leave.

I straightened my derby, tucked my conch shell under my arm and lumbered out the door toward another long, dull off-season.

3

MOM REACHED ACROSS the dining-room table and loaded my plate with colorless meatloaf and lumpy mashed potatoes.

"Why can't we live in Atlantic City all year round?" I asked for the hundredth or so time.

Dad shook his head. "Because it's *dead* all winter," he said.

As usual, before she cooked it, Mom had washed the raw ground beef until the color was gone. The meatloaf had a rubber-like consistency and no taste. The potatoes were dry. Dad said the lumps gave them character. Ketchup helped.

Neither my mom nor Skip's knew how to cook. Skip's family had a maid, a black woman named Willa who visited three times a week, cleaned the house, did the laundry and fixed meals. We didn't have a maid. And it wasn't until a few years later that I learned not to wash red meat before cooking it—or that green beans should simmer for three minutes, not be kept at a rolling boil for an hour and a half.

It wasn't Mom's fault she couldn't cook. Dad told me that no one had ever expected her to. She was supposed to marry a big businessman and hire a maid. Her parents sent her to art lessons, not cooking classes. She couldn't cook a meatloaf, but she could paint one.

"Nothing happens on the boardwalk all winter," said Dad. "A couple conventions, but that's it. Mr. Peanut's around, but Planters is a national chain. They don't make money on the boardwalk during the off-season. Nobody goes out. It's too cold."

"Before you know it," said Mom, "third grade will be over and we'll be back in Atlantic City. But right now, your job is school, young man. Nobody says you have to like it, but you do have to be there. You *have* to pay attention."

I grunted, dragging a forkful of the drab meat through a smear of ketchup. "You know what happened at recess today? I was practicing, and this sixth grader walks up and pokes a stick right into my pattern."

"Why'd he do that?" Mom asked.

"How should *I* know?" I reached across the table for the ketchup bottle. "Just to watch me chase the balls. He interfered with my livelihood, Dad."

"On the other hand," Dad said, rubbing his chin thoughtfully, "if you're going to perform solo next summer, you'd better be prepared for people who act like jerks."

I mashed my fork at a clutter of peas on my plate. "Don't worry. Everyone who acts like a jerk goes to my school. And they don't go to Atlantic City in the summer."

"What about the talent show at the school fair next month?" he asked. "Do you plan to sign up?"

"Why should I?" Chin on my palm, I glumly twirled my fork on my plate.

"The talent show sounds like a terrific idea," said Mom. "It'll give you a chance to try out your act before you take it to the boardwalk next summer."

As much as I hated anything having to do with school, I had to admit that Mom and Dad could be right. "I'll think about it," I said.

"I'll take the afternoon off to come and watch you," Dad said.

I worked a forkful of potatoes into my mouth. "We'll see."

"LADIES AND GENTLEMEN! Boys and girls! Teachers of all ages! I am Jason the Magnificent . . ." I paused. The narrow white spotlight blazed the backs of my ears. A bead of sweat trickled out from under My Edna's derby and down the side of my neck. ". . . And these are my balls." The sixth grade section erupted in laughter. I winked like Henry the Juggler and began with a simple cascade. Wide pattern; steady rhythm. "Please note," I said, "I may purposely drop one or more in order to make my act look *extremely* difficult."

I worked the cascade up and down, throwing high and then low, maintaining a minuscule pattern until it drew applause. Under my legs, around my back, off my head and off each foot. It was like being on the boardwalk, like working a marionette and surfing a wave of laughs, holding the moment until the people almost stopped laughing, then landing a joke or making another high throw to hold their attention. I ended the routine by throwing one ball high into the air, spinning three hundred and sixty degrees on my heels, and making the catch in the nick of time. I took a bow, basking in the generous applause.

Offstage, my heart pounding, I found the bench where I'd left the little yellow suitcase Mom had given me for my juggling gear. On the outside of the case, she'd painted three gleaming red balls and "JASON THE MAGNIFICENT." I packed the balls and derby, straddled the bench and closed my eyes. Drenched in sweat and panting like a puppy, I took several slow, deep breaths—in through my nose, out through my mouth—the way Bobby had taught me to handle the jitters. I recalled his advice: *Don't forget to breathe.*

After the final act, people from the audience rushed backstage to congratulate the performers. Mom hugged me. Dad reached out and shook my hand. "See where practice gets you? You knocked 'em dead!" he said.

"Ed," said Mom, "I'll bet you're glad you took the afternoon off."

"And how!" Dad put his hand on my head and mussed my hair. "And the best part was that I didn't have to ask anybody's permission. Son, when you grow up, whatever you do, be self-employed at it."

Dad was happier than ever now that he owned his own pretzel bakeries and didn't have to "punch a goddamn time clock like a day laborer." He never came home complaining about his boss anymore. But a week before the talent show he got into a fight with Peppy the Clown, who, when he wasn't doing his Saturday morning TV show, owned a farmers market where Dad had a pretzel bakery. I assumed that when Peppy the Clown came to the farmers market he'd be wearing his rainbow-colored costume and his big shoes. But Dad said he looked like a regular adult. "The bastard heard my sales were good, so he tried to raise my rent," Dad grumbled. "I held my ground. 'Go ahead,' I told him, 'just try to throw me out!' I've got a lease. It's a legal document. That goddamned clown's an opportunist."

At bedtime on the night of the talent show, I took Floppy out of my closet, where he'd been hanging since September. Clutching the stuffed dog, I climbed into bed. In the dark, I reached for Lita's conch shell on my night table, put it to my ear and listened to the ocean. I recalled something Bobby had told me during the first season when we were both up early one morning, looking at the ocean: "You look out as far as you can, and you see to infinity," he said, pointing at the horizon. "As far as you can see to the left and right: Infinity." We stared at the horizon. "Boardwalk people— all day long we can see to infinity. Who else does that? Nobody. Except for sailors. And maybe cowboys, depending."

And now, as I lay in bed, I wondered: Was Bobby gazing at infinity on the shore of another ocean? Was he waiting tables in Miami? Standing in line to visit the Gypsy King? "Jason, man, when you get older I'll teach you about girls," he'd promised me.

Dad poked his head into my room. "Still up?" he whispered. The hallway lights silhouetted his balding head and sturdy shoulders.

"Mm-hmm."

He opened the door wider. The light from the hallway wedged its way inside. Dad came over to my bed, patted the blankets, bent down and kissed my cheek. He'd returned to his bakery after the talent show, and now he smelled like dough. "I'm proud of you, son. And it's not just the juggling. I know you're trying harder in school, and you're doing better."

I drew Floppy to my chest. "Um, Dad?"

"Yes?"

"Who's going to teach me about girls? Bobby said he would but now he's invisible."

Dad patted my blankets. "Don't worry," he said. "When the time comes, you'll know everything you need to."

"Who taught you about girls?" I asked. "Jimmy?"

He chuckled. "No. Definitely not Jimmy."

"*Your* dad?"

"My dad died when I was a little boy—about your age, actually. He was only forty-two years old."

I sat up in bed. "How did he die?"

"He had a heart attack," Dad said. "His heart stopped beating because he had a disease that nobody knew about back then. But my mother didn't tell me. One day when I came home from school, she said my father had 'gone away on business.'"

"How come she lied?" I asked.

Dad looked at the floor. He picked at the flour under his wide, flat fingernails. "She didn't exactly lie. She was so young. She didn't know what to say. She didn't know how to tell me so she didn't say anything."

"Who's gonna die first?" I asked. "You or Mom?"

"We're both going to live for a long time," Dad said. "There's nothing for you to worry about."

"No going away on business?"

He hugged me. "No going away on business." He tucked Floppy and me under the covers. Clutching my conch shell, I listened to the ocean until I fell asleep.

THE NEXT SUMMER, it was just Jimmy and four college kids working the marionette theater. Bobby didn't show up. No one knew where he was or when he'd be back.

Henry the Juggler didn't return, either. Jason the Magnificent was the only juggling act on the boardwalk. And I was a hit.

"Ladies and gentlemen, welcome to the show!" I'd announce in my sideshow barker voice, pulling two bright red rubber balls and a soft pretzel from my suitcase, then tossing all three aloft into an easy cascade. Some of my patter was my own, and some I'd learned from Henry the Juggler. "Jason the Magnificent will now attempt to eat one of these objects while he juggles." I'd work the pattern, manage a few behind-the-back and over-the-shoulder catches—the balls bobbing up and down smoothly while the pretzel twirled awkwardly. "Can you guess *which* of these objects Jason the Magnificent will attempt to eat?" Everyone laughed. They applauded and whistled. And just as Madam Diane had predicted, they threw lots of cash into my derby.

The only thing that made me unhappy was the thought of returning to Philadelphia. I envied Norman because he kept the arcade open all winter. "You guys are so lucky that you get to be here year-round," I told him one afternoon when I'd stopped by to play pinball.

"Why shouldn't I?" he asked. "I pay rent for the winter. I make a little extra money. Kids after school, conventions. They come in out of the cold, play some pinball."

"Dad says it's dead all winter."

"Dead for a pretzel man, but only slow for a pinball man," Norman said. "Middle of January your father bakes an oven full, sells a half-dozen and the rest what he feeds to the pigeons." He laid his hand across the glass cover of the machine before us—a flashy black and green game called Godzilla vs. Tokyo. "But pinball machines don't get stale."

Around us, the Two for One teemed with kids and teenagers banging and shaking the machines, working the flippers, angling their sweaty bodies, trying to control the silver balls through sheer will. Buzzers blasted and buttons clicked. I slipped a quarter into the coin slot and pressed the button for my first ball. Godzilla roared to life.

"The trick," Norman explained, his reedy voice rising above the din, "is to catch the ball in the flipper every time what you can. Stop the spin, get control." I pulled back and released the spring-loaded knob, propelling the ball into play. "Keep the ball up top as long as you can," Norman said, watching over my shoulder and reaching around me to point through the glass top. "Flip it through that gate—you see, *boychick*? Light up the bumper." He pressed an ink-stained finger to the glass. I batted the pinball with the flippers, slammed it into the bank of blinking red lights and racked up ten thousand points. "Don't shake side to side," he said, "or you'll tilt it. Gentle, back and forth." I missed a flip and lost the ball, smack down the middle.

"It's like your juggling," he said.

"Except nobody throws money in my hat for playing pinball."

Norman scratched his chin. I noticed a neat little row of blue numbers tattooed on his forearm. "What are they?" I asked.

"It's a long story which I'll tell you another time. But you know what? You juggle in front of your father's bakery and in front of Jimmy's place, right? And you draw the crowds? So how about you juggle out front of here sometimes and I give you free games?"

"Sure!" I said, looking away from the game to shake Norman's hand. He dug into his apron and handed me a fistful of quarters.

I played for another half hour until Dad came for me. During the walk back to our hotel, I told him about my deal with Norman. "Why don't you talk with Irene's Fudge?" Dad asked. "You could juggle out front and bring them some business in exchange for fudge."

The next day I asked, and Mr. Lambert the owner said yes. By the end of the season, I was doing five shows a night and earning more money than the college kids who worked for Dad.

4

"Can you still juggle?" Ruth asks. This is the longest she's been at my side all day. Preposterous as it sounds, neither she nor Eileen has seen me juggle. They know I used to perform on the streets of Philadelphia, and later in Boulder, New Orleans and San Francisco. And they know I quit. Cold turkey. I'm a recovering juggler.

"Oh, I'm sure I can," I say glibly. "It's like . . . riding a unicycle." Ruth snorts. Eileen looks away. The joke falls flat. I remind myself: Don't aim for funny or clever or sentimental. Just tell the story.

Despite the music blaring from the casino entrances, we can hear the waves rolling up on the beach, like the sound of a crowd clapping. The old Convention Hall still stands—a grand sweep of deco columns and copper domes. A good old building. Jennifer from work, who grew up in Atlantic City, told me she ushered at Convention Hall when she was in high school. According to her, they can't tear down the building because it's a historic landmark. It looks out of place next to the sleek, angular Trump Plaza, like a frumpy dowager posing next to a supermodel. I wonder if Convention Hall is still the home of the Miss America Pageant. Posters outside promise an upcoming Neil Diamond concert and a series of minor-league ice hockey games.

Now Ruth trails behind us, gaping at shop windows and hotel doors.

"When we took Ruth to Seaside Park and Coney Island, it always reminded me of this," I tell Eileen.

"You must have felt weird." Eileen's voice rings with disappointment.

"I didn't know how to bring it up. I'd been private about it for so long by then."

"*Private?*" She glares at me. "Spare me the euphemisms. You know what's private? A fetish. A crush. But a beach house? That's not private, that's secret."

"Okay, it was my secret," I say. I want to add, *"At least I'm not having an affair. There are worse things than covering up that I own a house."* But that's not the point. Eileen wants to know why I wouldn't tell her, and I'm still working up the courage to explain.

We stop in front of a video arcade, and I suddenly realize where we are. I blink at the front window. The music from the casinos thrashes in my brain like someone is beating my head with a tennis racket. Improbably, on both sides of the arcade there's new construction—a hotel and shops.

No remnants of the pretzel bakery or the marionette theater—and that's almost a relief.

I can hardly believe the arcade itself is still here. I assumed everything was gone. Did I want everything gone?

There's no "Two for One" sign outside. But it's the right place. I cross the boards and stop at the entrance. Cupping my hands around my eyes to shield the glare, I peer through the glass door like we did earlier at the house. Inside, I recognize almost nothing. The old pinball machines have been replaced by video games. A middle-aged Asian couple patrol the aisles. Each wears an apron for carrying change and bills. Teenage kids throng the games. The Asian couple make change. The man says something to the woman, and then he retires to the corner office, like Norman used to do.

Ruth has caught up with us. I point to a spot across the boardwalk. "Right there's where I did my first shows," I say. "My dad's pretzel bakery was here." I nod at the construction. "That's where the marionette theater used to be."

There's a grab in my throat. I have to think of a way to steer the conversation away from what's most painful. "Ruth," I ask abruptly, "do you know what a shill is?"

My daughter looks puzzled. She weighs the word, presses her lips in concentration. "No," she says. "What's a shill?"

But I can't answer her because I'm about to cry.

ON A DRAB winter afternoon when I was in seventh grade, a box arrived at our front door with my name written on it. No return address, just a postmark from Miami, Florida.

"Open it," said Dad.

"I'm trying," I said, hunching over the box at the kitchen table, digging my fingernails under the packing tape. "Where's Mom?"

"She's staying overnight at the hospital so she can take a test first thing in the morning," said Dad, opening a drawer and grabbing a pair of scissors. "Let me try." He jabbed a hole in a corner of the box and snipped around the edge.

"*Again?*"

"She needs a couple more tests." Dad snipped all the way around the box, cutting through the packing tape. Underneath was a layer of ochre-colored masking tape. "She'll be home tomorrow. In the meantime, I'm in charge of dinner."

The tests had begun a month earlier, after Mom got her ears pierced. The holes kept getting infected. No matter what her doctor tried—medicine, new holes, creams and solutions—her ears wouldn't heal. Now they were doing "tests." Lately when I arrived home from school, Mom was usually at the doctor's.

I unpeeled the masking tape and opened the box. Inside was a new derby—an exact replica of the old one, only bigger. No card. No note. I hadn't seen My Edna in four years. She hardly ever came to Atlantic City, and when she did, she didn't venture out of the marionette theater. I'd forgotten about her promise of a derby for life.

I lifted my new derby out of the box and held it between my fingertips. Pitch-black, with a broad brim that curled into a perfect, shell-like curve around the edge, which was slightly frayed, exactly like its predecessor.

"Dad, look." I stroked the smooth edge of the brim. "It's worn in just like mine is. But it's a new derby!"

"Is that right?" Dad asked, barely looking up. "It's beautiful," he said. "Make sure you write Edna a thank-you note. I'll try and dig up her address in Florida."

I took the derby upstairs to my bedroom, where I tried flipping it into the air and catching it on my head for about a hundred throws, until I managed three in a row. Satisfied with my progress, I reached under my bed and pulled out my yellow suitcase to put the new derby away. The new one should fit right over the old one, I figured, like Mom's set of suitcases where each case fit inside one that was a little bigger.

But when I opened my suitcase, I discovered that my old derby wasn't inside. I tromped downstairs and stuck my head into the den. "Dad? Have you seen my old derby?"

Dad swiveled his chair around to face me. "No, why? Did you misplace it?"

"No way," I said. "It was in my suitcase."

"Mom probably put it somewhere."

Puzzled, I went back upstairs to my bedroom and worked on twirling the hat, balancing it on my nose and catching it on my head for another hour until I heard Dad shout "Pizza!" from the bottom of the stairs.

"YOU CAN ARGUE until you're blue in the face," said Dad on a Sunday night during dinner, "but you're having a bar mitzvah whether you like it or not."

I rolled my eyes. "Yeah, well, in case you haven't noticed, my face doesn't get blue when I argue."

"It's an expression," said Mom.

"Well, it's a dumb expression."

"Don't be rude!" Dad barked.

"I'm not," I said. "I said it was a dumb expression. I didn't say *you* were dumb."

Glowering, Dad pointed his finger at me as if to say *enough*.

"It's so arbitrary," I said. "We don't go to synagogue. You never made me go to Hebrew school. And now, three months before I'm thirteen, all of a sudden I'm supposed to cram for an idiotic bar mitzvah?" I turned my head away from him. "Her father was right," I muttered. "You *are* a hothead . . ."

We'd never even gone to a synagogue for the Jewish holidays. Skip thought I was the luckiest kid on earth. His mom and dad dragged him and his brothers to a stone and stained-glass temple a bunch of times every fall. Each time poor Skip was stuffed like a sausage into a tight brown suit. Plus he had to go to Hebrew school two days a week after school and on Sundays.

Now, out of nowhere, Mom and Dad were acting like Skip's parents. "You guys aren't religious," I said, challenging their unilateral decision. "You didn't have bar mitzvahs. We went to Passover at the Y that one time, like a thousand years ago. What's next? Are you going to send me away to *camp* this summer?"

They wouldn't budge.

A few days later, Mom picked me up at school and we drove through the wintry streets across the city line and into town to see a rabbi who would help me "learn my part." She explained that bar mitzvah boys were expected to read Hebrew from the Torah and lead the worship.

"It's bad enough I have to go to real school," I said. "Now you want me to give up three afternoons a week for private bar mitzvah lessons?"

"Your bar mitzvah is important to me," she said softly.

I pressed my forehead into my palm and stared out the window. Over the past few months, Mom had gotten skinny—and she'd lost even more weight during her recent hospital stay. Dad did almost all the cooking now, which mostly involved ordering pizza. Usually, when I came home from school, I'd find her asleep on the living-room sofa.

Now she turned left onto Chestnut Street. It was a losing battle, but I soldiered on. "All this, plus regular homework," I said. "Really takes the cake."

"Too bad, buster," she said.

I looked across the car seat. Mom was so thin that the sun actually shone through her wrists, turning her pale skin an unnatural shade of blue. She caught me looking and tugged at the sleeves of her blue wool coat.

"Do I *have* to do this?" I asked, gazing at shoppers and businessmen bustling along Chestnut Street, bundled in overcoats and scarves, stopping to look in store windows, waving their gloved hands at taxicabs.

"Please stop whining," she said, her eyes on the road.

Pressing my nose against the car window, I realized that I could probably juggle on a street corner and draw a decent crowd.

"Will I have to come into town for my bar mitzvah lessons?" I asked. "Or is this just where we're meeting the rabbi?"

"Your lessons will be here," said Mom. "But I can't drive you most days, so you'll take a bus from school to the 69th Street terminal, then the El train into town."

Mom parked the car in an indoor garage. We walked one block to a three-story stone temple. We climbed the cement stairway to the big wooden front door. Inside we found ourselves in a dark hallway. The air smelled damp, like the back of Jimmy's marionette theater. On one wall were signs with arrows pointing in different directions: *Sanctuary. Education Director. Rabbi's Office.* "Rabbi's office," said Mom. I trailed her past a dingy lobby to the rabbi's office at the end of the hall. The door was ajar. Mom tapped on it.

"Come in," called a man's voice from inside.

Mom pushed open the door and led me in.

"You must be Mrs. Benson," said the man, rising and extending his hand.

"Nice to meet you, Rabbi," said Mom. "This is Jason."

"Shalom, Jason. How do you do, son?" We shook hands. He invited us to sit.

Rabbi Greenblatt was a wiry, delicate-looking man with oak-brown hair, a neatly trimmed beard and a small white skullcap on his head. Three of the office walls had floor-to-ceiling bookshelves. The fourth wall bore framed certificates and pictures, and a window with a view of Chestnut Street.

"Are you prepared to study?" asked the rabbi.

"I guess," I said, shrugging my shoulders and glancing out the window.

"Why do you want to be a bar mitzvah?"

The rabbi waited, stroking his beard. "I don't, actually," I said. Mom and Rabbi Greenblatt exchanged glances. "My parents are making me."

The rabbi smiled tenderly. "Well, I admire your honesty. We're taught to honor our parents, right? So, we'll begin on Wednesday. Your mother told me school lets out at two-thirty. I'll expect you here by three-thirty." Mom nodded her approval. "Oh, and here," he said, sliding a book across his desk. "If you have some time between now and Wednesday, take a look at pages 512 to 515. That's your Torah portion. See, the English translation is down here at the bottom. Read it, and then we'll discuss."

Outside the window, on Chestnut Street, I could see a black man playing a saxophone. Several people had gathered to listen. His case lay open on the sidewalk. Soon, an old man in a fedora and an overcoat dug into his pocket and tossed something into the sax case.

"Any questions?" asked the rabbi.

"What time will I get out?" I asked, eager to salvage something from this farce.

"Lessons are ninety minutes, give or take."

Glancing out the window again, I saw two more people throw money into the sax case. I calculated: in at three-thirty, out at five. I could catch the rush-hour crowd. One or two quick shows; try out my new five-ball ballet before attempting it on the boardwalk next summer. Suddenly life seemed less bleak.

I also realized that getting out of the neighborhood three afternoons a week wouldn't be so bad. Lately, Skip had been making me nervous. The day before Mom and I visited the rabbi, Skip and I were hanging out at the edge of the neighborhood where construction workers in bright yellow hardhats were building six houses. It was four o'clock. Skip looked around. No one in sight; the crews had gone home for the day. He bent down, picked up a rock the size of a baseball, wound up and threw it at one of the houses. It crashed through the front bay window.

I gasped. "Skip! What the hell!" Jagged shards of glass hung from the window frame like icicles on an underpass. One dislodged and fell to the ground, landing silently, point first, like a dagger in the fresh earth beneath the window.

"Your turn," said Skip, grinning maliciously.

It was wrong to break other people's windows, even if no one lived in the house yet. After all, someone would have to pay for a new window and clean up the broken glass. But I didn't want to let Skip down. Stone in hand, I arched backward and pitched it at a smaller first-floor window. My aim was perfect. The stone hit the glass smack in the center. The window wobbled in its frame like it was trying to breathe, like it was trying to expand and absorb the blow without falling into pieces. Then it shattered.

Now, in the rabbi's office, I stood up and offered my hand to Greenblatt. He looked surprised, but he shook it. A minute later, as Mom and I left his office, he patted me on my head. I glanced back. He was studying me. It reminded me of how Madam Diane looked at me sometimes, like she was worried. The rabbi pressed his lips into a placid smile and raised one hand to gesture goodbye.

Mom and I walked down the hallway and back out to Chestnut Street. Men and women hustled past us, bundled against the chill, puffing steam with their breath. We passed the saxophone player. A small crowd stood around him, bobbing their heads and swinging their hips. He seemed to be playing not a particular song but a tune of the city, capturing the mood of the frosty bustle and the cars and buses and pedestrians. Mom was shivering, so I didn't ask if we could stop and listen. But I thought his bouncy bopping music would be nice to juggle to.

On Wednesday I took my juggling stuff to school. When the final bell sounded, I dashed out the building to the end of the block, where I caught a bus to the 69th Street terminal, then the El train to downtown Philadelphia. White winter sunlight pierced the chill, warming the city's concrete and asphalt surfaces. It was cold but not windy. Not a bad day for juggling.

At the synagogue, Rabbi Greenblatt rolled up his sleeves and sat next to me. "On the day of your bar mitzvah, you will be called to the Torah," he explained. "The scroll. Every bar mitzvah boy reads a section from the Torah at a *Shabbat* service on the Saturday morning closest to his thirteenth birthday." He set a thick leather-bound book before me and opened it to a page that was marked with a slip of paper. "Here's your part. Of course, this isn't the scroll you'll read from, but it has the same words."

I thumbed through the brittle pages. On the right were foreign, squiggly letters; on the left, English characters forming words that made no sense. As if reading my mind, the rabbi said, "On the right is the Hebrew. On the left is what's called *transliteration*. It's English letters, you see? But they spell Hebrew words. Now, let's read aloud." He put the tip of his index finger on the top line of the left-hand page, sounding out the words to coach me as I made my way through the section.

"Ba . . . rook. Atta. Ah-dough . . . nye," I said.

"Good," said Rabbi Greenblatt. "Don't squirm."

"Alu . . . henu meleck . . ."

While I read, the rabbi rested his chin on his middle knuckle and scratched at a tiny mole on his cheek. The office air was stuffy. I wriggled in the wooden chair. A radiator hissed. "Are we almost done?" I asked.

The rabbi looked at his watch. "It's early, son. Let's try the next section, beginning on page two hundred and seventy-four, with a tune. I'll sing a line and you repeat it."

First he chanted, and then I chanted. The melody was strange. Plaintive. After a few minutes he stopped and patted me on the shoulder. "By Jove, I think you've got it!"

"Isn't that pronounced *Jehovah*?"

The rabbi laughed. "It's *Jove*. 'By Jove' is from the musical *My Fair Lady*. The other is God's name, which, we're taught, we should never utter."

"Sorry," I said. "I hope I'm not gonna get struck by lightning." As if a forced bar mitzvah wasn't punishment enough.

"It's okay," the rabbi chuckled. "You didn't know. And God is forgiving."

"Yeah, right," I said under my breath.

"Do I detect a note of sarcasm?" he asked, a mischievous grin on his face.

"I don't really believe in Him. Sorry."

He raised his brows. "You don't believe in God?" I was afraid he'd be angry, but he was still smiling.

"Even if I did," I said, "I read some of the book you gave me, and God wasn't so forgiving." I thought about something Skip had said: *There is no God. And even if there is, He's an asshole.* Skip had a point. The Old Testament God was angry. That's how He described Himself to Moses and the Israelites. God told the Israelites He was "vengeful" and "jealous" too. He didn't call Himself an Asshole, but he might as well have.

"You certainly landed a tough Torah portion," the rabbi said. "It must seem mysterious—all those rules about the holy of holies, and the guilt offerings."

It didn't seem mysterious, just bizarre. "It's kind of . . . weird," I said. "I mean, it starts with God telling Aaron he'd better not enter the temple the way his sons did, or God would have to kill him too. And Aaron doesn't even argue. He doesn't say, 'Hey, God, why'd you kill my sons?' And then, before you know it, God's telling him how to dress for Yom Kippur, and how to put the Israelites' guilt on a scapegoat, and how they're never supposed to drink blood. And it ends with the rules about uncovering nakedness."

"Sort of a mixed bag," said the rabbi, good-naturedly.

"I hear stuff about God all the time. Like what you said about Him being forgiving. And I saw a bumper sticker that said 'God is Love.'" I pointed to my book. "But this . . ."

The rabbi closed his book. "It's a good question, and enough for today. I will see you next week. We'll work on Monday, Wednesday and Thursday."

I slipped into my coat and then grabbed my school bag and juggling case.

Rabbi Greenblatt stood up. "What's in the suitcase?"

I opened my case and showed the rabbi my clubs, balls and derby.

"You juggle?" he asked.

"Yes, professionally," I said.

"You're an interesting character, Jason Benson. I'll see you on Monday afternoon."

I snapped the suitcase shut. "Thanks. So are you."

Outside, it was so cold I could see my breath. I searched for the saxophone player, walking three blocks in one direction, past display windows, office buildings and banks, back to the synagogue, then three blocks in the other direction. No sign of the musician, so I set up shop under a streetlight on Chestnut, about a block from the synagogue. I opened my case, put on my derby and pulled out three red rubber balls.

"Ladies and gentlemen," I shouted, "for the first time ever . . ."— and then added, under my breath, "in this exact location"— ". . . Jason the Magnificent!" A couple people stopped to watch me, and then a few more. By the time I finished my routine and began making my way through the audience, derby in hand, there were maybe a dozen people huddled in the cold, laughing and clapping—women carrying shopping bags from Wanamaker's; men in suits, holding briefcases, with newspapers under their arms. The take was small compared to Atlantic City—only about seven bucks—but at least now I had somewhere to perform off-season.

Over the next few weeks, Mom and Dad hired a band and a caterer. They rented the ballroom at the Warwick Hotel and planned a lavish luncheon for one hundred and fifteen guests. They told me I could invite my entire homeroom class. But no thanks. I didn't like school and I didn't like the kids there. We didn't just live in different neighborhoods; we lived in different universes.

"I'll invite Skip," I said as we sat in the living room, looking over the engraved invitations that Dad had brought home from the printer that afternoon. "And Jimmy and My Edna, and Madam Diane, and Norman, Betty and Lita."

"We can invite them," Dad said. "But don't be disappointed if Jimmy's family can't make it. They don't like to travel north in the winter." Norman and Betty might come, but neither of them drove a car, and they'd have to close the arcade for the day.

"What about your mom and dad?" I asked Mom. "Will they come from California?"

"Of course!" said Mom. "They wouldn't miss your wedding for the world!"

Dad and I turned to Mom. *"Wedding?"* we asked in unison. "Did you say 'wedding'?"

Mom made a high-pitched laugh and covered her mouth with her hand. "Bar *mitz*vah. They wouldn't miss your bar mitzvah for the world." Then she changed the subject to a conversation she'd had that morning with the caterer. Something about salmon mousse.

Dad interrupted, waving one hand insistently. "I told you to go with the other caterer. But you insisted on that idiot on Locust Street."

"He is not an idiot." Mom shuffled a neat stack of the stiff white RSVP cards and slid them back into their box. "The caterer you liked had a pre-existing commitment. Remember? This is short notice."

Dad didn't reply. He was proofreading an invitation, his index finger skimming over the text and his lips silently pronouncing each syllable. *Ed and Judith Benson cordially invite you to the bar mitzvah of their son, Jason . . .*

Mom looked happy. The invitations, RSVP cards and envelopes piled on the coffee table looked like newly opened Christmas gifts. "Just ten weeks and there's so much to do!"

RIDING ON THE BUS and the El train to and from bar mitzvah lessons, I often thought about my missing derby. How could the new one be frayed and worn in exactly like the old one? And what happened to the old one? Mom and Dad didn't seem to care. Whenever I asked them about it, it was always the same. "It's no big deal. You obviously misplaced it."

Every few days, inspired by a surge of curiosity, I carried out a new search, intently combing our basement and closets. I searched Mom's studio in the attic. I looked through Dad's file cabinets and the cardboard boxes piled up in the boiler room. I searched the garage, where we stored spare parts for the pretzel equipment. But the missing derby never turned up.

5

THE BALD TAILOR with the bushy mustache squatted behind Dad, pressing a measuring tape against the back of his pants and fingering the bottom of his cuffs. "When I quit Westinghouse and went to work for myself," Dad said, "I thought I'd never wear a suit again." The tailor clenched a small arsenal of pins between his teeth, the blunt ends sprouting from his mustache like silver stalks. He stepped back to scrutinize his work, folding his arms and raising an eyebrow.

The shop was on the sixth floor of a downtown building—a bright white-walled loft with earthy hardwood floors and rows of black metal racks bearing suits for men and boys. There were cotton, wool and mohair suits; black, brown, tan, white, powder blue and navy blue.

Mom had picked matching double-breasted, navy blue wool suits for Dad and me. For herself, she'd bought a floor-length floral-patterned dress with long sleeves and padded shoulders. It looked bulky, but it did the trick: you couldn't tell she'd lost about twenty pounds and that her arms and legs looked like pick-up sticks.

It was the end of February. The bar mitzvah was less than a month away. All the details had been handled. The invitations. The menu. The band. The flowers. The napkins. Even matchbooks with my name and the date of my bar mitzvah—March 24, 1973—printed on them.

Skip was preparing for his own bar mitzvah, scheduled for three months after mine. But he was having a rough time practicing. "The reading lady says I have *dyslexia*," he told me. We were at the shopping center, about half a mile from our neighborhood, waiting for women to come out of the Acme with their loaded shopping carts. It was one of the rare days when neither of us had a bar mitzvah lesson. We sat side by side on top of a train of shopping carts. Skip had figured out that we could help ladies unload their carts and make a few bucks in tips. "My old man took my allowance away until I study harder," he'd told me on our way to the Acme. "Fuck him. I'll make my own money."

"What's dyslexia?" I asked.

"It's the way I read. When you read you see the letters in order. Like your name: you see a . . ." He paused. "J. Then you see A and then an S-O-N, right? But I see it mixed up, like S-A-J-N-O."

I shook my head, unable to comprehend his condition. Skip just shrugged his shoulders and looked down at his sneakers. "My brain's fucked up," he said. "I'm stupid."

"No you're not," I said. The cold pricked my cheeks and nose.

Skip rubbed his hands together, cupped them and blew into them. A tall woman emerged from the Acme pushing a shopping cart loaded with brown paper grocery bags. He hollered to her, "Hey, ma'am! Need some help getting that into your car?" Hoisting himself off the carts, he jogged after the woman, angling in to offer his services. Deftly, Skip maneuvered the cart across the parking lot toward the woman's wood-paneled station wagon. She opened the back; he loaded it up and accepted her tip. "Thanks!" he said, stuffing the coins into his pocket. He returned to our perch and boosted himself back up beside me. The steely cold carts clanged under his weight. "Thirty-five cents," he said. "Not bad for two minutes' work!"

"Sorry about your dyslexia," I said. "That must make the Hebrew transliterations impossible."

Skip spat on the ground. "It's fucked up as a shithole, and all my old man ever says is work harder." Skip's dad thought Skip was lazy. I knew he wasn't stupid *or* lazy. If he didn't work hard like I did during the season, it was because his parents never asked him to rake leaves or mow the lawn or help around the house. They had Willa and a gardener for that. But Skip worked at his craft. All week long, he planned, hunched over his desk like a general in the field, making diagrams of the neighborhood and timing our getaways.

One Saturday night, Skip used his Acme tips to buy a red gas can and a gallon of kerosene at the Texaco station next door to the Acme. "We're going camping!" he told the attendant who pumped the fuel into our can. I knew we weren't going camping, but he wouldn't tell me what he was planning. "It's a surprise!"

We took turns lugging the kerosene back to the neighborhood, the can clunking against our hips, the liquid splashing and ringing inside. When we got to the bottom of my hill, Skip set the can by a sewer vent at the four-way intersection. Stretching his back, he looked around to make sure no one was watching. Then he poured the liquid down the sewer. He dug his hand into his blue-jean pocket and pulled out a pack of matches.

"Skip, wait a sec," I said, alarmed.

Ignoring me, he lit a match and tossed it into the sewer. We stood back and watched the flames leap out. After a few seconds the fire died down. Skip looked disappointed. He'd wanted to blow a nearby manhole cover into the air. "We need at least a few gallons," he said.

The fire was out, but now the intersection stunk. "We should go," I said. "You need to shower. You smell like a gas station."

"Yeah, whatever," he said, scrunching his face and staring down at the smoking gutter, silently recalculating the amount of explosives required to do the job.

I WASN'T THRILLED about my bar mitzvah, but I knew it would be over soon and I'd make a pile of gift money. Skip, on the other hand, was dreading his. He couldn't read and he wasn't accustomed to performing in front of crowds. His brothers, away at college, weren't even coming to his bar mitzvah. Instead, they were going to Washington, DC, to march against the war. According to Skip, they were hippies now. I imagined them with long hair and headbands, calling each other "man" at rock shows and protests. I wouldn't be at Skip's bar mitzvah either, because I'd be in Atlantic City.

One day in February when we were hanging out in Skip's bedroom after school, I offered to help him prepare. I knew his mom wasn't helping him; whenever I came over, she was in pajamas and fuzzy slippers, dozing in front of a muted TV. Skip said she was high on pills.

Today bar mitzvah books were scattered across his bed and his desk. "Want help practicing?" I asked, clearing some space on the bed and plopping down. On Skip's bedroom walls hung red and gray pennant flags from his summer camp—Camp Tonkino—and black and white posters from *The Man from U.N.C.L.E.*, with Napoleon Solo leaping out of a helicopter. On the inside of the door was a poster of Steve McQueen from the movie *The Great Escape*. He was on a motorcycle, jumping a fence, getting away from the Nazis.

Skip sat backward on his desk chair and faced me. "Fuck no. I'll let Rabbi *Ass-spits* handle it. That's what my folks pay him for." Skip's rabbi's name was Auspitz.

I opened a hardcover prayer book. "I have this one. I have to lead the *Shema*. 'Hear O Israel, the Lord our God, the Lord is one.' Do you have to do that one too?" I asked, handing Skip the book.

Skip flung the book at the wall above his bed. I ducked as it flew past my head. "Don't know, don't give a fuck," he said. "Ass-spits calls my old man like every week. 'Duh, Skip's not working hard enough. Duh, Skip's heart isn't in it. Skip isn't learning his part.' My old man's an asshole *and* he's a dick." He gnawed on his thumbnail, which was chewed down to a fine crescent embedded in a pad of pink flesh. "He's a dick hole."

"Okay," I said, "your old man's a dick hole, but don't eat your thumb. You might need it someday."

Skip studied his mangled thumbnail. "Fucking fuck it." He gnashed his raw cuticle with his front teeth.

Bar mitzvah lessons were less traumatic for me. I was pretty good at sounding out the English letters—*Ba-ruk at-tah*, etc. It was easy to imitate the rabbi's melodies and intonations and to memorize my part.

Once, after Rabbi Greenblatt and I wrapped up the back-and-forth Hebrew singing, he asked if I had any questions.

"What's the deal with the goats?" I asked. "Why does God tell Aaron to put the people's guilt on a goat?" The Torah story struck me as absurd and random, not unlike my bar mitzvah itself.

"When people talk about 'scapegoating,' what do you think they mean?" asked Greenblatt. "You've heard the expression, right? You've heard about Jews being scapegoated?"

I nodded my head and took a sip of water from the tall glass the rabbi had brought me from the synagogue's kitchen. I'd heard the expression, and I understood that actual goats were no longer involved. When Dad told me about World War II and the Nazis, he said that the Germans had scapegoated the Jews, blaming them for all of Germany's economic problems. Mom and Dad had also told me how their grandfathers got beat up because they were Jewish.

The rabbi tapped his fingers on his desk. "If you look around, you will see that there are still scapegoats. Take the stereotype of the greedy Jew. Greed is a human trait. *People* are greedy. Some people are greedier than others, but it's not as though gentiles as a whole are generous while Jews are not. But some gentiles believe that. And maybe even some Jews. Greedy people don't always feel so good about themselves. They feel guilty. They're ashamed because they know better. So what do they do? They project their guilt on someone else—outsiders, *others*."

"Like Jews and blacks," I said.

"How about the stereotype of the violent black man?" the rabbi asked. "What do you think about that? Are black people violent?"

I didn't know many black people. Skip's housekeeper Willa was nice. She baked peanut butter cookies and she called me "Mr.

Jason" even though I was only twelve. And the saxophone player I'd seen on Chestnut Street didn't look violent. "I don't think Jewish people are greedy or black people are violent," I said. "No more than anyone else."

The rabbi leaned forward. He spoke slowly. "Son, if you remember only one thing about our work together and your Torah portion, I hope it will be this: When people . . . when *we* put our guilt and our anger on others . . . that's scapegoating," he said. "You see? It's like when God told Aaron that one goat would bear the Israelites' guilt. This is what people do. It's part of the human equation. What we loathe about ourselves we project onto others."

While I took a long drink of water and pondered all this, the rabbi eyed me the way Madam Diane did—like he knew what I was thinking. "Let me ask you something," he said. "Have you ever done something you felt guilty about? You don't have to tell me what it was. But you know what I'm talking about, right?"

I knew exactly what he was talking about. I felt guilty about breaking windows with Skip.

The rabbi asked another question: "Ever get mad at somebody who was connected to what you felt guilty about—maybe even the victim—but you can't put your finger on exactly why you're mad at them? It's not like they insulted you or took your place in line or stole your lunch. They didn't hurt you. And maybe you even hurt them. But *you're* mad at *them.*"

I thought about the people who owned the houses whose windows we'd broken, who had to fix their windows before they even moved in. It was a rotten way to welcome new neighbors. Skip said they were a bunch of assholes for building houses where the woods used to be. "But this whole neighborhood used to be woods," I'd said. "They cut down the woods to build the houses, including yours and mine."

"When my folks bought their house it was already a house," said Skip. "Same with yours. But these pricks . . ."—he hitched his thumb at the new homes with the shattered windows—"they tore down the woods. My brothers used to play there, but you and me can't."

Back in the rabbi's office, it began to look clearer to me. The homeowners hadn't done anything wrong, so why was Skip mad at them? Because, if you're angry or guilty or ashamed, you won't have a problem finding somebody else to blame.

"What are you thinking?" asked the rabbi.

"I guess people like to keep their scapegoats handy."

He raised his eyebrows and leaned back in his chair. "That's profound, young man." Once again, he gazed into my eyes like a fortune-teller. "As you go through life," he said, "when you're angry, before you blame somebody for how you feel, step back and look at yourself."

"WHAT'S A SHILL, Dad?" Ruth asks again, trying to call me back from my stupor while I stare grimly at the imposing hotel under construction where the bakery used to be.

Men and women pass us on the boardwalk, consulting tourist maps that flutter in the wind like tent flaps. Do any of them notice this guy scrunching his face like he's going to sob?

"Technically," I say, wiping my eyes and gathering enough composure to answer, "a shill is an accomplice. A decoy—somebody posing as a customer to make a vendor appear more valuable. But down here, it was anybody who stood in front of a business trying to woo customers in."

I used to be a shill. Right here on this spot my life was remarkable before I spent two decades holding back my memories. I'm the Hoover Dam of nostalgia. Now the dam has burst. Recollections flood my head—stuffing steaming hot pretzels in brown bags on days so sweltering that people on the boardwalk looked wavy; ringing up sale after sale; scraping salt that had caked on the wooden pretzel boards and the oven; the daily spectacle of men and women, boys and girls ambling up and down the boardwalk.

I can't stand the sight of what's no longer here. So I turn my back and walk on, fast, Ruth and Eileen scrambling to keep up. I can't tell if their faces are sympathetic because, right now, I can't even see where I'm going.

THE FIRST HINT that the dam had a leak came a few months ago, during a meeting with my company's HR director. *Can you stop by my office before COB today?* That's what Allen's email had said. A few hours later, when I popped my head into his office, I assumed he was going to give me bad news about two new hires I'd requisitioned. I knew the drill: Allen would push back, explaining that funds were tight, and I'd stand my ground, arguing that we needed at least one more senior-level copywriter to handle projects already in the pipeline.

"Jason, come in!" said Allen, welcoming me into his cluttered office with a sweep of his arm. "Have a seat." He gestured to the empty chair across from his desk. A tall, scarecrow-like man around my age, with thinning hair and nerdy T. S. Eliot glasses, Allen was one of the few people at the firm who wore a tie to work. Around the office, with its modern mesh of stainless steel and glass, Allen looked out of place—a tweedy anachronism. But he looked like he belonged here in his cove, isolated from the agency's day-to-day events and its legion of hipster staffers decked out in black.

"Let's cut to the chase," I said, taking a seat across from him. "I need two copywriters, you're going to tell me there's a freeze and I can't hire any, so can we settle on one and get out of here on time for once?" I shot Allen a friendly grin and drummed his desktop with two expectant fingers.

Allen tightened his face and drew a deep breath like he was in pain.

"You okay?" I asked. "You look like you have a toothache."

"This . . . isn't about new hires."

I surveyed his office—a jam-packed space, files piled on the desk and a bookshelf crammed with legal journals, trade magazines and a sagging row of self-help and management books.

"What's up?" I asked.

"Well, it's never easy, you know."

I sat upright like a bolt, suddenly nauseous. "Oh, shit! Am I getting fired?" After fifteen years, this is how they let me go?

Allen waved his arms. "No, no. Sorry . . ."

Shaking off my panic, I asked, "What's this about then?"

"There's been a complaint."

"About what?" I asked. He regarded me in silence. "*Me?*"

He nodded his head, slowly and unenthusiastically. I hadn't fired anyone in over a year. I hadn't even disciplined anyone since I could remember. But even as I furrowed my brow to give the appearance of confusion, I knew.

"What kind of complaint?" I asked. Allen hesitated, his face compressed like he was warding off an ice cream headache. "What *kind* of complaint?" I repeated.

"It's um, harassment." His voice was barely a whisper, like he was pronouncing a bleak diagnosis. *It's AIDS. It's cancer.*

I met Allen's eyes with my own. "It was Jennifer in Marketing."

Allen brushed this off. "I can't reveal who complained. But it will be taken seriously, I will investigate it, and if the investigation turns up anything—if this escalates . . ."

"Aw, fuck that!" I said.

"Hey, guy," he said. "Watch the language."

"Sorry, but there's nothing to investigate. Call her now. Get her up here."

Allen's lips curled into an impatient, professional smile. "Jason, please don't order me around."

"Then don't accuse me . . ."

"I'm not accusing."

"Just call her?" I placed my hand flat on his desk. "Invite her up, let her look me in the eye."

Allen held his palms up, silently pleading for me to stifle myself. "That's not how it works. Don't make this any . . ."

"I'm not making this *any*thing!"

"Will you tone it down?" he asked tersely.

My heart pounded. "I'm not making this anything," I said in the most matter-of-fact register I could muster, like I was lecturing a five-year-old. Gentle. Direct. "Nothing happened."

"I understand," he said, folding his hands on his desk. "The complainant is saying one thing and you're saying something else—and it's my job to investigate fairly and discreetly."

"Did you just say 'complainant'? You sound like a fucking prosecutor!"

"I'm not going to ask you again to watch your language and control yourself."

"I'm being falsely accused!"

"Then you have nothing to fear."

"We talked," I said. "That's all—and never about anything inappropriate."

"Noted," he said. "And remember, I'm not at liberty to reveal who made the complaint, so don't assume . . ."

"I *know* who it was," I said, struggling to keep my volume low and my indignation muted, wiping my hand across my sweaty forehead.

Allen looked uncomfortable. He scraped his bottom teeth against his upper lip. "Right now," he said, "do your job and I'll look into this. It could be just a misunderstanding."

"I did nothing wrong."

"If you did nothing wrong, how can you be so sure who made the complaint?" He raised his eyebrows as if to crow "gotcha."

My heart pulsed in my throat. Allen shuffled a couple of papers, patted his desktop and looked at his watch. The meeting was over. But I wasn't ready to leave. "Theoretically," I said. "If it was her, what did she accuse me of?"

"This is not the time or place," he said.

My cheeks and forehead flushed, I stood my ground. "Did she tell you something happened between us? If she did, I'm filing a complaint against her because that's a false accusation!"

"No one alleged anything like that," he said.

"All we did was talk. If she's claiming something else, she's lying."

Allen raised his chin and perked his ears to show he was listening to me. "Then why, when I brought this up, were you immediately certain of who made the complaint? You talk with a lot of people, right?"

"It's because of what we talked about. We didn't talk about work or which restaurants or coffee shops to go to, or any of the usual bullshit people talk about here. We talked about Atlantic City. We're both from there. She's the first person I've met from there in twenty years."

Allen folded his hands on his desk. "How often did you talk about Atlantic City? How often did you show up at her desk? How many emails, how many instant messages and how many texts did you send her? How many times over the past two months did you invite her out for coffee?"

I put my head in my hands. "Oh, for Christ's sake. I invited her for coffee so we could reminisce when we weren't on company time. That's not harassment. It's good judgment."

"Did you get the feeling that your nonstop invitations might have made her feel uncomfortable?" asked Allen. "Did you consider that because she's new and younger than you and because you're a lot higher up on the org chart, she felt she *had* to meet you, she *had* to talk with you every time you showed up at her cube? Theoretically, I mean."

"No," I said. "There's no way I made her uncomfortable."

"How can you know that?" Allen asked. "Isn't it at least possible that you made her feel uncomfortable without intending to?"

I gazed directly across the desk at the man who wanted me to leave his office. "I know, because this is bullshit." I stood up. "Look, do your investigation. I won't say a goddamned word to that girl."

"Good plan," said Allen, rising from his chair and extending his hand across his desk. I shook it and turned to leave his office. "One thing before you go . . . ," he said.

I stopped and turned, my hand on the doorframe.

"We've known each other a long time," he said. "So I'm suggesting, not as your HR guy, but as your friend. Nothing official, just to remind you about the agency's employee assistance program. It pays one hundred percent. If you want to talk to somebody."

He wanted me to see a shrink. Now my job could be in jeopardy. I'd never cheated on Eileen, and if I were going to, I wouldn't be dumb enough to carry on with somebody from work. This was insane. "Thanks, sure, whatever," I said, stepping out of Allen's office.

"Thank *you* for listening," he said from the doorway, as if handing me a bromide. I raised one arm without turning around. I fought off the urge to flip him the middle finger.

As I made my way down a flight of stainless steel stairs and across to my desk, I worried about who else Jennifer had told. My cheeks and ears burned. I gazed at the floor, avoiding eye contact from colleagues in the cubes and hallways around me. When I arrived at my desk, I sat down, my face in my hands, feeling like a pariah.

I'd discovered Jennifer's origins by accident, sitting at her boss Rosemary's desk, absently thumbing through a half-dozen resumes. "Atlantic City High School 1994" leapt off the page. "Whoa!" I said. "Did you hire this one?"

"Yep, started a week ago," said Rosemary, the manager in charge of the marketing group. "Rutgers. Scholarship kid. Good listener. Gets in early."

According to Jennifer's resume she'd held summer jobs on the boardwalk and an internship at the *Atlantic City Press*. Could I detect a whiff of ocean air? Had she printed her resume on beach-scented paper? A minute later, drawn like a riptide against my better judgment, I stood at Jennifer's cube. She was a good-looking girl in her early twenties, with curly strawberry blond hair tucked into a wide ponytail and a dewy, freckled face. She stared intently at her computer monitor, deciphering numbers on a spreadsheet.

"Jennifer?" I asked. She looked up. "Jason Benson." I extended my hand. "Creative director, Editorial."

"Oh, hey, nice to meet you." She sized me up. I liked that: a girl who didn't back down, didn't feel intimidated by a workplace superior. I knew I had that effect on some of the younger ones.

"I was just over at Rosemary's desk, I saw your resume and had to come meet you," I said. A hint of uncertainty crossed Jennifer's face. "Nothing's wrong," I said. "I'm glad you're here. Guess what. I'm from Atlantic City too!" It felt like a confession but sounded natural, as though I'd been saying it for years.

Her face lit up. "Oh, cool!"

"I left in '78."

"I was two years old then."

"Your family still down there?"

"Yeah, my father's a manager at Bally's," she said.

"I haven't been down there in forever. My dad and I ran a pretzel bakery on the boardwalk at Texas, and I used to juggle on the boardwalk."

"Back in the day," she said. "Magicians, guitar players . . ."

"When I close my eyes it all comes back," I said. That was a lie. For twenty years I did not close my eyes and it did not all come back. "Your parents probably saw my act. I was Jason the Magnificent." I hadn't uttered the words "Jason the Magnificent" since I was Jennifer's age. But it felt natural.

"Small world indeed," I said, extending my hand again. She took it, but when she withdrew, I must have held hers for an instant too long. Her discomfort was subtle—a millisecond lurch of her fingers.

"I gotta run," I said, "but I'd love to talk with you more about Atlantic City."

"That would be nice."

"I'm upstairs, in Editorial. Stop by."

Jennifer never made it up to Editorial, but I stopped by her desk several times to reminisce. Did she remember the Two for One Arcade? Did Madam Diane ever tell her fortune? Did she remember Jimmy? What beach did she hang out at? Did her parents buy pretzels from us? Did they ever catch my show? I hadn't spoken of Atlantic City for two decades. I hadn't allowed myself to think about the place. New Yorkers don't go to Atlantic City. We're more a Seaside Heights crowd. I hadn't gone out of my way to avoid Atlantic City in conversations, just didn't bring it up; nor did anyone else. Until I picked up Jennifer's resume and got a whiff of my past.

The day after my meeting with Allen was a Saturday. Ruth had slept over at a friend's the night before. Outside it was icy cold and sunny. Eileen and I lay in bed, snuggling, sipping coffee, the window curtains pulled open and the sun streaming in. I could not get my talk with Allen out of my head. I tried the usual tricks— breathing consciously like Bobby had taught me; visualizing the day ahead. But I could not *not* think about it.

Eileen nuzzled me. She likes nuzzling her face against my stubbly beard. I thought we were going to have sex. Under the blankets, I twisted my legs to press against hers, hoping for a distraction from yesterday's meeting. But she wanted something else.

"Mmmm, listen. We need to talk," she said, pulling away from my embrace, planting herself upright against the headboard. She took her coffee mug from her nightstand and waited for me to pick up mine.

I fussed with the blankets and hoisted myself up until we were side by side. "What's up? Are you worried about my heart? Don't be. They're gonna put me on Zocor. I'm gonna live to be a hundred. And sex will not give me a heart attack."

She sipped her coffee. "You're right," she said. "I'm not worried about that."

"Okay, so what's on your mind?" I asked.

"Over the past few months . . ." She paused, casting her glance at the ceiling. "You've changed."

"I don't know what you mean," I said. But I knew exactly what she meant. I'd been even more distant, worried about Jennifer mentioning Atlantic City to Eileen at the spring gala.

Eileen laced her fingers around her coffee mug and took another sip. What could I tell her? That I'd been falsely accused of harassment? Practically interrogated by my HR director? The subject of an investigation? That a twenty-three-year-old woman had complained I was stalking her? That I'd sent two dozen text messages inviting her out for coffee and to talk about a part of my life I'd never even mentioned to Eileen? That although the girl had been frightened by my attention, I remained oblivious until she filed a complaint?

"You have this edge," Eileen told me. "You're distracted. And you screamed at Ruth in front of her friends. That's not you. It's out of character. What's the matter?"

"I lost my temper. I told her I was sorry. What am I supposed to do?"

"You wake up in the middle of the night. You toss and turn. Whatever was bugging you then is still on your mind." She stroked my arm. "I wish you'd tell me."

Some weeks before, Ruth had had a raucous sleepover on a Saturday night that ended at three o'clock in the morning when I called her friends' parents and demanded they come pick up their "obnoxious daughters" whose wild laughter and moody, pretentious music were keeping me awake. Eileen had tried to stop me from making the calls. She pleaded. Ruth tugged at my arm when she heard me on the phone with the parents, begging me to put the receiver down. "Check-out time!" I yelled, hulking in the doorway to the basement playroom where the girls were spread across the floor in their sleeping bags.

Ruth covered her mouth with her hand, then spun and darted out of the basement and upstairs to her bedroom. "I hate you!" she shrieked. "I hate you!"

"Everybody pack your stuff!" I yelled. The girls scrambled out of their sleeping bags and began putting jeans on over pajamas, hopping around the basement like kangaroos. "Your parents are on their way because you're all too rude to let other people sleep!"

Ever since that night, Ruth had avoided eye contact with me, offering only grunts and glum one-word answers. But wasn't that typical teenage bullshit? Wouldn't she spurn her father no matter how he treated her?

Now, sitting in bed beside Eileen, I looked up at the ceiling. "Sorry. I guess I can be a real asshole sometimes."

"Actually, lately, it's a lot of the time."

"Oh, come on. At worst I'm a part-time asshole."

She faced me, propping her chin on her palm. "This isn't something you can brush away with a joke."

"Other fathers yell more than me."

"You're right!" she said. "Like I just said, it's not you. You're more distant than ever. You're disaffected. You're two paces removed from the rest of life. Ruth needs you. She's struggling in school. She's losing her confidence."

"I'm here for Ruth," I said.

"No you're not! You're physically present, but you're not engaged. You're stuck in your own head. Do you know what I mean?"

I knew exactly what she meant. I'd heard it before. "No," I said dryly.

She pursed her lips, searching for the right words. I watched her rib cage expand and contract. "The other day Ruth asked me what you were like when we met," she said. "She wanted to know what attracted me to you. I told her how funny you used to be, and that you made me laugh every day."

Her use of the past tense was making me nervous. "And what did she say to that?" I asked.

"She asked how someone like the man I married could become such an asshole. She told me she got mad at you the night of her sleepover party, and now she can't get un-mad. She's stuck being mad at you."

It felt like a kick in my teeth. "*She* said 'asshole'? But I'm not like that," I said. "I'm funny." This sounded pathetic even to myself. Arguing that you're funny is pretty much the opposite of being funny.

"You *can* be funny," Eileen told me. "But mostly you're moody and withdrawn. Ruth says you never listen to her. She's right. And you don't listen to me, either."

She paused. I braced myself; sipped my coffee, looked out the window at the puffy winter clouds. Her next remark landed like a fifty-pound sack of flour.

"I think you should talk to someone about what's going on."

This was the second time I'd been diagnosed with clinical assholism in twenty-four hours. When Allen told me, it felt like a manageable disruption in my juggling pattern—like dropping one ball and recovering mid-bounce. But Eileen's warning was like watching all the balls bounce away in every direction, out of reach, unrecoverable. It made me want a cure, or at least a treatment. Hopefully clinical assholism could be managed, like diabetes. Or heart disease.

"Or . . . what?" I asked.

She pressed her hand to my shoulder, her eyes rimmed with tears. I sank my head. She didn't answer. No ultimatum, no conditions. "I love you so much," she said, her voice a whisper.

ON THE WAY HOME from the tailor shop after our bar mitzvah suit fittings, I asked Dad why he was spending so much money on my bar mitzvah. The pretzel bakeries were doing well, but blowing a wad of cash on a fancy party wasn't his style. He clenched his jaw, pressed the wiper and washer button and cleared some gray-brown slush from the windshield. "It's important to your mother," he said.

"I know, but why?" I asked. The Old Testament stories were dumb. No one lived to be a hundred and forty. Parting the Red Sea, drawing water from a rock—Moses' water tricks were like my disappearing derby. I don't know how he turned his staff into a serpent, but I'd seen boardwalk magicians do the same thing with a handkerchief and a rabbit.

"Seriously," I said to Dad. "Why am I doing this?" I stared across the car seat.

Slowly the muscles in his neck tightened. He turned around to check for traffic behind us, and then he stepped on the brake pedal and swerved into the parking lane, screeching to a stop. He took off his glasses, revealing dark rings under his eyes. He pointed his index finger at my face. "Mom. Wants. This," he said. Stern. Irrefutable. Mom. Wanted. It. He pulled back out into traffic.

I should have muttered "Okay" and then stared glumly out the window. But against my better judgment I said, "You're basically telling me that Mom wants it because Mom wants it. But that's ridiculous. If she's so hot to trot, maybe *she* should have a bar mitzvah."

This time, Dad didn't pull over. He drove and yelled at the same time. "Why are you so ungrateful? We're doing this for you! It's your heritage! Why can't you just appreciate it? You'll make money! Stop your goddamn bellyaching!"

"I'm not bellyaching. I'm just asking why. The rabbi says it's Jewish to ask questions."

"It's Jewish to honor your goddamn parents!"

"I *am*!" I said. "I'm doing the bar mitzvah. I'm going to Greenblatt three times a week. You and I got matching suits. We look like the Temptations. I'm honoring the hell out of you! All I'm asking is why this particular honor!"

It came like a surprise wave that catches you from behind, buckling your knees, tossing you like a rag doll and filling your lungs with salt water. "Shut up!" Dad bellowed in my face, splattering me with spit. "Keep your damn mouth closed!" His breath smelled like stale coffee and his words cracked like fists.

I reeled against the passenger door, pressed my forehead to the window. After Dad finished yelling, he didn't say anything. We were on the West River Drive by the Schuylkill River. The sun was setting. It was chilly outside. Scull boats glided like water bugs on the river's surface. With Dad's outburst echoing in my ears, I watched the racing boats as we passed them. My head spun. I thought about how the water flowed from the Schuylkill to the Delaware, to the bay, and eventually to the ocean. *Next summer, when I'm looking at the ocean*, I thought, *I will think about how some of the water will have come from the Schuylkill River.*

At last Dad took a deep breath. He relaxed his grip on the steering wheel and slowed to a normal speed, stared out the window into the dusk. The river reflected lights from the boathouses along its banks. When Dad stopped at the traffic light before we left the drive, he turned to me again. This time he spoke softly. "I'm . . . sorry."

I grunted and wiped the back of my hand at my eyes. Neither of us said anything else the rest of the way home.

6

RABBI GREENBLATT HAD walked me through the service so many times that I knew the drill like a three-ball cascade. On the morning of the big day I wasn't even nervous. Before the service, I sat in the rabbi's office while the guests filed into the sanctuary. I looked around, taking it in one last time: the hissy radiator with the peeling yellow paint, the water glasses, the rabbi's desk piled high with leather-bound volumes, the flocked wallpaper.

The rabbi came in wearing a long black robe and a hat that looked like one I'd seen the Pope wearing in *Time* magazine. He handed me a prayer shawl and showed me how to drape it over my shoulders. He stepped back and looked me up and down. "It's time," he said, squeezing my arm and straightening my yarmulke. We marched out of his office, down the musty hallway to the back of the sanctuary. He opened the door. I followed him to the altar. He walked over to the pulpit while I took a seat next to the ark of Torah scrolls.

I scanned the crowd. Almost everyone was a stranger: Dad's business acquaintances, relatives I'd never heard of until a month earlier when their RSVPs began to arrive, and synagogue regulars. One night six weeks earlier, while the three of us sat at the dining-room table licking and sealing invitations, I'd asked, "Who's Harriet Benson?"

"She's my aunt," Dad said. "My father's sister, which makes her your great-aunt."

"Do you think she'll come?"

"Who knows?" said Dad. "I haven't been in contact with anyone from Cleveland since I was seventeen."

"Why not?"

He shook his head. "When I was eighteen I went into the army. After my father died . . ."

I interrupted: "You mean after he went away on business?"

"Right," he said. "After he went away on business I never saw much of the family—just my Uncle Joe who brought me to Atlantic City for my first summer."

"The doctor," I said, constructing a mental timeline of Dad's early years. "So he brought you down there the summer between eleventh and twelfth grade?"

"And after high school I did my hitch in the army, then started at Penn, and my mother went away on business, and then I was either working on the boardwalk or in school."

I tried to picture Dad as an orphan. What would I do if that ever happened to me? Leave and never return like he did?

Now, on the big day, men in suits and women in fancy hairdos stared back at me, winking their encouragement and whispering to one another. Skip was there. He looked small, wedged between two women I didn't recognize.

In the back of the synagogue, sitting alone in the very last row, were my grandparents, whom I hadn't seen since their big fight with Mom and Dad in front of the pretzel bakery six years earlier. We'd talked on the phone for a few seconds every month when they called Mom from California. "How are you? How's school?" Then I'd hand the receiver back to Mom. They sent me birthday cards with cash inside, and I sent them polite thank-you notes. But I didn't know them. Here at my bar mitzvah, they looked the same as I remembered: he with slicked-back hair and a pencil-thin mustache; she, dark, severe and matronly, her hair pulled back so tight it made my scalp scream.

The organist played a doleful tune. I took a deep breath to focus my thoughts on the service that was about to begin.

Rabbi Greenblatt warmed up the crowd with a few Hebrew blessings. I sat next to the carved black walnut ark, in a red velvet chair with a high back, my nose buried in my prayer book. My neck itched. The rabbi turned to the ark and removed the Torah draped with an embroidered gold and white cover, a shiny silver breastplate and dozens of sparkling bells and epaulets. That was my cue. I stood and walked to the pulpit. While Rabbi Greenblatt held the scroll, I removed the Torah cover. Hands steady, so that the tiny bells on the silver handles didn't jingle, I placed the Torah's adornments on a wooden rack.

It was time for my Torah reading. Mom and Dad joined us at the altar, where they sang a blessing in Hebrew, reading the transliteration from a cue card scotch-taped on top of the pulpit. Rabbi Greenblatt unrolled the scroll and handed me a pearl-handled silver pointer. I'd memorized my part, so I didn't even have to read from the English-lettered cheat sheet that the rabbi had brought along. But I did pretend to use the pointer as if I were actually reading from the Torah. From the corner of my eye, I caught several nods of approval from the front row. At one point, just to add tension, I stumbled over the words a little.

After working my way through the Hebrew, I read the portion in English:

Then he is to take the two goats and present them before the LORD at the entrance to the Tent of Meeting. He is to cast lots for the two goats—one lot for the LORD and the other for the scapegoat. Aaron shall bring the goat whose lot falls to the LORD and sacrifice it for a sin offering. But the goat chosen by lot as the scapegoat shall be presented alive before the LORD to be used for making atonement by sending it into the desert as a scapegoat.

When I finished, everyone sat silently for a few seconds. I swiped my finger at a bead of perspiration on my neck. Finally Rabbi Greenblatt signaled to Mom and Dad, and they all sang another blessing. I helped the rabbi dress the Torah and everyone stood while he returned it to the ark. Rabbi Greenblatt gestured for Mom and Dad and me to come over to the ark. He put his hands on my shoulders and whispered a blessing in Hebrew. Then, louder and in English, he said, "I've enjoyed getting to know you these past few months, Jason. I'm impressed with your diligence, your discipline and your character. Today you are a man. Where your life will lead, only God himself knows. And God generally doesn't reveal our destinies to us."

"That darn God," I mouthed to the rabbi.

Mom and Dad held hands. Their faces were taut, their jaws strained. Why was this a big deal to them?

Somebody in the congregation sniffled. Somebody else said, "Shh!" Rabbi Greenblatt closed his eyes and placed his hands on my head. He whispered something in Hebrew. I closed my eyes too. When I opened them, he was looking straight down at me. It was my turn to say a few words.

I looked out over the crowd, like I was about to launch three balls into the air. This was something I'd learned from watching Henry the Juggler. You don't just dive straight into your patter. You take a breath, you hold back; you wait until they're a little hungry.

"Thank you for being here," I began. "Yesterday I was a boy. Tomorrow I'll be a teenager again. But today I am a man." The crowd chuckled. "And as a man for a day," I continued, "I would like to thank my mom and dad, Ed and Judy Benson, for their support. And thanks to Rabbi Greenblatt. If you have to have a bar mitzvah, make this man your go-to rabbi. You won't regret it.

"These days, God's not in our faces like he was in Moses' and Aaron's. But we all know what's right. We know how we're supposed to live. The Torah shows us how to treat one another. Sometimes it shows us how not to. Like scapegoating. God tells Aaron how to make a scapegoat. Now, today in 1973, I don't think God actually expects anybody to put their guilt on goats and fling them off cliffs. But maybe if we look at that part of the Torah through modern eyes, we can learn something about how we put our guilt on others. Sometimes when I hear people say, 'Lazy hippies!' or

'You can't trust *those people*,' I think there could be some scape-goating going on."

I paused to look at the crowd again. My speech wasn't meant to be sad—just stuff I'd learned from Greenblatt. Yet about a quarter of the audience looked like they were about to cry. A few were even wiping away tears. Sure, people cried at weddings. But bar mitz-vahs? It made no sense. I glanced to my right. Mom's weight had dropped even more over the past two weeks. She was so skinny, even in her puffy dress. Her legs looked like pencils.

Suddenly I realized I wasn't the only one watching her. Most of the crowd was, too. And Dad didn't just have his arm around her. He was holding her up.

And then I began to say something about how a scapegoat doesn't even know he's a scapegoat. He just feels really bad. And it hit me: Mom had accidentally called my bar mitzvah a wedding because she knew she wouldn't be at my wedding. I tried to speak, but the words got caught in the back of my mouth.

I was a veteran performer who could handle drunken heck-lers showing off to their girlfriends. But I had no clever tricks to save this moment. Tongue thick and cheeks burning, I felt like I'd been grazed by a freight train. I sucked in my breath, my cheeks and forehead burning. My voice cracked. A hot tear rolled down my cheek. I tried again, but it felt like I was choking on the words. I swallowed, gulping air and tasting bile.

The rabbi materialized beside me, his hand on my shoulder. After a moment, he began to speak. I couldn't make out his words. But the next thing I knew, he was crying too. He didn't fall apart; he just sniffled a little, told the crowd what a great student I'd been and how it had been an emotional day for everyone. Now the en-tire congregation's eyes were on him.

At that moment, the rabbi pulled off a trick as mysterious as My Edna's gift-for-life derby: He made my embarrassment disappear.

The organ kicked in and everybody sang in Hebrew.

After the songs, Mom and Dad and the rabbi and I climbed down the stairs to the sanctuary floor. The organ music stopped, and a guy up front made an announcement in Hebrew. Everyone shook hands, then went to the doors and got in line to shake hands with us. My aunts from Cleveland pinched my cheeks. At the end of the line were my grandparents. Up close, they looked older than I remembered them. They hugged and kissed Mom and shook hands with Dad, who greeted them warmly, using both of his hands to shake each of theirs.

By now, the mood was festive. People slapped me on the back, told me how well I'd done (as if I hadn't frozen up and cried at the end) and congratulated Mom and Dad.

In the synagogue lobby Rabbi Greenblatt stood before a table that held several bottles of wine, dozens of little plastic cups and a long loaf of braided bread studded with raisins. The rabbi raised a cup of wine while two old men in baggy suits and white yarmulkes filled the little cups and passed them around. When everyone had a cup of wine, the rabbi made a short blessing in Hebrew and everyone drank. Skip held a cup of wine in each hand. He drank them both, then made his way back to the table, where he grabbed at a third and fourth before one of the men shooed him away.

Soon it was time to leave the synagogue for the big reception.

We walked six blocks to the Warwick Hotel, stopping twice along the way for Mom to sit on a bench and catch her breath.

"Should I go back and get the car?" asked Dad at the second stop, his lapels rippling in the breeze.

"No," said Mom. "Don't fuss. I'm fine. What a big morning."

Dad looked worried. "You sure?"

"Absolutely," Mom said, patting the bench for me to sit beside her. "I love you," she whispered.

"I love you too, Mom. Thanks for all this."

She clasped my hand in hers. So now I knew. And she knew I knew.

A wind gust ruffled my suit jacket. Mom extended a hand for Dad to help her up. "A block and a half to go," said Dad, delicately pulling Mom to her feet. We walked the rest of the way to the Warwick with Dad and me on either side of Mom, who held tightly to our arms.

The Warwick's ballroom was rimmed by twenty round tables, each bearing a white tablecloth, delicate china place settings and a centerpiece that Mom had made with wicker fruit baskets filled with Dad's soft pretzels. Somehow I managed to put my dismal new knowledge aside. It was like juggling. I could let it float aloft and deal with other, more immediate items. With mental effort, I could blot out the crowd, the hecklers and the traffic. Focus on the pattern, on each ball hitting its peak before the next throw, and don't think about what's beyond your next toss.

While the band played a mix of big band, sixties soul and rock and roll, I went from table to table greeting our guests, who stuffed envelopes into my hand. After a while, I ducked into the men's room, tore open a few and peeked inside. Savings bonds. Checks. Cash. I estimated my total take: two, maybe three thousand bucks. Not bad for three months of lessons and a morning's work.

The Cleveland relatives sat around three tables—an odd-looking lot: paunchy, bald men in checkered suits, and women with layers of makeup caked on their faces. They all seemed happy to meet me. "Jason," gushed Uncle Sam. "Your Hebrew's as good as my rabbi's!" He shoved an envelope at me with one hand while licking salmon grease off the other. "A little something," he said.

"I'm your Aunt Harriet from Cleveland," announced a fat red-headed woman across the table from Uncle Sam.

I walked around to shake her hand. "I remember you from the invitations," I said. Aunt Harriet grabbed hold of me and drew me into a long, wrenching hug. Underneath her heavy perfume she smelled like meat. She knew about Mom. I could tell by the way she held my shoulders and looked into my eyes.

The band was playing "Light My Fire" (probably the most un-danceable song ever recorded). Aunts and uncles bobbed and ducked, making goofy, swishy motions with their necks. When they saw me watching they'd smile and wave like they were posing for a picture.

Someone came up behind me and took hold of my shoulders. I turned around. It was my grandfather. "Pretzels still three for a quarter?" he asked affably.

We shook hands. "Are you kidding? Quarter apiece, five for a buck," I told him.

"Come over to the table, *boychick*," he said, handing me an envelope, which I stuffed in my breast pocket. "Your grandmother wants to talk to you."

The band launched into a rendition of "Do You Like Soul Music? (That Sweet Soul Music)." When I arrived at their table, my grandmother kissed my cheek and patted the empty chair next to her. I sat down between my grandparents and leaned in so we could hear one another over the music. I could tell right away she didn't know about Mom. If she knew, she wouldn't be smiling.

Mom was so thin and weak. Why hadn't I guessed before? Because I didn't want to know—like my grandparents didn't want to know. Now I was thinking about it again, and my head grew warm, my neck tense. Breathe, I reminded myself. Breathe and concentrate on the current throw.

"How's school?" asked my grandfather.

"It's okay," I said. "I keep my grades up so I can juggle downtown."

They glanced at each other suspiciously, like I'd confessed a bank robbery. "What's the matter?" I asked, looking back and forth between them, a wily half-smile on my face.

"We don't understand," said my grandfather.

"I'm a juggler," I explained. "Every summer on the boardwalk. And now I do it here in town. People give me tips."

"On the streets?" asked my grandmother. "You *beg*?"

"It's not begging!" I said, rattled by her question.

"Does your mother know about this?"

"Yeah, of course," I said. "I'm not doing anything wrong, and I'm not even allowed if I don't keep my grades up." Now I was beginning to understand why Mom and Dad avoided Mom's parents.

But I didn't want to quarrel, so I changed the subject. "Anyway, how are things in California?"

"Beautiful," said my grandfather, sounding relieved to avoid an argument. "You should visit."

I stood up. "That'd be really neat." I kissed my grandmother's cheek and shook my grandfather's hand. "See you guys later," I said, starting across the ballroom to find Mom and Dad. Halfway across, I spotted them on the dance floor, clasping each other tightly, slow-dancing to "Papa's Got a Brand New Bag." I remembered the funny chicken dance they used to do, pigeon-toed with arms splayed, strutting around the kitchen. But today Mom's arms were draped over Dad's shoulders, clutching him for support.

By now, lots of people were on the dance floor twisting and grinding. And in the middle of it all, Skip was dancing with a lady I didn't recognize. She was about my parents' age—a first or second cousin once or twice removed. She and Skip were really going at it! She held a drink in one hand while she danced, and every time she wiggled her backside, she spilled some on the floor. Skip hopped up and down and waved his arms like a lunatic. His tie was loose, his shirt untucked. I'd never seen him like this before. He was usually pretty quiet around adults.

Dad came over to me and put his hand on my back. "Looks like somebody got into the Mogen David." It took a few seconds for me to register that Skip was drunk.

When the song ended, Skip and his dance partner exchanged wobbly bows and stumbled off in separate directions. Walking past an empty table, Skip grabbed a partially finished cocktail. Dad scrambled across the ballroom and grabbed his wrist to stop him. Skip yanked his arm out of Dad's grasp, but he tugged too hard and lost his balance. Dad tried to catch him while Skip grabbed hold of a metal cart filled with dirty dishes. The cart toppled—plates, saucers and drinks crashing on the floor. And there lay Skip—his glasses half off and his suit covered in thick, white blue-cheese dressing.

Dad didn't yell. He just signaled to one of the waiters that he needed a hand. They guided Skip to his feet, steered him to an empty table and sat him down. Mom came over and whispered with Dad for a minute while waiters and busboys cleaned up the mess from the overturned cart. Mom said, "I'm going to call Skip's parents from the pay phone. Can you give me a dime?"

Dad looked down at Skip. "You stay right where you are, young man," he said, shaking his head in disgust. Skip, covered in salad dressing, mumbled something unintelligible. Dad and I looked at each other. "God damn it," said Dad. "I sure as hell hope this teaches you something about liquor." At that moment, Skip bent his head and vomited on the floor. I stepped back reflexively. Dad wrinkled his nose and summoned a busboy.

Mom returned from the lobby. "His father will be here in forty-five minutes," she said. She looked down at Skip in his blue-cheese-and-vomit-slathered suit. "Oh, my," she said, grasping the table.

The band played two more songs while the waiters served Baked Alaska. A janitor came around with a mop and bucket. While the waiters wiped down Skip's suit and shoes, the janitor mopped the floor. Skip stayed in his seat, head hung low, making an occasional whimper. "You okay?" I asked.

"Nnph-hmnn," he said.

"Want to give him some coffee?" I asked Dad. I'd seen that in the movies and on TV. Somebody gets drunk, you sober them up with black coffee.

"I don't know if he's allowed," said Dad. "I'd hate to see him get in even worse trouble when his father gets here."

"His mom lets him," I said.

Dad signaled for a waiter to bring coffee to the table. Then he asked me if I wanted a cup too.

"Sure," I said. "Why not? Today I'm a man."

A waiter came over and poured coffee for Dad, Skip and me. Skip could barely pick up his cup. Dad helped him lift it to his lips. Skip sipped tentatively.

I blew on my coffee the way I'd seen adults do. I held my face over the cup and saucer, savoring the steam. I took my virgin sip. "M-m-m," I said. I blew onto the surface again, and then slurped a little more through my lips. I swished it around and swallowed tentatively. Sweet. Rich. Warm. I sipped again. "This is great."

"Take it easy," Mom warned. "You'll be up all night if you drink too much."

My brain raced. I isolated each thought like a toss and a catch. Focus. Breathe. "By the way," I said, "there's something I've been meaning to ask you guys." Mom and Dad leaned in so they could hear me over the din. "I can still come into town to juggle after school, can't I?" My plan was to find the sax player and put together a musical juggling show that would attract bigger crowds than either of us could do on our own. After each of my lessons with the rabbi, I'd combed two or three blocks in search of the musician before setting up shop and performing solo.

Mom and Dad looked at each other, then back at me. "Seeing as how today I'm a man and all?" I asked. Even as I grinned, my pulpit-realization ringed the periphery of my consciousness like a satellite. Once again, I pushed the thought out of my mind and concentrated on the question at hand.

"As long as you keep your grades up," said Mom.

The band let out an awful roar, the brass piercing the ballroom's air like thunder. I sat upright. Mom looked startled. She glared at the musicians. Skip shifted in his seat, raised his head and moaned.

"Ladies and gentlemen," announced the bandleader, "everybody on the dance floor!" He raised one arm and the musicians made their instruments blare again—a deep rumble punctuated by the clarinet's high-pitched trill. "Everybody on your feet for the *Hora!*"

The guests pushed themselves out of their seats and converged on the dance floor. "Where's the bar mitzvah boy?" asked the bandleader. "Jason Benson! On the dance floor! Mom and Dad, you too!"

Dad gave Skip a stern look. "Do not move a muscle, young man," he said. He took Mom's elbow and helped her out of her chair. Everyone else was on the dance floor by now, holding hands in a circle. The band played "Hava Nagila," slowly at first. Mom and Dad and I joined the circle. Dad and I managed to keep Mom propped up.

The circle grew bigger as more dancers joined in. Soon a second circle formed inside it. The band played faster. As our circle gained speed, I thought again about my revelation on the pulpit. *Mom was really sick.* There was so much happening—arms waving, sweaty grins and wide eyes, fancy waiters carrying silver trays, clinking crystal glasses, blurred curtains and plush purple seats.

Nearly overwhelmed, I broke it down like a juggling pattern. True, she was sick. But she was alive. She was laughing and dancing. She was here and now.

7

A LITTLE WAY up the boardwalk, I can make out Million Dollar Pier, or what's left of it. Fire damaged, the charred skeleton of pilings and planks juts into the ocean. I recall reading about a fire in the early eighties. At the time, I was in the back of a van, crossing the Texas panhandle on my way to a renaissance fair in Albuquerque. No one in my troupe even knew I had come from Atlantic City. By then I'd buried my past, expunging all signs of the Jersey shore from my professional resume, remaking myself as a street juggler from Philadelphia. Not exactly a lie, not exactly the whole truth.

Now as we approach the pier, I clear my throat and tell Eileen and Ruth about the rides and attractions—the bumper cars, the house of mirrors, the flying saucers and the roller coaster. But it's just small talk. I'm thinking about how a little white lie can grow and spawn big ugly lies. Some—*I'm fine, thanks*—fade away. Others—*She needs a few more tests* or *He's away on business*—will come back and kick your ass.

Eileen and I met in October 1984, at the New York Public Library, where she was interning while getting her master's from Columbia. I was new in town. An art director from Brodsky & Brown had seen me juggling on Bourbon Street in New Orleans. He liked my patter, gave me his card and invited me to the studio to record a few voiceovers. *Are you looking for a career in architecture, design or electronic engineering? Call the American Institute of Design! Call today!* I was good at it, and I had some ideas, and soon I was writing the copy and they sent me to New York. Since the rest of my resume consisted of juggling, hawking soft pretzels and shilling for a marionette theater, I went to the library to study trade magazines. A pretty reference-desk librarian helped me find them. I told her about my new job and how I'd arrived in New York after years on the road. When she laughed at my jokes, I invited her to join me for coffee on the front steps overlooking Fifth Avenue. It was a windy, blue-sky Monday. Fifth Avenue rumbled, a river of cream-colored Checker cabs, Hondas and Volvos, stepvans and police cars, swerving and honking. We had ten minutes. Eileen had to get back to work and I was scheduled to record a public service announcement.

A few nights later we met for dinner at an Ethiopian restaurant off Washington Square. Between servings of steamy lentil stew and braised goat meat on spongy injera bread, we talked for five hours. By the time I stepped on the F train headed for my apartment in Brooklyn, I was in love. Eileen was everything I wanted: sexy and alluring, grounded and practical, wistful and wholesome.

My parents were dead; I had no siblings, no relatives to speak of. No attachments. I told her everything. Except about the house.

Nor did I mention the house on our second date—the movie *Footloose*. At the time, I told myself it was no more than an *I'm well, thanks* lie. In 1984 Atlantic City wasn't cool, and owning an investment property didn't fit with the savvy vagabond image I wanted to project.

But it was more than that. I'd been watching the copywriters at my new job, so I knew about revisions. I was making a simple revision. I came from Philadelphia and my parents were dead. After high school I hit the road. Essentially the truth, reorganized to avoid the messiness of how and why I left Atlantic City.

IN THE MONTHS after the bar mitzvah, I'd wake up in the morning, snug and toasty under the covers—for about ten seconds. Then I'd remember, and the sadness would take hold.

Still, by concentrating on what was in front of me, I got through each day. I roamed the neighborhood with Skip, did my homework, juggled in town, occasionally filled in at a bakery on the weekend, looked forward to the season in Atlantic City—all without dwelling on Mom. This was the great lesson from juggling: maintain the pattern, one throw at a time.

Meanwhile, I learned how to cook by watching *The French Chef* and *The Galloping Gourmet* on TV. I could roast a chicken, make a casserole and throw together a salad. I functioned day-to-day, going to school, juggling, doing homework. School remained boring, but my grades were pretty good. It would be years before I made the connection between learning to juggle and no longer receiving "Fails to pay attention" and D's on my report cards.

Though I felt relieved to be free of my meetings with Rabbi Greenblatt, I was glad I'd studied. Skip, on the other hand, wasn't bothering to prepare for his bar mitzvah at the end of June. He spent his free afternoons roaming the neighborhood on his Sting-Ray bicycle.

One day we were wandering around the neighborhood, at the top of one of the hills, when he told me he had a plan. He had his bike with him. I didn't have mine, so he just pushed his while we roamed up and down the hilly streets.

"Hi, Mrs. Peters!" Skip shouted to a neighbor midway down the hill. She was getting out of her station wagon, its back end crammed with grocery bags. "Watch," Skip whispered to me. He mounted his bike and coasted down the hill to the station wagon. I didn't know Mrs. Peters, a short sturdy woman with thick thighs and a clipped helmet of silver hair. "Can I help with your bags?" Skip asked as he skidded his bike to a stop, gracefully fishtailing the rear wheel and, in one gesture, hopping off, leaning his bike against the station wagon's fender and grabbing a grocery bag from the back of the car. Before Mrs. Peters knew it, Skip was leading her up her path toward her front door, hugging two bags of groceries. Looking over his shoulder, he gestured for me to lend a hand. I scrambled down the hill, grabbing two bags from the back of the station wagon and tagging behind Skip and Mrs. Peters.

It took three trips to get all the bags inside the house. Then, standing outside the front door, Mrs. Peters handed us each fifty cents. We thanked her and resumed our aimless walk around the neighborhood, Skip guiding his bike by the back of its seat. "That was pretty neat," I said. "Let's keep an eye out for more incoming moms." I didn't really need the money, but I knew that Skip was saving up for a new can of kerosene and a box of CO_2 cartridges to add to his next sewer attack.

Skip reached into his pants pocket and fumbled with something. I thought it was the change that Mrs. Peters had given him, but it turned out to be three little yellow pills. "What are they?" I asked.

Skip grinned. "Something I found."

"They're pills," I said. "Where'd you find them?"

"In Mrs. Peters' medicine cabinet." He displayed the pills in his palm like tiny trophies.

"I can't believe you did that!" I said. When I'd grabbed the last two bags and Mrs. Peters came out to close up her car, Skip had lingered inside her house. In that time, he must have dashed upstairs to the bathroom, gone through the medicine cabinet and swiped the pills. "What are you going to do with them?" I asked. "Do you even know what they are?"

"Valium," he said. With that, he popped them into his mouth and swallowed.

My jaw dropped. "How do you know?" I asked.

"Same shit my mom takes. Valium. Five-Point-O MG."

"What if they were actually *fifty* MG?" I asked. "You have dyslexia, you can't trust decimals!"

"They don't even come in that strength. Valium's two, five or ten. The yellow ones are five. I've been studying my mom's pills for like six months. I'm dyslexic, not colorblind."

"What does Valium do?"

"Relaxes you."

I rolled my eyes. "Oh, great. Like booze?"

"Fuck you, dick-breath." Skip surveyed the neighborhood, probably casing for his next drug heist.

About twenty minutes after he swallowed the yellow pills, Skip began walking funny, weaving across the sidewalk. "Are you okay?" I asked. I took over pushing his bike.

"Whaa?" he asked. "Yeah. Oh, man. This is far out." His eyes were glazed, his lids heavy.

"Are you high from the pills?" I asked.

"Huh? Yeah. Shut up," he said. "Like, just stop talking." Skip sat down on the sidewalk, crossed his legs Indian style and slumped his head forward like a drowsy teenage Buddha. I stood over him, holding his bike.

"We should get you home," I said, worried that Skip's dad or a police car might drive by and spot us. I bent down and tried to pry him into a standing position, but he wouldn't budge. Skip wasn't a big guy, but he was dead weight. Since his Sting-Ray bike had a long, banana-shaped seat, I figured my best bet was to heave him onto the back and ride him to his house. I looked up and down the block. No traffic; no one in sight.

Skip stretched out on his side like a beached whale. He wasn't unconscious, but he wasn't cooperating either. Somehow, grunting and sweating, I managed to hoist Skip's floppy body onto the bike's banana seat, grasp him with one arm and the handlebar with my other hand, and coast downhill to his house, past the blooming magnolia trees and wood-paneled station wagons.

Thankfully, his dad's car wasn't in the driveway and his mom was conked out on the living-room sofa. We lumbered up the stairs to his bedroom—with me clutching his torso and waist to prevent him from tumbling backward.

Skip collapsed on his bed with a hefty bounce and a dreamy moan. Thirty seconds later he was snoring. I crept back downstairs. Outside, I guided Skip's bike from the front porch to the garage. It was six o'clock, still light out. Birds chirped in the trees. Traffic rumbled in the distance. My legs ached. I wiped a band of sweat from my forehead and headed for home.

"*Jason Benson, please report to the Front Office.*"

On a dewy morning in May, I was in seventh grade biology class, trying to talk my way out of dissecting a frog, when Principal Rickert's announcement came over the intercom system. Everything in the lab stopped; everyone turned toward me. Miss Fibb cleared her throat and eyed the intercom speaker mounted on the wall above the door. "*Jason Benson, please report to the Front Office.*" She spun around, walked to her desk and snatched a pink hall pass from the top drawer.

Mom was gone. I swallowed hard. My temples prickled. I'd known since my bar mitzvah two months earlier. She'd been in the hospital for the past three weeks—her longest stay. Dad and I never talked about it. I hadn't told anyone, not even Skip. Since the bar mitzvah, the unuttered truth had lain there, like a stench in the room you didn't want to mention, because if you did it meant you'd have to call a plumber, who would have no choice but to demolish your wall. So you told a white lie and you didn't think about the consequences.

"How's she doing?" I'd been asking Dad each night.

"She needs a few more tests," he'd say. "Thanks for making dinner and doing the laundry. You're really stepping up. It's important for Mom's recovery."

I should have pressed him. "*Dad, how is she really doing? Tell me. I can handle it.*" But I was as afraid to know as he was to tell me.

Some nights, Dad came home early, ate the dinner I'd fixed and then rushed out again to visit Mom. Most of the time, he left me at home. "She's just sleeping," he'd say. "You may as well stay here and do homework or practice your juggling."

"*Jason Benson, please report to the Front Office.*"

When I entered, the typing and mimeographing stopped. A somber-looking office lady rose from her swivel chair, ushered me in and asked me to sit and wait for Dad. .

"Is this about my mom?" I asked.

She curled her lips into a polite smile and promised that Dad was on his way. Turning her attention back to her typewriter, she resumed her work. I sat in a stiff-backed vinyl chair the color of lime. Drawing a deep breath to try to fill the growing pit in my stomach, I concentrated on the warm sunlight streaming through the great windows—windows you see only in schools, with tiny patterns of chicken wire embedded in the glass—illuminating bits of dust in the office air. Typewriters clattered and hummed. Somewhere down a hallway, a janitor buffed the floor with an electric machine.

Soon Dad arrived, pale and disheveled. He was still in his white bakery pants. Clumps of dried dough stuck to his forearms. His glasses were flour-flecked, his eyes red and puffy. I stood up. The office ladies typed and copied. Dad jutted his chin toward the door. "Let's go."

We walked across the black asphalt parking lot. The sun pulsed against the back of my neck, a warm invisible hand urging me forward. Halfway to the car, Dad put his arm around me.

Neither of us spoke during the drive home. I felt my breath going in and out, heard myself sniff and clear my throat a couple of times, heard Dad sigh. I looked out the window at an incongruous bright blue sky. Puffy white clouds tickled the horizon. Sunlight tickled the rooftops and glimmered through the tree branches.

When we arrived home, we walked down the front hall and into the dining room, where we sat, facing each other, at opposite ends of the polished walnut table. Dad took off his glasses and rubbed his eyes. He drew a slow, deep breath as if what he was about to say would require a room full of air.

"She's gone," he murmured.

I moved my head up and down, trying to absorb what I already knew. Chin up, chin down, watching Dad as he stumbled out of his seat and around the table to me. He wrapped me in his arms, sat in the chair next to me and pulled me until I slid onto his lap. Then we were both bawling. Pretty soon, my face was drenched and my neck and arms stiff. The telephone rang. Neither of us made a move.

Eventually, I raised my head from where I'd had it buried against Dad's chest. "I think I'm kind of all cried out for now." Dad's shirt felt cold and damp. My tears had soaked through. "Think we should eat something?"

Dad massaged his neck. He reached across the table for his glasses and slipped them on his face. "Are you hungry?"

"I don't know," I said. "I guess. You?"

"There's not much in the house," said Dad. "I should shop tomorrow."

"I'm gonna go see what's in the kitchen."

It felt good to have a plan. I got up, fished the percolator and the coffee filter out of the dish drainer, started a pot of coffee. Meanwhile, Dad came in and rummaged through the cupboards. He found a jar of Tang, which he mixed with water in a pitcher, and a box of Trix. We sat at the table. Dad shook up the Tang and poured each of us a glassful. He poured dry Trix into two cereal bowls. Dad said he'd call Rabbi Greenblatt and schedule the funeral. Then he'd call Mom's parents in California and his relatives in Cleveland.

"You have to call everyone in Atlantic City," I said.

Dad raised a spoonful of Trix to his mouth. "Norman and Betty I can reach." He chomped absently on the cereal. "But Jimmy and Edna—we never found an address for the bar mitzvah invitation. I'll try."

"Bobby told me they visit the Gypsy King in Florida every May."

"Florida's a big place," said Dad. "I doubt the Gypsy King is in the phone book."

I forced a smile. "Look under *King, Gypsy*."

Three days later, on Sunday, Dad and I donned our matching bar mitzvah suits one more time. We waited in front of the house, under the blossoming dogwood. A black limousine pulled up and we climbed into the back seat. The sunshiny, puffy-clouded day felt absurd. It should have been raining.

Our first stop: my grandparents' hotel in town. We took the West River Drive past Boathouse Row. Scull boats breezed up and down the silver-blue river. Herons and gulls circled overhead, scanning for fish below the surface. I rolled down the window and let some cool air into the stuffy limo. Silently we watched the boathouses across the river—those broad, sturdy, century-old buildings where rowers stored their sculls and teams gathered in the morning fog to slide their racing boats into the river.

Soon we were cruising down the Benjamin Franklin Parkway. Dad put a hand on my knee. "As difficult as this is for us," he said, "bear in mind, it's worse for your grandparents." The worst thing in the world, he told me, is losing a child. "I can't even imagine." His eyes brimmed. I pressed my face into my palms. "No matter what they say today," he told me, "show them love and respect."

After another block, I rolled up my window against the horns and screeching brakes. Pressing my face to the glass, I watched the men and women go about their business, hustling in and out of stores, dodging traffic.

My grandparents were outside their hotel, huddled together, dressed in black. They looked different than they had at my bar mitzvah—smaller, more wrinkled and stooped. My grandmother didn't look like a prim marionette anymore. She looked like a sad old lady.

The driver pulled the limo over. He got out and helped my grandparents into the back seat next to Dad and me. When we were in traffic again, my grandmother heaved a great sigh. "Why?" she implored no one in particular. "Why?" My grandfather put his arm around her. She sank against his shoulder, sobbing.

"*Why?*" Maybe I'd ask the rabbi. But like Jimmy when I asked about Bobby, he wouldn't give me a straight answer. That's because there wasn't one.

My grandfather cleared his throat and dabbed at his eyes with a handkerchief. He drew in a deep breath and announced: "Only the good die young." Dad grunted in agreement, but I knew he was only being polite. Everybody dies. And everybody lies about it or talks around it.

Two days before the funeral, as news about Mom swept through the neighborhood, I'd run into Skip's maid, Willa. She was walking toward the bus stop near the Acme, an umbrella under her arm and a big plastic shopping bag in her hand. When she saw me, she bustled across the road, waving and calling, "Mr. Jason! Mr. Jason!"

Willa set her shopping bag on the sidewalk. She wore a checkered raincoat even though it was sunny and warm. She held out her arms. "Poor baby, come here." I hugged her. She smelled like fresh laundry. "Everything happen for a reason." She squeezed my ribs. "Your momma an angel now."

I was grateful to Willa for her comfort but I didn't believe her, and her confidence in "a reason" wouldn't have satisfied my grandmother any more than it did me.

We pulled into the parking lot next to the funeral home, a dull glass-and-stone box of a building in a run-down commercial district. Two somber men in black suits and dark glasses escorted us out of the limo. They looked like Secret Service agents. They ushered the four of us, squinting in the sunlight, through a back entrance and into a windowless room where Mom lay in a burnished tan coffin in her floral bar mitzvah dress. Eyes closed, hands folded neatly over her belly, she looked good—except for being too thin. I'd never seen a dead person before. Her hair and makeup were perfect. Dad and my grandparents cried over the open coffin. They held her. I just stood there sniffling, my head throbbing. I wanted to kiss Mom's cheek but I was afraid—and ashamed that I was afraid. I studied Mom's face and my throat constricted. Dad held her right hand, my grandfather her left. My grandmother cradled Mom's head in her bosom. I gripped the side of the coffin and squeezed my eyes shut, stubbornly hoping that this was all a bad dream.

When I looked up, Rabbi Greenblatt had arrived. He hugged all four of us—me last and longest. The guys in the black suits returned. They straightened Mom's body, refolded her hands back over her chest and closed the coffin.

The air in the chapel was warm and stuffy. My grandparents, Dad and I sat in the front row. People streamed in—the Cleveland aunts and uncles, people from our neighborhood, men who knew Dad from his days at Westinghouse; they shook our hands and grunted and hugged us and told us they were sorry. Almost everyone from my bar mitzvah was there. So were Norman, Betty and Lita. Since Dad hadn't been able to reach Jimmy or Madam Diane, they wouldn't know about Mom for another month.

Skip and his mom were among the swarm of guests. It was the first time I'd seen Mrs. Schwartz outdoors and dressed. She looked like a normal mom, not one who spent her life high on pills, sleeping in front of the TV. Her red hair stood high on her head. Her face was strong, with an angled chin and a sharp nose; her eyes wide and blue, like Skip's. She wore a black skirt and a black jacket. When she came over to hug me she whispered that Mr. Schwartz was out of town but sent his condolences. She moved on to shake hands with Dad and my grandparents.

Now it was Skip's turn to greet me. He wore a new suit—a black one. And like his mom, he looked clear-headed, not high on stolen pills like he was most days after school and on weekends.

"Sorry about your mom," said Skip, awkwardly shaking my hand.

"Thanks," I said. "Thanks for coming."

"No big deal," he whispered. "I mean, it got me out of Sunday school." He looked around the chapel. "Same difference anyway. I mean, you know. Hey, how come you didn't tell me your mom was so sick?"

"Because nobody told me."

"No shit. That blows." Skip reached out and we shook hands again. Then the surge of guests swept him along like a stubby little log in a river.

Next thing I knew, another Cleveland aunt whose name I could not remember held me in her grip while Skip shook hands with Dad and my grandparents. My grandparents wailed like wounded animals in the front of the chapel, the way Dad and I had cried at the dining-room table on Thursday night. Somber guests approached them, introduced themselves, shook their hands and whispered lies. "*Only the good die young. Everything happens for a reason. She's in a better place.*" Yeah, right. I believed that like I should have believed "*She needs more tests.*"

Then Lita was standing in front of me, with Norman and Betty behind her. Even though it was Mom's funeral, I was glad to see them. Lita was eleven and growing up. Since I only knew her in the summer, I'd hardly ever seen her wearing shoes before, not to mention a smart, gray skirt with a black blouse, her hair brushed neatly and rolling down her back. Lita didn't say anything, just reached up and hugged me, clinging to my neck and kissing my cheek. Her lips were warm and she smelled like honey. My face flushed. She moved on, and in a moment Norman and Betty were clasping me, tears in their eyes.

When the mob of guests finished shaking our hands and hugging us, everyone took a seat. The air felt heavy. I turned around from the front row to survey the crowd. The chapel was full. Four men from the funeral home wheeled the coffin into the chapel and parked it in front of the pulpit. Rabbi Greenblatt made a few blessings. He spoke about Mom, how generous she was and how much she loved Dad and me. How she had followed Dad back to Atlantic City and "risked everything" on a summertime dream; how she'd worked so hard at the bakeries and helped Dad to be a success. Tears blurred my vision. I shut my eyes and leaned my head against Dad's shoulder. When I looked up again, the men were wheeling Mom's coffin up the aisle and out of the chapel.

We got back in the limo while everyone else filed into their cars. The procession crawled across town, through red lights at gritty intersections, down a broad, litter-strewn boulevard to a cemetery. The men from the funeral home escorted us across a manicured lawn to a ring of soft, freshly dug soil. Rabbi Greenblatt recited some more Hebrew prayers while a steel pulley lowered Mom's coffin into the earth. Dad stood to my right, his arm around me. To my left, my grandparents crumpled against each other. The pulley rattled like a freight elevator. The coffin descended and Mom was gone. Somebody handed Dad a spade filled with dirt. He threw the dirt into the grave, then handed me the spade. I stooped and filled it up with moist earth, held it over the grave, turned my wrist and watched the dirt land on Mom's coffin.

The afternoon was a blur. Neighbors arriving at the house with cakes; the smell of lasagna heating in the oven and coffee dripping in a large silver percolator; trays of smoked fish and sliced meats; a din of condoling voices, murmurs of sympathy, more silly and bland pronouncements about angels and only the good dying young. There were neighbors I knew, and neighbors I'd never met before—neighbors armed with cheesecakes and baking dishes covered with aluminum foil. Norman, Betty and Lita came, but they stayed for only a short time and I barely had a chance to talk with them. Norman and Lita sat like glum strangers at a bus station while Betty busied herself in the kitchen, unwrapping cakes and spooning smoked fish onto plates.

That night, after the last of our visitors had gone, Dad and I— too exhausted to clean up and too wound up to sleep—took off our jackets and ties, made a fresh pot of coffee and sat across from each other at the dining-room table. Outside, a steady spring rain thrashed against the windows.

Dad poured coffee and set the silver percolator in the center of the table. I blew on the surface of my cup and took a tentative sip. Neither of us said anything for a while. We just drank our coffee and listened to the rain. Finally I spoke up: "Everybody but me knew how sick she was."

Dad leaned on the table, resting his chin on his open palms. "Not everybody."

"All you ever told me was that she needed more tests," I said.

Dad took off his glasses and rubbed his eyes with the back of his hands. "I was hoping for a miracle. Remission, you know?"

I studied the tiny styrofoam ridge that circled the rim of my coffee cup. "Who else knew?" I asked. "Did school know?"

Dad blew on his coffee while I waited for his answer. "Principal Rickert," he said at last. "And your teachers."

"Oh, God," I said, hanging my head. My stomach churned. "This is humiliating."

Dad put his glasses back on his face. "You shouldn't feel that way . . ."

"Maybe I shouldn't," I said sharply, "but I do!"

Dad couldn't even look at me. "Rabbi Greenblatt knew," he said. "He told me I should tell you. We had an argument about it."

I winced, imagining Dad yelling at Rabbi Greenblatt, *He's my goddamned kid! Don't tell me how to raise my goddamned kid!*

"Jesus, Dad, you should have listened to him."

Dad slapped his palm on the table. "I didn't want to hurt you. I kept telling myself she'd get better. And the worse she got, the more I couldn't bring myself to tell you."

"I should have had a chance to say goodbye to her," I said. "What did you think would happen? How did you think it would end?"

Dad heaved a sigh. "I wanted a miracle."

I looked out the rain-spattered window, at the moonlight now shining in the beads of water. "What about Mom's parents? Did they know?"

"She didn't want them to." Dad had been right: losing a mother was tough, but at least it was natural. He swirled his coffee and shook his head sadly. "Like I told you this morning, they're suffering terribly right now. We have to be good to them."

"Did they ever even give you a chance?"

Dad set his cup on the table. "When Mom and I announced our engagement they made a big scene. They made her choose between me and them."

I put down my cup. "That's crazy."

"They thought Mom would back down and marry somebody they approved of. But they were wrong. And now they're too proud to admit it, and to admit that I'm doing well and supporting my family."

"Why didn't they like you?"

"They said I lacked ambition. They called me 'small-time.' Your grandfather said I was a 'glorified accountant' at Westinghouse. Even after I got promoted twice. And then when I struck out on my own, they felt my dreams were too small."

"But you own a chain of pretzel bakeries . . ."

"A chain of *four*," he said. "To them, it's small time. In their minds, retail's dirty. Cash businesses are undignified."

"But Mom loves you," I said, instantly realizing I should have used the past tense.

"Their parents were dirt poor," Dad went on. "Immigrants who never learned to speak English. They lived in tenements. Some days there wasn't enough food. Your grandmother begged for pennies on the street. Your grandfather sold rags."

I recalled the story Mom had told me about her mom getting fired in the middle of a blizzard. Then I pictured my grandfather as a teenage rag boy, lugging around a wagon full of scraps. I could hear his pathetic cry, "Rags for sale!" I thought about the sideshow barker pitching for the Bearded Lady. "Step right up! Step right up!" And my own cries of "Hot pretzels! Get 'em while they're hot!" Now I understood why Mom's parents were ashamed of my juggling on the streets. But I wasn't a beggar or a rag seller. Street performing was different. Rabbi Greenblatt might say they were doing what God had told Aaron to do: putting their shame on me, scapegoating me, making me into the dirty street kids they themselves had been.

Outside, the rain picked up again, gusting against the windows and beating the roof like a stampede. I looked at my watch. It was a few minutes before midnight. My arms and legs were weary, yet in my caffeinated state my heart raced and my fingers trembled.

"How long did you guys know Mom was sick?" I asked, pouring myself another cup of coffee. I recalled Mom's ears not healing after she had them pierced. "Was it when she got her ears pierced?"

"I was afraid even before that," said Dad. "We wanted to have another baby—this was when you were five or six—and she had three miscarriages." Dad poured himself more coffee, nearly emptying the pot. "I suspected something was wrong. And I think Mom did too. She couldn't stay pregnant and she couldn't gain weight. By the time they opened her up, she had cancer practically everywhere."

I stared at the table. "How does that happen?"

"Nobody knows," he said. "The doctors tried everything. Radiation. Drugs. Surgery. Experimental treatments."

I imagined the doctors cutting Mom open, like a frog on a lab table at school. A wave of nausea came over me. I drew a deep breath, bit my lower lip and chugged down the rest of my coffee. "You should have told me what was going on," I said, resting my arms and head on the walnut table, its polished surface smooth and cool. I listened to the rain outside. My head ached and my eyes burned. I squeezed my eyelids tighter and tighter until I saw flashes of light and colored patterns.

"You're right," said Dad. "I'm sorry." I opened my eyes. Dad looked like a boxer who'd taken a body blow. "Listen," he said, "I think you and I ought to concentrate on getting our lives back to normal, establish a routine. For one thing, I don't want you coming home to an empty house every day."

"But I've been coming home to an empty house for eight months."

"You could take public transportation to whichever bakery I'm at, do your homework in the back and we'll go home together."

"I *could* do that," I said, "but I'd rather go into town and juggle. I can take care of myself. I'll get my homework done."

"We'll see," he said. I knew that was the best I could get out of him for now.

We stayed up and talked for another few hours, until the rain stopped and the moonlit sky glowed like red velvet. In those wee hours Dad told me more about his life than he had before. The loneliness of growing up without a father. The poverty. The drab winters in Cleveland. He joined the army right after high school, but he missed World War II and spent four years working as an accounting clerk at a military base in North Carolina.

In the middle of Dad's first year at Penn, his mother died. Instead of returning to Cleveland that summer, he stayed on the East Coast, sharing a summerhouse in Atlantic City with friends from college. He got a job selling souvenirs in a gift shop on the boardwalk. Two summers later, he met Mom on Steel Pier. They danced to big-band music all night long and fell in love. On their third date, Dad proposed. "Money was tight," he told me, "but we were happy. On our wedding night we had a loaf of bread, a pot roast and two carrots. Your mother scrubbed the pot roast and boiled it for half a day. Her first meal." He stood up and stretched his back. "I've got to get some sleep." He scooped up the creamer and the percolator and took them into the kitchen. I followed with the styrofoam cups. There wasn't much more to say. In a few hours, the mourners would be here again.

It was almost dawn by the time I went to bed. I couldn't sleep. I lay there for three hours, thinking how getting through the next four years would be like juggling four balls. You break it down; you think about juggling two balls in each hand. You concentrate on each set of throws and catches. Think too much, you'll drop the balls. You'll never bring your mom back, but you don't have to think about her all the time, either. You can release the two red balls exactly when the blue balls peak; you can time your throws to the jazz rhythm on the radio or a song in your head, or that saxophone player if you ever run into him. When you're juggling, there's no past or future—just throws and catches and your breath going in and out like ocean waves.

I knew that's how I'd survive: set a pattern, breathe in, breathe out. One day, one night, and then another day and another night. A throw, a catch, a throw, a catch.

8

On a scorching Saturday afternoon in early July, the board-walk was so hot it could melt a wad of bubblegum in fifteen seconds. You couldn't go barefoot or you'd get second-degree burns.

I was juggling in front of the pretzel bakery for about thirty people. It was our first summer in Atlantic City without Mom. "Ladies and gentlemen!" I shouted. "Jason the Magnificent presents, for the very first time—at this exact spot—the Payroll Juggle!" Here I caught every third throw overhand, shouting "Gimme!" as I snatched the ball before it hit its peak. "Ladies and gentlemen, the Social Security tax." Next, I sped it up—overhanding every second throw. "State taxes. Gimme. Gimme. Gimme." Finally I shifted to every catch overhand. The balls whizzed in a tiny arc, my hands and arms blurring like a chainsaw. "And let's not forget the federal wage tax! Gimme-gimme-gimme-gimme-gimme!!!"

After that, I launched into my "Eat the Pretzel While Juggling" routine, during which I'd sneak in a pitch for Dad's pretzels.

In the front of the crowd stood a group of girls about my age. One had shiny jet-black hair that fell to her lean, tanned shoulders. She wore a light blue bikini top and a pair of red denim cut-offs that were so short her front pockets dangled against her bare thighs. Her brown sandaled feet were covered with beach grit. She wore a teeny little ankle bracelet made of colored beads.

Despite knowing better, I allowed my gaze to shift for a split second to the girl's thighs, at which point I dropped both balls.

"Vsh pt mm glm," I mumbled, my mouth stuffed with pretzel.

The audience roared with laughter as I chased the bouncing balls across the boardwalk, got a real nice view of the girl in the red cutoffs' smooth brown legs—while holding the crowd by mumbling incoherently but emphatically through the fistful of pretzel lodged in my mouth.

Regaining both composure and juggling balls, I swallowed, proclaiming, "Ladies and gentlemen, you have just witnessed Jason the Magnificent's legendary Juggle du Gravity! Please note, when I released two balls, they simultaneously obeyed the law of gravity while I—Jason the Magnificent—consumed an entire pretzel, thank you very much! And what a delicious pretzel it was, ladies-and-gentlemen, boys-and-girls. Purchased for a quarter—one thin quarter!" I swept one arm dramatically toward the bakery. "Ladies and gentlemen, I offer you today an unsolicited testimonial for these fresh-from-the-oven soft pretzels! The saltiest and tastiest on the boardwalk!"

Across the boards, Dad watched from the counter. I made the rounds with my derby, scoring decent tips for a midday performance. "Do you doubt, sir, that my endorsement was unsolicited?" I asked a man who'd snickered at my patter. With a flourish of mock indignation, I called to Dad: "Sir! Have we ever been introduced?"

"No, son," Dad deadpanned.

The crowd laughed and applauded, and the man stuffed a five-dollar bill into my derby. As I worked my way through the small mob with my derby held out for tips, I made eye contact with the girl in the red cutoffs. We smiled. When I approached her, she did something incredible: She poked me in my stomach, gently, with her index finger.

I blinked. Something inside my head *popped.* It felt like my brain had sprung a leak. "Hi," I managed to say.

"You're really good!" she said. She moistened her lips with her tongue and brushed at her bangs with her fingertips.

"Thanks," I said, struggling to get a grip on my pounding heart. She bit her lower lip, shifted her weight to one hip and waited for me to say something. She wore a little bit of mascara around her purplish-blue eyes. "I, uh, work there too," I added, jutting my chin toward the bakery. My forehead pulsed. "I'm a pretzel twister, like my father before me." I searched for words like a blind man reaching for a doorknob. "But . . . not like his father, you know, before him. I'm . . . second generation." My mouth felt like sandpaper. "I'm Jason," I said.

She put out her hand. "I'm Annie."

I wiped my sweaty palm on the back of my shorts and took her hand in mine. She had a firm grip. I breathed deep, steadied myself. "So, um, Annie," I said. "Would you wanna, like, do something? Later?" My voice cracked. I sounded desperate. Put me in front of a hundred people and I can patter away without thinking. But one poke in the stomach by a girl in red cutoffs and ninety percent of my vocabulary goes missing.

Annie nodded. "Wanna go to Million Dollar Pier tonight?" she asked.

We agreed to meet in front of the pretzel bakery at nine o'clock.

That night, my shift dragged on forever. When Dad asked me to hand-twist a batch of jumbo pretzels, I rolled the hunks of dough and dreamily worked them into letters:

A N N I E

What would she be wearing? The red cutoffs? Maybe something fancier—like a clingy summer skirt and that sexy ankle bracelet. Was she a year-round Jersey girl? Or maybe she lived in Philadelphia. Maybe near me! Then we could see each other all the time; hang out after school and on weekends. I imagined Annie and me strolling the boardwalk, hand in hand. Looking up over our ice cream cones (vanilla for her, coffee for me) into each other's eyes, we giggle and coo. We ride the roller coaster. Annie clings to me . . . I slip a comforting arm over her bare shoulder. Calmly, as we free-fall, I explain the principles of aerodynamics, saying something witty like, "Well, my dear, that's centrifugal force for you." The roller coaster grinds to a halt. Annie wraps her slender arms around me and smooches my cheek.

I blush. "What was that for?"

"Just for being you."

Rolling and twisting the jumbo pretzels that night, I pictured our senior prom. By then we'll have been a couple for more than three years. People will say our names together, in one breath: *Jasonanannie.*

The evening dragged on. My guts churned like a dough mixer. I kept goofing up orders—misbagging pretzels, miscounting change.

With nine o'clock approaching, I took every opportunity to lean over the counter, pop my head out like a nervous groundhog and scan the crowded boardwalk. Each time I caught sight of a girl with black hair, my heart lifted—and then sank when I saw it wasn't her.

I looked at my watch: five minutes past nine. I imagined Annie pressing through the pulsing crowd. At a quarter past nine my shift was over. I ducked under the counter and dodged across the boardwalk. I stood on a bench for a better view. Gritting my teeth, I scanned down to the lights of Million Dollar Pier. No Annie. I looked the other direction toward the big hotels. No Annie.

I sat on the bench, forlorn, until the crowds thinned out. Long past midnight, head bowed like a defeated boxer, I trudged back to the hotel. I was glad I got to our room before Dad. I undressed and got into bed. When he came in a half hour later, I pretended I was asleep.

That night, I dreamed about Annie. But Mom was there too. I was in the front passenger seat of Dad's station wagon, parked in front of our house in Philadelphia. The car faced downhill— its front wheels wedged against the curb. Annie was in the back. "It's my mom," I told her. "She runs late too." I pointed out the car window to the second-floor window of the house, to my parents' bedroom. Mom's face was in the window, watching us. I gestured for her to open the window. "She's going to love you," I promised Annie.

I awoke with a start. It was still dark. My sheets were damp. She'll come in the morning, I assured myself. She'll arrive bright and early, in her red cutoffs, all set for a day at the beach. I'll buy her some fudge and we'll sit on a bench at a shady pavilion, feet up, watching the people tramp up and down the boards. Then, hand in hand, we'll walk down to the ocean. We'll step into the surf up to our waists, and we'll cringe in anticipation of the foamy wave splashing us. Hands clasped tightly, we'll count to three and cast ourselves into the water. We'll bob up and down, laughing and holding each other's waists and kissing as a wave breaks over our heads. Cool water. Blue sky. White sand. Jasonanannie!

I WONDER WHERE Annie is today. Married, with kids? Does she bring her family here? Does she ever think about the juggler she met on a blistering afternoon twenty-six years ago? Now Ruth stands on the exact spot where Annie once stood. Did Jennifer from work, who accused me of harassment, ever stand here when she was thirteen, attracting boys, dreaming of New York City? It's too cold for red cutoffs and flip-flops. Ruth's bundled in her army coat, ripped jeans and scruffy boots. I'm sure that boys look at her the way I looked at Annie. I know her smile can make a boy's heart flutter, and her empty promise can crush him. But my daughter and I don't discuss boys. Lately, our discussions are more pedestrian. I tell her to get out of bed or she'll be late for school. She grunts in my general direction. But not today. Today, at long last, she's listening.

OVER THE NEXT two weeks, I dropped my juggling balls during at least half a dozen shows, burned my thumb on a hot oven door and dropped three batches of pretzels on the bakery floor. Even though I had barely mentioned my disappointment about Annie, Dad understood, or tried his best to understand. "Look, I know you're upset," he told me one night after he took me aside while the college kids baked and sold. "You need to pay more attention, son, or you're going to get hurt—or hurt somebody else."

I puffed my cheeks and exhaled a burst of air. "Sorry, Dad."

He looked at me sternly and pointed his index finger in my face. "I'm telling you this as your boss. Not as your dad."

"Sorry, Boss."

Jimmy and Norman and Betty treated me like an injured rabbit. One day Betty brought me a cheesecake. "Eat, *bubula*. You'll feel better," she said, sliding the cake across the counter and stroking my cheek with the back of her hand.

That season, Jimmy had put together a new marionette show, a takeoff on *Gilligan's Island*, with puppet castaways in costumes that My Edna had spent the winter in Florida making. While the puppets clunked each other on the head, Hawaiian music played in the background. People were packing the theater, but Jimmy still found time to spend with me once or twice a day, pumping me full of his philosophy.

"I gotta tell ya," he told me one morning as we walked the boards to the inlet and back, "girls are funny people." He put his arm around me, drawing me close. Winking conspiratorially, he gestured toward three college-aged girls, riding their bicycles toward us. "A beautiful sight, huh? The tits, the legs, the hair— look at 'em. But they're unpredictable. Now watch me and learn a thing or two."

As the women glided passed us, Jimmy grinned at them, announcing grandly, "Ladies . . ." One smiled and winked at him. One smiled at me. The third rolled her eyes and sped up her pedaling.

Jimmy turned to me. "What'd I tell ya? Three girls. One wink. Who can predict?"

When we arrived at the inlet the tide was high; the ocean rumbled up the beach and rippled under the boardwalk. We stopped at a small diner that opened early for the fishermen.

"Girls'll make ya crazy," Jimmy said, rubbing his hands as a waitress set our coffee on the table. "But *good* crazy. Did I ever tell ya how I met My Edna?"

I shook my head.

He leaned across the table and lowered his voice. "Actually, I was bangin' her big sister. But then one day I'm over the house, I see this scrawny little fourteen-year-old nuthin' hunched over a sewing machine in the kitchen. 'I didn't know you had a sister,' I say to my girl. I look over at the kid sister and she looks at me. She smiles, I smile. We're all smiles. You ever notice My Edna's smile? Well, before ya know it, the older sister's history even though her tits were bigger." Jimmy raised his palms in wonder. "You see my point?"

"Sorry, you lost me," I said, shaking my head.

"I'm sayin' girls are a mystery which you ain't gonna figure out. Sometimes you get your heart broken, and sometimes you get My Edna."

"But she hurt me," I said.

Jimmy tore off a piece of his strawberry Danish and stuffed it in his mouth. "It's like a scar," he said. "You cut yourself, and when it heals, you get a scar, and then it don't hurt as much the next time. Know what I mean? You get a little older, a little wiser, it ain't so bad." He chomped on his Danish and slurped a glob of red jelly filling off his knuckle.

Neither of us said anything for a minute. Coffee cups clinked, steam hissed behind the lunch counter and the waitresses shuffled back and forth, arms loaded with trays of coffee cups, waffles and pancakes.

"You miss your mom?" Jimmy asked.

I nodded and sipped my coffee. The morning sun blazed through the window by our table, warming my eyelids. I pressed my tongue to the roof of my mouth, savoring the coffee's bitter aftertaste. I opened my eyes, leaned toward Jimmy until I was close enough so no one else could hear. "Ever hear from Bobby?"

Jimmy waved me off. "Don't worry about him." He put his index finger to his lips. The subject of Bobby was off limits.

We finished our coffee. "By the way . . . ," I said after the waitress had returned with the check. "What's the story with that new derby My Edna sent me?"

"What—" said Jimmy with a roguish grin. "Don't it fit?"

"It fits perfectly, but when the new one came, the old one disappeared."

Jimmy brushed me off. "You don't need it no more."

"That's not the point. Would you mind asking My Edna about it?"

He stood up and stretched his back. "Oh, sure, I'll ask her." He fished a wad of cash out of his pocket, peeled off a five-dollar bill and left it on the table.

IN TRUTH, I wasn't thinking much about Mom. And when I did, I felt guilty for not thinking about her more. That summer I thought mostly about girls. Girls in bikinis bopping along the beach—their bodies tanned, hair blowing, shoulders glowing with ocean mist. Girls on the boardwalk, licking cotton candy and cuddling the teddy bears their copper-toned boyfriends won for them at the softball toss and the Wheel of Fortune. Jimmy was right; girls were good. I wanted one.

All summer long I anticipated her, watched for her as I juggled and baked, as I banged the pinball machines and stalked the boards. *Jasonan_____.*

The season drew to a close like the others before it. Except Mom wasn't there this time, beaming at Dad across the table when we celebrated at the Italian restaurant. Over antipasto, garlic bread and big white bowls of steaming mussels, Jimmy, Dad and Norman took turns raising their wine glasses and toasting the summer of 1973. Jimmy's *Gilligan's Island* show had been wildly successful.

"Repeat business!" Jimmy boasted. "All summer long, they kept coming back for the same show! A toast! *To the boardwalk!*"

9

DURING EIGHTH GRADE Skip graduated to Dexedrine, which had the opposite effect of Valium. "There's a pill that makes you nervous?" I said. "Jesus, Skip. Is that why your hands are jiggling?"

"What?" he said, like he didn't know he was practically vibrating all over and his forehead was sweating. "Listen, my brothers are coming home this summer. And guess what? I'm going to score some weed when they're here."

"You mean they're going to give you some?" I asked. "Or do you plan to *find* some in their backpacks?"

Skip smiled playfully. "That's up to them."

We'd been curious about pot ever since I brought home an anti-drug brochure from school. My Health teacher, Mrs. Rader, gave them out for us to take home and look at with our parents. The brochure had a section about each kind of drug that kids were taking: uppers, downers, pot, acid and heroin. Some of the descriptions were scary. "*An LSD trip is like a nightmare that can last for years!*" "*Diet pills, when abused, will wreak havoc on your central nervous system.*" "*Barbiturates and sedatives may cause extreme drowsiness.*" I knew that waking nightmares, a whacked-out central nervous system and extreme drowsiness weren't good for my juggling career. But marijuana sounded different. "*This plant, when smoked, causes mild euphoria for two to four hours.*" A little mild euphoria never hurt anyone.

By the time I left for Atlantic City, though, Skip's brothers hadn't shown up. That summer, while I baked pretzels and juggled and watched the girls, I sometimes looked curiously at the college-age kids sneaking tokes in what they thought were secluded places. But mostly, I was too busy to think about pot.

Skip's brothers finally came home for two weeks at the end of the summer. Whenever they were out of the house, Skip rummaged through their bureau drawers, closets, guitar cases and jacket pockets. On their last night, Skip found their stash—a nickel bag wedged into a hidden compartment in a backpack. If his brothers realized it was missing before they returned to college the next morning, neither one questioned him. "What were they gonna do?" Skip asked me later. "Call the cops? Tell the old man? Hah!"

The first weekend of my freshman year, the manager at Dad's Pennsauken, New Jersey, bakery called in sick, so Dad had to fill in and work double shifts on Friday and Saturday.

"My dad won't get home until after midnight," I told Skip on the phone on Saturday afternoon when he called to tell me he'd scored the weed. I sat at the kitchen table twirling the phone cord. Skip was cagey on the phone; he didn't say "grass" or "pipe" or mention anything illegal. Instead he spoke in a secret code like the one he'd overheard his brothers using with their friends. "I have that *thing*," he said. "And we'll need another *thing* to do it with. If you guys have any tinfoil or something?"

"You mean tinfoil to make a pipe to smoke the weed in?" I asked.

"Jesus fucking Christ!" Skip said, his voice a harsh whisper. "Not over the phone, ass-wipe. You want to get me busted?"

"Skip, do you actually think your phone is tapped because you swiped a nickel bag of grass from your brother?"

"Shut the fuck up!"

"Okay, sorry," I said. "Come over at seven. We can order a pizza and, um, do that *thing*—and yes, I have some of that *stuff* we can make a *thing* with, so that we can *you-know-what* the *other* thing in the first thing."

That night, as soon as Skip arrived and confirmed that Dad wasn't in the house, he led me upstairs to my bedroom like a spy on a mission. "Give me a double album," he said, motioning to my small record collection. I fingered through the albums—Rolling Stones, Cream, Donovan, Led Zeppelin, Humble Pie and James Taylor—and handed him the Beatles' *White Album*. Sitting cross-legged on my bed, Skip opened the album cover on his lap and crumpled a pinch of the grass onto it. I watched. With nimble fingers, he crunched the dry brownish buds almost into a powder. Then he shook the album cover, gently separating the seeds and twigs from the grass.

I'd made a pipe in the kitchen by wrapping a sheet of tinfoil around a pencil, fashioning a bowl at one end and sliding the pencil out—like I'd seen a guy do in the movie *Woodstock*. I handed the pipe to Skip and stood by with a pack of matches while he put a pinch of grass into the bowl. "Open the window. We should blow the smoke out the window," Skip said. "Don't want your old man to get a whiff when he comes home."

I opened my bedroom window. Skip climbed off the bed, pipe in hand. I lit a match and held it to the bowl. He took a long, deep drag, held the smoke in his lungs and fought back a cough. When he exhaled out the window, the smoke from his lungs wafted with the wind. I could smell the grass—sweet and pungent, not like cigarette smoke, and not unfamiliar. I'd smelled it under the boardwalk from time to time, and occasionally in the boys' room at the junior high school.

Skip handed me the tinfoil pipe, and I handed him the matchbook. He lit a match and I took a puff. "Don't cough!" he said. "Hold it in." I sucked the stem. The embers in the bowl glowed red hot. My lungs felt like they were about to explode. I handed the pipe back to Skip, who held it next to the window and fanned the smoke with one hand. Then he took another drag.

"It's spent," he said, pointing his nose toward the bowl full of gray ash. I held in the smoke as long as I could before exhaling out the window. Skip refilled the bowl and took another toke; and then I took another. "We'll keep smoking until we're high," said Skip, tapping the ashes out my window and filling up the bowl for the third time.

At first nothing happened. But after about ten tokes each, it was as if a switch had been thrown. I was looking at the world through an amber-colored filter, like on stage at a talent show. The light in my room crackled silently; the air was charged. I felt the blood coursing in my veins, and my heart beating, and my lungs expanding and contracting.

"I'm high," I said.

"Me too," said Skip, looking around my bedroom like he'd discovered a new continent. "This is . . . fucking . . ."

"Am I talking too loud?" I asked. "Man, I want cantaloupe."

"That doesn't go together," said Skip.

I grinned. "Does too. Cantaloupe goes with everything. Ever hear anyone say, 'Hold the cantaloupe'?"

Suddenly we were laughing hysterically, crumpled on the floor. "You're too loud," Skip giggled. "Have some cantaloupe."

I couldn't remember the last time I had laughed so hard. I got up and walked giddily to my album collection, knowing what I wanted to listen to: Emerson, Lake & Palmer's *Tarkus*. Epic. Majestic. Highly juggleable. I slid the album from its cover and placed it on the turntable. The music started and I turned up the volume. The first song, "Eruption," rattled fast, angular, edgy, with Keith Emerson's wailing organ climbing higher and higher, reaching new plateaus, and then taking it one step higher—and another and another. Usually I juggled to jazz, timing my throws to the lines in the sax, vibe, piano, drum and bass. But now that I was high, I wanted rock. I knew how the surfers felt when they rode a wave that crashed over their heads while they hurtled horizontally under the arc of water. Shooting the tube, they called it. And now I was inside a tube and everything around me was crystalline, like coagulated water molecules or Superman's Fortress of Solitude.

"This is amazing," I said, still unsure about my volume. Skip lay on his back on the bedroom floor, his eyes closed. "I mean, this is me," I said. "I am *me*. I am the inner me of me."

I pulled my suitcase out from under the bed, flipped open the top and grabbed three white lacrosse balls. I counted off and pitched all three aloft to the frenetic screech of the ascending organ. I grabbed the balls from mid-air, planning to launch into a three-ball cascade—a simple maneuver I'd done thousands of times. But two of the balls clunked each other on the way up. One careened left, bouncing off Skip's back, startling him. The other shot out of reach under a bookshelf. I scampered around on my belly, laughing and retrieving the balls, standing up and launching into a cascade, but my timing was off.

"Hey, cool it," said Skip impatiently.

Dispirited, partly by Skip's annoyance and partly by my inability to juggle, I stuffed the balls back in my suitcase and sat on the floor next to Skip. I looked at the patterns of light playing across the insides of my eyelids. Had those lights been there all along? It was like a fireworks display projected inside me.

Sitting on my bedroom floor, I understood why getting stoned was called "turning on." I felt plugged in. I saw the world differently—with more weight, more color. I knew that a lot of musicians got stoned when they played. Skip said he had read in his brothers' *Rolling Stone* magazine how one guitar player said that smoking weed tuned him in to the other players. But when I juggled, I juggled alone. There was no one to tune in *to*. And I didn't have as much control over the balls. My mouth was dry as well. If this were a show, I'd stumble over my patter.

I thought again about the cantaloupe in the kitchen, ripe and ready. "The cantaloupe in the kitchen calls," I said, enjoying the alliterative thud of consonants against the roof of my mouth.

"The call of the cantaloupe," Skip murmured, rolling to his side. "My mouth is fucking dry."

"Mine too," I said. "How does this compare to pills and booze?"

Skip looked confused for a second. Then he said, "Different. This is a head high. Pills and booze are body highs."

Although I hadn't tried alcohol, Valium or Dexedrine, I'd seen Skip on them. Weed was different. He wasn't out of control like when he was drunk. He wasn't twitching and bouncing his knee up and down and talking at 600 miles an hour like on Dexedrine. And he wasn't druggy sleepwalking like on Valium.

I liked being high, except my juggling sucked. I wanted to be outside where I could see the night sky, lie on my back and drink in the galaxy, connect my breath to the breeze until the night breathed me.

But first: cantaloupe.

Giggling, we clomped downstairs. In the kitchen, hunched over the table, I sliced the melon in half. Skip dove into his half face first like he was bobbing for apples. I sliced mine into chunks. The soft, sweet, orangey melon flesh called like a siren. I ravished the fruit, sating my thirst and letting it drip down my chin. Skip's face was smeared with cantaloupe pulp. Seeds stuck to his chin and his glasses. Breathless and wild-eyed, he looked like he'd just run a mile through fruit salad.

We slurped and cackled, and rinsed our faces over the kitchen sink. Then, stepping unsteadily into the purplish autumn night, we beheld the canopy of stars. I felt microscopic in the deep purple air, overcome by the expanse of cosmic orbs suspended in outer space.

Crisp cold air blew against my cheeks. I imagined the wind was God's breath, the night sky His workshop. I had an urge to call Rabbi Greenblatt, tell him that maybe I believed in God after all. How else to explain endless heavens and moonlit night clouds that looked like Mr. Peanut and Floppy and ice cream cones? How to explain the moon—which was almost full, floating, gazing upon us like a friendly, corpulent uncle?

I walked down our hill, feeling the gentle pull of gravity and the resistance in my legs, admiring the mysterious choreography of movement: how I cast my attention where I planned to go and then my body responded, naturally calibrating to the hill's angle. I spread my arms, leaned forward, picked up my pace and jogged downhill against the wind. I turned and saw Skip tromping behind me, mouth open, glasses reflecting specks of white light from the street lamps. Nature was God's perfect equation: every rustle and crack, every flash of moonlight and twirling leaf, every curve of every tree limb. Never before had I realized how beautiful lines were—electrical wires, tree trunks and branches arcing gently in space, obeying gravity's silent will.

In the distance, the rumble of cars on Township Line Road sounded familiar. I stopped, closed my eyes and listened. It was like Lita's conch shell. I could hear the ocean.

From the bottom of my hill, we made our way to the new development where we'd broken windows a couple of years earlier. Now Skip had no interest in smashing windows or igniting Molotov cocktails in sewers. Instead he stared at his open palms. "What are you looking at?" I asked.

Skip showed me his palms, glistening a bluish hue under the stark streetlights.

"Fish," he said. I looked harder. "Real small. Palm fish." His palms were empty except for a few tiny, paisley-shaped reflections of light from the moon and a streetlamp.

For the first time, my neighborhood was as cool as the boardwalk. The moonlight and the streetlights beamed shivery rays. I timed each breath to the universal pulse, to the ocean of traffic in the distance, attuned to every faraway brake squeal and shift in the wind, to the whoosh and rumble of a passing car, to the squawk of a distant night bird. The lights and the noises weren't discrete but melded. Sounds and colors: all one. In the distance waves rumbled and splashed. I knew then that wherever I was, I could summon the ocean.

I scanned the gutter, spotted several rocks scattered near the curb, picked up three and launched into a basic cascade. No patter, no jokes. Just seeing if I could maintain a pattern. But I dropped the rocks after a half-dozen throws. "Too juggled to stone," said Skip, reading his palm fish like he was studying a manual.

We arrived back at my house at ten forty-five. When I walked inside, the light shifted from outdoor darkness to indoor iridescence, causing a ripple in my brain. "Ah, that's cool," I said. "I love light, man. Starlight, moonlight, kitchen light—I swig light with my eyes."

Skip, stepping through the back door into the kitchen behind me, blinked at the floor tiles. I remembered back when we first met, swimming on his kitchen floor. "Oh, wow," he said. "Cantaloupe bomb!"

I surveyed the puddles of cantaloupe juice on the counters and floor, dabbing a sneaker toe into a sticky spill. "We should clean the kitchen."

"Nah, let's go upstairs and smoke the rest first," said Skip, halfway out of the kitchen.

That surprised me. I was just beginning to come down—and curious how long it would take before I could juggle again. And I didn't want to be stoned when Dad got home. It was fun, like riding a roller coaster. But my ride was over. "None for me, thanks," I said. "You go ahead and I'll be up in a few minutes."

I tore two paper towels from the roll next to the sink, dampened them with water, squirted some dish soap and wiped up the sticky cantaloupe juice from the counter and the floor. The mess didn't look like God's creation. Meanwhile, Skip tromped upstairs to finish the weed.

NINTH GRADE was a black hole. I trudged up and down bleak concrete halls, a prisoner on a cellblock, haunted by memories of life on the outside. Sometimes on my way to class, I'd stop, close my eyes and try to hear the ocean, smell the marshy air that filled the car when we approached the shore. If school was prison, then riding the bus into town to juggle on Chestnut Street was like a work furlough.

My homeroom teacher, Mr. Page—whose job each morning was to take attendance and hand out smeared, unreadable blue mimeographs from the office—sputtered up and down the rows of desks like a rusty lawn mower, coughing and hacking, occasionally stopping to idle, mumbling to himself over an empty desk, reengaging his throttle and making a notation in his roll book.

"Didn't I see you juggling in the student lounge yesterday?" he asked one morning in October. As he leaned over my desk, I detected the faint odor of ink and wondered if he drank the stuff.

I looked up from the ocean I was sketching in my blue canvas notebook. "I'm working on five balls, and the lounge has really high ceilings."

"You should try out for the talent show," he said, poking his chalky finger at the announcement sheet for tryouts, which he'd just deposited on my desk.

"I don't know," I said, hedging to try and be polite. "It's just that I'm, you know, a professional."

Mr. Page scratched his head. "But it would be fun," he said.

"It would be work, too."

Mr. Page hiked his gray pants and lurched up the aisle, shaking his head and clearing his throat.

Jimmy had impressed upon me the importance of professionalism. "Never give it away or they won't respect ya. Ya stick the hat in their faces, make 'em pay up, 'cause you deserve it. You ain't no amateur." Besides, rehearsals would interfere with my street juggling. It would be like paying to be in the talent show.

Almost every day, Mr. Page handed out notices about afterschool clubs, plays and sports. I'd never played anything on any team. I'd never even played a game of catch.

One day in the middle of November, Mr. Smeer, the gym teacher and football coach, called after me in the hallway when I was coming out of the cafeteria. He asked if I would juggle at a pep rally.

"What's a pep rally?" I asked, smirking.

Coach Smeer rolled his eyes. "You know what a pep rally is." The coach was tall and thick, in a tight black polo shirt and powder blue sweatpants with our school's insignia printed on one of the legs. "Why are you such a wiseass, man?" he asked.

I gazed up innocently. "Me, *man?*"

"Yeah, you. You glom around here with a chip on your shoulder. Somebody tries to talk to you, you act like they're in your way." He put up his hands. "You're a super juggler, but you're unkind to your audience . . ."

"You mean in the student lounge? I'm *practicing.* They're not my audience."

The coach shook his head. He wasn't irritated any more; it was something else. He leaned in closer to me, lowering his voice. "I heard your mom passed away last year."

Pity. Of course.

"I'm sorry," he said.

"Well, it's not like you killed her, but thanks."

He flinched. "You don't have to be a football fan to have a good time," he said. "There's a big game against Upper Darby on Saturday. You could juggle on the sidelines, come out at halftime and put on a show."

"I'm busy Saturday."

"Well, then, two weeks from Saturday. Marple Newtown . . ."

"I'm busy that day too," I said impatiently. "I don't have time for stupid football games."

The coach stepped back. "No time for stupid football? Hey, suit yourself." He was done with me, and that was fine. I watched him retreat down the hallway.

Other than the high ceilings in the student lounge, the only thing I liked about school was English. The teacher's name was Miss Smith. Mostly she gave us books to read—novels by Thomas Hardy and Upton Sinclair, Edgar Allan Poe stories, Tennyson poems like *The Lady of Shallot*. We wrote about them for homework and talked about them in class. She gave us writing assignments too. Once she asked us to write an expository essay about our favorite place. Naturally I wrote about the boardwalk. A few days later, Miss Smith asked me to stay after class.

"Jason," she said, motioning me to an empty seat in the front row while she sat at her desk. "I enjoyed your essay on Atlantic City."

"Oh, thanks." I smiled. Miss Smith was nice. Mid-thirties. Bright-eyed. Good posture. Brunette hair pulled into a tight bun. With her knee-length gray flannel skirt, her thick, dark stockings and sensible brown Wallabee shoes, she looked like she got her clothing from a catalog called *The English Teacher's Nook*. "You don't want me to juggle at a pep rally for the English team, do you?" I asked.

Miss Smith laughed. "You're funny," she said, slipping her metal-rimmed glasses off and dabbing at one eye with the tip of her pinky. "I think that's the first time I've seen you smile."

More pity from my captors, albeit a nice one. I flicked my eyes at the ceiling. Miss Smith must have picked up on my defensiveness. Instead of saying anything further, she stood up and motioned toward the door. "You mustn't be late," she said smoothly.

I stood up and flung my backpack over my shoulder.

"If you ever want to talk," she said as I reached the door, "come see me." By now, the throng of kids rushing to their classes was beginning to thin out.

I stopped and turned toward Miss Smith. She knew about Mom because I'd mentioned it in my essay. "Thanks," I said, stepping out of the classroom and into the hallway.

MIDWAY THROUGH ninth grade, Dad consented to let me go to Atlantic City by myself. "Just for the day," he said. "We'll see how you do. Next year, we'll talk about weekends."

The bus ride from downtown Philadelphia took an hour and a half. I looked out the window over the icy Delaware River and the reedy fields and pine forests of South Jersey, at rickety wooden billboards for Coppertone suntan lotion, at gleaming silver diners and squat strip malls, gas stations and car washes. By now I recognized every billboard, every cheap motel and roadside bar on the Black Horse Pike. Even with the bus windows sealed closed, I could smell the salt air as we approached the bay, placid under the white winter sun.

When Skip heard I'd be away all day on Saturday, he wasn't happy. "We have your place to ourselves and I've got Columbian Fucking Gold. Stay and we'll get wasted!" But I didn't want to get wasted. Over the past few months I'd gotten stoned twice more with Skip. It was fun, but it always screwed up my juggling.

When the bus pulled into the station, I bundled myself in my coat and black wool watch cap, slipped on a pair of ski gloves and hustled down Ohio Avenue three blocks to the boardwalk.

It was freezing outside. The streets were nearly empty. The boardwalk too—just a few old men bundled against the cold, hiking briskly, their breath steaming. The wind whistled up the sands from the ocean. I leaned over the railing and looked out at the Atlantic, studying the horizon from left to right—a perfect, simple line dividing ocean from sky. I shut my eyes and listened to the waves smack the shore.

It was too windy to juggle, so I visited Norman and Betty's arcade, one of the few places on the boardwalk that was open. Inside, a small group of high school guys crowded around a row of machines, smoking cigarettes, their thumbs hooked in their jean pockets.

"Pretzel Man!" one of the kids shouted after I'd pulled off my hat and unbuttoned my coat.

In the back office, Norman, Betty and Lita sipped tomato soup from Campbell's Soup mugs.

"Jason!" Betty said, rushing over to embrace me. "What a nice surprise. Where's your poppa? You want a little soup? Norman! Heat some soup!"

"Thanks," I said. "It's really cold out there!"

"Where's Ed?" Norman asked, sliding open one of his desk drawers and taking out a can of soup. He opened it with a penknife can opener and poured it into a small saucepan on a hot plate.

"Dad didn't come down," I said.

"Who would if they didn't have to?" Lita asked sarcastically.

"Me for one," I said. "You ought to try a week where I have to live."

"I'd love it!" she said. "Let's trade places."

Norman laughed. "Yeah, yeah. The grass what's always greener."

After I warmed up and drank a mug of tomato soup, Norman gave Lita and me a handful of quarters for pinball. "We got a new machine," said Lita, taking my hand and leading me from the office to a row of flashing games. "It's a rodeo game." She put a quarter in the coin slot and played the first ball, showing me which bumpers to go for and how to light up the specials to score free games.

"Pretty cool," I said, as she flipped the ball up a chute to score an extra ten thousand.

We played for an hour. Afterward, I ate a steak sandwich at a sub shop on Pacific Avenue. Then I caught the 4:30 bus back to Philadelphia. At the station's newsstand I bought a copy of the *Atlantic City Press*, and during the ride home I read a few of the stories. It seemed like every one had something to do with a special vote to legalize gambling.

AS NINTH GRADE drew to a close, the weather got warmer and more people went "down the shore" for the weekend. I spent less time on Saturdays playing pinball with Lita and more time juggling on the boardwalk. Most Saturdays, I invited Skip to join me. His parents would have let him, but he never wanted to. At last he agreed to visit me in Atlantic City at the beginning of summer, after school ended and before his camp started.

10

LIKE ME, RUTH prefers tacky souvenir shops to extravagant casinos. She stops, peers into the smudged windows, smirks at the dumb slogans printed on the cheap polyester shirts. I catch her eyeing one with a large marijuana leaf printed on the front. "They didn't sell shirts like those when Skip came to visit," I say, jutting my chin at the shop door. "You want it?"

Ruth giggles. "No. Thanks."

I know better than to ask her if she's smoked weed yet. This is not the time for a "Keep away from that stuff" lecture. Besides, judging from her pierced-faced, mascaraed friends and her penchant for black clothing and moody rock and roll, it would be a good bet.

"The thing about Skip," I say, trying not to sound preachy, "is that he didn't have anything else. His mom was zonked out on painkillers and tranquilizers for pretty much his entire childhood; his dad was always at work. At first I thought he had freedom, but eventually I realized it was more like neglect."

When it came to getting his hands on drugs, Skip had a touch of genius. He taught himself how to fake accidents that landed him in the emergency room. One time he staged a hit-and-run by a driver nobody saw that left him bloody-nosed and splayed in the middle of the street, a rusty nail puncturing his palm. An ambulance took him to the hospital, where he swiped a prescription pad. Then this dyslexic kid who could barely read wrote his own prescriptions for painkillers and filled them at local drug stores—half the pills for him, half to sell at school. He used the pill money to buy weed.

Ruth gazes through the shop window, nodding her head almost imperceptibly. A shock of wind blasts across the boardwalk. I adjust my wool hat. Ruth shivers and folds her arms. I put my arm around her and she doesn't pull away. We look through the shop window at a table filled with snow globes of Atlantic City.

"In the summer," I tell her, "they take the window out and all this stuff is out on the boardwalk in front of the store." I sweep my arm. "Up and down, like a street fair."

"We should come back," says Ruth. "In the summer . . . for a day, you know, whatever."

I swallow. "Maybe stay at the house," I say.

"LADIES AND GENTLEMEN! Welcome to Atlantic City. I am Jason the Magnificent. . . . And these are my balls."

It was June, but it felt like April. A chill swept up and down the boardwalk. Billowing, saffron-colored clouds threatened rain. But it was the first night of the season, and as long as it wasn't pouring, I was going to perform.

Dad and I had arrived in time for lunch. Jimmy had already been around for a week, hiring three or four college kids, teaching them how to work the marionettes and rehearsing his new show—a spoof of *Little House on the Prairie* with marionettes of covered wagons, horses and girls in braids. The three of us walked to Nathan's Famous Hot Dogs, stopping at stores along the way to say hi to the shop owners. Among the merchants, the buzz was about the upcoming vote on legalized gambling in Atlantic City. Practically everywhere we stopped—the orange juice stand on Florida Avenue, Laura's Custard across from Million Dollar Pier—everyone wanted to know whether Dad and Jimmy thought gambling would pass.

I didn't know why it was such a big deal. As far back as I could remember, you could put a quarter down on a spin of the wheel and take a chance on winning a prize. That was gambling, right? What did it matter whether you were playing for cash or a teddy bear?

"They'll raise everybody's rent," Jimmy said over lunch at Nathan's, hunched over the table, slurping from a clamshell. "Everything's gonna change. They build a casino, nobody's gonna be on the boardwalk no more. Ghost town, ghost boardwalk."

Dad bit into his foot-long hot dog. "Let's wait and see what happens with the referendum," he said, swabbing at a glob of mustardy relish that had spurted out of the roll. "No point in getting worked up about it now."

Jimmy sucked down another clam and stretched back in his seat. He pulled a pack of cigarettes and his silver lighter from his shirt pocket. "Diane says the gambling's gonna put her out of business." He lit a cigarette.

Tired of Jimmy's negativity, I tried changing the subject. "How *is* Madam Diane?"

"She's coming up today or tomorrow," said Jimmy. "Bullshit legal problems in Florida. Sons-of-bitches set her up. Tore her place apart over abso-fucking-lutely nothing! An expired license."

"Who, the police?" I asked.

Jimmy took a deep drag on his cigarette and blew three or four smoke rings. "Entrapment. Bullshit."

After lunch Dad and I went back to the bakery, where we cleaned the mixer, scraped the ovens and fiddled with the rolling machine. We oiled the oven doors, rinsed the dipping pot and scraped the gunked-up salt deposits off the wooden pretzel boards. By dinnertime we were greasy and sweaty.

"Dad, if I'm gonna do a show tonight I'd better go back to the hotel and shower."

Dad looked surprised. "It's miserable out there. It's going to pour."

I looked at the sky and back at Dad. "It's not raining yet and it's my first night."

He rubbed my head with his knuckles. "I admire your optimism," he said.

I wiped my hands on my greasy white tee shirt and brushed chips of hardened dough out of my hair. I ducked under the counter and stepped out onto the boardwalk. It was good to be home.

My first show of the season was a disappointment, though. Too windy for high throws, too cold for big crowds, and I didn't even attempt the seven-hundred-and-twenty-degree spin on my heels while all three balls were in the air that I'd been practicing since February.

Sure enough, just as I began working my way through the crowd of shivery onlookers, derby in hand, I felt the first few raindrops. I'd collected only about six bucks when a thunderclap burst and the sky opened. No more shows for the night, and none tomorrow because Skip was coming. He'd stay for two days and one night, and I'd arranged for a couple of the college boys to take my bakery shifts while he was in town.

The next morning, walking up Ohio Avenue to meet Skip, I noticed that most of the big wooden boarding houses needed work. Salt air was unkind to paint jobs. Several of the porches buckled; their thick, peeling floorboards were bloated and curved like ocean waves. Three or four houses were boarded up altogether.

The bus station smelled like disinfectant. I sat down on a hard brown plastic seat, my elbows on my knees, staring across the domed airy room at the big board with bus numbers and arrival times. I watched a janitor—a lean black man about Dad's age—mop a swath of the bus station floor outside the men's room.

Soon a bus rumbled into a stall outside the glass doors. Passengers stepped off—people on day trips, mostly, young families with whiny kids clutching their plastic buckets and shovels, moms with beach bags, dads with cameras and binoculars hanging from their necks. And there was Skip. Backpack in one hand, small brown overnight bag in the other, he wore blue jeans and a Penn State sweatshirt that he'd probably swiped from one of his brothers. I waved and he came directly to the glass doors.

"How was the ride down?" I asked.

"Sucky. Long. But guess what . . ." He lowered his voice to an urgent whisper. "I've got hash!"

"Cool," I said. I'd heard about hash. Stronger than grass. "Maybe we can smoke some tonight."

"Nah, let's get wasted now."

"But it's only twenty after ten," I said. "Don't you want to see the boardwalk first? Say hi to my dad? Meet Jimmy? Remember Lita, from my mom's funeral? And Norman and Betty?"

Skip shook his head. "I'd rather get stoned first."

"If you say so," I said. "But take off that sweatshirt. It's warm out there." We had to stop at the hotel so Skip could drop off his stuff anyway, and I didn't have to work at all that day, so I figured it was okay to get stoned before we did anything else. We could smoke, gargle some mouthwash, put on our sunglasses and no one would know.

The hash was brown and sticky like clay. It smelled like weed but sweeter. We took two tokes each, surreptitiously blowing the smoke out the window while keeping an eye out for neighbors sticking their heads out their own windows.

"I'm stoneder than ever," I said. I closed the window and Skip buried his stash deep inside his backpack.

"My brain's ass-fucked," said Skip.

"Let's go up to the boardwalk," I said. "I'd better avoid my dad while I'm this high, though." My voice sounded to me like reverb had been added.

"My folks never know when I'm stoned," Skip said.

Well, yeah, I thought. *That's because your mom's brain is more ass-fucked than yours, and your dad's never around.*

I led Skip down the stairs and out to St. James Place, then up the block to Pacific Avenue. Skip had been to Long Beach Island with his family, and they'd gone to Florida a few times, but this was his first time in Atlantic City. I wanted to take him up the boardwalk to the inlet, but I stuck to Pacific Avenue for the first five blocks so we wouldn't run into Dad, Jimmy, Madam Diane or Norman, Betty and Lita while we were high.

"What a shithole," Skip said, snorting at a dumpy, one-story neon-decked motel next to a liquor store with faded yellow paint flaking off the grated front entrance.

"Don't worry about it," I said. "We'll head up to the boardwalk in another block." I had to admit, Pacific Avenue didn't make a good first impression. The shops needed a coat of paint. But wait until Skip got a taste of the boardwalk at night. He'd love it.

At Tennessee Avenue we turned right and walked the block toward the water. When we climbed the ramp to the boardwalk, Million Dollar Pier's cavernous entrance obscured our view of the beach. "The ocean's right over there," I said, pointing past the pier. "Can you hear it?" The Atlantic Ocean: my favorite sound in the world. The rumble-wash filled my head. I must have looked stupid standing there, in the middle of the boardwalk with my eyes closed and my mouth hanging open, listening to the waves lap the shore and splash against the moorings. I shifted my concentration to take in the ocean breeze and the carnival music floating across the boards from the rides on the pier.

"Hungry?" I asked.

"Yeah," said Skip. He pointed at a Belgian waffle stand. "I want one of those." At last he was smiling.

We got in line. The late morning sun bore down on my neck and ears. In the wake of last night's storm, the air was balmy and still. "Hey, there's Mr. Peanut!" I said, pointing to the Planters mascot strutting like a dandy, swinging his cane and waving to little kids. "He isn't allowed to talk. Like a guard at Buckingham Palace."

Skip furrowed his eyebrows. "Huh?" Annoyed, he shook his head and stared absently at the waffle menu. Remembering his dyslexia, I tried to help him out. "I usually get one with everything."

"Okay," Skip said. "That's what I want."

The waffles were mind-blowing. "These should come with instructions: 'Eat While Stoned,'" I said, slurping strawberry juice and whipped cream from my wrist. Skip's face was slathered with whipped cream and pecan crumbs.

When we finished eating we walked down to the ocean to rinse off our sticky hands. We watched the waves for a minute or two, then went back to the boardwalk and walked about a mile north to the inlet at New Hampshire Avenue where the boardwalk ends. Across the inlet was Brigantine Island, the next island up from Atlantic City. The water smelled like fish. All around us, fishermen cast their lines from the boardwalk into the ocean. High tide. No beach visible at the inlet—just water, lapping under. One guy reeled in a flounder. Another used a pair of pliers to yank a hook from the mouth of a blowfish, which he tossed over the railing and back into the ocean. Skip and I watched the men and boys bait their hooks with slippery gobs of squid and pensively cast their lines into the ocean. "Sometimes you can see dolphins swimming right out there," I told Skip. "They get really close, but they piss off the fishermen, because if you see dolphins you know they're feeding and you won't catch shit."

We walked around the corner to Captain Starn's, a big seafood restaurant and commercial fishing dock. "What the fuck are they?" asked Skip, pointing at the cement enclosure of sea lions that kids could feed.

"Sea lions."

"They look like my grandmother."

We watched the sea lions wriggling and yowling in their pens. A little girl and her dad fed them fish from a blue bucket that said "Captain Starn's" on it. The sea lions barked and clapped and slurped down the fish.

Captain Starn's looked worn down. It needed fresh paint and the roof sagged. But the sounds were great—squeaky jibs, seagull caws and a salty breeze.

After a while I wasn't feeling stoned anymore. "Want to head back, say hi to my dad and all?" I asked.

Skip scratched his head. "Huh? Yeah, I guess," he said. "Whatever."

We leaned over the metal railing and took a last look at the sea lions. Skip stooped and picked up a cigar butt from the ground, wound up and pitched it into the pool. The sea lions didn't notice. "Why'd you do that?" I asked.

Skip snickered. "Huh? I dunno. I thought they'd eat it."

"But that might make them sick."

"Bullshit." Skip scanned the ground for something else to throw.

I didn't want to argue. How do you reason with a kid who's intent on feeding a cigar butt to a sea lion? I tapped the metal railing with my fingertips. "We should head back."

Sunlight splashed the boardwalk as we made our way to the bakery, stopping to watch glassblowers and listen to a pitchman demonstrate his handy-dandy-automatic-floor-sweeper-and-damp-mop to a huddle of moms in beach robes and sandals. Despite the breeze, it was hot out. I was glad I'd persuaded Skip to change into short pants and a tee shirt at the hotel. But he looked tired. Bored. "Want to check out Steel Pier?" I asked. "Want to watch the diving horse? All the time I've been coming here, I've never seen the diving horse. Too much else to do."

"Not really," said Skip.

"What do you want to do?"

"Go back to the hotel, get high and hit the beach?"

"Okay," I said, leading him past the pier and down the boardwalk toward the bakery. "First we'll just pop in and say hi to Madam Diane and then go see Dad and Jimmy. 'Kay?"

"Whatever," he said moodily.

Our first stop was Madam Diane's. I hoped that getting his future told would cheer Skip up.

"Hey, Madam Diane," I said, poking my head through the beaded curtain that separated the waiting room from the fortune-teller's work area. Madam Diane was unpacking a box. She stopped, came out to the waiting room and kissed me on my cheek. "This is Skip. Skip, this is Madam Diane."

Madam Diane extended her hand in a grand, royal gesture. Skip shook it reluctantly, eyeing the purple silk curtains. Madam Diane tried to make eye contact with Skip while she held his hand, but he wouldn't meet her gaze.

"You want to have your fortune told?" she asked.

Skip blew air through his lips mockingly like he knew this was bullshit. "How'd you know *that*?" he asked. Madam Diane raised her eyebrows and stole a side glance at me.

Skip sat down across from her at the small, round wooden table while I leaned against the wall behind him. "Let me see your palm—your right hand," said the fortune-teller. Skip complied, holding his right palm open on the table. Madam Diane took his hand in hers. Skip looked uncomfortable and small.

Squinting, she studied the lines on his palm, tracing them with her fingertips and occasionally glancing up to look Skip in the eye. Each time he avoided her gaze.

"What do you see, Madam Diane?" I asked. Skip clucked his tongue.

Madam Diane raised an index finger to her chin and massaged it, like she was applying an ointment. After a couple of long minutes she said: "You . . . are a very smart young man. Sometimes too smart for your own good. Do you know what I am talking about? Yes, you do. You hear, but do you listen? You see, but do you read?"

Skip spun toward me. "You told her about my dyslexia!"

I held up my hands. "No way, man."

"Look at me," Madam Diane told Skip. "Stop biting your fingernails."

Skip turned and faced her. Then he said something that surprised me. "When am I gonna die?"

Madam Diane remained calm. She looked at his palm some more. "You're going to be around for quite some time," she said. "And I can tell you this: You will die . . . in . . . a foreign country or something like it."

Skip looked like he'd been shaken out of a dream. "*Wha—?*" he asked.

Madam Diane clasped Skip's hand in both of hers, then released it. "Boys, I'm busy. I'm still unpacking." She tilted her head at a half-full cardboard box on the floor of her work area. "Off you go. Come back later. I promise, a full reading."

We arrived at the pretzel bakery at around one o'clock. Dad was at the cash register, talking with Jimmy, who stood on the boardwalk, one elbow on the counter.

"Good to see you, Skip!" said Dad, extending his hand.

"Hey, Mr. Benson." Skip offered Dad a limp handshake.

"Where were you guys all morning?" Dad asked.

"We walked to the inlet and watched guys fish for a while. And we had Belgian waffles," I said.

"What do you make of Atlantic City so far?" Dad asked Skip.

Skip yawned. "It's okay."

I tried to sound more upbeat. "We're going back to the hotel to change, then we're gonna hit the beach."

"Jason's a regular tourist!" Jimmy said, mussing my hair. "Days off. Beach time."

"Oh, sorry," I said. "I didn't introduce you guys. Skip, Jimmy. Jimmy, Skip."

Jimmy extended his hand to Skip. "Welcome to the soul of America. Jason tells me you never been down here before. Unique, right?" Jimmy smoothed his hair with his palm and leaned back against the counter.

"Huh? Yeah," Skip said quietly.

Back at the hotel, Skip and I each took three more tokes of hash. My brain didn't get as ass-fucked this time, which was fine with me. Hash was intense. I didn't like that I couldn't tell how loud I was talking, and it made me feel clumsy with my words—too many "ums," too many pauses while I tried to remember what I wanted to say.

But I put on my best face for Skip. "This is really cool," I said as we changed into our bathing suits and flip-flops. "Like Jimmy said, I never get to go down to the beach until the last day of the season." I grabbed a couple of bath towels from the bathroom closet.

Skip folded a layer of tinfoil around the remaining lump of hash. "Plenty left for tonight and tomorrow." He stuffed the pipe and the hash into the bottom of his backpack.

"Ready for the beach?" I asked.

"Yeah. Let's go. This room smells."

"I told you to blow it out the window."

"Not hash. Mildew."

I sniffed the air. "There's no mildew here."

"Is too," said Skip.

"If you say so, Skip. Let's hit the beach."

Lying on my back, on my beach towel, a little high and a little sleepy, eyes closed, the rolling waves filling my ears, the sun glinting down on my chest and warming my eyelids—this was heaven. I was happy to have the day off with my best friend from Philadelphia, even if Skip wasn't exactly falling in love with Atlantic City. Suddenly a spray of sand whipped the top of my head. I flipped over to look around. "Lita! Hey!" I said. "Cut it out. Remember Skip?"

"Hey, Skip," said Lita.

"Hey," said Skip.

A little earlier, he had asked me if Lita got high.

"No way, man. She's only thirteen!"

"So what? That's old enough. Even twelve-year-olds at my school get high."

I made some room on my towel and patted it for her to sit next to me. Lita wore super-short, cut-off blue jeans and a bikini top. Over the winter her breasts had grown into firm mounds. Her wavy brown hair was uncombed and tangled, giving her a wild look. She sat down beside me, drew her knees to her chest and jabbed her toes at the sand. Skip scooped a handful of sand and tossed it at her legs. She shot him a dirty glance, brushed off the sand and flung some back in his direction. Skip stared at the ocean. I lay down and listened to the waves for almost an hour.

That night we hit the boardwalk. "When I was a little kid everyone used to dress up at night," I told Skip as we shuffled along, my pace sluggish and eyelids heavy, stoned for the third time that day. "The old ladies wore mink stoles, and the old men wore white shoes. My mom would go back to the hotel like at three o'clock to dress up for the boardwalk on nights when she didn't work a shift. She'd have her hair in curlers all afternoon."

"Curlers?" he asked dully.

"Huh? Yeah, hair curlers; you know, like moms put in their hair to make it curly?"

"I know what curlers are, asshole."

I stopped so suddenly that the young family walking behind us nearly crashed into me. "Why'd you call me an asshole?"

Skip grunted.

"I'm serious," I said. "What's going on? Okay, I get it. You don't like Atlantic City, but all day long you've been in a shitty mood, you were a dick to Lita and Madam Diane, and you barely spoke to my dad or Jimmy."

"I'm gonna die in a foreign country?"

"She said 'a foreign country *or something like it.*'"

"Well she's an asshole, *or something like it.*"

"She's a fortune-teller," I said. "It doesn't mean anything! It's just for fun. It's a goof."

"It's bullshit! *Or something like it.*"

I led Skip over to the railing, away from the crowd. "She's not an asshole," I told him. "She's my friend."

"You think you're hot shit 'cause your mom died!" he spat. "Everyone feels sorry for poor little Jason. You think you're better than everybody else with your juggling and your 'Oh, poor me, my mom died.' It's bullshit and you're plastic."

"Plastic?"

"Phony! Fake! You're one thing in Philly and you're another thing here." Skip was getting loud. A dad scooted one of his kids past Skip by her elbow. "And now I know where your bullshit comes from. When you're in Philly all you ever do is act like that fag with the earring. 'Oh, I have a magic hat. Look at me. I can hear the ocean in my toilet . . .'"

My face prickled. "Jesus, Skip! Jimmy's not a fag, and I don't imitate him."

"The fuck you don't!"

"I love it down here," I said. "And I hate Philly. So, yeah, maybe I act different, but that doesn't make me phony. I'm happier here. What do you want me to do? Break windows with you? Set shit on fire? Get high every day? Then I'm just imitating you!"

"Bullshit!" said Skip. "When we were kids you were the one who always had to throw rocks at windows. I was just doing it 'cause you were."

"No way!" I said, my heart pounding in my throat. "It was *your* idea, you went first and I'm sorry I played along."

Skip turned his back and headed off into the crowd.

"Wait up!" I shouted, tagging behind him, dodging around the throngs of tourists and sidestepping a rolling chair. "Skip! I'm not going to chase you, and you don't even know how to get back to the hotel!"

Skip slowed down and let me catch up. Exasperated, I led him back to the railing, my knees wobbling. Skip was out of breath and sweaty, his face bright red.

"Your juggling's stupid," he said. "If you want to meet chicks you should have taken guitar lessons. Chicks don't like clowns. They like musicians."

"I'm not a clown," I said. But what was the point? "Know what? Fine. Let's go back to the hotel."

Now he was silent. He took hold of the boardwalk's rail, tightened his jaw and gazed at the empty beach. For the longest time he just stood there, looking out, his lips shut tight. Finally he spoke. "My mom almost died and nobody gave a flying fuck."

I wasn't expecting that. "What do you mean?"

"When I was in first grade. My old man took my brothers on a ski trip to the Pocono Mountains."

"What happened to your mom?"

Skip stared into the darkness over the beach. "She . . . fucking tried to off herself! O*kay*? And I was there."

He loosed a long, rapid, vulgar spew about finding his mom on the kitchen floor—in the same spot where we play-swam a year later—beside a puddle of Janitor in a Drum, her breath smelling sweet. And he stood there listening to her babble into the puddle on the floor. And he watched her fall asleep. And then he went into the den to watch TV, and *Bowling for Dollars* was on. And when his dad and brothers came home a little while later they found her on the floor and called for an ambulance, and Skip's dad yelled at Skip and called him "stupid." His mom came home from the hospital with her pills, and after that she watched TV all day, and no one ever said a thing about her drinking Janitor in a Drum. Like it never happened. And Skip had never told anyone until now, on the boardwalk, on the day he learned he would die in a foreign country or something like it.

"I am so sorry," I said. "That's the worst . . ."

"Everybody feels sorry for you because your mom died. But when mine almost died it was my fucking fault, and I got shit on for it, so fuck that, and fuck you, and fuck your asshole father and your weird friends."

My jaw was set tight as marble, my teeth clamped shut. I felt like throttling Skip. He was acting like such a shithead. At the same time, I couldn't help feeling sorry for him. Unsure of what to do, I just stood there.

"And fuck your boardwalk," Skip said. He spat on the boards, drawing glares from people around us. "This place sucks. My old man's right: Atlantic City's all fat people and crappy old rides."

We walked a few blocks without speaking, past arcades, hot dog stands, wheels of fortune and tee-shirt shops where up until a few minutes earlier I'd hoped Skip would want to pick up a souvenir.

"We should turn around," I said. "Ready to head back?"

Skip shrugged and we reversed our route.

When we were almost at the bakery, I tried again. "Hey, Skip, I'm sorry about your mom. You didn't know. You were too young. Your dad shouldn't have blamed you."

"Yeah, well, what was I supposed to do? My dad's a fuck face, just like yours."

"Yeah, my dad can be a trip, man, but he's a lot nicer down here than he is in Philly." By now we were in sight of the bakery.

Skip pointed across the boardwalk at the bakery. "There's your nice dad." Dad was inside the bakery, leaning over the counter to yell at some teenagers. I couldn't hear him, but he was jabbing his finger at the kids, who looked annoyed as they backed away. They'd probably been hanging out in front, blocking customers and disrupting business. "Your dad's an asshole no matter where he is. You just imagine all this bullshit about Atlantic City, like you imagined me breaking windows first. You don't notice your old man's an angry asshole because *you're* an angry asshole."

The next day, Skip and I barely spoke at all. We ate breakfast at the Belgian waffle stand and then spent most of the day on the beach, with Skip trekking to the hotel three times to smoke his hash. By nighttime, he'd be gone and I'd do a show with my first-ever seven-hundred-and-twenty-degree spin. After my shows, I'd visit Madam Diane and ask her about when I might meet a girl.

Late in the afternoon, Skip packed his bag and took a few hits of hash for the bus ride home. We left the hotel and walked up St. James to Pacific, then over to Ohio Avenue and the bus station. "Want me to wait with you?" I asked, looking up at the big clock on the wall and the giant board listing departures and arrivals. According to the board, Skip's bus to Philadelphia would leave in fifteen minutes.

"Nah, I'm good," he said, dropping his overnight bag and back-pack on the wooden bench and plopping himself down beside them. I felt awkward. Skip looked up at the board.

"Have a great time at camp," I said, extending my hand. He shook it like his mom was making him. His hand felt like a dead fish.

"Have a good ride back," I said. "When you're on the Atlantic City Expressway, keep looking out the window into the woods, maybe you'll see a deer."

"Like I give a fuck about asshole deer."

Rabbi Greenblatt would have said that anyone who calls anonymous deer "assholes" probably feels like an asshole himself. *Scape-deering.* I left the station, exhausted from Skip's foul mood and glad to be rid of him.

Back at the hotel, I stretched out across my bed and stared at the ceiling, unnerved by Skip's visit, by his odd insistence that I was the one who'd first thrown rocks at windows, and by the image of his mom lying on the kitchen floor—our emerald-colored make-believe ocean a death pool of Janitor in a Drum.

"LADIES AND GENTLEMEN, boys and girls, dudes and dudettes," I announced that night as I was about to close my first show. "For the first time in public, I—Jason the Magnificent—will attempt to complete my three-ball ballet with a full seven-hundred-twenty-degree spin while all three balls are in the air. That's two full turns for you non-math majors. If I succeed, I hope you will throw a few bucks in my derby. And if I fail . . . ," I said with mock earnestness, "tell my wife I loved her."

I'd learned the seven-twenty by watching Michael Jackson dance on TV. The wind was low. I turned on my portable cassette recorder and juggled to Emerson, Lake & Palmer, building my cascade to the rhythmic progressions—higher and higher until I nearly lost the balls in the glare of the lampposts. Then, as the music picked up its pace, I made my cascade smaller and smaller until the three balls barely left my hands, making a blur in perfect rhythm, eight throws per beat—eliciting oohs and aahs from the crowd. As the song neared its end, I steadied my pattern, took a deep breath and launched all three balls as high as I could, spun twice on my heels, caught all three balls, held my arms out triumphantly and took a deep bow.

That night I did four shows, averaging thirty dollars each. I made a quick projection: the money people threw into my derby plus the thirty bucks a day I earned at the pretzel bakery would make me the richest kid on the boardwalk. But I understood that when I was living in Atlantic City all year round, I'd see this kind of income for only twelve weeks a year. So I'd need to save and budget.

After my final show that night, I walked to Madam Diane's. "Come in!" she said. I went in and sat down across from her. She looked older than she had last season. Her hair was still jet-black, but her face had more wrinkles. "Lemme see your palm," she said. She studied the lines on my hand, pausing every few seconds to gaze into my eyes. "What do you want to know?" she asked me. Before I could answer, she held up her hand and pressed her index finger to her lips. "You're seeking someone . . ."

"Like you didn't already know that," I said sarcastically, but with a smile.

Madam Diane smiled and squeezed the back of my hand. "Don't lose faith. She will come. You must be patient."

"Will it be this summer?"

Madam Diane gazed at the ceiling, shaking her head innocently. "How should I know? When it happens, it happens."

"Okay," I said, underwhelmed.

Madam Diane looked into my eyes. "He's troubled, your friend."

"Skip? Yeah, I mean, he has issues." I couldn't believe he'd blamed me for breaking those windows.

"What does he live for?"

I shook my head, exhaling through my nostrils. What did Skip live for? Drugs. I wasn't going to say that out loud, but she was no fool. She *had* to know I'd been getting high too. I changed the subject: "So, about a girl, okay, I understand you can't tell me when I'll meet her, but you are saying that I definitely *will* meet her, right?"

To my relief, Madam Diane raised her head and smiled. "Jason, you will marry, you will have a family; you will know life. Stop worrying!"

"I hate Philly," I said. "If a guy like him is my best friend there, what's that say about the place?"

"Nothing," said Madam Diane. "What does it say about you?"

"That my parents bought a house in a neighborhood with no other kids my age. That I'd be happier if I lived here."

"No, you wouldn't," said Madam Diane. "Never think a new place will make you happy. Temporarily? Oh, sure. Like a coat of paint. But if you're not happy, it don't matter where you live."

"I'd be happy if I met a girl," I said. I leaned back in my chair and gazed out the open door to the boardwalk. It was almost midnight. Outside, the crowd thinned while merchants shut their shops. Madam Diane watched me silently. I stood up. "I should go."

Outside the shop, a guy and a girl in their early twenties peered in, scoping out the chairs and table inside. "She's incredible," I said. "It's like she's known me my whole life."

"MEETING GIRLS is like juggling. It takes practice," said Jimmy.

It was a glorious sunny afternoon, the last week of July. The temperature was in the mid-eighties and the ocean calm. A lazy wind fanned the beach, which was lined with people stretched on their backs and bellies, on blankets and beach towels, like sausages grilling under the sun. The ocean teemed with rubber rafts and body surfers.

"You're scaring 'em off," Jimmy said, plucking a cigarette from behind his ear. Deftly he slipped it between his lips, cupped his hands against the breeze and lit up. "I seen you talk to the girls at the counter. You come on too strong. Girls don't like desperation."

"But I *am* desperate," I conceded.

Jimmy dragged on his cigarette. "Just don't let 'em see it. Like when you juggle, you're working hard, but you make it look easy. Invisible, no? Same thing here. Just lighten up. You meet a nice girl. You ask her for a date, a night on the boards. You buy her a cotton candy, put your arm around her. Tell her she looks great. Make her feel like a million. A girl wants to feel like that, you know? Maybe you get a kiss at the end of the night. Maybe you cop a feel. But that's it. You don't get laid and she don't get no ring."

It wasn't until the second week of August that I had my first prospect—a petite, bouncy redhead named Janis, who watched me juggle on a Saturday night and stuck around after the show. She introduced me to two other girls—her thirteen-year-old cousin and a friend from Cherry Hill, New Jersey. Although I was certain that my one and only wouldn't have freckles, Janis was pretty.

Thick, wavy hair. Green eyes. Thin lips stretched into a wide smile. One of the straps of her purple and black bikini top had slipped down her shoulder, where it dangled alluringly against the flesh on her arm.

She whispered to her companions, who burst into giggles, flitted across the boardwalk and disappeared inside the Two for One. Janis turned her attention back to me. By now the audience had dispersed. I emptied the coins and bills from my derby into my old yellow suitcase, stuffed my juggling balls and derby in as well, snapped the top closed and ran my hand through my hair. "So," I began, leaning against the boardwalk's railing and gazing up at the moonlit ocean. "Where do you live year-round?"

Janis faced the boardwalk, clasped her hands behind her and leaned back on the railing. "Elkins Park," she said. "Outside Philadelphia. You're from down here, aren't you?"

"Uh, well, basically, yes." It wasn't a lie, exactly. I'd simply omitted part of the truth: the part about living in Philadelphia from September through June. "It's pretty quiet down here all winter. But that's good, because a juggler needs time to practice and think."

"You're pretty deep." She slid along the railing until she was next to me. When our hips brushed against each other's, my loins tingled.

"Nah, it's just the air down here," I said. Janis giggled. She looked across the crowded boardwalk, then down at her feet. "Wanna go to Million Dollar Pier?" I asked.

"Sure," she said, taking my hand in hers. Her delicate fingers, entwined in my own, were smooth and inviting. "C'mon," she said, tugging me into the pedestrian traffic. "I need to tell my cousin where I'm going." I complied, her loyal puppy, skittering across the boardwalk after her. "Did you see where they went?"

"Yeah," I said, steering her toward Norman and Betty's. "They're in the Two for One."

There was a long line at the pretzel bakery. Dad, hurriedly bagging pretzels and working the register, was too busy to look up as we passed.

When we walked into Norman and Betty's, we spotted the girls Janis had introduced me to. Just then, Norman came around the corner, staring into his money apron and sorting the bills and change in its bulging pockets. When he saw Janis and me holding hands, he did a double take.

"Hiya, *boychick*," he said, grinning. He eyed Janis and winked his approval.

"Hi, Norman," I said. "This is Janis. We're going to Million Dollar Pier. Okay if I leave my juggling stuff in your office?"

"Sure. Leave it by Betty." A bunch of kids crowded around him to exchange their dollar bills for quarters. Janis whispered and giggled with her cousin and her friend while I dashed to the back office and tossed my suitcase inside.

Then, hand in hand, we made our way along the crowded boardwalk to Million Dollar Pier. We walked through the grand entrance, stopping in front of the carousel, next to where Bobby, Lita and I had spied on the Bearded Lady. Raising my voice over the tinny organ music, I asked, "What do you want to do?"

"I don't know," Janis said, demurring. "What do *you* want to do?" The pier was mobbed, its midway lined with attractions: games of chance; chickens that played tic-tac-toe inside glass boxes; a House of Mirrors; a syrupy-smelling cotton candy counter; and farther down, the giant steel roller coaster. All the rides were going full tilt: the spinning teacups and saucers, the big salt and pepper shaker that turned you upside down, the haunted house at the end of the pier. All around us, people squealed and laughed.

"We could ride the roller coaster," I said. "Or get something to eat. Or we could see what's going on under the boardwalk."

Would Janis slap my face? Storm off in a huff? Retreat to the Deauville Hotel and tell her parents that a perverted pretzel boy had tried to take advantage of her? I was too well known on the boardwalk to avoid a vengeful father for long.

"What's under the boardwalk?" she asked.

My jaw trembled. "Oh, well, nothing, really . . ."

"Let's go," she said, just as boldly as she had taken hold of my hand. We left the pier, walked half a block along the boardwalk and climbed down a wooden stairway to the beach. When we hit the sand, Janis paused to slip off her sneakers. I took off mine too. We ducked under the boardwalk and sat beside each other in the cool, damp sand.

In the darkness, Janis's freckles were invisible. I held both her hands in mine and caressed her fingers. "You're really nice," I said.

"So are you."

I leaned over to kiss her on the lips. Unfortunately I missed, my mouth landing on her nose. She didn't pull away as I feared. Instead, she giggled sweetly and returned the kiss, but with better aim. Her lips were dry but warm, and slightly parted. Her breath smelled like licorice. We sat for a minute or more, attached at the lips—the muffled drumming of people's feet and strains of carousel music above our heads. After a little while, she pressed her tongue into my mouth. Soft. Wet. I answered back with my own, mashing it against her tongue. Her breathing grew heavy.

After about fifteen minutes of kissing, Janis told me she had to go find her cousin. We emerged from our gritty love nest, climbed up the stairs to the boardwalk and shook off the sand.

"I can't believe I have to go home tomorrow," Janis sighed, holding my arm for balance as she slipped a sneaker on.

I took Janis by the hand and led her across the boards to Irene's Fudge. The shop was crammed with customers, the air sweet and thick as caramel. The owner, Mr. Lambert, had a son my age named Lew, who was working behind the counter, slicing fudge with a big two-handled knife, weighing and boxing saltwater taffy, deftly working the big green electronic cash register like a concert pianist.

"Lew," I whispered, worming in between the customers waiting to be served. "Slip me a large variety pack?"

Lew snagged a box of fudge from the shelf behind him and flipped it over the heads of the customers and into my waiting arms.

I handed the box to Janis, who cradled it in her hands like a prize. "How'd you do that? How'd you get him to do that?" she asked.

"I juggle out front sometimes and draw a crowd so they give me free fudge."

Walking Janis back to the Deauville, I felt like I owned the boardwalk. Outside the hotel we kissed some more, Janis leaning back against the boardwalk railing, her back arched, her body lithe and tanned. At long last I was one-half of the kind of teenage couple I'd been watching since I was seven. I cupped the small of Janis's back, pressed my lips to hers, tasted her damp breath and her daring tongue. When we finished making out, Janis promised to look me up next summer.

"Thanks for the fudge," she said, darting into the hotel and disappearing into the gleaming yellow lobby.

11

WHEN DAD AND I returned to Philadelphia after Labor Day, we found a cardboard box wedged between the front door and the storm door. A foot high by a foot long, with several layers of gray packing tape wrapped neatly around it, it had no return address and no postmark. Just my name handwritten in black magic marker: **TO JASON BENSON**.

Inside, I used Dad's Swiss army knife to make slits under the flaps. I opened the box to find my third derby. It was bigger than the last. The same smooth black felt and rounded bowl. The exact same stitching, tiny and precise, like miniature train tracks circling the hidden inside lip of the perfectly balanced brim. As I had done twice before, I clasped my new derby between my fingertips, admiring its simple beauty, inspecting its satiny, hand-stitched inside. Slowly, ceremonially, with an easy double-twirl between my fingers, I placed the derby on my head. A perfect fit.

In recent weeks I'd noticed the old derby feeling a little tight. I hadn't seen My Edna in years; I wondered how she knew my hat size. Dad probably snuck over to my bed when I was asleep, wrapped a string around my head and mailed it to Miami. But he'd never admit it to me because they'd made him swear to a gypsy oath.

I pushed aside the empty box and rushed out the front door into the balmy night. "I'll be right back!"

"Close the door behind you," Dad said. "AC's on."

New derby on my head, I raced to Dad's station wagon parked in front of the house. I opened the wood-paneled back door and rummaged through the suitcases and boxes until I got a grip on my yellow juggling suitcase. I yanked it free from underneath a cardboard box filled with blankets and towels, flipped it open and discovered that derby number two was gone. I ran back to the house.

"Daaaaad!" I yelled up the stairs.

When I cornered Dad on the second-floor landing, he swore he had nothing to do with the derby switch. He looked sincere. I would have believed him if there were a logical explanation. The old derby had been in my suitcase the night before, in our hotel room. I'd put it there after my last show.

"It had to be you," I said. "Where's my old derby? What do you do? Mail it back to My Edna? Then she sends it to some other kid? C'mon, tell me!"

"I don't know," he said.

"Then what do you *think* happened to the derby that I'm a thousand percent sure was in my suitcase?"

Dad puffed his cheeks and took off his glasses. "You misplaced it?" he asked, shaking his head like he didn't even believe that himself.

"That's impossible!" I said. "I lost the first derby on the day the second one arrived, and I lost the second on the day the third arrived! So let me ask you: What else have I lost? My keys? My wallet? My juggling stuff?"

Dad looked confounded.

"I don't lose things, your theory's irrational and you've lied to me before. When Mom was sick. You knew she wasn't getting better. But all you told me was she needs more tests, she needs more tests."

"I apologized for that," Dad said. "And I have not lied to you since then. I can't think of any other way it could have happened, but the simplest answer is usually the correct answer—even though, as you say, it's uncharacteristic of you." He looked me square in the eye. "It wasn't me."

We stood at the top of the landing, at a silent impasse. If Dad knew anything, he wasn't going to admit it. He was right: the simplest explanation was usually correct. And the simplest explanation was that he was involved.

I inspected my new derby. The rim was slightly worn just like the rim on the previous derby. I tilted my head back, knees bent and arms out, and balanced the derby on the tip of my chin. "It's perfect," I said, straightening up and letting the hat slide easily into my hands.

Dad whistled. "Damndest thing."

By now the air conditioning had kicked in. Dad tromped downstairs with My Edna's empty box under one arm. "You have school tomorrow," he said from the first floor, "but we have to empty the station wagon tonight. Let's go."

As soon as school let out on the first day, I rode the bus into town to juggle on Chestnut Street. I'd forgotten about the saxophone player I'd seen almost three years earlier. But the search for him had been fruitful: I knew my way around downtown Philadelphia as well as I knew the boardwalk in Atlantic City. I knew the spots with the best foot traffic, the small parks where business people hung out during their coffee breaks. Sometimes I juggled for the shoppers on Chestnut Street; sometimes by the riverfront where tankers and freighters arrived and where tourists meandered on the paths; sometimes at Rittenhouse Square, where wealthy old ladies and their little dogs in plaid jackets mingled with college students, bums and construction workers; and sometimes on South Street, where the hippies congregated and the air pulsed with soul music, cheesesteak grease and marijuana smoke.

On the corner of 15th and Chestnut, my new derby snug on my head, I was just getting started juggling four balls, making the pattern nice and high to draw a decent crowd, when I spotted the saxophone player about half a block away, opening up his case. I stopped my juggling, stuffed the lacrosse balls into my backpack and hustled down the block.

"Hey!" I said.

"What's up, man?"

"I've been looking for you!"

The man eyed me suspiciously, fingering the valves on the saxophone that hung around his neck.

"Oh, no, no," I said. "Nothing weird. I'm Jason. I'm a juggler."

"Blue Dawson," he said, extending his hand. I told him how I'd seen him and heard him play and how I wanted to juggle to his music.

He looked at me, then at my backpack. "Let's do it, man." He poked the reed into his mouth and blew three loud, wet blurts. Several passersby stopped and turned their heads. I dropped my backpack on the sidewalk, took out three balls and flung them aloft, launching into a three-ball ballet in time to Blue's be-bop melody.

About a dozen people gathered to watch. We must have been a sight—a white teenage juggler and an older black jazz musician. But we hit it off immediately. Blue set the pace and I juggled to it, flipping the balls high and low, bouncing off my head and knees, slapping my palms, adding percussion to the snappy music.

The crowd loved us! They clapped in the middle of the act, and when we finally came down from a crescendo and found a nice place to end the first tune, they exploded with applause and threw dollar bills into my derby and Blue's case.

After the show, when we split the take, we each ended up with more than either of us had ever made in Philadelphia on our own.

"We gotta do this again," I told Blue while I put my juggling balls away and he wiped down his instrument with a yellow cloth.

"Can't, man, splittin' tomorrow. Cruise ship gig." He pressed his sax into its case between the velvet lumps like he was tucking in a baby.

Disappointed, I wondered if cruise ships hired jugglers.

Blue snapped the case shut. "Cold weather fuck up my chops. Gotta get out when I can."

"Ever play Atlantic City?"

Blue waved a hand, dismissing my question. "Naw, man."

"I made four grand juggling on the boardwalk last season. If you and me teamed up we'd knock 'em dead!"

He laughed. "And I'd get my ass hauled off to jail 'fore I get my reed wet."

"Where did you hear that?"

"How many black folks you see working them boards?"

A lot of black people worked at the bus station, and there were black guys pushing the rolling chairs on the boardwalk and selling ice cream on the beach. But now that I thought about it, I couldn't recall a single black person working at a pizza place, sub shop or souvenir store. No black lifeguards except for the guys at Chicken Bone Beach, the Negro beach near Missouri Avenue popular with black families who came down from Philadelphia for the day. There were no black ride operators or ticket sellers on the piers; no black magicians or musicians on the boardwalk. All the college kids Dad hired were white—mostly pug-nosed preppies from Penn or Italian kids from South Philadelphia. But these were modern times, I figured. Atlantic City wasn't a "whites only" town.

"You'll be with me," I told Blue, "in front of my dad's pretzel bakery, mostly. No one's gonna give you shit."

Blue chuckled. "Gotta catch a train to Germantown. See you 'round, man." He shook my hand again. "You all right."

"You're all right too," I said, tagging along after Blue up Chestnut Street toward Suburban Station. "I think we should do something again."

"Just not down the shore, man. You and me ain't seen the same A.C."

"It's not like it's segregated," I said.

Blue clicked his tongue. "Call it what you want, my man."

A block from the train station, Blue picked up his pace. "Can't be late for my gig." We said our goodbyes at the escalator that led down to his train. And we promised to look for each other on Chestnut Street between Broad and 20th, in the spring when the weather got warm.

A FEW WEEKS LATER, on a frosty autumn morning, I was sipping coffee in the student lounge, looking at a newspaper before first-period social studies. A group of students were chatting nearby. When someone said something about Atlantic City, my ears perked up.

"A referendum," the guy was saying. "They're gonna have a statewide vote to see if people want gambling down there. And if they do, they're gonna open a bunch of casinos."

I knew all about the referendum. Dad said that if it passed, he'd do okay even if his rent skyrocketed, because he could probably get a deal to supply the casinos with soft pretzels. The *Atlantic City Press* had called our pretzels "Best in South Jersey" for five summers in a row. We'd be okay, but not Jimmy or Norman and Betty, and especially not Madam Diane. Gambling and fortune-telling go together like ocean swimming and stomach cramps.

One of the girls in the group was Sarah Gilquist. Sarah was one of the smart kids. She didn't hang with any one particular crowd; like me, she was usually alone. I glanced at the pile of books at her side: *Trigonometry. French II. Biology II.* We'd never had a class together, but I'd seen her in the lunchroom and at assemblies. Last year she was a mousy-looking girl I never paid attention to. Now I found myself studying her more closely. She'd changed over the summer, growing prettier, her body filling out. She wore stiff, brown corduroy slacks, a white silk blouse, a gray wool vest and a pair of suede Wallabee shoes. Dark blond hair tumbled down her back in a sensuous wave. Slender and delicate, with doe eyes and gold, rectangular wire-rimmed glasses perched on top of her head, she listened to the conversation while chewing on the eraser end of a yellow pencil.

"Atlantic City's dying," said one guy. "Inflation, crime and shit. Who wants *that* when they can do Avalon or Wildwood or Ocean City?"

"My father says it's going to be all black there in five years," said one girl disdainfully. She whispered *black* like it was a scalp condition.

"We go to Beach Haven," said another guy.

They all chimed in where their families went to the shore. "*Wildwood.*" "Ocean *City.*" "Cape *May.*" *Nyah, nyah, nyah.* They sounded like magpies.

Sarah Gilquist said that she'd never been to Atlantic City. Her voice was soft. Tentative.

"Never?" I asked. She turned toward me, looking surprised that I was joining in the conversation. I caught the strawberry scent of her hair.

"We go to Cape Cod," she said.

"Isn't that in a foreign state or something?"

She smiled. "It's in Massachusetts, silly."

I returned the smile. "I couldn't get in. No passport."

She laughed. I liked her laugh. Smart. Throaty. Her eyes were like two perfect almonds. "You should definitely check out Atlantic City sometime."

The guy who was talking about the referendum snickered. "Atlantic City's dying, man," he said. "It's not a happening place. It's a fucking ghost town."

I glared at the jerk. "Then I'm a fucking ghost 'cause Atlantic City's my fucking home!"

"Well, fuck you," he said.

"No. Fuck *you*!" I glanced at Sarah Gilquist. "I'll bet you didn't know I'm on the debating team," I said with a sly grin.

The guy leaned toward me, but when he moved, the bright orange plastic material covering the bench he was on made a farting sound.

I smirked at him. "You trying to fart—er, I mean, start something?" I asked. The guy chuckled, just enough to break the ice. I seized the moment. "Atlantic City's my home," I said. "You shouldn't talk about a guy's home like that, you know?"

The bell rang for first period. The guy huffed and puffed and then got up and left. The other kids grabbed their books and their backpacks. Before I knew it, Sarah Gilquist and I were the only ones there.

"That's neat how you handled him," she said.

"Oh. Thanks. No big deal. I get heckled by drunks when I do shows."

"Well, I've got trigonometry," she said, collecting her books and sliding them into her blue canvas backpack.

"Sorry," I said. "Isn't there a lotion?"

She laughed. I stood up and grabbed my stuff. Sarah was shorter than I. Petite. "Which way you going?" I asked. "I'll walk you."

Jasonansarah. Jasonansarah.

That afternoon, instead of catching the bus into the city, I waited outside school for Sarah Gilquist. I couldn't see her among the throngs of kids pouring out of the building, but I didn't think she'd gotten past me. Walking her to trigonometry had gone so well that if she were to spot me among the crowd, she'd say hi.

After a while I returned to the building. There weren't many people in the halls. I poked around a little, sticking my head into the cafeteria and a few of the first-floor classrooms where the after-school clubs met. On the auditorium door was a notice: FALL PLAY TRYOUTS TODAY. I pushed the door open and peeked into the cavernous auditorium.

There was Sarah Gilquist, walking down the aisle, lugging a black, flapping lighting fixture under one arm. She was stage crew! I watched her climb the steps to the stage and disappear behind the curtain.

I wandered down to the front row, where two kids with clip-boards sat beside Miss Smith, my English teacher from last year. One of the students, a burly-looking girl in blue jeans and a hooded sweatshirt the color of a squirrel, looked up and whispered briskly, "Can I help you?"

"Is this where I try out?" I asked.

Miss Smith leaned over. "What a pleasant surprise, Jason. I'm so happy that you wish to audition. Our production this year is *Harvey.* Are you familiar with the play?"

The only theater I'd ever seen was Jimmy's marionette show. But here I was, and here Sarah Gilquist was. I seized the opportunity. "One of my favorites," I said.

"What have you prepared for the audition?" asked the big girl in the hooded sweatshirt. I must have looked hapless. Shaking her head, she thrust a beefy fist across the aisle and handed me a paperback book. "Harvey," it said on the cover. "By Mary Chase."

I climbed the stairs to the stage. Miss Smith and the girl with the sweatshirt and the other girl all sat there looking at me. I looked to my right. Sarah Gilquist was watching me from backstage! She smiled and waved. A bunch of other kids putting up lights around the darkened hall stopped to watch. Everyone knew me as Jason the Juggler who practiced in the student lounge but kept to himself.

I opened the book and began reading aloud. I didn't want it to sound too stiff. The girl in the sweatshirt interrupted: "Those are the *woman's* lines!" Somewhere in the cavernous auditorium, somebody snickered. I didn't like being laughed at, but Jason the Magnificent could fix that. I looked out over the auditorium, threw back my head, pushed out one hip and lapsed into a blaring, nasal falsetto. I overdramatized the woman character's lines, delivering them with broad, overdone feminine gestures, swishing around the stage to howls of laughter. I got through the speech and then improvised my way through the next scene, reading every character's lines, leaping from place to place. In the front row, the girl in the sweatshirt was doubled over laughing. Beside her, Miss Smith was giggling so hard she had to take off her glasses and wipe her eyes.

When I finished, everyone clapped, and I took a bow. It was fun. But I felt naked without my derby. On my way out of the auditorium, I got a few back slaps and "nice jobs" from kids I didn't even know.

Two days later, on an overcast October morning, Sarah and I met in the student lounge before first period. We sat opposite each other on a sprawling black vinyl sofa, our legs folded Indian-style, our knees touching.

I was in the middle of telling her about Atlantic City and how much she'd like it when Katie the stage manager swaggered in like a grungy pied piper, trailed by a bunch of kids who'd auditioned for the play. She tacked a sheet of paper to the bulletin board. The try-out results. Everyone swarmed around to see who was cast. Sarah and I wedged through the crowd until we could read the paper. I was surprised to see that I was cast in the lead role—Elwood P. Dowd. Over the ruckus, Katie informed me that Miss Smith had told her it was the first time in our school's history that a sophomore got a lead. Other kids crowded around to congratulate me.

Down at the bottom of the sheet, Sarah's name was typed under the heading CREW. We'd be together almost every afternoon. I smiled. "Congratulations," said Sarah, reaching out and giving my hand a friendly squeeze.

I wanted to kiss her. "So you don't want to act?" I asked as we returned to the vinyl sofa. "You just do stage crew?"

"It's the extracurricular activity that gets me out of the house for the longest," she said.

"Parental problems?"

"My mother won't allow me to do things that aren't school related."

"What is she, a Puritan?"

Sarah shook her head. "No. She's crazy."

I laughed. "Parents and their goofy rules."

She looked down at her shoes. "No. Seriously," she said.

Katie the stage manager, the hefty, freckle-faced redhead who carried a clipboard everywhere she went, possessed the authority of a teacher. She raised her hands and we settled down. Then she announced that rehearsals would start on Monday.

LIKE THE Two for One Arcade, Irene's Fudge still stands, looking much as it did decades ago. Ruth studies the shop's facade. "This is where you used to juggle."

The neon sign screams "Irene's Fudge" in a sparkly, diner-like typeface. "Same store, same spot," I tell her. "Hasn't changed."

We go inside. A few customers browse the steel and glass display cases that hold fudge and saltwater taffy. In the back, a man wearing a stained white apron and a powder blue hair net works a paddle over a slab of marble, stirring and thickening a batch of chocolate fudge. Behind the counter stands a girl who looks a year or two older than Ruth—a comely strawberry blond who reminds me of Jennifer, my accuser from work. The girl approaches us. "Can I help you?" she asks.

"Do the Lamberts still own this place?"

"Yep," she says. "Lew's my dad. He's off today. My grandfather's in the back. Should I get him? What's your name?"

I lean over the counter. "Jason Benson."

The girl walks to the back of the shop and turns a corner. A moment later, an old man in khaki pants and a white Irene's Fudge polo shirt shuffles out and approaches the counter. He looks at me and blinks.

"Pretzel Boy?"

I reach out to shake his hand over the counter. I introduce Eileen and Ruth.

"The crowds you used to draw!" says Mr. Lambert. "A hundred people, mob scene, three times a night. And he'd tell 'em, 'Irene's Fudge is the official fudge of the Olympic Juggling Association.'" I'd forgotten that bit of patter. We laugh at the memory.

Mr. Lambert reaches into the display case, takes out a box of fudge and places it on the counter. "Assorted?"

"Sure," I tell him, reaching into my back pocket for my wallet.

He puts up his hands. "Your money's no good here."

I thank him and take the fudge. "Ever hear from the old crowd?" I ask, handing the box to Ruth, who has this look in her eye that says maybe I'm not a complete asshole after all.

Mr. Lambert shakes his head. "Gone." He gazes over the counter and out his shop window, across the boardwalk to the ocean, to the horizon. "Norman and Betty long gone. You were friends with

Pinball Girl, right? She's been gone maybe five years. I think she's dealing blackjack in Vegas."

"What about Jimmy and his family?"

"The marionette man?" Mr. Lambert asks, shaking his head. "Not a clue. Disappeared, I don't know, ten years ago?"

We linger for several minutes, talking with Mr. Lambert about the old days.

"THE SCHOOL PLAY sounds terrific, but won't it interfere with your schedule?" Dad asked me at dinner when I told him about *Harvey*. "You'll have to give up juggling in town."

"That's okay," I said, using my palm to slam the bottom of an upside-down bottle of ranch salad dressing. It was hard for me to imagine that only a month ago I'd wanted to drop out of high school as soon as I turned sixteen. "Rehearsal's only three days a week, so I can still juggle in town on Tuesdays and Thursdays." I gave another whack and a couple hard shakes to force the thick white liquid onto my romaine lettuce and sliced tomato. "It's not like I need the money. I've got enough saved up for my car next year. And besides, there's this girl . . ."

Dad looked up from his salad bowl. "I knew it! I'd given up on extracurricular activities for you."

Sarah and I were becoming Jasonansarah fast: meeting in the cafeteria before school, walking to classes together, holding hands, hanging out after rehearsals before we boarded the "late" buses. One damp, chilly afternoon, with a half hour between the final bell and the start of rehearsal, she and I took a walk around the campus. Behind the school were tennis courts, empty on account of the weather. Holding hands, we walked out on the clay, which was wet from cold rains the day before; the wind gusted, blowing a few pieces of litter around.

"I'm freezing," she said, wrapping her arms around her shoulders and bobbing up and down. I put my arm around her and drew her toward me. We kissed. Sarah's breath was sweet, her lips moist and cool.

Hand in hand, we circled the grounds. Beyond the tennis courts, in the middle of the empty football field, two twelfth grade guys—one with long stringy hair and wire-rimmed glasses, the other with bushy, thick blond hair—passed a joint back and forth. They were about fifty yards away, but we got a whiff of the smoke.

"I'll bet you've never been stoned," I said.

"On grass? No way."

"No way *have* you ever or no way *would* you ever?"

Sarah poked her tongue in her cheek. "No way *have* I ever. But I'd do it with you."

"It's pretty cool, actually. I can get some, and when you come down to Atlantic City with me we could get high under the boardwalk. It makes you feel like everyday life is a neat adventure. Like a different perspective."

I couldn't wait to take Sarah to Atlantic City. Introduce her to everyone. Stop at Norman and Betty's for a little pinball. Take a long, quiet walk on the wintry beach. Feed the pigeons. Watch the winter sun set over the bay. Have a bowl of clam chowder at Captain Starn's. A nap in the bus on the way home—Sarah's head resting on my shoulder. If only her mom would let her go. If not, we'd have to concoct a plan.

"And it makes cantaloupe and Belgian waffles taste incredible," I went on. "But I can't do it much. Don't want to get a JUI."

"JUI?" she asked.

"Juggling Under the Influence. It fucks up my juggling for like four hours. So I can't do it too often. Unlike Skip."

"That guy you told me about? You shouldn't hang around with potheads," Sarah said.

"We've been friends for a long time. I can't just abandon him. There's a principle involved."

In fact, because of Sarah I was spending much less time with Skip. On the occasional day that I came home directly from school, we'd walk around the neighborhood together. He'd sneak tokes from his tiny wooden hash pipe, checking first for oncoming traffic and then offering me a clandestine hit, which I usually declined.

I felt sorry for him, wandering the neighborhood, getting high every day. On the other hand, he'd never apologized for calling me plastic. He didn't respect anybody, so why should anybody respect him? It was like Rabbi Greenblatt taught me: Skip was basically an asshole, so that's what he saw in other people. Classic scapegoating.

Still, when Sarah was ready to get high, I could score some weed or hash from him.

At long last, I was happy. For the first time ever, I looked forward to school every day.

12

REHEARSALS WERE going well. After every one, when Miss Smith gave the actors our "notes," she reminded me to look at the other actors and actually listen to their lines. "Try a little harder," she advised me one afternoon. "I can appreciate how challenging it must be for you. After all, you've been a solo performer for a long time. But sending and receiving lines is like playing catch. It's about intention."

"I've never actually played catch," I said.

"Never?" She sounded surprised. "Not with your father?"

I shrugged. "My dad and I don't play together. We work together."

"When someone delivers his or her lines," she said, "listen to the words. Process what the person says and respond with your lines. Think about where you're sending them. And *listen* to the other character. You have to trust that when you make the communication real, it will be real to the audience."

That night, Sarah called me. I was home alone, sitting at the kitchen table in my jockey shorts and one of Dad's University of Pennsylvania sweatshirts, trying to make sense of a geometry proof. We'd been Jasonansarah for a month, but this was our first telephone call because Sarah's mother didn't like her talking to boys on the phone.

"I have an idea," Sarah whispered. "We could visit Atlantic City three weeks from this Saturday." The weekend after Thanksgiving—the weekend after *Harvey* closed.

I got up from the table and danced around the kitchen with the receiver to my ear. "That makes me so happy!" I said. I stretched the phone cord across the counter, reached for the coffee pot and poured myself a cup. "But what about your mom?" I asked while I fished in the fridge for a carton of milk.

"Well. I don't really have to tell her where I'm going," she whispered. "I'll tell her it's a school event."

"Tell her it's a science project," I said, stirring the milk into my coffee. Cup in hand and phone receiver cradled between my shoulder and ear, I made my way back to the table. "Tell her you've got to go outdoors somewhere and measure shadows for twelve hours. Like a sundial. So she can't call you."

"I'll think of something."

"I love you," I said.

"I love you too," she murmured.

I pressed the receiver to my face, wishing I could squeeze myself through it.

"Um, about my mother . . . ," she said, lowering her volume even further. I put my mug on the table and plugged my free ear with my thumb. "She has problems, Jason. I don't want you to feel insulted about not meeting her yet. It isn't you. It's her."

After we hung up I bopped around the kitchen, in the same spot where Dad and Mom had danced their chicken dance on the night he announced that he'd quit Westinghouse and signed a lease for the first bakery. She loved me! I wanted to shout it out, tell the whole world.

Of course she'll fall in love with Atlantic City, I thought. I'll teach her to juggle and we'll learn how to pass. In the summer we'll perform together.

The day before *Harvey* opened, there was no rehearsal. At lunch, I asked Sarah if she would stay late and help me with my lines.

She dabbed a finger at the ooze from her peanut butter and jelly sandwich. "Sorry. Dentist appointment."

I decided to take a bus into the city after school and juggle for the rush-hour crowd on Chestnut Street. It was warm for November, with no wind; good juggling weather. When school let out, I dashed out the main entrance and across the street to the bus stop in time for the 2:47 into town. During the ride I looked out the window at the sun-splashed suburban streets. Maple trees stood strong, their red-orange leaves like fiery canopies.

A minute or two after I'd set up shop at my old corner, 15th and Chestnut, two hippies stopped to watch my act. One had frizzy blond hair that stuck out in every direction like a clown. He wore a thick flannel shirt over a Mickey Mouse tee shirt, blue jeans with patches over the knees and black army boots. The other guy had long, stringy hair tied in a ponytail. Giggling and snorting, they worked their way to the front of the crowd.

"What a rush!" the blond-haired guy said as I worked a full cascade behind my back. I could tell by their glazed eyes and gaping smiles that they were stoned.

After my three-ball ballet, I juggled four balls and then five. I ended the show by juggling three clubs high in the air, managing a triple twirl with each throw. "American Express is accepted," I said when I'd finished and was passing through the small crowd with my derby. "Please make your checks payable to Jason the Magnificent. That's spelled Jason *T-H-E* Magnificent."

After everyone else in the crowd had drifted away, the hippies came over and shook my hand, soul-brother style. The one with the ponytail tossed something into my derby. "Check it out, man," he said slyly. Then they took off giggling down Chestnut Street.

To my surprise I found a hand-rolled joint in my derby. Now I could turn Sarah on without having to ask Skip for weed. Our friendship had grown so strained, I felt guilty about coming to him only when I wanted grass. I tucked the joint into a can of Band-Aids that I kept in my backpack for when juggling gave me blisters.

THE LIGHTS FELT as hot as a furnace, and so bright I couldn't see the audience.

In Elwood P. Dowd's first scene, he is alone on stage, accompanied only by his human-sized rabbit, Harvey, whom only Dowd can see. The situation has already been set up in the previous scene, so the audience knows that Dowd believes he's not alone.

I walked across the stage, stopping once to regard my invisible friend. The audience cracked up. That felt good, like easing into a warm bath.

The rest of opening night came off without a hitch. I got a standing ovation. When the house lights came up, I saw Dad in the front row, beaming with pride, clapping like crazy.

Backstage, Miss Smith and Katie congratulated me. Sarah emerged from the lighting booth and wrapped me in a bear hug.

Soon Dad was backstage too, his eyes brimming with tears. "Your mother would be so proud," he whispered.

"Dad, this is Sarah Gilquist. Sarah, this is Dad."

Dad stepped back, composed himself and turned to Sarah. "Nice to meet you," he said, offering his hand. "I've been hearing quite a lot about you."

Katie the stage manager burst in, cutting a path through the crowd like she was the state police. "Cast party in Miss Smith's room! Friends and families welcome!"

Dad and Sarah and I made our way out the stage door and down the long concrete-block corridor to Miss Smith's room. Earlier, the stage crew had removed the desks and set up two long tables with cupcakes, potato chips and six-packs of Coca-Cola.

We hung around for about an hour, snacking and talking; then Sarah had to go home. We said our goodbyes, but before we were out of the room, Miss Smith tapped me on my elbow. When I turned around, she reached out her arms and gave me a hug.

"Good work," she said. "Just remember, you're not alone out there."

Sarah and Dad and I crossed the parking lot to the station wagon. It was cold; the sky was clear and filled with stars.

"You kids want to sit in the back?" Dad asked.

"Sure," I said. I opened the door for Sarah. She got in and I slid next to her.

The long day of classes, run-throughs and then the performance itself was catching up with me. The flashing of streetlights through the passenger window, the hum of the car's engine and the whooshing of other traffic created a gentle hypnotic effect.

"I love you," I whispered in Sarah's ear.

"Mmm . . . love you," she purred.

When we pulled onto Sarah's street, Dad slowed the car and Sarah instructed him where to stop. Her home was an enormous Tudor-style, set back a little from the road, sweeping across a vast lot, with about a dozen huge oak trees scattered about the front yard.

"Dad, can we pick Sarah up for tomorrow night's show?" I asked. "We have to be there at seven."

"I don't see why not," said Dad.

Sarah opened the car door.

Dad turned around in his seat. "Why don't you walk Sarah to her door?"

"No!" Sarah blurted. "I mean, thanks, it's okay."

Before I knew it, she was out the door and halfway up the narrow stone path leading to a gigantic front door, which opened—like in a horror movie—just as she approached it.

13

Two weekends later, at eight-thirty on Saturday morning, Sarah and I were aboard a bus, crossing the Benjamin Franklin Bridge, midway between Philadelphia and New Jersey. "They make you keep the windows closed 'cause it's cold out," I said. "But in the summer, you can open them and smell the salt air when you're about twenty miles from the shore."

The sun blazed through the bridge's cold steel beams, streaming through the bus's windows, radiating wintery warmth on our vinyl seats as we nuzzled each other.

I leaned over and kissed the side of Sarah's face, gently brushing her hair aside with my fingers. She spied around to make sure the other passengers couldn't see us, slunk down in her seat a little and kissed me on the lips with her mouth open.

Hesitantly I poked my tongue into Sarah's mouth. She snatched it between her lips. Squishy. Sexy. We scrunched closer together. Discreetly Sarah pressed her hand on my leg. I felt like my brain had melted and was now extruding through my ears.

"The first thing . . . I'm gonna show you when we get there is . . . ," I said, taking hold of her hand and guiding it to the erection in my jeans.

"What?" she asked breathlessly.

". . . under the boardwalk."

"Mmmm . . ."

Once we were off the bus, we raced like frisky puppies from the station to the boardwalk, nearly knocking over a bag lady in the middle of the intersection of Ohio and Atlantic avenues. We burrowed into the cramped crawl space between boards and beach, tumbling into a two-foot bank of sand behind a dank, splintery piling, protected from both the wind and the view of people on the beach.

"Wait," said Sarah, pressing her hands to my chest. I squatted in the sand. She took off her backpack and I squirmed out of mine. Crouching, she rummaged through her pack and, like a picnicker pulling sandwiches and tubs of coleslaw from a basket, she produced a blue wool blanket, a change of underwear and three condoms.

"I didn't think it would occur to you," she said, reading the astonishment on my face. "So I went to the drugstore." She spread the blanket on the sand.

We sat cross-legged, facing each other. Muted footsteps clunked and squeaked above our heads—kids chasing pigeons, old people strolling arm in arm, bicycles clomping over the tiny ridges of the boards.

Sarah said the sounds made her nervous.

"Don't worry," I assured her. "No one can see us, nobody ever comes down here."

"Let's sit for a minute," she said. "I need to get acclimated." A gust blew under the boardwalk and around our piling, whisking bits of sand in our faces. Sarah took off her coat and pulled half the blanket over her. "Come on in," she said. "Warm me up."

I crawled under the blanket and snuggled beside her. She put her arms around my neck. We French-kissed. She slipped her top leg over mine. My hands quivering, I unbuttoned her blouse and gazed at her taut nipples. Sarah squiggled up a little so that her breasts were at my mouth level. I kissed one nipple, then the other. Sarah moaned and breathed hard. She shifted her body and pulled down her jeans. She removed her white cotton socks and flung them into the sand. Then she took her jeans all the way off. Now all she was wearing was her unbuttoned blouse, and in another second she'd slipped out of that too.

I tugged at my own clothing, undressing like a small storm, whipping sand everywhere. When we were both naked, we pulled the blanket over us, our bodies entwining. With the combination of wool and body heat, it didn't seem cold.

"You know what?" Sarah asked with a naughty, throaty giggle.

"What?" I said.

"I'm going to eat you up." And with that, she plunged her tongue into my ear and took hold of my hardened penis with her hand. I groaned. She inched her way down, kissing my chest, licking my belly. At last she put me in her mouth. I gasped at the sensation.

After a minute she came back up and we kissed some more. I could taste myself in her mouth. Salty. Slightly sour. She unwrapped one of the condoms, placed it over my penis and unrolled it. I took a deep breath, afraid I was about to climax. We kissed again. She took hold of my hand and guided it toward her vagina. I used my fingers to explore this new territory; then slowly, gently, I poked my way inside her.

We copulated, grunting and grinding, covered head to toe with sand, sweating like it was the middle of summer. Sarah shifted under my weight, wriggling and pumping. I pumped too, slowly at first—afraid I'd hurt her. Realizing that my eyes were squeezed shut, I opened them to see what was happening. Sarah's eyes were wide open and her head thrown back, exposing her pale neck as she stared up at the bottom of the boardwalk.

With a lusty growl, she pressed her groin into mine. We thrust like mad, twisting and growling, savages in the sand, throwing off the blanket and nearly burying ourselves until I felt the familiar warmth and rumble of release. We groaned in unison, Sarah's thighs quivering as I came inside her. Then we were in each other's arms, breathless, coated with sand and sweat.

I rested my head on Sarah's chest and listened to her heartbeat—quick at first, then slow as she caught her breath and relaxed. I shifted my weight and pushed myself off her. She reached into her backpack, took out a tissue and wiped herself. I saw blood on the tissue, but Sarah didn't look alarmed. I recalled from health class that this is what happens the first time. She buried the tissue in the sand. We sat Indian-style, opposite each other, knee to knee, the blanket across our shoulders. We kissed. I traced her jaw line with my sandy fingertips.

Eventually we crawled out from under the blanket, brushing sand off our bodies. We got dressed. Then we sat in the sand where we had a clear view of the ocean about fifty yards before us.

I searched through my backpack, came up with the Band-Aid box and took out the joint that the hippie on Chestnut Street had given me a few weeks earlier.

"Oh my God, is that pot?" she asked. "Did you buy it from Skip?"

"Nah," I said, handing the joint to her. "Some guy threw it in my hat when I was juggling downtown."

"People just throw stuff in your hat," she said, shaking her head.

"Mostly money," I said, "but I thought this was a nice tip. Wanna try it?" I felt around the pockets of my army coat for the pack of matches I'd brought.

Eyeing the joint, she bit her lower lip and ran her fingers through her hair. "Okay."

It took about four tries to get the thing lit. I took a puff. The smoke burned my throat. I closed my eyes and held the smoke in my lungs for as long as I could before erupting in a fit of coughing. Sarah took a drag and immediately coughed her guts up.

"Hold it in as long as you can," I told her. We passed the joint back and forth, taking drags, until it burned our fingertips and I dropped it in the sand.

I felt the familiar buzz. It was strong weed—better than Skip's. Suddenly Sarah broke out laughing, making loud, goofy honking sounds.

"Are you stoned?" I asked.

Sarah looked around. "Yes." She grinned like a jack-o'-lantern. "I am stoned under the boardwalk with the man I love."

We gathered our stuff and crawled out from under the boardwalk, giggling like kindergartners. Pausing at the base of the stairs to the boardwalk, I gazed at the sparkling whitecaps on the water's surface. They looked like angels dancing on a wavy field of blue-green energy.

Sobered by the stinging wind, the sun's glare and our awareness of people on the boardwalk above us, we did our best to collect ourselves, appear normal and talk at a reasonable volume—like we weren't high, like we hadn't lost our virginity minutes earlier, like the passersby didn't remind me of gawking, rubber-faced cartoon characters.

I handed Sarah my backpack, motioning for her to open it. Then I reached in and took out three red balls. "A round of applause for my lovely assistant!" I announced to a small flock of gulls circling overhead. Since I was stoned, I knew I couldn't juggle as well as usual. No spins for now. No fancy patterns, overhand catches or behind-the-back tosses; just a simple cascade.

I juggled joyously, sloppily. People on the boardwalk stopped to watch, but it wasn't for them. I was juggling only for Sarah. I finished by flinging the balls behind me, dropping to my knees, scooping up handfuls of sand, throwing it into the air and letting it rain down upon me. I juggled the sand in a gigantic, manic whirl, my arms digging deeper and deeper into the beach, tossing handful after handful into the air, showering myself in a blustery, gritty hail. In the end I collapsed on the beach, flopping on my belly at the feet of my beloved.

When I looked up, I saw tears streaming down Sarah's face.

I scrambled to my feet, brushing sand from my eyes. I held her in my arms. "What's the matter?"

She clutched my arms and pressed her head against my chest. "Nothing," she sniffled. "I love you so much and this is all so . . ." She looked around at the boardwalk and the desolate beach. "This is all so much. Maybe it's the grass. Everything is so . . ." She reflected for a moment. "Intense."

I rubbed the sand off my hands and gently stroked Sarah's cheek with my thumb. She drew in a breath and relaxed in my arms. In a moment, I dashed off to retrieve my juggling balls and put them into my pack. By then Sarah wasn't crying anymore. We climbed the wooden steps to the boardwalk. At the top, we turned and looked back at the beach and the ocean. I put my arm around her.

"I love you," I said.

She clasped my waist and nuzzled the side of my face with her nose. "I love you too."

We kissed against the boardwalk railing—like I'd done with Janis, like I'd been watching teenagers do every summer night for almost as long as I could remember.

"C'mon," I said, taking Sarah by the hand. "Let's find an open custard place. I think there's one next to Convention Hall. Then I'll show you the bakery and we can play some pinball next door at Norman and Betty's and then take a really long walk."

At the custard stand, I bought us two large vanillas dipped in chocolate. We sat on a wooden bench in the middle of a mostly empty pavilion, licked our soft ice cream and watched the people walking by.

"This is incredible, don't you think?" I asked, smacking my lips.

Sarah agreed, taking a long sensuous lick around the edge where the ice cream and cone converged.

After our cones, we made out—our tongues chilled and milky with custard. Then we walked arm in arm, like Dad and Mom used to do, toward the bakery. "Doesn't it smell great?" I asked, filling my lungs and thrusting out my chest. "The ocean breeze blows all the crap out of the air—like recycling—so no matter how polluted the rest of the country gets, down here it's perfect."

We were almost at the bakery. The grass was beginning to wear off. Over the past two months I'd fantasized about this moment hundreds of times. And now that it was actually happening, it still had a dreamy, fantasy quality about it. There was the bakery, the "See Them Twisted—See Them Baked" sign Mom had painted and Dad had hung years before. There was Jimmy's marionette theater, boarded up for the winter. And there was Norman and Betty's pinball arcade—its flashing neon sign one of the few splashes of color on the drab, off-season boardwalk.

We stopped across from the tiny row of stores. I put my arm around Sarah the way I remembered Dad had done to Mom on the day they hung the sign and began our boardwalk life.

"What do you think?" I asked.

"Oh, it's really neat," she said. But she looked disappointed, like one time a package came to the house for me; I was sure it was a derby from My Edna, but it turned out to be a mohair vest from Aunt Harriet in Cleveland. "I'm sure it's more colorful in the summertime," Sarah added consolingly.

I had to admit that it wasn't much to look at. "You're right," I said. "You should see it when people are lined up to buy pretzels, and we're in there twisting and baking like crazy."

Meanwhile Sarah had diverted her glance from the bakery, up the boardwalk toward Million Dollar Pier. I realized how unfair it had been for me to expect her to be impressed by the sight. What was there to see? A boarded-up storefront, a cheap wooden sign? Sarah nudged my ribs with her elbow. "Check out this nut job," she said. I was still looking at the bakery, thinking it needed a coat of paint, when someone called my name. Sarah gasped. I turned to look.

"Jimmy!" I shouted in surprise. "I can't believe it! What are you doing here? You never come here off-season." I turned to Sarah. "He never comes here in the winter!" Jimmy wore bell-bottom pants with wide purple and yellow stripes running up and down the legs, a bright yellow wool sweater and a green felt cowboy hat. His breath smelled like garlic.

"Jimmy," I said, "this is Sarah Gilquist, my girlfriend. Sarah Gilquist, this is Jimmy . . ." I paused for a moment. I'd known Jimmy forever, but I didn't know his last name. Sarah stared blankly. "From the marionette theater," I said.

Jimmy extended his hand. Sarah shook it. "Jason, how you doing, kid?" he asked. "How's your old man? You down for the day, just the two of you? Ed around? He should take down that sign. The weather."

"No Dad today," I said, clasping Sarah's hand. "Just us."

"Is that right?" said Jimmy, grinning slyly and winking. He *knew*—either about what we'd done under the boardwalk or about the grass. Maybe both.

"What are you doing here?" I asked Jimmy.

In one smooth gesture, he pulled a cigarette from his shirt pocket, lit it in his cupped hands and took a deep drag. "Business," he said, blasting a jet of blue smoke out his nose. "I had to see a man about a license." He took another drag. Then he brightened. "But hey, I get to see my Jason and his beautiful lady friend." He stepped back to admire us as a couple. I squeezed close to Sarah, as if Jimmy were taking our picture.

"Beautiful couple," he said. "*Beautiful!*"

"Thanks, Jimmy," I said, offering a playful punch on his arm. It was great to see him, but I wanted to take a long walk with Sarah.

Jimmy must have been reading my mind. "Hey, kids, I gotta go," he said apologetically. He hugged me and planted a kiss on each of Sarah's cheeks. "I gotta catch a guy down on Baton Rouge Avenue, says he'll pay me two hundred bucks to drive his car to Miami. Tell Ed I said take that sign down." With that, Jimmy spun around and whipped down a ramp toward the street. "See you in a few months," he called over his shoulder, waving his arm and disappearing around the corner.

"What a character," said Sarah.

"He's a great guy," I said. "By the way, I think he knew. What we did. Not the weed. The other."

Sarah's face grew tense. "Don't worry," I said. "He's cool."

"If you say so," she said. "But I'd rather not meet anyone else today."

"But what about Norman and Betty? And Lita?" I asked, motioning toward the arcade across the boardwalk.

"Next time?" she asked, wringing her hands and lowering her voice. "I hope you don't mind, but next time would be better. I think I'm still high and it's making me kind of nervous."

The "next time" part was heartening. It meant she wanted to come back. We walked about twenty blocks, stopping to peek through the fence at Million Dollar Pier and pick up a bag of roasted peanuts at the Planters store. Clasped in each other's arms, we ambled toward the inlet at the end of the boardwalk.

"What are you thinking?" I asked her.

"I hate my mother." She looked like she was going to cry again.

"If you don't want to talk about it . . ."

"No. I do. I'm glad I finally can."

I listened attentively, thrilled she was confiding in me. This is what Miss Smith meant by "sending and receiving."

"I don't remember my father," she said. "He died when I was three."

"At least I got to know my mom," I said.

Three or four seagulls hovered in my periphery. I could remember everything about Mom. I recalled her voice, her laugh—the feel of her fingers when she mussed my hair and tucked me in at night.

"My mother never even talks about him," said Sarah. "It's like she can't face the fact that he's dead, so she ignores it and it's off limits."

I reached my fingers into the bag of peanuts that Sarah held in her free hand. I removed a few, snapped the shells between my fingers and tossed the insides to the sea gulls. They swooped toward us to make the catch. "My father's father died young," I said. "When he died, my grandmother told Dad that his father had gone away on business. Then, when my mom was dying, Dad didn't have the guts to tell me she was sick. It was like everybody in the world knew except for me. The longer she was sick, the worse he felt about keeping it from me. He says it was a white lie because he didn't want to hurt me. But I think it was a regular lie because he didn't want to feel shittier than he already felt. People say they lie to protect other people's feelings, but I think it's to protect their own."

"My mother never leaves the house," said Sarah. "She went to a psychiatrist for a while, then she stopped because she won't go outside."

"*Literally* never?" I asked. At least Skip's mom had gotten out of bed for my mom's funeral.

"Not in a year. She doesn't even shop for groceries. We get everything delivered now. She didn't even go to the Cape last summer."

That immediately got me thinking. If Sarah's mother didn't leave their house, then, theoretically, next summer Sarah could claim she was at Cape Cod when actually she'd be in Atlantic City. It would take some planning, but we could pull it off. I wrapped my arm even tighter around her and whispered in her ear, "I'm your family now."

Glancing to my left, I saw a familiar face: an old lady from India who sold souvenirs and pigeon food year-round out of a cramped shop wedged between a pizza place and a doughnut stand near Kentucky Avenue. She sat on a milk crate in front of her store, wrapped in a purple and orange sari under a blue down vest. When our eyes locked, she grinned and made juggling gestures with her hands.

Sarah, unaware of my exchange with the old woman, confided, "Sometimes I feel so alone."

"You shouldn't," I told her. I kissed her cheek. "I'll never leave you." I turned and looked back. The old Indian woman was still watching us. When she saw me looking, she made more juggling motions with her hands. I raised my free hand and waved to her.

"Who's that?" Sarah asked.

"A lady I know from the summer," I said. "She sells dried rice for people to feed to the pigeons."

Sarah turned and looked back. "What's she doing?"

"She's telling me to keep juggling."

We walked all the way north to the inlet, where Skip and I had visited the summer before. Captain Starn's was closed and the tide was out, so there weren't any fishermen casting off the boardwalk into the ocean. "In the summer they have sea lions over at Captain Starn's," I said, jutting my chin toward the boarded-up restaurant and marina. "When Skip came down, he tried to feed them a cigar butt."

"Why?" Sarah asked. Before I could answer she said, "What a jerk."

"Skip's been through a lot," I said. "It's like, you and I have one parent, right? Well Skip has one and a half. His mom's on pills and she doesn't really do anything all day. I mean I've known her since I was seven, and I've only seen her dressed once—at my mom's funeral. She's like a ghost on that couch. And Skip's brothers are gone, and his dad's hardly around . . ."

Sarah interrupted. "He sounds like a sociopath."

"Nah, he's just dyslexic."

Maybe I shouldn't have told her about the sea lions or the Molotov cocktails, or breaking windows. But Skip hadn't set fire to anything other than the tip of a joint in a couple of years.

"At worst he's a *recovering* sociopath," I said.

"There's no such thing, and you don't have to defend him."

"Just try not to judge him until you meet him, okay?"

"Why not?" Sarah asked. "What will he do? Set fire to my house?"

"He grew out of that," I said. "He firebombed a sewer. Big deal. He was farting around. It's not like he's cruel to animals."

"Tell that to the sea lions," she sniffed.

"He missed the pond," I said.

"You're awfully forgiving."

"I'm loyal."

"I know you are, but what about Skip?" she asked. "Is he as loyal as you? Is he as good a friend to you as you are to him? Sometimes loyalty is just, you know, needing to be liked."

"If I needed to be liked I'd be a lot friendlier at school," I said. "Skip and I go back a long time."

Lately I hadn't even been that loyal to Skip. I was spending every day after school at rehearsal or juggling in town. I'd only hung out with him once since September. Of course, he'd told me

I was phony and plastic and he'd insulted my friends. But he'd come to Mom's funeral; he was there when I needed him. "Skip's complicated," I said. "Don't judge him too fast. Okay?"

I didn't want to talk about Skip or about Sarah's mother; I wanted to plan the rest of our lives. But something told me to wait until summer when Sarah could see Atlantic City in full bloom. To the uninformed eye, Atlantic City looked rundown in the off-season.

At four o'clock we lumbered down the ramp at Ohio and went into a small restaurant on the corner of Pacific. I ordered clam chowder and coffee. Sarah had a grilled cheese sandwich and a Dr. Pepper.

At the bus station, with fifteen minutes before the next express to Philadelphia, we cuddled on a wooden bench. The near-empty building echoed with the padding of feet, the occasional sneaker squeaking on the concrete floor and the distant rumble of buses idling outside. The same skinny black janitor who'd been mopping the floor when I came to meet Skip was there again. I thought about what Blue Dawson had said—"You and me ain't seen the same A.C." Lately it seemed that no one saw the same A.C. as I did.

Sarah picked grains of sand out of her hair and off her arms and clothing. "Oh, God!" she said, like she'd discovered a fruit fly infestation. Frantically she brushed her forearms with her hands.

"Don't worry," I said. "We have the whole ride home. Plenty of time for a proper de-sandification."

I called Dad from a pay phone to arrange for him to meet us, and ten minutes later we were on our way home. Before we even made it to the mainland, Sarah took her hairbrush from her pack and began whisking sand out of her hair and scalp. I took the brush from her, twisted around and positioned myself behind her. While Sarah went methodically over every square inch of her body, rubbing and flicking at each grain of sand, I brushed her hair, stroking it over and over until each section was sand-free and lustrous. The soft wooden brush handle fit nicely in my hand, like a juggling club.

I brushed for almost an hour. We talked about everything: How Dad *had* to be behind My Edna's magic derbies, but he wouldn't admit it. How I'd figured out that the elaborate bar mitzvah they'd suddenly thrown before Mom died was really her chance to give me a wedding, and how that made me cry in front of the whole congregation. How Sarah's mom went from being strict to weird. How she had to be there for her mother to make sure she got out of bed in the morning and didn't just sit around in her pajamas all day, staring at the walls.

"Sometimes," Sarah said, "she seems fine. If you were talking to her you'd never know. Then all of a sudden it's like she's in another world."

We talked more about Skip and getting high. "The grass was fun," Sarah told me. "I'd definitely do it again . . ."

"But?" I asked.

"Just promise me you won't take anything stronger."

"No way. I don't like what it's done to Skip. You know how he gets his drug money? He steals pills from neighbors' medicine cabinets when he helps them carry their groceries in from their cars. That's his scam. All these moms have Valium and Dexedrine in their bathrooms."

Sarah gazed out the window into the blurry pinewoods. "My mother's on pills too."

"No shit. What is it with these moms?"

"The doctor gave her something for depression—"

"Let me guess," I said. "He gave her speed for depression, then he gave her something to help her sleep?" Sarah's mom was like Skip's mom, and like the half-dozen or so other moms in the neighborhood with the loopy smiles and the uppers and downers in their medicine cabinets that Skip stole when he carried in their groceries.

At last Sarah's hair was sand-free, and I sat back and looked out the window. The trees and road signs began to blur; the hum of the bus engine droned in my head and my eyelids grew heavy. Sarah rested her head on my shoulder. Before I knew it, I was nodding off.

When I came to, we were halfway over the Benjamin Franklin Bridge, almost in Philadelphia. A light rain had begun to fall. Through the steamy bus window we watched people duck out of the drizzle into restaurants and shops on Market Street. Inside the Greyhound terminal, Dad was waiting at the gate.

We didn't talk much on the way to drop off Sarah or the drive home from her house. When Dad asked about Norman and Betty, I told him that we didn't have time to see them since we took such a long walk. I mentioned that the pretzel sign needed an upgrade—and that we'd run into Jimmy. At the house, Dad held the front door open for me. "Go upstairs and take a shower, then come back down and we'll talk," he said.

What a day. It was only eight-thirty; but with the sex and the grass and all the walking—not to mention Sarah's being so emotional about the sand and her mother—the bus ride that morning seemed like a hundred years ago.

Upstairs in the shower, the water hit the top of my head full force; when I looked down I saw sand building up near the drain. I scrubbed my legs, back and chest; let the water spray into my mouth, behind my ears, between my toes and under my balls.

After the shower, I put on my bathrobe and went down to the kitchen. Dad had made a pot of coffee and set a bag of pretzels from the Pennsauken bakery on the table. The coffee was strong. I finished one cup and poured a second. The caffeine took effect— a steady, zippy rush through my belly and up my spine. Soon I heard Dad's footsteps coming down the stairs. I got up and poured him a cup.

After he'd stirred in his cream and sugar and taken a sip, he asked, "How was your day?"

I reached into the pretzel bag, took one out, twisted off the little nubs at the ends and popped them into my mouth. "Great."

As I was taking another sip of coffee he pulled a fast one. "Did you use protection?" he asked matter-of-factly.

"Well, yeah." That was a surprise. I cleared my throat and raised my eyebrows.

"Don't misunderstand," he said. "I'm not encouraging you. But if you're going to be active, you have to use protection."

"We do," I said. We sat silently, sipping our coffee. "How'd you know?" I asked.

"Be good to her," was all Dad said. When I looked up, his eyes had moistened and his face looked heavy and burdened.

I knew he was thinking about Mom. "You miss her, don't you?"

Dad's chin quivered. He took off his glasses and suddenly he was crying—chest heaving, tears streaming, snot dripping. He covered his face with his hands and rested his elbows on the table. I got up, went around to his side of the table and hugged him. He held me tight. His crying sounded almost like his laughter: rapid little titters punctuated by inverted wheezes—*huh-huh-huh-heeeeeh, huh-huh-huh-heeeeeh.*

When he'd wound down to a whimper, I went to the sink, doused a paper towel with cold water and handed it to him.

"I like her," he said, dabbing his face. "You look good together, like a real couple."

"We *are* a real couple."

"I know. But you're young."

"What are you saying?"

"Just be careful."

"Jesus, Dad, o*kay.*"

14

A COUPLE OF DAYS after our trip to Atlantic City, I visited a print shop a block from school. Wedged between Goodman's Five-and-Dime and the Hot Spot pizzeria, the store smelled musty and inky. The walls were rimmed with sagging shelves crammed with gray cardboard boxes—print jobs waiting for customer pickup, I guessed. When the printer told me that production for a three-color brochure would run five hundred bucks, I didn't blink. "Is cash okay?" I asked.

"Cash is perfect," said the printer, a bald man with blue-stained fingertips. "How many copies? Ten thousand? Twenty?"

"No, just one or two," I said.

"There's almost no price difference between a thousand and ten thousand."

"No, no," I said. "Just plain one or two."

The printer stared at me like I had a smudge on my forehead. "You're making a brochure for an overnight camp, and you need two copies?" He eyed me up and down like a border guard. "Either it's an exclusive camp or you're putting me on."

"I'll pay in advance," I promised. "I'll be back in a week with the money and a bunch of pictures and everything written out the way we want it."

That night, the Pennsauken Mart closed at five o'clock because it was snowing, and Dad came home early. After making sure he was in a good mood, I asked if we could sit in the living room for a man-to-man talk. Dad settled into his black leather recliner; I sat on the love seat next to him. Ordinarily our time together was spent hustling between bakeries and racing out the door. Sitting in the living room reminded me of the old days, when Mom and Dad would snuggle on the love seat and drink coffee after dinner.

A shrill wind beat at the windows. Surveying the room, I noted for the first time that the eggshell-colored walls needed new paint. In one corner, where the ceiling met the wall, a small rust-colored spot marked water damage. Dad had taken down one of Mom's paintings from its place below the stain. The painting sat on the floor, propped against the wall. Two years ago, Dad would have called a plumber, but now he let it go.

We started with small talk about pretzel sales and the lack of good help at the Pennsauken Mart. "It makes no sense," Dad said. "The Camden schools are failing, they're graduating morons who can't operate a goddamn cash register—and then the voters shoot down a referendum to invest in education. Now they're going to lay off teachers!"

I shook my head in sympathy. Dad was getting agitated. If he got any more upset, it wouldn't be a good idea to ask him about my Summer Strategy.

"So, Dad," I began. "I have this idea, and I want you to listen, and don't interrupt, and when I'm finished, I'll just say, 'over.' Okay?"

Dad nodded and I launched into a description of my plan for a fictitious summer camp at which Mrs. Gilquist would enroll Sarah, but Sarah would actually come down to Atlantic City for the summer. I showed him the printer's estimate and a couple rough sketches for the brochure. There'd be a "visiting day," and Sarah's mom wouldn't come. Once a week, Sarah would write her a letter, and one of us would take a bus to central Pennsylvania where the "camp" was and mail the note there so it would have the right postmark.

"Are you finished?" he asked.

"Yes," I said. "Over."

Dad sat for a moment gazing at the wall, his lips pursed. He then said, "I'm proud of you for being creative, but you cannot actually go through with this."

"But she won't let Sarah out of the house. What are we supposed to do? We can't go all summer without seeing each other!"

Dad waved his hands, cutting me off. "If her mother allows her to spend the summer in Atlantic City, Sarah may have a job at the bakery and a place to stay."

"Her mother won't allow her out of the house for a fucking ice cream cone after school!"

"I understand how you feel," Dad said, "but I will not condone blatant deception."

"Oh, don't gimme that!" I said. "You blatantly deceived me when Mom was dying and everybody in the entire universe knew except for me!" It was just like Rabbi Greenblatt said: Dad felt guilty about lying to me, so he turned his guilt on me, made me the dishonest one.

Dad wagged his finger. "That's not fair. I didn't fabricate. I only withheld . . ."

"That's a bullshit technicality," I said.

"No, your analysis is apples and oranges. It's not the same as when Mom . . ."

"It is too!" I yelled. "It's life and death! I can't go twelve weeks without her! Why don't you get that? What are you, an idiot?"

"That's no way to talk to your father."

"Hypocrite!"

Dad stood up. "This conversation is over."

"Not for me," I said.

Dad was about to leave the living room. I stood and faced him. *"Fuck you!"* I bellowed in his face, like a blast from a steam whistle. He grabbed my arm and yanked me away from the love seat. I thought he was going to hug me. So, he was sorry, was he? Well, it was too late for that.

Dad slapped my face.

He'd never hit me before. My face burned. My lips contorted into a scowl. "I hate you!" I shrieked, my pulse pounding inside my temples. I spun on my heels and bounded out of the living room and up the stairs, slamming my bedroom door behind me.

My life was turning inside out: Instead of living for the summer, I dreaded it; instead of pining for a winter weekend in Atlantic City, I counted the hours until Monday, when I could be with Sarah again. Instead of being able to talk to Dad about anything, I was pulling away, punishing him with hostile glares and cold silence.

Since Sarah had to report home immediately after school, like a prisoner on work release, my afternoons were free. It was the middle of the winter—too cold to juggle downtown most days. One bleak, windy Wednesday, I sat at the kitchen table, drinking a cup of coffee and eating a bowl of tuna salad. I had an hour or two of homework to do, and I planned to practice my five-ball routine for another hour. But it was only three o'clock. I finished the tuna salad, rinsed out the empty bowl. Outside it was seventeen degrees. No Sarah. No juggling.

I reached for the telephone and dialed. After two rings, he picked up. First a long silence, then a dreamy "Hullo?"

"Hey, Skip," I said. "It's Jason. What are you doing? Want to come over and hang out?"

"Is your old man around?" I knew he'd ask that.

"He's gone until late." Dad was at the Montgomeryville Mart bakery until five or six, then driving all the way to Reading—about an hour and a half northwest of Philadelphia—to buy some parts for a rolling machine. He'd told me not to expect him home until ten o'clock.

Fifteen minutes later Skip was at the door. Shivering, he took off his down-filled parka and his mountain-climbing boots. "Want some coffee?" I asked, beckoning him to the kitchen.

"Yeah, man, and check this shit out." Skip sat down at the table and pulled a pipe and two 35-mm film canisters from his jeans pocket. He opened a canister and offered me a whiff.

"Damn, Skip, that smells strong!"

"Hawaiian," he said, his voice low, like the weed was classified information. He tapped a bud from the vial and inspected it on the kitchen table before crushing it between his thumb and his forefinger. Then he opened the other vial. "Now take a whiff of *this* shit."

I recognized the odor right away. "Hash."

"Black hash from Afghanistan. Best shit on earth." Next to the pile of weed, Skip crumbled a mound of the hash. He put a pinch of the weed in the metal pipe, and a pinch of hash on top, then a pinch of weed and another of hash—weed then hash until the silver metal bowl was brimming. "It's a parfait," he said.

The weed and the hash were stronger than anything I'd ever smoked. I coughed up a cloud of thick, pungent smoke. Skip laughed. I coughed some more, sipped my coffee and waved off another toke. Ten seconds later, I was stoned out of my mind. Skip took two big tokes and passed the pipe back to me. A trail of blue-gray smoke plumed from its stem.

"Did I tell you I turned Sarah on?" I asked. I'd already told Skip about Sarah. He wasn't interested, but I figured that if the story involved weed, he'd listen.

"She got off her first time?" he asked suspiciously. "Almost nobody gets off the first time."

"*We* did."

"That's because it was good shit and we kept toking until we got off, man."

"Same with Sarah and me," I said. "Some hippie in town gave me a big-assed joint and we smoked the whole thing under the boardwalk."

Skip took a final toke. He inspected the pipe, tapping the ashes onto the tabletop.

I pressed my finger into the pile of ashes, afraid that an ember might burn the table.

"It's spent," he said. He looked dazed, his eyelids drooping. He leaned back and stared at the ceiling.

Sometimes I wondered why we were even friends at all. Skip had treated me like shit last summer. Which reminded me . . .

"Oh, hey, by the way, you were right. My dad *is* an asshole."

Skip snorted. "Stop the presses. My dad says your dad's lawsuit-happy." That came as a surprise because I didn't know that Skip's father even knew Dad. "He told me your dad sued Peppy the Clown and lost."

"Bull*shit!*" I spat. "Peppy the Clown tried raising my dad's rent after he saw how well the pretzel bakery was doing."

Skip filled another bowl with layers of hash and grass and slid it across the table to me. "Not what I heard," he said.

I waved him off. "No more for me." Skip took back the pipe and lit up. "What did you hear?" I asked. "How does your old man know?" My mouth felt like cotton.

"He's Peppy the Clown's new accountant," he said, smoke seeping from his nostrils. "Peppy told him your old man put in three ovens instead of two, and he was using storage space he wasn't allowed to, so Peppy added more to the rent and your old man freaked the fuck out and took him to court."

This was news to me. Dad hadn't told me about the lawsuit, just about Peppy the Clown being a *goddamned opportunist*. "It was years ago anyway," I said.

Skip shook his head. "Didn't make it to court until like last year."

"My dad lost?" I got up from the table and filled two glasses with water.

"Fuck yeah. Cost him a shitload." Skip produced a house key from his pants pocket and used it to stir the remaining mixture in his pipe. I handed him his water. He took a long drink.

Dad had lied. Again. I reached across the table for Skip's pipe and took a long, slow hit. The smoke burned my throat. I stifled a cough and chugged half a glass of water. I decided not to ask Dad about Peppy the Clown. What was the point? He'd probably just bullshit me.

MY CELLPHONE BUZZES in my pants pocket. The vibration makes me jump. There's a text message from the man who sold me the house all those years ago and who has been the property manager this whole time. *"sorry to miss you pretzel boy, key in coffee can under back door porch. don't be a stranger."*

"Good news," I say, returning the phone to my pocket. "We can get in the house."

Ruth hugs the box of fudge Mr. Lambert gave us, doling out sticky chunks to Eileen and me like a prudent parent. I've been cutting back on the fat, avoiding butter and cream ever since learning about my cholesterol the same week I heard that Jennifer grew up in Atlantic City. But today I make an exception, happily gobbling down whatever Ruth hands me. Soon, though, she lags behind us again.

We are past the casinos and their loudspeakers, almost at the inlet. It's quiet. Old people sit on benches, bundled in coats and blankets, chatting and watching the ocean.

With Ruth out of earshot, Eileen probes me about Jimmy and Madam Diane, Norman and Betty. "When we got married, they were all still here," she says, accusingly. "You told me you didn't have anybody. But they were all still here."

Helpless, I shrug my shoulders. "I'm getting to that."

"Did lying to your family bother you?"

I clear my throat. "Only when I thought about it."

"That's your M.O.," she says flatly. "Don't stress what you don't think about. Nice trick."

"It's a by-product of juggling," I explain. "Did I tell you about the mindfulness training they gave us at work last fall?"

"No. You never talk about work," Eileen says. "Don't you realize that? You talk about exactly what's in front of you. Drive Ruth to Sharon's. Eat Cheerios. Watch the news. Or else you make glib, self-deprecating jokes. You use humor like Skip used drugs. It's a mask. And when I talk to you about ideas or news or opinions, you hear me . . ."

"But I don't listen," I say.

Eileen sighs. "You keep the world at arm's length."

We walk in edgy silence. I think about a mask. Phony. Plastic. Like Skip said.

"What about the mindfulness training?" she asks.

"They gave us a workshop. This guy came in and taught us how to meditate. You know, breathe in, breathe out, and you pay attention to your breath, you know? Follow your breath with your mind. Which was basically what Bobby taught me when I was eight, when he showed me how to beat the jitters. After the workshop people were going around saying 'Wow, it sounds so easy, but it's impossible.' But for me it *was* actually easy. I've been doing it my whole life. Up and down, like a cascade, up and down, throw and catch, and the rest is just incidental."

"That's the wall you've built," says Eileen.

"Maybe I'm an accidental Buddhist."

"Bullshit," she says.

15

I KNEW HOW TO play to a hostile crowd, and I was confident I could win over Mrs. Gilquist. So one morning in the cafeteria before first period I broached the subject of meeting her. "Give me a book," I told Sarah. "I'll come by your house tonight to return it. Tell your mom I'm a friend and you accidentally left it with me, and you need it. And then I can meet your mom."

"Why is it important to you?" she asked, poking at her coffee cake.

"Because we're supposed to know each other's families, not be each other's secret. I don't want to be someone you lie about. You know my dad, I should know your mom."

"But isn't that what you're asking? You want me to lie about you to my mom so you can get in the door."

"No. This is different," I said. "It's a white lie to get us to the truth."

With a cluck of her tongue, Sarah handed me her Social Studies textbook. I slipped it into my backpack.

That night, as I was leaving the house for the five-mile walk to Sarah's, Dad asked me where I was off to. When I muttered my answer, he asked if I wanted a lift. "It's a long walk," he said, setting his newspaper and coffee mug on the kitchen table. "I'll drive you."

"No thanks," I said, slamming the door behind me. Soon I'd have a driver's license and a car and I wouldn't need Dad for anything. He'd lied about Mom and about Peppy the Clown, and he was probably lying about the derbies too. But God forbid he should bend the truth for the sake of Jasonansarah.

Our neighborhood was solidly upper middle class—sturdy, single houses built of stone and brick; well-trimmed hedges glistening with frost on an ice-cold February night; Volvos, wood-paneled station wagons and Buick sedans in the driveways. Our house was as big as most of our neighbors', but the window frames were flaking, and out back the garage door had been broken since last fall when Dad tried to cram in a new dough mixer. Sputtering and cursing, he had forced the door closed and it popped off its track. In fact, our house's shabbiness had begun to remind me of the pretzel bakery in Atlantic City. I knew that Dad had taken out a second mortgage to pay for some of Mom's "experimental" treatments that weren't covered by insurance. Now that I knew about the lawsuit with Peppy the Clown, I wondered how much else he wasn't telling me about his finances.

About half a mile from Sarah's, I launched into a slow jog. Her neighborhood was more upscale than ours, the homes twice as big, sprawling across great lawns, with carports in the front and swimming pools out back. Under my army jacket I wore a crew-neck sweater over a white button-down shirt, along with corduroy slacks and a pair of Wallabee shoes (the kind Sarah wore). When I arrived at Sarah's house, I stopped outside to catch my breath and smooth my hair.

I lifted and released the handle of the big brass door-knocker. A few seconds later Sarah opened the door. She flashed a nervous smile and bit her lower lip. "Come in," she said, welcoming me with a shy kiss on my cheek. "My mother's upstairs. She just woke up from a nap. She'll be down in a few."

She led me into the biggest living room I'd ever seen, filled with stiff-looking furniture. I sat on a red couch that was as cozy as a cinder block; Sarah sat across from me on a pretentious, strawberry-colored chair that looked like it belonged in a museum.

Sarah cleared her throat. "Did you bring the book?"

"What book? Oh, shit. Sorry." I grimaced.

Sarah stood up. "It's okay. She won't remember. I'll go see what's keeping her." She padded up the stairs.

After a few minutes I heard footsteps on the stairs—Sarah, followed by her mom. I stood up when they entered the living room, but the sight of Mrs. Gilquist almost knocked me back down. Far from the handwringing, disheveled lunatic I'd imagined, she looked normal. Shoulders back, head held high like she'd just stepped out of a beauty parlor.

I extended my hand, trying not to gape. "It's nice to meet you, Mrs. Gilquist."

Smiling pleasantly and pumping my hand, she said, "How do you do. Won't you have a seat?"

I returned to the couch. Sarah sat in the love seat and Mrs. Gilquist stationed herself in a rectangular recliner in the corner of the room. I turned to Sarah, raised my eyebrows and grinned. We were off to a good start. Mrs. Gilquist didn't look crazy. She had the same almond-brown eyes as Sarah, only set farther apart. She wore an aqua-colored pants suit and expensive-looking leather pumps.

Instead of initiating a conversation, Mrs. Gilquist stood up and walked over to a wheeled cart stocked with liquor bottles and an ice bucket. She put three ice cubes in a tumbler, poured some liquor in, stirred it around with a plastic stick and took a long gulp. She looked up from the glass, a warm smile on her face. I smiled back.

"So, Jason Benson," she said, returning to her chair, "what can I do for you?"

Stumped, I fumbled for something to say while Mrs. Gilquist took another long sip of her drink, finishing off almost half the glass.

I cleared my throat. "I just wanted to introduce myself," I began, "and see if it would be okay for Sarah and me to be friends and hang out after school once in a while and maybe go to a movie sometimes on a Friday or Saturday night. We'll be home early. You can drive us, or my dad can if you're too busy." Pretty clever, I thought, asking her to drive, as if she actually would.

"What does your father do?" asked Mrs. Gilquist. "What's he in?"

In? On my way here, I'd rehearsed answers to her questions, but this was one I hadn't anticipated. *He's in aeronautics. He's in law. He's in banking.*

"Pretzels," I said, optimistically. "He owns four pretzel bakeries. One in Atlantic City during the summer, and the others are at the Downingtown Farmers Market, the Pennsauken Mart and the Montgomeryville Mart."

She polished off her drink, stood up again and made her way back to the cart. "What's a mart?" she asked while she poured her second drink.

"You know, like a farmers market, with lots of little stalls— stores and stuff. Like clothes and tires, and books and sneakers. Frozen custard."

While Mrs. Gilquist's face was buried in her tumbler I stole a glance at Sarah, who eyed me back cautiously.

"So what do you say?" I asked. "Do you think Sarah and I could go out together once in a while? As friends?"

Mrs. Gilquist looked up. She seemed surprised to see me. She pointed her index finger at me. "*Pretzels?*" she asked.

"Fresh baked," I said. "Would you like me to bring you a bag? On my next visit? I'll bet you like yours extra salty."

"More or less," she said.

"So, maybe, next weekend I can come by for Sarah so we can go to a movie or something—my dad can take us—and I'll bring you a bag?"

Mrs. Gilquist took a long gulp of her drink.

"Slow down, Mother," Sarah said. She called her mother "Mother." Jesus. Didn't that go out of style last century?

"We'll see," said Mrs. Gilquist.

Breathe, I told myself. Remain calm. Each line of dialogue is a throw and a catch—what Miss Smith calls sending and receiving. Stay with it. You send a line, and when it reaches its peak, the other person sends you a line, which you consciously receive.

"Mr. Gilquist was the youngest senior vice president in Campbell's history," said Mrs. Gilquist, drink in hand.

"He was in soup," I joked. Mrs. Gilquist squinted at me. Against my better judgment, I tried to explain. "You know, like my dad's *in* pretzels?"

Mrs. Gilquist brushed away my attempt at humor. "Mr. Gilquist went to the Harvard Business School, you know," she said, rising once again to cross the room and refresh her drink. Having gone through nearly a quarter of the bottle in fifteen minutes, she was beginning to slur her speech.

I tried keeping the awkward conversation going. "I'm not surprised he went to Harvard. Sarah's so good in school."

Mrs. Gilquist turned to me, a look of confusion on her face. "What does that have to do . . . ?" Her voice trailed off. So much for sending and receiving: Conversing with this woman was like juggling Jell-O. Maybe she wasn't crazy after all; maybe she was just a drunk. Either way, she needed help. But if she went away for treatment, Sarah couldn't live alone.

I drew a deep breath and forced a smile as Mrs. Gilquist returned to her recliner, a fresh drink in hand. She set the glass down on a lamp table. She looked at Sarah, then at me. "Extra salty," she said.

"Will do," I told her.

"Expect a dinner invitation," she said. Then, curiously, she added, "Maybe." She sat in her chair, crossed her legs and closed her eyes. A few seconds later she was snoring.

Sarah looked like she was going to cry. I forced a tight little smile and mouthed, "That went well, right? A dinner invitation? Maybe?"

Warily Sarah slid out of her seat and led me to the front door. "What happened?" I whispered.

Sarah bit her lower lip. "She takes pills. And she drank on an empty stomach."

Pills. Of course. I had two friends outside of Atlantic City—and both their moms were on pills.

I opened my arms and hugged Sarah. "I'll see you in school tomorrow."

"I won't be there," she said. "It's an early dismissal—remember? I have a doctor's appointment in the morning and then I have my social studies report."

Tomorrow was Friday, so I grimaced at the thought of three days without her. "I love you," I whispered.

"Love you too."

When I got home, Dad was hunched over the kitchen table, studying his bakery ledgers, a pen scrunched in his hand. He looked up from his work. "How'd it go?"

"Okay, I guess," I said anemically.

"Will Sarah's mother let you date?"

I nodded. I didn't like the word *date*. It was too casual. We didn't *date*. We were *together*. Jasonansarah.

"Well, that's progress," said Dad, raising his eyebrows. "Congratulations."

I poured myself a glass of water and gulped it down. "I've got homework," I said.

The more I looked around the house, the more I saw stuff in need of repair: spidery cracks in the dining-room ceiling; a worn-out living-room sofa with frayed cushions; and outside, the peeling window frames.

The next day, school let out early and Sarah had her doctor's appointment. I arrived downtown at one-thirty, got off the bus at City Hall and walked south for a block, past banks and plazas filled with office workers. It was cold but nearly windless. Sunlight poked through the skyscrapers. Around 15th and Chestnut, hearing a saxophone squawk like a seagull, I followed the sounds to Blue Dawson, who was playing for a small audience. Surprised to see him back from his cruise ship gig, I jostled my way through the crowd and unpacked my juggling stuff. When Blue saw me, he nodded his head and picked up his tempo. It felt great to work with live music—Blue holding a note while the ball arced into the air or took an extra bounce off my knee.

We did a number that lasted about ten minutes, culminating with a four-ball juggle in which every other throw bounced off the sun-speckled pavement. As we were taking our bows, right before I headed out into the crowd with my derby extended, I noticed a young man in the audience, a hippie in his mid-twenties bundled in a green army coat, corduroy pants and bright red high-top sneakers. His long hair was pulled back in a neat ponytail, and he carried a rainbow-colored backpack. I made my way through the crowd. The man in the ponytail stood back, watching me. After the crowd dispersed, while Blue cleaned his sax and counted the change in his case, the man approached me.

"Nice work," he said, his voice resonant. He tugged at the colorful backpack slung over his shoulder. "I'm a juggler too."

"Wait a second. Are you Henry the Juggler?"

"Oh, wow. I feel famous!" he said.

"I used to watch you juggle in Atlantic City, in front of Steel Pier."

"Were you the kid who used to hang with the gypsies? Did a gypsy kid teach you how to juggle on the beach?"

"That was my friend Bobby! I'm Jason Benson," I said.

"Right on," said Henry the Juggler, extending his hand to me. "I haven't been in Atlantic City in years, man."

"I've been doing shows there every summer."

Blue Dawson had packed up his sax and helped himself to his share of the tips. "Blue Dawson," I said. "Meet Henry the Juggler. Henry is actually the only other professional juggler I've ever known."

"Solid," said Blue, clasping Henry the Juggler's hand soul-brother style, overhand. "I gotta cut out. See you 'round, man."

"Later, Blue," I said, returning my attention to Henry the Juggler.

"It's coming back," said Henry. "You used to watch me with your mom and your gypsy friend sometimes, right?"

"Yeah, that was Bobby!"

"And your father ran a doughnut shop?"

"Pretzel bakery. Still does . . ."

"I remember Bobby showing you how to juggle on the beach, next to where the potheads were trying to get their shit together."

"The day Bobby taught me how to juggle, the cops came down to the beach and busted one of those hippies."

Henry the Juggler laughed. "The cops hassled me about it. They were like, 'You're their leader,' and I was like, 'Bullshit, man. I'm nobody's leader, and those cats suck at juggling, and I don't do drugs and why don't you give me a lie detector test?' But once they figured out it was your boy dealing to the potheads . . ."

Huh? My boy? "What do you mean?" I asked.

"Bobby," said Henry the Juggler. "You didn't know?"

I stared at him blankly.

"He was dealing weed. Right. You didn't know. You were just a kid."

"What happened?" I asked.

"Got busted, skipped bail," he said with a good-natured shrug.

It felt like a smack in the face. Bobby was a dealer! That explained his game of being invisible to the police. He had to lie low for the rest of the season. And when he left me out in front of those stores, he was going inside to sell weed!

I hadn't thought about Bobby in a long time, but now the memories washed in. Bobby with his big dancing marionette bear, and me with my little Floppy the Stuffed Dog marionette, side by side, drawing the crowds from the boardwalk.

"Do you pass?" asked Henry the Juggler.

"Huh? Oh. No," I said, shaking off my confusion. "Sorry. I'm solo, but I want to learn to pass because I'm teaching my girlfriend and we're going to do an act once she gets good. We're going to move to Atlantic City and live there year-round after high school."

"Far out," said Henry the Juggler.

"Where do you live?" I asked him.

"L.A.," he said. "I'm in town for my cousin's wedding. But man, I'm on the road nine months a year. Festival circuits, theaters, street malls, colleges."

"That's what me and my girlfriend are going to do," I said. "Work Atlantic City all summer, then head where the weather's warm in the winter."

"How are your parents?" he asked.

"My mom died. She had cancer."

"Oh, man," said Henry the Juggler, clasping my arm in sympathy. "Sorry to hear that."

"Thanks," I said. "It's okay. We're doing all right."

"How's your dad? Still hollering at customers across the counter?" He winked.

"Nah, he's cooled out," I said.

Henry the Juggler reached out his hand. "I gotta split," he said. We shook soul-brother style. He adjusted his backpack and rubbed his hands together in the biting air. "Get your girlfriend up to speed and work on your passing, man. Passing's where it's at."

I watched Henry the Juggler blend into the crowd on Chestnut Street. The news about Bobby had taken the wind out of me. But it would be great to learn to pass with Sarah, to make one gigantic pattern of balls or clubs.

On Monday morning, Sarah and I met on the school steps and walked to her first-period class. "What did your mom say?" I asked. "Don't you think it's neat that she opened up to me about your dad and sort of said we could go out? I mean, a dinner invitation. . . . Maybe."

"Don't get your hopes up," said Sarah. "She changes her mind all the time." She glanced into the classroom. "I think my mother actually liked you."

"You seem surprised!" I said, beaming.

"She asked if you were Jewish."

"What did you tell her?"

"I said you were, but you weren't religious. And she said as long as we weren't getting married it didn't matter." My stomach flip-flopped. Of course we were getting married.

"Don't push," she said when she saw the look on my face. "I have French." She spun around and entered the classroom without looking back.

16

June 20, 1976

Dear Sarah,

I love you so much!!! I'm surviving, but Atlantic City is not the same without you. It's like there's only half of me here. I miss you! How are things in good old Cape Clod? (Ha-ha.)

This summer everybody's yakking about gambling. I don't read much of what's in the newspapers, but there was a vote and now a bunch of casinos are definitely going to open. Before, there was a vote that was for gambling in New Jersey, and that lost. But the new vote was just for Atlantic City and gambling won, so here it comes! Now Dad says it won't be good for business for a lot of the boardwalk stores, including ours. He figures that if a gambler is losing he's not going to leave the casino and buy a pretzel, and if a gambler's winning he's not going to leave the casino and buy a pretzel either. So he's going to try and sell to the casinos, and he feels like he can definitely make a good deal with them because our pretzels are so popular.

But the good news is that the casinos will be open year-round so we can work at the bakery all winter when we're living down here full time. But the bad news is that the rent will probably double so we may not even be on the boardwalk in a couple of summers. We'll have to rent a space off the board-walk just for baking.

But guess what! Jimmy closed his marionette theater! After fifteen seasons! Now he's telling fortunes and guessing people's weights out of a storefront across from Million Dollar Pier. Things are really changing down here.

I miss you like crazy. And I especially miss doing the stuff we like to do (if you get my drift. By the way, can I write about that stuff to you, or will some nosy relative of yours read your mail?). There are all these girls here, and some of them like to meet me after my shows on the boardwalk at night. But you don't have to worry as I am completely faithful and true to you. As loyal as a puppy dog. I'm counting down the days until we will be together again (80½).

I have my learner's permit (I'm memorizing the manual for the written test they make you take, and I'm going to get my license and buy a car as soon as I get back to Philadelphia), so don't you think eleventh grade will be really cool? I'm a great driver. It was really easy to learn and Dad lets me drive his car around sometimes when business is slow.

It was so great going out on Saturday nights the last few weeks of school! I told you, you didn't have to be afraid of your mom. See? I think she is definitely going to get better, especially when she sees how happy we are in eleventh grade. And next year will be even better because I'll have my license.

Dad says hi. He drives back and forth to Philadelphia and to his other bakeries so mostly I'm managing this place all summer. Plus I do my shows at night so you can bet I'm super busy. That's good, because it makes the time go fast, and I know that before too long I'll see you again. Also, I am mak-ing really good money this summer (Dad pays me 270 a week for managing the bakery and I make about another 400–600 juggling). What kind of car should I get?

We gave up our usual hotel room this summer—just try-ing to save a little money. My room behind the bakery is about

10 × 10 and all it is really is where somebody threw up four panels and cut a chunk out of one and stuck an air conditioner in. I have a cot and a night table and a portable TV. Most nights Dad's in Philly, but he sleeps here two nights a week on a second cot, which gets a little crowded but oh well.

I know it's early but I've been looking at some year-round rental properties. We can get a place from September through May, but we'll have to move out for the summer season. Or maybe we could even buy a little place. And by the way I also learned that you can be a New Jersey resident after you have lived here for a year, so then you can go to Stockton State College or maybe Rutgers. I know how important college is to you.

That's about it for now. Write back soon. You are the love of my life and I need you and I love you! I'm counting the days until September 9th when I can finally see (and feel!) you again.

Love,

Jason

July 1, 1976

Dear Jason,

I love you too. Nobody here reads my mail. I have more privacy than at home. Thank you for the kind words about Mother. I worry about her, but I think she's getting better too. We talked on the telephone yesterday and she was very clear and funny. She even asked if I had heard from you! Please give your father my regards. I miss you, too. Sometimes I almost forget what you feel like when we're in each other's arms, and I wish we could be together and hold each other again, wrap up in a blanket on a sand dune and watch the sun set. Jason, you can't imagine how beautiful the sunsets are here! You'd love it. It's so laid back. I told Aunt Joan and Uncle Jerry about you, and they said that you are welcome to come up and visit for a couple days if you can manage to take some time off.

This has been a good summer. The weather's beautiful. The water's warm. My aunt has a pool and I spend most of my days there reading and tanning. You may not recognize me when you see me! My aunt keeps saying I should get my hair cut short. What do you think? She says it will make me look perky. She thinks I look too bookish. Do I look bookish to you? (Not when we're in bed, I'll bet.)

My aunt and uncle don't discuss Mother. She told them she was too busy to make it up here this summer. Too busy doing what? They're acting like that's perfectly normal, when they know she doesn't work. You were right when you said that when adults bullshit, they're only bullshitting themselves. They haven't seen my mother in over a year, and they act like nothing's wrong. I told Aunt Joan that Mother drinks and takes pills all day and never leaves the house, and she said, "Well, I'm sure that's a bit of an exaggeration." I said no, it's not an exaggeration. She literally never leaves the house! Aunt Joan patted me on my head like I was a dog. That's one thing I love about you. You are so honest and you talk about things that are important, instead of stupid stuff like sports and gossip. You're talented and original and funny instead of just repeating dumb jokes that somebody else told you.

Not much else to report. I miss you too. I'll see you in 70 days. Write back soon. (And don't have too much fun with those girls who watch you juggle!)

xxxxxxooooooo

Sarah

OF COURSE I couldn't accept Sarah's invitation to visit her because I worked seven days a week while Dad commuted between Atlantic City, Pennsauken and Downingtown. I did two or three shows a night, slipping away from the bakery, entrusting it to the other kids who worked for us—Scott, a pre-med major from Camden, and Michelle, a high school senior who lived year-round in Atlantic City. After I'd twisted enough pretzels to carry us through the night, Scott baked, Michelle sold and I ducked out to juggle. On a good night I earned as much in ninety minutes as the kids I went to school with made in a week of flipping burgers or lifeguarding at swim clubs.

"Ladies and gentlemen," I'd announce. "Jason the Magnificent will gladly juggle any object that you can lift and toss!" The audience would throw me stuffed animals they'd won at the pier, cotton candy, single peanuts, sandals, you name it.

Late at night, after doing my shows, sweeping the bakery and scraping out the ovens, I'd stand at the counter and watch the neon lights from the boardwalk shops flicker off, like fireworks fading in the night. I'd turn out the bakery lights, go to my little room and crank up the air conditioning. Too tired to study my Pennsylvania driver's manual, I'd step out of my clothes, climb under the covers and masturbate to fantasies of Sarah; and sometimes of girls who skittered across the boards from the beach in the daytime to buy pretzels and who, a few hours later—freshly shampooed, wearing pressed jeans or light summer dresses—watched me juggle, intoxicating me with their giggles, brushing my wrist with their fingers when they dropped coins into my derby.

It was weird not having Jimmy next door. The marionette theater was now a discount bookstore called "Beach Reader"—the first bookseller on the boardwalk, according to the sign on the awning. Jimmy dropped by each morning for a cup of orange juice, and then once or twice during the day to chat with Dad or me. Usually the conversation came around to gambling.

One night early in the season, a man accused Jimmy of trying to pick his pocket when Jimmy was guessing his weight. The man called the cops. He wanted them to arrest Jimmy, but all his stuff was still in his pockets. The next morning Jimmy was mad.

"You shoulda heard that sonofabitch," he said, stomping out one cigarette on the boardwalk and immediately lighting another that had been tucked behind his ear. "'I felt his greasy fingers in my pockets!' The cops asked him what's missing and he tells 'em that ain't the point, that he felt my greasy fingers in his pockets. 'Greasy,' he says." Jimmy held up his hands for my inspection. He spat on the boardwalk. "Fat bastard had gas." Jimmy polished off his orange juice and crumpled the paper cup in his fist. "If these fuckers think I got *my* hands in their pockets, wait till the casinos get hold of 'em." He looked up and down the boardwalk, took a deep drag off his cigarette and shook his head.

It was chilly. A dozen surf fishermen lined the ocean's edge, their long poles rising like antennae from the sand. Down by the water, the lifeguards were perched in their blue and white Atlantic City Beach Patrol stands or tinkering with the oarlocks on the big wooden rescue rowboats that lay upside down on the sand.

Jimmy took a deep breath through his nose, his nostrils flaring. He exhaled sharply, shook his head in disgust and muttered something under his breath.

"What's the matter?" I asked.

"It don't smell right."

"What doesn't?"

"Everything."

I stuck my head over the counter and took a whiff: Damp, salty morning air. Suntan oil. Doughnut grease. Jimmy's smoke. "It smells okay to me. Maybe you should put out your cigarette."

Jimmy took another sniff. "It's changing, kid," he said ominously.

"Like with the gambling?"

Jimmy crushed his new cigarette on the boards, but a moment later reached into his pocket and produced a lime-green can of tobacco and a pack of rolling papers. He opened the can with one hand, gingerly tore a pinch of the moist, shredded tobacco, closed the can and slipped it back into his pocket. "In the old country, my old man's family had a traveling circus," he said. "Istanbul, Cairo, Paris. One night my grandfather says it don't smell right."

"What didn't?" I asked.

Deftly Jimmy rolled his cigarette with one hand. "Europe." He lit up and took a deep drag. "They pull up their stakes, and before you know it I'm ten years old, reading palms on the boardwalk which beat getting gassed by the Nazis."

"Jesus, Jimmy. I had no idea. You got out because Europe didn't smell right to your grandfather?" I took a long, slow sniff and shook my head. Not smelling anything out of the ordinary, I decided to change the subject. "By the way, I need to ask you something."

Jimmy leaned over the counter, smiling like an imp. "Girl stuff?"

"Hat stuff. The derbies from My Edna. How does she do it?"

Jimmy shrugged. "A long time ago her mother taught her how to make a derby. And she got good at it."

"You know what I'm talking about," I said. "How do they disappear?"

"Disappear?" He blinked like he was baffled.

"You must know something," I said. "There has to be a logical explanation."

Jimmy rolled his eyes skyward. "Who says I gotta be logical? I made it this far, right?"

"Tell me how they disappear," I demanded. "The new one arrives and the old one's gone."

Jimmy smiled. "Maybe when you were a little kid, Diane put a gypsy spell on you. Now you get a phone call, somebody says the secret word and you go into a trance, like a zombie. You ditch the old derby yourself, then you snap out of it." He puffed his cigarette. "It's logical. Hypnosis. Ask a scientist."

I smirked. "Yeah, right."

"There's a hundred explanations," he said, "if that's what you want. I don't know if any of 'em's true. And you don't, neither. All you know is shit's happening and you can't explain it. That's half of life. Oh, but you want logical."

"If it happened to you," I said, "wouldn't you want to know what was going on?"

"How do you know it *don't* happen to me? Maybe that's how I get my clothes." He swept his hands up and down his small frame. "Where ya think I get my tobacco? Ever seen me buy it? And what makes you sure there's a how?"

"What do you mean?" I asked.

Jimmy leaned in toward me until our noses almost touched. "Sometimes things just happen," he whispered. "There ain't no *how* until afterwards when somebody goes, 'Hey, what the hell?' Nobody asks how until after it happens, right? The explanation comes after. The thing comes first. The *what* got there before the *how* did." Jimmy stepped back, took a long drag off his cigarette and exhaled a shaft of bluish smoke through his nose. "All right," he said. "You tell me—logically. Seven, eight years ago, I'm standing right over there watching two kids down on the beach and the big one's teaching the little one to juggle."

"I remember," I said.

Jimmy held his palms in the air, entreating me. "So where's the little kid now?"

"That was me," I said, confused. "I'm right here."

Jimmy shook his head. "No, where is he now? You say you're him, but you're bigger than he was. You're funnier. You're only half as annoying." He looked me in the eye. "Where's that little kid? Is it still you? Or are you somebody else now? You see what I'm saying?"

"Not really," I said. "I'm growing up. What's the big deal?"

"That's life," he said with a grin. "Things change and you can't explain everything."

"If you say so," I said. "But you can't compare a living person to an inanimate object like a derby."

"The hell I can't," said Jimmy.

A breeze kicked up and a row of storm clouds threatened the morning sky. A smattering of beach-goers began packing up their stuff and heading toward the boardwalk, clutching beach chairs and umbrellas, fishing rods and rubber rafts. They scurried like hermit crabs to their cars and hotels, to the shelter of store awnings.

Lightning flashed and thunder cracked over our heads. Jimmy took one last drag of his cigarette and flicked the butt about six feet into a small puddle that had formed next to the building. He winked, flashed a thumbs-up sign, pulled his windbreaker over his head and took off down the boardwalk toward Million Dollar Pier. Just then the sky opened. Heavy rain pounded the boards. I hoped it would wash away whatever Jimmy thought he could smell.

Watching the storm crash on the beach and boardwalk, I wondered whether I'd ever know the truth about the derbies. I closed the bakery, leaving the ovens on for later, emptying the register and hiding the cash in a cigar box under my cot in the back room. I put on my yellow raincoat, locked the front door and took off out the back. I ran around to the boardwalk and darted over to Norman and Betty's arcade.

"Come out of the rain, you crazy Pretzel Boychick!" said Betty when she saw me. "You look like a drowned rat!"

The arcade was practically empty, so I had my choice of machines. "After you play a little," said Betty, handing me a fistful of quarters, "come to the office for a nosh. I made a nice honey cake." She disappeared into the office, leaving me to the flashing pinball machines. One of my favorites was a "soccer" game where you had to flip the ball past a line of opposing players and into a goal to score points. I stepped up to the machine and slid a quarter into the coin slot. The machine knocked and rattled to life. I pressed the start button, pulled back on the knob and sent the first ball into play. I shook the machine gently back and forth, willing the silver ball to tap a bank of bumpers and ring up a thousand points. Shaking and swaying, I rang up two free games on my first ball. Each time I scored a free game, the machine signaled with a loud, pleasing knock.

At that point I realized I wasn't alone. Lita was beside me, watching me play. I caught the ball in the flipper again and turned to her.

"How ya doing?"

She shrugged her shoulders. "Pretty wet out there, huh?"

The rain slammed the roof so loudly that Lita and I practically had to yell just to hear each other. I released the flipper and shot the ball at the goal. It missed, ricocheting off the bumpers at the top of the machine. I tried maneuvering it back toward the goal by shaking the machine a little, but I was off the mark. After the ball bounced around a little, hitting some ten-point bumpers, it raced down the middle and I lost it between the flippers.

Lita had grown taller and filled out over the winter. She wore a touch of pink lipstick. Her ringlets of hair were a little unkempt, giving her a wild-girl look. She wore a sleeveless gray tee shirt and blue jeans cut off and cuffed above her knees. I couldn't help but glance at her tanned legs.

Lita rested her hand on the glass top of the machine, partially blocking my view of the game. Her fingernails were painted red, adding another dimension of womanliness to what had been girl-hood until now.

"Could you move your hand?" I asked.

Lita withdrew from the glass but stayed close. I pulled back on the silver knob, released it and sent the next ball into play. Shaking and flipping, ducking and shifting, I played this ball for two or three minutes. Lita stood at my side, equal parts cheerleader and back seat driver—bouncing, squealing and sucking her breath through her teeth. Eventually I overshot with the right flipper; the ball careened around a post and disappeared.

"You wanna play one?" I asked.

"It's still your game," said Lita. She reached into her pants pocket, pulled out a pack of Wrigley's Spearmint and offered me a stick. I stepped away from the machine and gestured toward it gallantly. "Go ahead, play one."

Lita stepped up, chomping her chewing gum. She jutted out her hips and pushed a strand of hair out of her face. She pulled the knob and released the ball with give-'em-hell grit, an attitude incongruous with the lipstick and nail polish. I found that kind of sexy.

Having spent most of her life in the Two for One Arcade, Lita was a pinball wizard. She worked the bumpers, defying gravity, keeping the ball at the top of the machine and not even using the flippers for the first full minute of play. Finally she let the ball roll to the flippers, then shot it effortlessly through the goal and back to the top of the machine to rack up five free games. After ten minutes she lost the ball when it rolled straight down the middle.

Grimacing, she stepped away from the machine.

Betty poked her head out of the office door. "Lita! Come! I have a little job I want you should do for me."

Lita tilted her head and twirled her hair with her fingers, then trotted off toward the office. I wondered if she had a crush on me. But what did it matter? Lita was still a kid even if she had a killer body, and besides, I was virtually engaged to Sarah. I swiveled my head to watch Lita, and at that moment she turned and caught me looking. I felt my forehead flush. Noting my embarrassment with a naughty smirk, she sashayed into the office, closing the door behind her.

Outside, sheets of rain slapped the boardwalk. It looked like it would keep up for hours. I bought myself a cup of watery coffee and a Snickers bar at the row of vending machines next to the office; then I returned to my game.

Even if it was still raining by the afternoon, I had plenty of cleaning up to do at the bakery. Rainy days were a good time to scrape down the ovens, change the lye mix in the dipping vat and order flour, yeast, salt and sugar. And I'd need to call Scott and Michelle and tell them not to come to work.

I played for an hour before the office door opened again. Betty stuck her head out and called my name, beckoning me inside. I finished the ball in play and abandoned the machine with six free games rung up on it.

Inside the office, Betty poured me a cup of coffee from the pot on Norman's desk. I straddled a chair. At a small table tucked into a corner, Lita counted quarters from the machines, making meticulous notations with a ballpoint pen in Norman's blue canvas-covered ledger.

Norman and Betty's office was tidy and bright compared to the dim arcade. It was soundproofed well enough—with old egg cartons that had been painted white and neatly affixed to the walls—to eliminate most of the tooting and grinding and general racket produced by the hundred or so pinball machines. In the middle of the wall was a big window so you could observe the comings and goings of the arcade, but you really couldn't hear much—only an occasional, muffled bonus bell or a burst of cheers from players huddled around a machine. A dark green metal file cabinet sat in one corner of the office. There were shelves on the walls, neatly crowded with items ranging from pinball machine service manuals to gleaming, freshly oiled machine parts to framed, sepia photographs of men with beards and women in babushkas in front of a small shop with Hebrew letters on its window. Most of the office was taken up by Norman and Betty's twin desks—drab, green and functional, with sliding drawers and locked cabinets—sitting face-to-face in the center of the room.

Rain kept pounding the roof like a herd of bulls. Betty cut a slice of honey cake from a big plate on her desk, wrapped it in a napkin and handed it to me. "No crumbology," she said in her thick Polish accent.

I didn't understand. "On Norman's desk," she said, "don't make no crumbs."

I laughed. "Crumbology. I like that."

Betty sat down at her desk. "What do you think's going to be?" she asked. "With the gambling on the boardwalk." She sounded worried.

"I don't think it'll be that big a deal."

"Then you could have another think comin'," she said. "Casinos gonna put us out of business."

"Why don't you just add a bunch of slot machines?" I asked. "Or pay prize money for high scores. You know, if you can't beat 'em, join 'em."

"Not without no casino license," she said. "And we ain't the type what's going to get a license, neither." I took another crumbless bite of the sweet, moist cake and washed it down with a gulp of coffee. "The casinos are going to do all they can to keep the people inside once they got them in there," Betty told me. "And all they can buy on the boardwalk—soft ice cream, peanuts."

"Pretzels," I said.

"Pretzels, you bet," she said, tapping a finger on her desk. "Everything what's for sale on the boardwalk the casinos gonna give away. God forbid anybody walks out with two quarters to rub together."

"So what are you guys going to do?" I asked.

"This season, then two or three more."

I set my coffee cup on the desk. "Then what?"

"We close here and go somewhere else."

"Off the boardwalk?"

"Away from Atlantic City," she said. "Philly maybe. You know where they built the nice mall on Chestnut Street?"

How ironic if Norman, Betty and Lita moved to Philly the same time Sarah and I moved down here. "That's where I juggle after school," I said. I imagined the busy corner at Sixteenth and Chestnut where guys in suits, students, office girls and moms pushing baby strollers stopped to watch my show a couple of afternoons a week when the weather was good.

"How's the foot traffic?" Betty asked.

"Not bad. I mean, it's not like it is here in the summer, but it's not dead in the winter either. There's a few arcades there already and I don't have any idea what the rent's like . . ."

"Norman's looking into that," she said, filling her own coffee cup and stirring in a spoonful of sugar.

Jimmy. Madam Diane. Norman and Betty. Dad. Everyone was talking about leaving. Like the people in Norman's photographs. Like Jimmy's grandfather. But it wasn't the same. Europe's been changing forever, I thought. Napoleon. Wars. Revolutions. But Atlantic City's always been Atlantic City. Things happen around it:

Vietnam. Politics. Baseball. But no matter what happened else-where, in Atlantic City, from Memorial Day until the Miss America Pageant, the boardwalk teemed with people seeking quick, cheap relief from the sticky, oppressive city summer.

Betty uncovered the cake and cut another slice. "And if you think they're going to let you do your juggling on the boardwalk," she said, "I wouldn't be so sure." I reached across the desk, napkin in hand, for my second helping of honey cake. Betty could be right. Putting on shows and passing the hat was technically illegal in Atlantic City, although no one had ever tried to prevent me from doing it.

So I'd get a job as an entertainer at a casino. And Dad could sell his pretzels to the casinos. All the doomsday talk was for the birds.

"Let me ask you something, Betty," I said. "This is going to sound weird, but how's Atlantic City smell to you?"

Betty looked at me like I was speaking Chinese. "How's it *what*?"

"Jimmy told me that Atlantic City didn't smell the same."

"Jimmy's crazy. Don't listen to no Jimmy."

"But he told me his grandfather said the same thing about Europe right before the Nazis came to power—and that's how they got out in time."

Betty drew a sharp breath, like an invisible fist had knocked the wind out of her. She put her hand on her chest. "I told you Jimmy's crazy," she said sharply. "I don't know what nobody smelled before the Nazis, but my mother and father had noses, and they didn't smell nothing. My aunts and uncles, my cousins . . ."

"I'm sorry," I said. "I didn't mean to . . ." I remembered the blue numbers tattooed on Norman's forearm. He had never told me what they meant, but that was one thing I had learned in school.

"I don't care what no crazy gypsy says," Betty said pointedly. "Nobody smelled nothing. And don't compare. It's two different things what happen in the old country and here. Atlantic City voted for slot machines, not Hitler."

"You're right." Jimmy was insane, or at least imaginative. This wasn't genocide; it was blackjack and slot machines.

"*Crumbology!*" Betty's scold yanked me from my reverie. I'd dropped a crumb on Norman's desk.

"Sorry," I said, pinching the culprit between my thumb and forefinger and popping it into my mouth. I stood up and put on my raincoat. "Good cake, Betty." I opened the office door; the din of the arcade rushed in, a wave of clattering skeeballs and rat-a-tat ringing of the pinball machines. "I'll see you guys around."

Betty blew me a kiss. "Stay dry."

I turned and winked. "No *soakology.*"

Poised at the arcade's exit, I pulled up my hood, contemplated the torrent outside and stepped onto the boardwalk. Shoulders hunched against the downpour, I hustled toward the bakery, raindrops smacking my hood like bullets. But after a few seconds I changed my mind. Thick rivulets wormed down the sleeves of my raincoat. Switching gears, I took a long, leisurely walk in the rain. I liked being the only person out. It felt as though I owned all the shuttered shops to my left and the vast expanse of soggy beach to my right. Like it was all mine. I was the King of Atlantic City. *Mr. Boardwalk.*

At Texas Avenue I trotted down the half-dozen wooden steps to the rain-soaked beach and rummaged through the sand until I came up with three hand-sized clamshells. Bounding back up to the boards, I held out the shells for the rain to wash the sand off, then continued my stroll while juggling the shells.

"Ladies and gentlemen!" I bellowed into the tempest. "Jasonansarah Productions is proud to present the one and only Clam Boy and his Twirling Exoskeletons." I juggled high, flipping the shells heavenward, catching them behind my back, then triple-tossing all three simultaneously and spinning three hundred and sixty degrees on my heels before making the catch and returning to the cascade. Between tosses I whacked the cold metal rail with my palms, making a sustained, hollow ringing.

It was more than juggling in the rain. It was a sacred dance, a celebration of amusement piers and saltwater taffy and dads teaching kids how to body-surf. I became the shells in their cascading pattern; became the crashing water; became the heart of the old wooden boardwalk, the rides, the bells and whistles of the night, the barkers shouting, "Step right up!"

I promised myself I would sustain the pattern with all my heart; take it with me at the end of the season; share it with Sarah; remember it through the long winter; care for it like a precious jewel or a magic derby.

ALL SUMMER LONG, merchants stopped by the bakery to ask Dad how he thought the casinos would affect their businesses. But he wasn't comfortable giving out advice. "I don't want the responsibility," he said one blazing hot Saturday in August. He was mixing up a batch of dough while I manned the register. "What if I advise someone to close up shop, and gambling turns out to be a boom? What if I tell them to stay where they are and they go under in two seasons? Why are they asking me, anyway?"

"You're the only Wharton grad they know," I said.

"I majored in accounting. I'm just a pretzel man." He lifted a fifty-pound bag of flour from the floor and, with practiced precision, poured half into the mixer.

"You're a Pretzel *King*," I said. "And you're smart."

Dad filled a bucket with water and added sugar, yeast and salt from the shelf above the sink. "Smart enough to know they'll double my rent next season. That's an entire year before the first casino opens. I should have bought this damned building when I had the chance."

"Why didn't you?"

"Too much else going on at the time." I didn't have to ask. Mom dying. Him losing his Peppy the Clown lawsuit. Not to mention whatever else he hadn't told me about. He punched the button to start the mixer and raised his voice over the blades' hum. "Everybody's got a theory, but I admire your optimism, son."

I walked back and leaned against the mixer, positioning myself so I could hear him over the whirring while keeping my eye out for customers. "What's your theory?" I asked.

"I don't think it'll do a damn bit of good for ninety-five percent of the year-round residents," he said bluntly. "City Council promises jobs, but will they go to Atlantic City residents?" He stopped the mixer, examined a bubble that had formed in the dough, prodding it with his finger. He restarted the machine. "The developers will pressure the casino owners to recruit help from outside. Face it, who are the year-rounders? Mostly black people who work in kitchens. Janitors. Back-of-the-house. Now they're going to get hired to deal cards? That's unlikely." He stopped the mixer and gave me a nod. The dough was ready. We each grabbed an armful, which we slapped down on top of a steel cart.

I recalled what Blue Dawson had said about Atlantic City—that black people weren't welcome on the boardwalk, except to cross it on the way to Chicken Bone Beach or to push rolling chairs.

17

ON OUR FIRST DAY back in Philadelphia, Dad drove me to the police barracks. The officer who administered my driving test made me zigzag through a course of orange cones, complete a three-point turn and then parallel-park between two blue plastic barrels. Inside the barracks, I took an eye test and a written exam. Twenty minutes later, I had my driver's license.

Sarah and I had agreed to walk to school early on the first day and meet outside the cafeteria. At five o'clock I headed out the door into the lilac-colored morning light. A breeze blew from the east, tickling the back of my neck. In a week or so I'd have my own car. And soon Sarah and I could start house-hunting in Atlantic City. I fantasized about shopping for condos and beach houses.

Sarah arrived at six-thirty. From across the misty parking lot, I saw her flash a smile and cock her head. I leapt off the brick wall in front of the cafeteria, bounded across the freshly paved asphalt lot and crunched her in my arms.

"Jason, I love you," she said, cooing and stroking the side of my face with her fingertips. Her going first with the I-love-you's was a bonus point. Because, let's face it: *I love you* means more than *I love you too.*

"I love *you* too," I said, trying to give my response a little oomph by emphasizing the "you" instead of the "too."

We hugged and kissed and entwined our fingers and stared into each other's eyes. Clutching and nuzzling, we headed into the cafeteria. Sarah's face beamed—golden-tanned and unblemished, her hair luxuriously brushed.

The cafeteria smelled like Pine-Sol and new sneakers. Holding hands, we waited in line for coffee, and then sat across from each other at a table in the corner. Sarah, wearing a white linen peasant blouse, khaki shorts and sandals, radiated summer beauty. Her hair seemed much thicker than I'd remembered it, with subtle streaks of red and brown. And I couldn't help but notice that her breasts had grown.

"What are you staring at?" she asked. "Were you looking at my tits?" She draped her body over the table, offering me a peek down the front of her blouse.

"I want you," I whispered. "I want to eat you up . . ."

I heard one of Sarah's sandals dropping to the floor, felt her bare foot brushing against the laces of my sneaker and then slowly, steadily up and down my calf.

I took one of her hands into mine, drew her index finger into my mouth and sucked on it. Sarah moaned. After a few seconds she withdrew her finger. "Let's cut school today," I suggested. "We can go to my house."

"Good Lord, it's the first day of school!"

"It's been twelve weeks," I said. "I might explode."

She clasped my hands in hers. "It's been hard for me too."

"Has it really?" I asked, elated. "That's so cool. Want to go down to Atlantic City on Saturday? It'll still be warm. You can see it in all its glory. Everything will be open."

Sarah winced. It was almost imperceptible—a quick gulp and a nervous, downward glance at the table. "We'll see," she said.

I had to be careful not to pressure her. A voice in my head told me to change the subject, talk about something else. The fall play, a movie I wanted to see, what kind of car I should buy—anything but Atlantic City.

"But you definitely want to move to Atlantic City right after we graduate, right?" I asked against my better judgment.

She hesitated. "Yeah."

"You don't sound excited about it."

"We're juniors," she sighed. "Can't we just focus on a great school year? We've got SATs . . ."

"That sounds like a consolation prize," I said, finishing off my coffee and crumpling the styrofoam cup in my hand. "Besides, I'm not taking the SATs because I'm not going to college."

The bell rang for first period. Sarah grabbed her backpack. The cafeteria echoed with students rising from their tables, hefting their book bags and filing out through the red lacquered doors like bees from a hive. We funneled out into the bobbing, shuffling swarm. The stairwell smelled of Clorox and fresh paint—and occasionally the sweet, pungent odor of pot wafting around giggly groups of kids who'd smoked a joint behind the school. The smell of pot reminded me of Skip, whom I hadn't even called when we got back from Atlantic City.

On Saturday morning, Dad and I visited a car dealership where Dad had bought his station wagons. "Something used, inexpensive and solid for my boy," Dad told the salesman, who led us across the asphalt lot and showed us four freshly waxed cars. I settled on a six-year-old powder blue Dodge Dart. It ran well, the radio worked and the back seat looked big enough for Sarah and me to lie down in.

"I'll take it," I said, putting the gearshift into park and squeezing the emergency brake toward the floor with my foot. The price was eight hundred and fifty dollars, plus some extra for the license plate and registration. I paid in cash and drove home behind Dad.

That night, Sarah and I told Mrs. Gilquist we were going to the movies. Instead, we went back to my house and fucked in my bedroom. When we were through, lying on our backs, our legs akimbo, I suggested she should send away for catalogs for Stockton State and Rutgers Camden. "They're the only colleges within a reasonable drive of Atlantic City. I mean, there are a couple junior colleges too, but that's pretty much just more high school . . ."

"You're right," she said, pulling the covers up over her head and burrowing into the mess of blankets.

I raised a blanket and announced into its folds: "'Cause if you want to go to college—and I'm not saying you have to, just if you want to—these are pretty much the only places you can go." She didn't answer. I got under the covers and clutched her naked arms. It was too dark to see, so when I leaned in for a kiss, I caught the side of her face. Sarah giggled. "Okay?"

"Mmm. . . . Okay, what?" she asked. Before I could answer, her tongue found my lips. She pressed through until I opened my mouth. Our tongues twirled around each other. I stroked Sarah's nipples with my fingertips. Her body was taut, ready for another round of sex. But I had something else in mind.

"Okay, will you call Stockton State and Rutgers and ask them to send you catalogs and stuff?"

"Jason!" she said sharply, loosening her embrace.

The phone on my nightstand rang. I wasn't going to answer it, but what if it was Dad calling to say he was coming home early? I didn't want him to find Sarah and me lolling around the house half-naked.

I rolled over, reached out from under the covers and grabbed the phone off the hook. "Hello?"

"Hey . . ." It was Skip.

"How's it going?" I asked. Sarah popped her head out from under the blankets. I covered the receiver with my hand. "*Skip*," I mouthed.

"What are you doing?" he asked. "Want to hack around?" He lowered his voice. "I've got a bottle of tequila and a nickel bag of Hawaiian."

"Well, um, Sarah's here . . . ," I said.

"Is he coming over?" asked Sarah.

I covered the receiver again. "Should I invite him?"

"Sure," she said.

"Come on over," I told Skip. "Give us like ten, fifteen minutes?"

Sarah and I got dressed, then I went down to the kitchen and made a fresh pot of coffee while Sarah fixed her hair.

Soon I heard a knock on the front door. On this warm, dewy night, Skip wore just a tee shirt and jeans, and he carried an army-green knapsack. He'd grown over the summer, his previously stubby body now an inch or so taller than me.

I greeted him with a friendly pat on his back. "Sarah will be down in a minute," I said like it was Sarah's house too. I led him into the kitchen. "We'd better go out back to smoke. My dad will be home in a couple hours and, with three of us smoking, I don't think we're going to be able to blow everything out the window."

"Right." Skip was an authority on getting high. He knew how long the smell lingered, how long your eyes stay red and your throat dry after you smoke.

"Coffee?" I asked.

"Nah." Skip opened the flap of his knapsack and produced the goods: a fifth of Mexican tequila and a black plastic film canister filled with grass. He arranged the pot, booze and paraphernalia on the table like he was setting up a chemistry experiment.

"So, how's school this year?" I asked, trying to make friendly conversation.

"Total bullshit. This year, next year, and then I am the fuck out."

"What do you want to do after high school?"

Skip leaned toward me, lowering his voice as if we weren't the only people in the room. "This guy I cop from knows a guy who owns land in Florida."

"You mean like real estate?"

"Like real estate for growing weed. Think about it: Florida is like Hawaii. Grass can't tell the difference."

"You're going to be a pot farmer?" It made sense. Skip's life had revolved around drugs for years now.

Sarah came into the kitchen, barefoot and coffee cup in hand, looking like she was at home, her hair piled atop her head and pinned back.

"Skip Schwartz, Sarah Gilquist," I said. "Sarah, Skip."

"Hey," said Skip, barely looking up from the joint he was rolling.

"Hey," said Sarah, looking Skip up and down, one hand on her hip.

"Lemme see your cup," Skip told Sarah. She handed him her half-full mug. Skip unscrewed the cap from the tequila bottle and poured a shot of the clear liquid into the coffee. Sarah lifted it to her nose and took a sniff. Skip raised the bottle and the two toasted across the table. Then they both drank, she from her coffee mug and he straight from the bottle.

Sarah wrinkled her nose and sucked in a breath to cool her throat. "Whew!"

After Skip chugged down about three gulps, he looked like his face was on fire. Sarah took another tentative sip, licked her lips and downed the rest of the coffee in one gulp.

Skip put the cap back on the tequila bottle. "Let's have a smoke out back."

We stepped out the kitchen door. Crickets chirped. A mild wind rustled the leaves on the big oak tree behind the house. Skip lit a joint, took a long hit and passed it to Sarah. She took a toke and passed it to me. I made a quick calculation: I had to get Sarah home by eleven; currently it was a little before eight. If I got high now, I'd be down enough to drive safely in three hours. I took a hit, held in the smoke, stifled the urge to cough and passed the smoldering joint back to Skip.

Inside the house the phone rang. It startled Skip. Instinctively he palmed the burning joint as if to hide it from whoever could see us from the telephone.

"I'd better get that. Could be my dad," I said. "In case he's coming home early." I took a second quick toke and darted inside. I was just starting to feel the high come on. "Hello?" I said into the receiver. Instantly I wondered if I was talking loud enough or too loud.

"Hi, Jason." It was Dad, his voice floating through the phone lines. "We're a man short."

I panicked. Was he going to tell me to come down to Pennsauken to help clean the twisting machine? I was high. But before I could say anything, Dad said, "I'm behind. I'm going to be home late tonight."

"Okay," I said, relieved. "Sarah's here. And Skip came over."

"Sounds like fun," said Dad. "Be good, and drive carefully. But do me a favor? Call Mike Simmons and ask him if he can come in an hour early tomorrow." Mike Simmons was one of Dad's managers. Mike usually worked at the Downingtown Farmers Market bakery, but sometimes he pulled a shift at Pennsauken. It was a long-distance call from Pennsauken to Mike's house, but a local call from ours to Mike's.

"If he can't come in early tomorrow, I'll call you back," I told Dad. "Otherwise, assume he can."

Outside, I heard Skip and Sarah laughing. I was glad they were getting along. I searched the phone list that we kept taped to the wall next to the kitchen phone. I dialed Mike's number and was happy to catch him at home—and happier still that he could make it in an hour early the next morning. Before I joined Sarah and Skip in the backyard, I stood over the kitchen table, held the tequila bottle in my hands and inspected it. Maybe I'd try alcohol one day. I was afraid it would make me vomit like Skip did at my bar mitzvah. Not that I'd be uncomfortable vomiting in front of Sarah. If you can vomit in front of your girlfriend, it's true love. But not tonight when I had to drive.

I went back outside. Skip and Sarah had finished the joint. They looked wiped out. Sarah wobbled. Skip stared at the night clouds.

"What do you think of booze?" I asked Sarah.

"I love it," she said with a loopy grin. She poked my ribs with her finger and when I turned, she planted a sloppy kiss on my face.

"Cool," I said, wiping a trickle of her spit off my chin with the back of my hand. "As long as you can walk a straight line in a couple hours."

"Yes, Mom," she said sarcastically.

I raised an eyebrow. "You probably shouldn't drink any more tonight because you have to be home at eleven and you look kind of fucked up as it is."

"She can handle her drugs and booze," said Skip.

"Yeah!" Sarah chimed in loudly. "I can handle myself, thank you." She elbowed Skip in his ribs, a friendly gesture I didn't like. Now they were laughing at a joke I didn't get—something to do with tiptoeing past comatose mothers.

Meanwhile, over at the Brookline Family Movie Theater, where *That's Entertainment II* was playing at seven-thirty and ten o'clock, in the middle of a song and dance spectacular, Jeanette MacDonald looked into the camera, thrust out her arms and announced: "*Your attention please, Sarah Gilquist, please report to the box office. Sarah Gilquist. You have a phone call.*"

We heard about Jeanette MacDonald from some kids at school who were at the show. If we'd been there, Sarah would have keeled over and died from embarrassment, and the theater manager would have gotten back on the phone and told Mrs. Gilquist, "She's not available. She's dead." Instead he said something like, "No one here by that name. Sorry."

A couple hours later, after Skip had gone home and Sarah had drunk a cup of coffee to sober up, we arrived in front of her house. As I walked her up the path to the front door, it creaked open ominously. Mrs. Gilquist stood in the entranceway, drink in hand, swishing an ice cube around the bottom of her glass. "She knows," Sarah hissed, shooting me a nervous glance.

"Bull*shit*," I whispered through the side of my mouth. "How could she know? She's drunk herself. When you're drunk you can't tell if somebody else is drunk. That's a known fact."

"Where'd you hear that?" Sarah asked.

"It's a law of thermodynamics. A vacillating object has no frame of reference from which to observe another vacillating object."

"Sarah!" Mrs. Gilquist barked.

"Fuck," I whispered. "She knows."

Mrs. Gilquist dispatched me with a condescending thrust of her chin.

Sarah's breath smelled like booze and weed, but it was too late for a peppermint Life Saver or a hit of mouthwash. "Call me in the morning," I whispered. "And try not to breathe around your mom. When she sways, you should sway in the same direction. Love you."

"Love you too," she said dutifully.

I skulked back down the path to my car, afraid to turn around for a final look at the woozy mother-daughter tableau.

When I arrived home, I was surprised to see Skip waiting outside the front door.

"Hey," I said.

"Hey," said Skip. "Want to go down the woods by the creek?"

"I think I had enough to smoke tonight, thanks."

Skip looked down at his sneakers. "Nah, I mean, to talk."

The night was still warm, good walking weather. I wasn't tired. "Yeah, sure, man," I said. We went down the hill and around the next block toward the woods. We didn't talk much along the way, just took in the night, the rippling leaves in the soft wind, the tail end of summer. The full moon glowed like a yellow doughnut.

In the woods we walked by moonlight down the root-strewn path to the creek. "Sarah's mom's a nut job," I said when we reached the clearing and sat next to each other on the pebbly bank.

"Lots of moms are nut jobs," said Skip, lying on his back, staring at the sky. "Half the neighborhood. Fucking crazy, popping uppers and downers all day."

"Which is what you do, basically," I said.

Skip turned to me. "At least I cop to being high. The moms don't. To them it's just life. You know?"

"And that's the difference?" I asked.

"Fuck yeah."

We lay on our backs, listening to the creek trickle and the leaves rustle. It felt like we were nine years old again, before Skip discovered getting wasted.

"Hey, Jason?"

"Hmm?"

"Sarah kissed me."

"Huh?"

"She kissed me."

I rolled over, propped my chin on my palm with my elbow on the ground. "Like, on the cheek? Like a friendly kiss?"

He didn't answer.

"Skip, what are you talking about?" I said.

He took a deep breath. "No. Like, with her tongue."

"Oh, bullshit," I said. Obviously he was so jealous of Sarah and me that he had to split us up. "I'm just going to forget you said that because it's so over the top that I must have been hallucihearing." I turned away, laid my head on the ground and stared straight up at the moon.

"I'm serious," he said. "I didn't know whether to tell you, I didn't think you'd believe me."

I hoisted myself up to a sitting position. "When?"

Skip still lay on his back, eyes closed. "When you were on the phone with your old man."

"You're full of shit."

Skip didn't reply.

"Okay then, how was it?" I asked, facetiously. "That was your first kiss, right?"

"No. There's this ninth grader, Dawn, she makes out for joints and she promised me a blow job for a quarter ounce."

"Sounds like true love."

"I'm telling you the truth," he said, pulling himself up to sit beside me. "You went inside and like two seconds later she's ramming her tongue down my throat."

"Sure, Skip. And what did you do?"

"I gagged. I was like, 'whoa!' So she stops for a second, and then she said she wanted to eat me up . . ."

That came like a kick in the stomach. How would Skip have known *that*?

"I'm really sorry, man," he said. "I tried to stop her. I pulled away. She was pushing her tongue against my teeth."

I'd never punched anyone before. I didn't know how it felt, didn't know whether it was like in the movies where one guy socks another guy's jaw and you hear a loud smack. I made a fist and swung it as hard as I could at Skip's face. The punch landed with a soft thud, like a rock hitting a bag of mud. And it didn't send Skip reeling like a movie punch. He just looked at me and blinked.

I threw a second punch. This time he caught my wrist, deflecting the blow. I heaved my other arm at his nose, and missed, and tried again, my fists hammering at his face and head. Skip caught both my arms and wrestled me back to the ground. I freed my knee and thrust it at his balls. Again I missed. He used his weight to hold me down. I hadn't even realized how strong and stocky Skip had grown in the past couple of years. The longer he held me, the harder I fought. Twisting and pulling, I tried to free my feet for a kick, my fists for a blow to his head. But Skip didn't try to hit back. "Fucking asshole bastard!" I yelled, writhing under his weight.

Meanwhile Skip pleaded with me. "I'm sorry, I'm really sorry."

Exhausted, punched out, teary eyed and covered in dirt, I let my body go limp under his. At last he stood up. Tentatively he backed away, his hands out, supplicating me not to go after him.

I sat on the ground, stared straight ahead, breathing hard.

"I'm really sorry," he said.

"You know what, Skip? Take your weed and your booze and your pills and don't come around anymore. Don't fucking call me. Don't come over and get me high. Just leave plastic, phony old me alone. *Okay*?"

Our eyes met. His were full of sadness, round and damp. He held out his hands to help me up. I didn't budge.

"I should have blown you off a long time ago, after you came down to Atlantic City and shit on me and my friends and my dad. I should have dumped you after my bar mitzvah when you made a jackass out of yourself."

Resigned, Skip turned and walked away, up the path and out of sight in the dark. I sat alone, trying not to think, just listening to my breath going in and out. I imagined that each inhale was a high toss and each exhale a slow, easy catch. I tuned out the woods and the creek and concentrated on my breath—in and out, like a big, wide cascade pattern. Nothing fancy. No tricks. No patter. Just high, wide throws and gentle catches. A sudden wind brushed my face. My eyes stung.

After a while I got up and brushed off my shirt and pants. I wiped my nose, scratched at the dirt behind my ears, ran my fingers through my hair and headed back to my house for a shower before Dad got home.

I want to eat you up. Yeah, right.

SARAH CALLED at seven-thirty the next morning. I picked up the phone in the kitchen, where I was drinking a cup of coffee. Dad was still asleep. It was his morning off. My arm muscles ached from wrestling with Skip the night before.

"Hey," I cooed into the receiver. "How do you feel this morning?"

"Okay," she said, her voice low.

"Hung over?"

"Not really."

"What about Atlantic City today?" I asked.

"Go without me. She's really mad. She called the movie theater last night. She knows we weren't there."

I got up from the table and walked to the cupboard above the oven, the phone cord stretching behind me. I took a cereal bowl and a box of Cheerios from the cupboard and grabbed the milk from the fridge. "What did you tell her?" I asked.

"I told her we were at *The Godfather II*," Sarah said. "I swore up and down. I told her she must have gotten it mixed up; I told her we already saw *That's Entertainment II.*"

Returning to the table, I poured the Cheerios in the bowl, then some milk. "Good thinking. I can swing by wherever *Godfather*

II's playing and pick a couple ticket stubs off the ground, so we can have something to show her."

"Don't bother," said Sarah. "She won't listen to reason."

I worked a big spoonful of cereal and milk into my mouth, chomped on it and swallowed quickly. "Are we going to have to wait all the way until Monday to see each other?"

"Jason, don't whine. Monday's tomorrow."

"You make it sound so casual."

"Go by yourself today," she said. "Maybe I can get away next weekend."

I flipped my tablespoon in the air for a triple twirl and caught it neatly between my thumb and forefinger.

"I think I hear her," said Sarah. "I have to go. I love you."

And she said it first!

I rubbed my sore shoulder. In the clear light of morning, Skip's accusation was absurd. "Before you go—," I said. "When I got home last night, Skip was still there. He told me . . ." I hesitated. "You . . . tried to kiss him." I could hear Sarah breathing on the other end of the line. "Which I know was total bullshit." I waited a few seconds. Sarah was silent. "I mean, it's total bullshit, right?"

"Yeah," she said. "I mean . . ."

I winced. "*What*?" I asked, louder than I'd intended. "You mean *what*?"

"I don't remember much," she said. "I remember getting home and my mom being really mad. And she kept asking me questions, like hammering at me—where were we? Why didn't I answer the phone at the movie theater? I was crying. I told her we weren't at *That's Entertainment*."

"But you didn't kiss Skip, right?"

"No, I don't think so," she said, her voice cracking. "I don't remember. I'm sorry."

"Don't worry about it. Skip's jealous and I'm sick of his bullshit. I should have kicked him to the curb a long time ago."

Sarah told me she had to go, and then she got off the phone pretty quickly. *I love you. Love you too, click.* I sat at the kitchen table, receiver in hand, listening to the silence on the other end of the line.

I had to believe her. Why would she kiss Skip? On the other hand, Skip had plenty of reasons to claim she had. If I split up with Sarah like he wanted me to, he'd have me all to himself. I'd be heartbroken and he'd bring me drugs. If she'd kissed him she'd remember it. Skip could go to hell. And he could take his weed and his booze and his ninth grade girl who would suck his dick for a quarter ounce with him. As far as I was concerned, Skip could suck *my* dick.

I STARRED IN *Arsenic and Old Lace* in the fall and *The Odd Couple* in the spring. In May, Miss Smith planned to hold upper-class-only auditions for next fall's production of *Inherit the Wind*. I worked hard on my acting—doing my best to share the stage, send the lines and receive the cues like Miss Smith suggested.

"I can't give it any meaning from my life," I told her at one rehearsal, after she said I sounded insincere. "The line doesn't mean anything to me."

"You have to discover the meaning," she said from the front row where she sat beside Katie the stage manager. "That's the magic of acting. Allow the words to transport you. And listen to the other characters. *Receive* their words."

Frustrated, I shook my head and circled the stage, script in hand. I didn't believe in magic. Not Miss Smith's. Not Jimmy's. I believed in pretending—and in practicing. Hats didn't disappear and reappear magically; there had to be a logical explanation. Theater was make-believe; words couldn't actually transport anybody anywhere. "Thanks," I said. "I'll try harder."

Most weekends, I got up early on Saturday morning and drove to Atlantic City. I'd hang out at Norman and Betty's, playing pinball with Lita until lunchtime. Lita was becoming weird. Sometimes when I was playing, she'd walk up behind me and press her body against mine. At first I thought it was accidental, and by the time I realized she was doing it on purpose, I was too embarrassed to say anything since I'd been letting it go for so long. It was one of those things—like owning a house you don't tell your wife about—that if you don't get in front of right away, it becomes harder and harder to come clean about.

At four o'clock I'd drive back home, take a shower and pick up Sarah at seven. Her mother was softening somewhat. We were allowed to go out every weekend. "I had a really great time today in Atlantic City," I said one Saturday night on the way to the movies. "Except for Lita. I mean, I like her and all, but God, she's all over me." I stole a glance across the car seat to see if Sarah looked jealous. But all she did was gaze evenly out the window. I was hoping for a flicker of suspicion on her part, something to show me that she thought rubbing other people when you were Jasonansarah was wrong.

"So, what do you think?" I asked.

"Lita sounds like a tramp," she said with a shrug.

"Well, I don't know about that. She's just a kid. But the point is, you don't approve of that kind of behavior, right?"

Sarah patted my knee. "Jason, I trust you, if that's what you're getting at."

As eleventh grade wore on, I grew increasingly anxious about the upcoming summer. One day in the spring, when Sarah and I were sitting on the bleachers behind school watching the track team practice, I asked her about spending the summer with Dad and me on the boardwalk.

"Not this year," she said as three runners raced past us, their green and white Adidas thudding softly on the track's clay surface. "My mother would never let me."

"Have you tried asking her?"

"If I asked her that, she wouldn't let me go out with you."

I made a sour face and shook my head disappointedly. In a little more than a year, we'd have everything exactly where we wanted it. We'd tell Mrs. Gilquist our plan, and if she didn't like it she didn't have to come to the wedding.

18

On a soggy Saturday morning at the end of April, I drove to Atlantic City to buy a house.

Instead of the speedy and direct Atlantic City Expressway, I chose the slower, intimate Black Horse Pike—a sluggish blacktop snaking through sleepy south Jersey towns, past strip malls and motels, trailer parks and biker bars, roller rinks and Dairy Queens; along fallow fields that in September would teem with soybeans, peaches and corn; past the dense pine forest to the marshes. As I crossed over the bay, Atlantic City's skyline looked like a painted backdrop, the tall hotels like cardboard cutouts tickling the brooding clouds.

I rolled down my window. The familiar aroma of salt air floated in. I took a deep breath. Exhaling, I thought about Sarah. Her mother wouldn't let her out this weekend because last Saturday Sarah had come home from *The Odd Couple* cast party an hour late. I'd driven back to her house as fast as I could, and once again her mom was waiting at the door, nightcap in hand, ominously swirling her ice cubes.

When I pulled onto Ventnor Avenue, I spotted an empty parking space in front of a real estate company office. It was a good omen. I darted into a tiny, cluttered storefront that smelled like stale cigarette smoke. Three desks took up most of the office's space. Two sat empty, and a pudgy, sandy-haired man wearing crooked wire-frame glasses and a white polyester shirt occupied the third. He was eating an omelet stuffed into a long Italian roll.

"I know you! Pretzel juggler!" said the real estate man, wiping his hands on a paper towel. He stood up to shake my hand in his meaty paw. "I'm a fan! My wife and kids, we've seen your act a hundred times!"

He handed me a business card. According to it, his name was Monty Dweck.

Monty Dweck steered me to an empty chair beside his desk. After some small talk about Dad, the bakery and the casinos, I explained that my girlfriend and I were planning to move down permanently after high school, and I didn't know whether we should buy or rent. I told him I had plenty of money saved up and that Dad would be willing to co-sign if he had to. This last part wasn't exactly true, but I had a plan for persuading Dad.

"How old are you?" Monty Dweck asked.

"I'll be eighteen." Which was technically true. I would be eighteen. In eleven months.

Monty Dweck opened his desk drawer and took out a loose-leaf binder filled with snapshots of houses.

"Look't this," he said, pointing his thick finger at a picture of a bungalow with a green metal fence around it. "Look't. Cute as a button. Virginia Avenue: Close to the bay, close to the beach. Can you beat that?"

Virginia Avenue was pretty nice. "How much?" I asked.

"Thirty-eight five," said Monty Dweck. He whomped his fist on his desk like an auctioneer pounding his gavel.

"Thirty-eight five," I repeated, taking my own earnest whomp at the arm of my chair. Monty Dweck lit a cigarette. "How high are the ceilings?" I asked.

He looked confused, but then he snapped his fingers. "So you can practice your act. Am I right? Want to ride over? Want to take a look?"

Outside Monty Dweck's office the wind gusted and seagulls cawed. Monty Dweck's kidney-bean-colored Nova sat in front of my Dart. I climbed into the passenger's seat. Inside, the car was neat, but it smelled like the morning breath of a chain smoker who hadn't brushed his teeth in a week. He started the car and I cracked my window.

"It's a good time to invest in real estate," said Monty Dweck as we pulled up to a red light in front of Tony's House of Subs on Atlantic Avenue. The sweet, greasy smell of cheesesteaks drifted into the car. "Property values will triple after they open the casinos." He whomped the heel of his hand against the steering wheel. "Triple!" He blew a thick smoke ring into the windshield.

Who cared about property values? I wasn't speculating. I was buying a home. The question was whether I could afford it. We'd be able to put a lot down—more than most young couples. I had almost $17,000 in my savings account. Even so, if the price did actually triple, we might never be able to buy.

Monty Dweck turned right on Virginia Avenue—a snug block of identical cottages—then made another right into a narrow concrete driveway. He opened his door and stepped out of the Nova, massaging his lower back and stretching as if he'd just driven across the Yukon Territory.

"It's got a decent garage," Monty Dweck told me. "Can you beat that?" Near the back door was the spigot and showerhead for when we returned from the beach. The backyard was about the size of a skillet. But who cared? Who needs a backyard two blocks from the beach?

I followed the realtor up three cement steps to a porch covered by a metal awning. The glossy white floorboards felt solid underfoot, and the green and white porch furniture looked homey and familiar. I imagined Sarah and me cuddling together on a porch swing on a rainy afternoon.

Monty Dweck opened the storm door; the hinges squeaked and the glass panes rattled. "Two or three squirts of 3-in-One. That's all she needs. Storm door's brand new."

Inside it was sparse—cheap furniture and a few framed prints of sailboats on the pale yellow walls. They reminded me of Mom's paintings on our walls at home, but Mom's were original. A faint odor of mildew mingled with the familiar, salty smell of the beach. A big TV sat in the living room, along with a scruffy oriental rug, an overstuffed green sofa and a couple of easy chairs. The first-floor ceilings were high enough for juggling. When Monty Dweck took me back into the kitchen, he seemed surprised that I knew my way around a gas range, nodding his approval when I tested each burner and turned on and off the broiler.

On the second floor were a big hallway closet, a tiny, white-tiled bathroom and three unremarkable bedrooms, each with a flimsy cot, a chest of drawers and four walls' worth of colorless, pattern-less, peeling wallpaper.

"So whatcha thinkin', Pretzel Boy?" asked Monty Dweck.

"I like it," I said. "The first-floor ceilings are perfect, and I love the showerhead out back. But I guess we'll have to buy a new bed because these mattresses look pretty cruddy."

"You may wanna refurnish," he said, wagging his fingers at the walls. "New wallpaper while you're at it, but hey, it's in move-in condition."

"Okay," I said. "So what happens next?"

He puffed his cigarette. "Make an offer."

I leaned back against the hall closet door. "I offer to buy this house."

"Nah, a written offer," he said. "I got a form in the car. You put down a deposit, and if ya can't get a mortgage, ya get your deposit back." Monty Dweck walked down the hall to the bathroom, where he took a final drag off his cigarette, tossed the butt into the toilet and flushed. "Ya hear that? Is that water pressure or what?" He patted the toilet seat like it was a dog. "Do you want this house?"

"Absolutely," I said. "I'll talk to my dad and my girlfriend to-night."

Back downstairs, as we were getting ready to leave, Monty Dweck said, "Not to rush you, but there's already interest. If you want it, I'm telling you, jump on it. Tell your old man to call me at home."

Monty Dweck locked up the house and we drove back to his office.

Before heading back to Philadelphia, I wanted to stop by the boardwalk for a box of saltwater taffy for Sarah and her mom. Leaving my car parked in front of Monty Dweck's office, I buttoned my big green army coat against the air gusts and lurched down Arkansas Avenue into the wind. The bright sunlight on the boardwalk strained to warm the air. With the wind to my back, I walked to North Carolina. In front of the old Chalfonte Hotel, a sign stopped me cold:

FUTURE SITE OF
RESORTS INTERNATIONAL CASINO

Underneath that, next to the name of the mayor and the architect and a bunch of other guys, it read:

ATLANTIC CITY:
AMERICA'S GAMING PLACE

A cyclone fence surrounded hotel, construction equipment and scaffolding.

I was confused. I didn't think that gambling was immoral, but it could look that way because it was against the law everywhere but here and in Las Vegas—like a dirty secret.

A half hour later, sweets in hand, I returned to my Dart, warmed up the engine and headed back to Philadelphia to tell Dad and Sarah about the house. While I understood that Dad faced a few financial hurdles on account of paying out of pocket for Mom's experimental treatments and losing his lawsuit against Peppy the Clown, I suspected he could still co-sign my mortgage. After all, I was going to put a lot of money down.

When I got home late that afternoon, I couldn't decide whether to tell Dad about the house first or to rush upstairs and call Sarah. I charged through the front door. Dad was sitting in the dining room, reading a newspaper and listening to an Artie Shaw tape.

"Slow down!" he said as I barreled upstairs. "Are you hungry? I ordered pizza."

"Yes!" I yelled from the stairs. "Be right down!" I flopped on my bed, snatched the telephone from the night table and dialed Sarah's number. After two rings somebody picked it up. I knew it was Mrs. Gilquist even before she said hello. I'd know that pause anywhere. Her voice was soft and numb. "Is Sarah there?"

"No."

Silence.

"Well, I sure hope you like saltwater taffy, Mrs. G." More silence. "Because I picked some up for you and Sarah when I was in Atlantic City today."

Thick, creepy silence.

Unnerved, I ventured, "Well, uh, could you ask her to give me a call when she gets in?"

"I'll inform her that you called."

After I hung up, I sat on the edge of my bed and buried my face in my hands. One year and two months to go. I could endure that.

The smell of freshly brewed coffee wafted into my bedroom, accompanied by the sweet, swinging strains of Artie Shaw's clarinet. I joined Dad in the kitchen, where he'd already poured us each a cup of coffee. "Thanks," I said, sitting down at the table across from him, stirring in some half-and-half and taking a sip.

"So," he said. "What's happening in Atlantic City?"

"I went by the Chalfonte on my way to pick up taffy for Sarah and her mom," I said. "You should see it. They're seriously gonna have gambling down there."

Dad took off his glasses and cleaned the lenses with a napkin.

"Oh yeah, and I bought a house," I added, trying to sound casual.

Dad raised his eyebrows and peered at me. Silently he finished wiping his glasses and put them back on his face. He took another sip of coffee, set down his cup and cleared his throat. "Is that so?" he asked.

"Well, not really. But there's this place on Virginia Avenue, and the guy said we'd better jump on it."

"Wait. Who?" Dad asked. "What guy?"

I showed him Monty Dweck's business card. "He's a good guy," I said.

"I'm sure he is," said Dad. "But he's a real estate guy. They all say you'd better jump on it."

"But it's a great house," I said. "Three bedrooms and a little spigot out back." Reaching into my pants pocket, I showed him the paperwork Monty Dweck had sent me home with: the form to put in our offer; a pamphlet about Monty Dweck's office; and a photocopied sheet with a picture of the house and a written description.

After reading everything, he looked up at me. "Are you sure about this?"

I held out my hands. "This is all I ever talked about. We're graduating next year and it's time to start looking for a place." I took a sip of coffee and lowered the black ceramic mug to the table. "Property values are going up, in case you haven't noticed."

Dad stared into his coffee. When he looked up, his glasses were foggy from the steam. "Yes, I've noticed. But you're only in eleventh grade."

"I *know*," I said, trying to keep myself composed. I didn't want to sound whiny. I wanted to sound like a rational, house-buying adult. "But come on, I'm not like other kids my age. I've been working since I was seven. What other seventeen-year-old has seventeen grand saved up?

"And the thing is," I said, trying to second-guess his next objection, "the house will be in my name, not Sarah's, because we're not married yet and she has no source of income. In case you're worried about a teenage couple buying a house together, because yeah, that would be impulsive."

Dad poked his forefinger at the bridge of his glasses. For several seconds he sat in silent contemplation. Then he said, "I'll make you a deal. You promise to take one college class every semester. You can go to Atlantic Community College. Do that and if I approve of the house, I'll co-sign."

I rubbed my chin and mulled his offer. "One class per semester? But not during summer, right?"

"Fall and spring," he said, picking up Monty Dweck's business card and studying it. "I've got to go down and see a pizza guy on Pacific Avenue about an oven he's got for sale. So I'll call this Dweck fellow on Monday and I'll drive down later in the week and take a look at the house, kill two birds with one stone."

I gulped. "Thanks!"

"No promises," he said. "I want to see the house first. It's a big step, son."

I smirked. "I'm not your stepson."

A car pulled up in front of the house, its headlights casting a glare into the dining room. "Pizza's here," Dad said, reaching into his pocket and handing me a small wad of cash. "Go pay the guy and I'll get the paper plates."

On Monday morning in the cafeteria before first period, Sarah was surprised to hear about the house. "You *what*?" she asked. "You bought *us* a house? Are you serious?"

"Buy*ing*," I said. "I'm buying us a house."

She glared at me. "Do I have any say in this?"

"Well, yeah, of course. But let's face it. Real estate values are going up, so it's like we're losing money every week. What was I supposed to do? Wait until the prices triple and we can't afford it? Sarah, it's the most incredible opportunity! We gotta jump on this. Dad's going to co-sign, but you don't have to do anything. I'll handle everything. You should see it. This weekend we can go down . . ."

Sarah lowered her head and stared blankly at the table. "We're seventeen," she said.

"But it's our dream home."

"*Your* dream home." She got up and stormed out of the cafeteria, leaving her backpack on a seat.

"You left your backpack!" I called after her. She didn't turn around. I picked up her green canvas bag. Her reaction to the news had stung, but she'd come around.

I decided to write her a love note and put it in her backpack. But when I opened the pack and looked inside, I forgot all about our dream home. There, on top of her spiral notebooks, a blue canvas loose-leaf binder and her French IV textbook, was a catalog from Greywood College in St. Charles, Missouri.

I felt like a freefalling skydiver, gaining speed and losing perspective. Not knowing up from down, the only thing I could grasp was the plain fact that no one commuted between Atlantic City, New Jersey, and St. Charles, Missouri.

19

"AND THAT'S HOW I wound up buying the house on Virginia Avenue. When I was seventeen."

Eileen, Ruth and I sidestep an ultramarine-blue tram hurtling toward us, its dozen or so cars enclosed in thick plastic sheets, offering riders a tradeoff: relative heat in exchange for the sensation of looking at the boardwalk through Vaseline. Posters slapped on the sides of the cars promote Trump and Harrah's and Resorts International.

"My dad was broke, and I bought a house," I say.

"Poor Sarah," says Eileen. "You must have been driving her crazy."

"I'm trying to picture you as a teenager," says Ruth.

"Picture the most insecure secure boy in the world," I say.

"Insecure," says Eileen. "You know how when I'm on my way out of the house you always ask where I'm going?"

I cock my head. "Do I?"

"All the time. I used to think it was just a habit. Then I thought you were being controlling, but that's not right, is it? You're actually afraid, in some unconscious way, that when I leave I won't come back."

"I don't know," I say. The wind blows harder. I tug at my wool cap, pulling it over my ears. "But I backed Sarah into a corner, I know that. We never talked about moving down here. It was always just me *telling* her about it—and her nodding. And then I . . . well, the way it worked out, I guess I kind of scapegoated Miss Smith."

"The teacher? How was she involved?" asks Ruth.

I RACED OUT of the cafeteria and down the main hallway in time to see Sarah disappear into the physics lab. Of course, I could be overreacting, I thought as I poked my head into the lab with about thirty seconds left before the bell. "Pssst! Sarah! Pssst!" When I finally got her attention, I waved the backpack at her, and she came to the door to retrieve it. I'd decided not to say anything about the Greywood catalog. Better to process this new information and approach it with a clear head. After all, it could be someone else's catalog. Maybe Sarah's idiot guidance counselor gave it to her, as if he knew what was best for her. There were many logical explanations. She wasn't necessarily secretly planning to break up with me and run away to Missouri.

But when Sarah stepped out the door, I shoved the backpack at her. "Why?" I asked, angrily. I could barely catch my breath. Sarah looked nonplussed. She shook her head. My temples thundered; tears welled in my eyes. "How can you do this to me? Were you planning on telling me, or was I supposed to find out on graduation day when the movers ended up half a truck short?"

Clutching her backpack, Sarah retreated two steps. "Don't be so loud!" she said, trying to worm her way back into the lab, but I blocked the entrance with my arm. "I don't know what you're talking about," she said. "But I've got Physics if you don't mind . . ."

"Greywood *fucking* College!" I said.

Sarah blushed. "Jason, keep your voice down!"

I gulped air. "Greywood," I said, tempering my volume into a harsh whisper. She stared at me blankly. I stomped my foot and spun on my heels as if I was about to storm off. I hesitated so that she could call my name, explain everything and ease my frantic, runaway imagination before the bell rang. But when I turned, she'd retreated to the lab.

I trudged down the hall to my homeroom. Screw the bell.

After Physics Sarah had English. At the sound of the bell, I raced to Miss Smith's room. No one had arrived there yet. I waited, out of breath, until Sarah showed up. She shook her head when she saw me. "How in the world did you get all the way over here? You're going to be late for class."

"I don't care. I've got to know about this Greywood place!"

"Don't worry about it. I'm not going to Greywood College."

"Seriously?" I heaved a sigh of relief.

"What were you doing in my bag?" she asked.

"Come on, Sarah. You know I could never fit in your bag."

"Don't make stupid jokes." She jutted out her hip and chomped on her lower lip.

"I was going to slip a love note in there, but I saw the thing from Greywood and it freaked me out. I'm buying this house for us and we're gonna have a life there. And I need to know you're not leaving me."

Sarah clasped my hands in hers. "I love you," she said. "I'm not leaving you. And if I were going to—which I am not, okay? But if I were, I would *tell* you."

I gave her a peck on her lips. "See you at lunch," I said. "Oh, and by the way, where'd you get that catalog?"

At that moment, Miss Smith arrived, carrying her briefcase and an armful of books. "Greetings and salutations, you two!" she said brightly. I held the door open for her. "Don't be late," she warned Sarah. "And I expect to see *you* at auditions for *Inherit the Wind* on Friday."

Sarah smiled and cocked her head toward the classroom. "She gave it to me."

"Gave you what?" I asked.

"The catalog. Did you forget already, silly?"

It felt like a sucker punch. I'd confided in Miss Smith, told her about our plan to live in Atlantic City. And now she turns around and tries to break us up? How could she do this to me?

"You should go," said Sarah. "You're late enough as it is." She disappeared into her English class, closing the door behind her, leaving me staring through the glass. Miss Smith saw me. She turned and smiled and shooed me away. I stared her down venomously. When she saw the expression on my face, she looked astonished. Slowly, sadly, I shook my head; then I walked away.

Over the next few days, I snubbed Miss Smith every chance I got—grimacing at her in the hallways, shunning her when she walked through the student lounge. She shook her head like she couldn't figure out why I was pissed. Yeah, right. Miss Innocence. I'd show her. Auditions for next fall's *Inherit the Wind* were set for Friday. That's when I'd give her a piece of my mind.

Miss Smith could inherit *my* wind.

Arriving at the auditorium on Friday afternoon, I pushed the big doors wide open in a grand, attention-getting gesture, making a regal entrance into the unlit hall, my chest thrust out like a rooster's. When I arrived at the front row where Miss Smith and Katie the stage manager sat, Miss Smith gestured toward the row of seats behind her. "You're first, but it's early. Let's wait until more people show up."

I sat two rows behind Miss Smith. She'd always wanted to see truth in my acting. Boy, was she about to get it.

Other kids filtered into the auditorium, trooping down the aisle and taking their seats. At last Miss Smith stood up. "Good afternoon, ladies and gentlemen," she said. "Welcome to upper-class auditions for *Inherit the Wind*. I'm excited about this production. We have several talented people trying out"—here she glanced at me—"who have contributed so much over the past couple of years. I have watched them blossom, and I am proud of their accomplishments." She paused to clear her throat. "Next year they will be seniors and I thought it would be a good idea to give them a chance to work on their roles over the summer."

Katie handed Miss Smith her clipboard. "Okay, everybody," Miss Smith said to the small assembly. "When I call your name, pick up a script from Katie and report to center stage. I will tell you what character to read. When I say 'thank you,' you may stop where you are, hand your script back to Katie and return to your seat.

"Jason Benson, Howard Melvoin, Leroy Binder, Linda Abraham, Peter DeMascio, Alexander Greenberg and Ronald Wertkin," Miss Smith said. I sauntered down the aisle, picked up a copy of the script and reported to center stage. "Act two, scene two," Miss Smith told us. "Begin at the top of the scene."

We all knew that *Inherit the Wind* was about the famous Scopes trial of 1925. I was Henry Drummond, the lawyer based on Clarence Darrow, who defends Bert Cates, a high school teacher who dared to teach evolution. In the audition scene I confronted Matthew Brady, a character based on William Jennings Bryan, a windbag lawyer who ran for president three times.

My first line, a page or two into the dialogue, was "Objection!" I shouted it like I was warning Ronald Wertkin that his hair was on fire.

Inside my head, my internal dialogue with Miss Smith raged. *Objection, bitch! How dare you drive a wedge between Jasonansarah? How dare you presume you know what's best for my future wife? I object!* All heads turned toward me. "I ask the court to remind the learned counsel that this is not a Chautauqua tent. He is supposed to be submitting evidence to a jury. There are no ladies on the jury." The "ladies" line was because Brady, in ridiculing the teachings of Mr. Cates, had addressed the jury as "ladies and gentlemen." But when I said my lines, I had something else in mind. "Objection!" I spat, like a vulgarity. In the front row, Miss Smith sat expressionless, her mouth hanging open. Obviously she had received my line.

Emboldened, I stewed in resentment while Ronald Wertkin read Brady's next speech. When it was my turn to recite Drummond's speech, I transformed into an indignant advocate, alone against the world, confronting a grievous injustice. I barked my lines, every word ringing with contempt for my enemy in the front row. I spoke the truth—my indignation palpable. The words were someone else's, but the meaning was all mine. I wasn't pretending to be angry. I *was* angry. "Then why did God *plague* us with the power to think?" I shouted. Miss Smith was a plague. "Mr. Brady, why do you deny the one faculty which lifts man above all other creatures on the earth: the power of his brain to reason?"

I stalked the stage, scowling and waving my arms, thrusting my lines like daggers. At the height of the Brady/Drummond confrontation, Miss Smith called out, "Thank you." The other kids looked up from their scripts and shuffled toward the edge of the stage. But I continued, yelling Drummond's lines as well as the other characters'. I took on the persona of Brady, hollering, "Ridiculous, ridiculous! There is only one great Truth in the world."

I stepped to my right and became Drummond again, yelling at the spot where I'd just stood as Brady. "The Gospel according to Brady! God speaks to Brady, and Brady tells the world! Brady, Brady, Brady Almighty!" Miss Smith knows what's right! Smug spinster high school teacher! Smith, Smith, Smith Almighty!

"Thank you," Miss Smith repeated.

I broke through the fourth wall, bellowing like a preacher, deriding the startled English teacher. "The Lord is my strength!"

"I said 'thank you,'" she said coldly.

"What if a lesser human being—a Cates, or a Darwin—has the *audacity* . . ."

Miss Smith stood up. "That is quite enough!"

I looked up from my script and directly into Miss Smith's eyes. "The *audacity* to think that God might whisper to him?" And I kept on reading, looking up occasionally to see Katie the stage manager recoiled in her seat, her head buried in her arms. Other kids stood with their mouths agape like they were watching a head-on collision.

"Extend the Testaments!" I shrieked. "Let us have a Book of Brady!"

Miss Smith walked all the way to the edge of the stage. She put out her arms; I couldn't tell whether she wanted to hug me or yank me off the stage.

"Aw, fuck you!" I said, flinging the script halfway to the back wall. The auditorium felt as silent as a canyon. I stared into Miss Smith's astonished eyes and said one word: "Greywood."

At first she seemed puzzled. Then a look of recognition began to work its way across her face. She squeezed her lips shut.

No one stirred. I hopped off the stage and stormed out.

THE NEXT MORNING, the ringing phone awakened me. Groggy, fumbling for the receiver, I hoped it was Sarah calling to tell me that she'd heard about my confrontation with Miss Smith and wanted me to know she was on my side. I glanced at the clock: six-thirty. It could be Miss Smith calling to apologize. Most likely, though, it was Dad calling because he was short-staffed in Downingtown and wanted me to fill in after school.

"Hello?" I said sleepily.

I was surprised to hear Skip on the other end.

"How's it going?" he asked. In the background someone was yelling, but I couldn't make out the words.

"Pretty good." I glanced at the clock again. "What's up?"

"My mom's dead."

"Skip, what do you mean?"

"When my dad woke up he found her," he said. "She took all her pills before she went to sleep." I realized that the yelling in the background was Skip's dad. It was more like wailing, like my grandmother at the funeral home when we buried Mom.

I sat up with a jolt. "Oh my God, Skip. Want me to come over?"

"Uh, okay," he said.

As I got dressed, I recalled Skip telling me about his mom drinking Janitor in a Drum, and I thought about her on that couch, every day, year after year, with the lights dim and the TV on with no sound and the pill bottles lined up on the coffee table like bowling pins.

After I got dressed and poured myself a cup of coffee, I called Dad at his Downingtown bakery and told him the news. Then I chugged my coffee and headed out. When I arrived at Skip's, the front door was open. I popped my head in. "Hello?"

Skip answered from the second floor. "Come on up."

On my way to his bedroom, I peeked over the banister into the living room. The couch was empty and the TV off.

Skip was sitting cross-legged on his bed, using his thumb to crush a large white pill between a nickel and the cover of a math book. "Hey," he said without looking up, pulverizing the pill into white powder.

"My dad said to tell you he's sorry about your mom."

"Yeah, it sucks."

"What's that?" I asked, pointing at his lap.

"Percocet," he said. "Snorting gets it to your brain faster."

"That's good to know," I said, trying to sound earnest, not sarcastic. On one hand, it made perfect sense that Skip would be taking a painkiller. He was in pain. On the other hand, it was seven o'clock in the morning and his mom was dead—from pills, no less. On a small table next to Skip's bed lay three large joints. He saw me eyeing them. "Want to do one?" he asked.

I waved him off. "Thanks, no, maybe later. Where's your dad?"

"At the hospital, dealing with shit."

Now Skip was rolling up a dollar bill. With one finger, he slid the pile of white powder across the textbook and into a line about an inch long. He licked his finger, and then he bent over and snorted the crushed pill in one breath. He thrust his head back and closed his eyes.

So here we were: Skip getting wasted and me sitting by his side hoping he hadn't taken too much. Just like the old days.

All morning long, we sat in his room. He crushed and snorted pills. I occasionally went downstairs to refill our water glasses and grab some leftovers from the fridge. Around noon his dad came home. By the time he made his way upstairs, Skip had managed to slide the powdery textbook and the three unsmoked joints under his bed. I stood up. "Hi, Mr. Schwartz," I said. "I'm sorry about Mrs. Schwartz. My dad sends his condolences too."

Skip's dad's face was drained of its usual color. Normally dapper, he hadn't combed his hair or shaved. He wore a pair of dress slacks with a green pullover sweatshirt, and tasseled loafers on his feet, but no socks—obviously the first clothes he could grab after he called the ambulance. He didn't say much to Skip—just asked how he was getting along—and he thanked me for being there. "Boys," he told us, "I have to go to the funeral home. Will you be okay? There's tuna in the fridge. I'll be back around three." Skip sniffled, either on account of his mom dying or the dollop of Percocet lodged in his sinuses. He looked like a zombie, but his dad didn't notice. Grieving and being stoned look a lot alike—blot-faced, droopy-eyed.

There wasn't much to discuss. Skip wasn't my friend anymore, but I was his. If Dad were to die, it wouldn't even occur to me to call Skip. I'd call Sarah, and then I'd call Mom's parents, and Aunt Harriet in Cleveland, and Norman and Betty.

Around one o'clock we went down to the woods, to our clearing by the creek, where we'd spent so much time as kids and where, back in the fall, we'd had our big fight. Now he silently lit a joint and we passed it back and forth, taking long hits and staring at the creek. As always, when I looked at the water, I thought about its path to the ocean. I wondered how long that trip took. The silvery swirl carrying a twig might arrive in Atlantic City the same day as Dad and I. Unlike me, however, the water didn't long to reach its destination. It just went with the flow. I could do that when I juggled—no past or future; no expectations; no worry about Sarah keeping her promise to move to Atlantic City—just the pattern before me, and all my attention invested in maintaining it. I wanted my life to be like that. Like juggling. Like water flowing toward the ocean.

We smoked two joints all the way down until they were glowing roaches that stained our fingertips. We flicked them into the creek and watched them float away like water bugs. We sat in the clearing and listened to the creek and the wind riffling through the trees and looked up at the strands of clouds scattered across the flower-blue April sky. I was pretty stoned, and I wondered how

Skip managed to keep his shit together. In addition to the joints, he'd snorted about six Percocet pills. His eyes looked dazed, but he sat upright on the cool ground. Over the past four years he'd learned how to hold his drugs.

We didn't do much for the rest of the day—just skulked around the neighborhood, barely talking, mostly lost in our own thoughts. At around six o'clock, I told Skip I should get home.

"Yeah, me too," he said. "Some asshole aunts and uncles are coming over tonight."

Skip's mom's parents were both dead, and his dad's parents wouldn't arrive until tomorrow for the funeral. Same with Skip's brothers, who'd moved to San Francisco after college and hardly ever visited.

I reached out and clasped Skip's arm. "My dad's taking off to-morrow. We'll be at the funeral." We arrived in front of his house. "You going to be okay for now, man?" I asked.

"Yeah," he said, reaching out his hand, which I shook. He turned and walked up his driveway.

When I got home I went upstairs, took off my clothes, ran a hot shower and stepped in. I opened my mouth and tilted back my head, raised my arms and grasped the showerhead above me with both hands, like a soul singer clasping a microphone. The spray landed hard on my face, rivulets of water squiggling down my neck and chest and legs, circling the drain to the sewer, to the creek, to the river, to the bay, to the ocean.

Skip's mom's funeral was at her graveside, in a Jewish ceme-tery across town. When Dad and I arrived, I saw Skip, his dad, his brothers and a huddle of strangers standing around in their stiff suits, eyeing the fresh-dug grave with the dull black casket sus-pended above it by green nylon straps. A rabbi arrived. I recalled a few of the prayers from the Saturday morning service I'd learned for my bar mitzvah and recited again at Mom's funeral.

The service ended quickly. Afterward everyone went to Skip's house for smoked fish and cold cuts. Skip and I filled our plates in the dining room and took them upstairs.

"I don't even know those assholes," Skip said of his aunts, uncles and cousins who milled around downstairs, consoling one another with deep sighs and sober pats of elbows. Skip and I sat on his bed, plates balanced on our knees, smearing cream cheese and whitefish with plastic knives.

"Maybe you should go back down and get to know them," I said.

Skip looked at me like I was a turncoat. "Why the fuck would I do that?"

I shook my head. "Never mind."

For the rest of the day, Skip and I hung out in his room, slipping out for occasional walks around the neighborhood or down to the woods to smoke a joint, while his brothers and dad and relatives and friends swarmed the buffet.

Early in the evening, the rabbi arrived and handed out prayer books and yarmulkes. Skip's dad came upstairs to fetch us. Stoned out of our minds, we dragged ourselves downstairs. The moment Skip's brothers spotted us they knew we were high. I could feel their disapproving glares.

After the blessings, everyone stood around for about an hour. Dad had gone home earlier to make dinner, telling me I should stay as long as Skip needed me. But Skip didn't need me. He just needed to be high. When he invited me back up to his bedroom, I said, "No thanks, I gotta get home." Surreptitiously Skip slipped his hand into his shirt pocket and took out the remaining joint. Palming it so no one could see, he handed it to me. "Thanks," I said, discreetly pocketing it.

We shook hands. Downstairs, I offered my condolences to Skip's dad and brothers. His dad thanked me for being a good friend to Skip, for "always being there." I felt like a hypocrite. I was only there because I'd been plunked there, like a juggling ball that landed at a bad angle and bounced into somebody else's act.

20

CRUISING ALONG the Black Horse Pike on a muggy morning in June with the windows rolled down and the hot air slapping my face, I tried to sort out the conflicting thoughts that raced through my head. I felt simultaneously euphoric about the coming season and despondent over another Sarah-less summer.

Just one year remained before we could move to Atlantic City. For years, imagining the long wait as a juggling routine, I'd always found the strength to slog through: one throw, one catch, one day; one throw, one catch, another day. A week. A month. A year. When I worried about spending the summer apart, or about Mrs. Gilquist grounding Sarah for a petty infraction, or about Sarah changing her mind about Atlantic City, I'd slow down and concentrate on each breath as though it were a throw, a catch—an easy up and down.

It wasn't until I was miles down the Pike that I remembered I hadn't said goodbye to Skip. We'd seen each other two or three times after his mom died. One night we went down to the woods, smoked a joint and talked about our mothers.

"Remember the first time we met?" I asked as I passed the joint, its ember trailing like a mini fireworks display.

"Huh? No," he said.

"Yes you do!" I told him. How could he not? "Your kitchen floor? The pretend ocean? We swam on it, on our bellies."

Skip took a long toke. The ember glowed so bright I thought it would explode. He held the smoke in his lungs and closed his eyes. "Remember now?" I asked.

He shook his head and handed the joint back to me. I studied its ash, sniffed its plume of smoke. He exhaled. "Sorry, but it's not a big deal."

"Never mind," I said. "You're right. It doesn't matter. As long as you have plenty of good memories of your mom . . ."

He shrugged his shoulders. "I remember her getting wasted mostly. And her and my dad took us to an ice hockey game one time."

"Ice hockey. That's neat. I didn't know about that," I said, way too enthusiastically.

Now I was passing familiar farmland, a pine forest, glitter-green ponds and gas stations.

Sarah had yet to see the house on Virginia Avenue. During the school year, whenever I had invited her, she'd offered a good excuse: Curfew. Grounding. Mother needs her. But she had promised to move there after graduation, so I held on to that.

Passing a road sign that read ATLANTIC CITY 40 MILES, I thought about the final six weeks of eleventh grade, and how when Sarah heard about my *Inherit the Wind* audition she got mad at me.

"I can't believe you said 'Fuck you' to her," Sarah said when she saw me in the cafeteria my first day back after Skip's mom's funeral.

"It wasn't a big deal," I said. "Poor Skip."

Sarah sighed. "I'm sorry about Skip's mother, but you can't talk to people the way you talked to Miss Smith."

"You're right. I'm sorry."

"It's not me you owe an apology to."

I set my white styrofoam cup on the table and held out my hands ingenuously. "She tried to break us up."

"No she didn't! All she did was give me a catalog to look at, and you overreacted. Jason, you need to do something about your anger."

"I'm not angry. I'm principled. You don't go around undermining people's relationships."

"Shut up!" she said. "There is no principle. Everyone's saying you had a nervous breakdown."

I shook off her criticism. "Do I look nervous? Do I look broken down?" I set my elbows on the table and rested my chin in my palms. "No. I look principled."

"You're not funny," she said. Then she stood up and walked away.

Miss Smith barely spoke to me for the rest of the school year. And to no one's surprise, I wasn't cast in the show.

ATLANTIC CITY 20 MILES. I stuck my head out the window and inhaled a deep breath. Soon I'd be snug in our cozy house. I missed Sarah, but it was comforting to know that this was the last time we'd be apart. Despite the anxiety of temporarily being only half a Jasonansarah, I felt pretty good. Dad was coming down the next day and he'd be staying with me at the new house all summer. He'd insisted on paying rent in addition to what I earned working at the bakery. All that, plus the money I'd make from juggling, and I'd pay a whole year's worth of the mortgage before Labor Day.

I had a new routine worked out—a five-ball ballet set to bebop jazz from a boom box I'd bought at a pawnshop on Chestnut Street. When I changed the direction of the first two balls—bouncing them off the ground instead of tossing them high—three balls remained aloft, creating a pattern that stretched from the ground to ten feet in the air, making it look like I was encircled by balls.

Back on the road, I could smell the salt air. Swerving to avoid hitting a turtle crossing the causeway between Atlantic City and the mainland, I watched the blood-orange sun cut through the mist over the marsh. Soon I was crossing over the bay, its surface silky and calm. Under the bridge a motorboat towed a water skier wearing a shiny black wetsuit. A plume of water trailed from behind each ski.

Atlantic City High had two more days of school to go. Out front, kids milled about, smoking cigarettes. Along Ventnor Avenue, shops were opening their doors and rolling up their venetian blinds. In front of the Super Sub Shop, the owner—a rotund man about Dad's age wearing a white apron—sprayed the sidewalk with a green garden hose. I tooted my horn; he looked up, saw me and waved. "Pretzel Man!"

At long last: my *real* bar mitzvah. Yesterday I was Pretzel Boy. Today I'm Pretzel Man.

The house smelled of mildew. I opened the windows, installed a couple of window fans. It took me an hour to unpack, straighten up the living room and set up the kitchen. After that, I headed to the boardwalk, planning to walk all the way to the inlet and back, stopping off at Norman and Betty's and checking to see if Jimmy and Madam Diane were in town yet.

The Chalfonte Hotel, which by next summer would be Resorts International Casino, was still under renovation. Guys in hard hats, setting up scaffolding on the North Carolina Avenue side of the building, hooted and whistled at girls on the boardwalk. I wondered if casinos might brighten up Atlantic City a bit. Pretzel sales had been sluggish over the past few seasons. The boardwalk was still crowded at night, but not as jammed as it used to be. A lot of the shops needed paint jobs. The "See Them Twisted—See Them Baked" sign Mom had painted still hung out front of our bakery, faded and tired-looking, but that was another story. Dad could afford a new sign, he just wasn't ready. Jimmy and Norman had stopped telling him he should get it fixed, because every time one of them mentioned the idea, Dad would get choked up, wave his hands and change the subject.

"*Bubula!*" said Betty, stepping out of her office when she saw me enter the arcade. "Mr. Homeowner! Look at you, all grown up." She kissed my cheek. "Your mama would be so proud of you! Norman's not here—he's in Vineland looking at new machines. Did you see Lita out there? She's been gone all morning and there's work what she has to do."

"I haven't seen her," I said. "I haven't seen anybody yet."

Exasperated, Betty shook her head. "Norman and me worry about her—out all night, and with the older boys it's not so good."

"Lita's a good kid," I assured her. "Don't worry about her."

"Uh-uh," Betty said, wagging her finger at me. "She ain't such a kid no more." It was true. Lita, fifteen, had blossomed over the last two years. "She smokes. And she runs with the wrong crowd."

"Cigarettes? Yuck," I said. "That sucks, but she'll be all right."

Betty reached into her apron for a handful of change. "From your lips to God's ears. You gonna play a little? You want a few quarters?"

"Nah," I said, turning and starting for the door. "I just came to say hi. If I see Lita, I'll send her back."

Then I was on my way, moving briskly along the boardwalk—past the bakery and the building next door where Jimmy's marionette theater used to be (this summer it sat empty, a rarity in Atlantic City). The ocean was too cold for swimmers, and the beach too windy, but the boardwalk was warm and sunny. Together, these conditions were usually good for business. I stopped in front of Million Dollar Pier and watched the Ferris wheel spinning in the sun. People milled about; pigeons fluttered and pecked at scattered peanuts. Seagulls swooped overhead, languidly welcoming the early summer crowd. Old people sat in rows at the pavilion next to the pier, some with blankets across their laps.

"Jason!" Someone called my name. I turned. It was Lita coming up behind me.

I kissed her cheek. "How's it going? Betty wants you."

Lita puffed on the cigarette she held between her bright red fingernails. "Fuck Betty."

"You sound like Skip," I said.

Lita puffed on her cigarette and jutted her hip defiantly. "They won't let me do anything."

"I notice you're not sneaking under the boardwalk for a smoke," I said. "You're pretty much doing what you want, right? You should see the bullshit my Sarah's got to deal with. Her mom *really* won't let her do anything. Norman and Betty are neglectful compared to her. Sarah's not even allowed to drink coffee."

"I'm running away," she said.

"Oh, Lita . . ."

"Don't 'Oh, Lita' me. You sound like them."

"Norman and Betty are cool. They do let you do shit and they let you grow up on the boardwalk, which is more than my dad let me do."

"At least you can talk to your dad," said Lita, flicking an ash from her cigarette onto her frayed blue denim shorts and rubbing it into the material with the palm of her hand. Her feet were bare and around one ankle was a delicate-looking strand of beads. All in all, with her white shirt knotted above her belly button and her thin, already-tanned legs emerging from her cutoffs, Lita had become ultra-sexy.

She dropped her cigarette on the boardwalk, looked down helplessly at her toes and back up at me. "Stomp on that?" she asked. I complied. "How's your house?" she asked.

"It's great. Except Sarah won't be down until next season."

"Can I come see it?"

"Stop by any time."

Lita reached out and brushed my arm with the tips of her fingers. "*Any* time?" she asked.

I felt a little uncomfortable, recalling the times she had rubbed against me while I was playing pinball. But I belonged to Sarah. Besides, Lita was like a little cousin.

"You should go back now because Betty needs you," I said.

Lita huffed, lit another cigarette and took off across the boardwalk down the ramp toward Atlantic Avenue. "Bye, Jason," she said over her shoulder, in a singsong, flirty voice.

I continued on my walk, stopping in to see Jimmy for the first time since last summer.

"Jason!" Jimmy shouted, darting out of his big easy chair next to the scale in his stall, and embracing me in a bear hug. "Where's your old man? He better fix that sign. How ya doing? Still with that girl?" He mussed my hair with his hand. Then he looked out over the ocean. "This is the last season."

"Right," I said. "Next year Sarah's going to move down year-round." We stepped outside, where I gripped the metal boardwalk railing with both my palms. Side by side we gazed at the foamy green ocean. Out beyond the rolling swells, the water was as calm as the bay had been when I'd driven in earlier.

"Nice about Sarah, but not what I meant," said Jimmy. "This is the end of the boardwalk life as we know it."

"Why do you always have to be so dramatic?" I asked. "Where do you come up with this crap? It's one casino, and you're acting like it's the Invasion of the Body Snatchers."

Jimmy chuckled.

"Is this about the smell?" I asked. "Because ever since you told me that, I've been smelling this place very carefully."

Jimmy put his arm around my shoulder. "I'm glad to know that," he said, pulling me close to him. "And what does your fine nose tell you?"

"That half of what you say smells like bullshit." I gave him a playful punch on the arm.

"That's true," Jimmy laughed. "But which half?" He squeezed my shoulder. We watched the ocean.

After a minute I turned around, my back to the shoreline, and leaned against the railing. "I think I'm gonna keep walking," I said. Jimmy didn't reply, just stared at the water.

I stepped into the crowd, swaggering as confidently as I could. Jimmy and his "last season" crap had made me a little sad. I hoped he didn't plan on keeping this up all summer long.

Making my way toward the inlet, I noticed several more empty shops. Merchants were scramming when nothing had even happened yet! It was ridiculous. I returned to my house late in the afternoon, put clean linens on my bed and Dad's, took a long shower and made a pot of coffee in case Jimmy stopped by. At six-thirty I walked over to Pacific Avenue, bought a pizza and carried it back to the house. I opened the box on the coffee table in the living room and smelled the fresh, steaming pie. I was just about to dig in when I heard a knock on the door. So, Jimmy had decided to come over after all. He'd probably apologize for sounding so gloomy earlier in the day. I rushed to the door, threw it open and was surprised to see Lita, looking like a lost puppy.

"How you doing, Lita? Norman and Betty with you?" Lita shook her head and walked inside. She settled into the couch and helped herself to a slice of pizza. I followed her, taking a seat next to her and digging into the pizza box myself.

"What do you think of my place?" I asked between mouthfuls.

"It's pretty cool," she said approvingly, licking a glob of tomato sauce off her pinkie finger. "You're staying year-round?"

"After next school year, yeah," I said. "Sarah's coming down . . ."

"When?" Lita asked. "This week?"

"No. I told you. Next summer."

Lita slipped out of her white sneakers and squirmed around in the couch, positioning herself so that her feet pressed against the side of my leg.

"Want to see what's on TV?" I asked, discreetly trying to wriggle my thigh away from her toes.

"Nah," said Lita. I was getting nervous. I couldn't ask her to take her feet off my leg. She wasn't actually doing anything, just massaging me with the balls of her feet. It was innocent, basically, for two kids who'd known each other practically all their lives and had spent their summers in a place where nearly everybody went around shoeless half the time. It was no big event. Except it felt pretty good.

"So what's the deal with Norman and Betty?" I asked in what must have sounded like an awkward attempt at everyday conversation.

Lita grimaced. "The deal is they suck."

"You really do sound like Skip. His mom died. Did I tell you?"

"No," said Lita. "How?"

"Pills. Suicide."

"That blows."

Neither of us said anything for a few seconds. Then Lita raised a foot and rested it on my leg. Her toenails were painted bright red. Her legs were smooth. Instinctively I raised one hand and was about to rest it on her thigh, when I came to my senses and lurched up from the couch, startling her.

"Cup of coffee?" I asked, sputtering. "I . . . I've got a fresh pot on."

"Sit," Lita said. She patted the couch with her palm and raised her feet for me to sit. When I was reckless enough to comply, she set both her feet on my lap, crossing her ankles. I was stuck—too embarrassed to say anything. Actually, it was good that she didn't want coffee because if I'd tried standing again, my hard-on would've given me away. Keep talking, I told myself. Don't forget to breathe. Remain calm. "You should give Norman and Betty a chance," I said.

"I'll give them a chance to jump out a window."

"You are so lucky that you get to grow up here," I said. "I'm jealous."

"Yeah, right," she said. "Like you have any idea what it's like here in the middle of the winter."

That hurt. "Hey, I do!"

"Yeah," she said. "You come down on Saturday, play pinball and hang out. But day after day it's boring as shit."

"Yeah, well, you should see where I live. Except for Sarah it's the Night of the Living Dead. School's totally idiotic. The teachers are Nazis. My English teacher went out of her way to try and break Sarah and me up."

"You think Atlantic City High's any better?" asked Lita. "White kids and colored kids fighting in the halls? Stinky girls' rooms you can't even go in without getting jumped? You don't know how much it sucks! You think it's a fairy tale down here!"

Secretly happy that she was becoming annoyed with me, I hoped she'd cut back on the foot action.

"You don't know how lucky you are," she said, lifting one leg and tickling my ribs with her big toe.

I lurched. "Cut that out!"

Smiling coyly, Lita returned her foot to my lap. "Your dad's the coolest," she said. "He treats you like a grownup. But Norman and Betty treat me like a kid, even though I've worked all my life and I've never been in trouble."

"Change of subject," I said. "What happened to your real parents?" I'd known Lita for a decade, but this was essentially the first conversation we'd had that wasn't about pinball or the size of the boardwalk crowd or the ocean temperature. Everyone knew that Lita wasn't Norman and Betty's actual kid, but no one knew whose she was.

"Norman and Betty knew them before the war," said Lita. "In Poland. They were like second cousins or something. And they all wound up at a DP camp in Germany. Displaced Persons. My parents survived the concentration camps and the DP camp, but they came out really sick. My mother had typhoid and my father had scarlet fever. Norman and Betty came back to Germany and got me."

Without any thought, I rested my hand on her ankle and traced its surface with the tips of my fingers. "So you've got two dead parents," I said.

"Right," said Lita, grinning playfully. "And you and Skip got one each. So I'm winning."

Soon we were laughing, and both the tension and the shameful pleasure I'd felt from Lita's feet on my thigh disappeared. I looked at her sitting across from me on the couch, giggling and wiping her eyes, her curly brown hair swept across her face. Despite the makeup, the nail polish and the cigarettes, she was just a kid.

Suddenly, though, she hoisted herself forward, grabbed my neck and kissed me on the lips. I pulled away, but she grasped my chin between her hands and kissed me again.

I gasped. When I opened my mouth, she jammed her tongue in.

Coughing and sputtering, I pulled back and grasped Lita's wrists in my hands. "Aw c'mon!" I said. "This is uncool!" I thought about Skip and Sarah. This is what he'd claimed she did to him.

Lita pouted, leaned back and rested her feet on my lap again. "Why?" she asked. A rash of warmth spread across my cheeks. She giggled. "Jason, you're blushing!"

"Well, *yeah*! Who wouldn't?"

She grew serious. "You can do anything you want to me," she said.

For a moment everything stopped and we just looked at each other. She rubbed her foot up and down my thigh. I thought about fucking her right there on my couch. Under my blue jeans I was hard as a rock. She licked her lips, beckoning, drawing her face closer to mine, her eyes hungry. She kissed me again. I scrunched my mouth closed, felt her tongue grazing my teeth, her fingers tugging at my belt.

"Look, wait," I said, pulling free and sliding back on the couch. "Number one, I have a girlfriend."

Lita retracted her feet from my lap and whistled under her breath. "What's number two?"

I held up my hands. "I don't think there's a number two." After a few moments of awkward silence, I asked, "More pizza?"

She pouted.

"I'd definitely rather play pinball with you than with her," I said consolingly.

"Oh, thanks a lot," she huffed, reaching down and snatching her sneakers off the floor.

"Come on, Lita, you know what I mean," I said. "I love you like family. And you've gotten really cute the past couple seasons. Congratulations on being so foxy."

She paused, one sneaker dangling seductively from her big toe. "So she's moving here even though she's never even seen your place? How come she never comes down?"

I took another slice of pizza from the box. "Her mother. She's not allowed to do anything."

"Do you guys do it?" Lita asked, working her heel into her sneaker and tying the laces.

"Me and Sarah? Yeah." I was finally beginning to relax. "And I can't do it with anyone else," I added. "Sorry."

Lita stood up. I got up too. "Don't leave yet," I said. "You want to watch TV? Want to see the rest of the—" I stopped there, not wanting to show her my bedroom. "Did you see the spigot outside so we can wash the sand off our feet before we come in from the beach?"

"What the hell are you talking about?" she asked as she crossed the living room toward the front door.

I didn't want her to leave angry. I was afraid of feeling gawky every time I was around her. "Hey," I said. She stopped at the door and turned to me. "You want to go up to the boardwalk, see what's happening?" Lita shifted her weight to one hip, poked her tongue in her cheek and considered my offer. "I'll buy you an ice cream cone," I said with a sheepish smile.

"Well . . . okay," she said, stepping outside while I grabbed my juggling stuff. A minute later we were on our way to the boardwalk. Behind us the sun was setting over the bay and a breeze had kicked up, adding a springy chill to the air.

"Madam Diane wasn't around when I stopped by today," I told Lita as we walked past cottages that owners and renters were airing out on the first night of the season—their front doors and windows open wide, cardboard boxes, steamer trunks and suitcases piled on porches. "Wanna go up there and say hello to her now?"

Lita shrugged indifferently. "Mm-okay. As long as I don't have to deal with Norman and Betty for a while."

"Just promise you won't run away," I said.

She grinned roguishly. "I won't. But it's nice to know that if I did, you'd worry."

"I wouldn't be alone," I said. The traffic light at Atlantic Avenue was taking forever to turn green. Lita stepped gingerly in front of a Volkswagen convertible that was moving toward us. The lady behind the wheel honked and Lita retreated to the curb, giving the finger to the driver as she sped past us with her horn blaring. As soon as there was an opening in the traffic, we dashed across the busy street, walked one more block and climbed the ramp to the boardwalk. I made sure to clasp my suitcase in my right hand and keep Lita to my right as well. That way she wouldn't try to hold hands or slip her arm through mine. I didn't want anyone getting the wrong idea.

On the boardwalk, the crowd was thin and the air chilled. We walked for about an hour, stopping for ice cream and to check on Madam Diane, who hadn't yet arrived for the season. Her shop was dark and her sign wasn't in the window. "Madam Diane better get her ass in gear," I said, peeking through the shuttered door into the fortune-teller's den.

"All she has to do is set up her table and her stupid cards," said Lita.

"She's gotta get the place smelling right."

Lita huffed. "Jesus Christ. Not you too! Jimmy's been talking that shit."

"No," I said. "I mean spices and incense to make her studio smell mysterious."

Lita sniffed disdainfully. "Norman says if Diane could tell the future she'd be rakin' it in on Wall Street or betting on college football."

"Maybe that's what she does off-season."

She tilted her jaw and made a face that said *you're an idiot*. She was probably right. Most of Madam Diane's predictions were vague. Skip was going to die in a foreign country or something like it. There were a lot of ways you could interpret that.

Lita turned from the fortune-teller's studio, scooted over to my left and took hold of my arm before I could switch my suitcase to the other hand. "Norman says if Madam Diane could really tell the future she would have done the Jews a favor and warned them about the Nazis."

We walked another half a block in silence. Lita stopped and released my arm. She fished a cigarette from the pocket of her sweatshirt, slipped it into her mouth and lit up. Then she blew a puff of smoke in my face. "Do you get high?"

"I have," I said. "But I don't. And it was just grass. No pills or anything. How about you?"

Lita raised her eyebrows. "Where would I even get it?" I looked at her, but she averted her eyes. She was lying. She was going into tenth grade at Atlantic City High and hanging out with older kids. She could get it in the girls' room, in the cafeteria, in front of the school, behind the school, under the boardwalk. Now I realized that even though Lita had wanted me to fuck her, she saw me as an adult, a *gadjo*, one of *them*.

At ten-thirty I walked Lita back to Norman and Betty's. The boardwalk was nearly empty. I went home. *Home*. I loved the way that sounded. I ate a slice of cold pizza, undressed, brushed my teeth, curled into bed and thought about Sarah: I pictured her delicate face, her arms and her neck. I recalled the herbal smell of her hair; I thought about how she wrapped her slender legs around my hips when we had sex. I closed my eyes, reached my hand under the sheet and began slowly to stroke myself, all the while thinking of Sarah's lips, her fingers and the feel of her flesh pressed against my own.

Afterward I thought about writing Sarah a letter. Should I tell her about Lita? We'd always been completely honest with each other. But nothing had actually happened with Lita, everything had ended okay, and I would have hated for Sarah to resent Lita for the rest of our lives. Despite a pang of guilt for having been attracted to Lita and not having stopped her earlier, I decided not to write Sarah for another day or two, until I could figure out exactly what, if anything, to say.

"STEP RIGHT UP, ladies and gentlemen! It's time for original joltin', jivin', jazz-juggling of Atlantic City's own Jason the Magnificent!"

On a busy Saturday night in the middle of July, stationed under a street lamp, Louie Armstrong Dixie jazz playing in the background, I bounced five gleaming white lacrosse balls in time to the music, off the boardwalk, high into the air under the silvery streetlight. When the balls soared toward the lamp, the light shimmered; when the crowd looked into the light and then down at the boardwalk, their eyes had to adjust for a second, which enhanced the effect of the glimmering balls encircling me like white fire.

I ended the routine by bouncing all five balls off the boardwalk and high into the air. Hands free, I took off my derby, turned it upside down and caught the balls in it. The crowd burst into applause. I bowed, emptied the balls into my old suitcase and stepped into the audience, derby extended.

Tips had been great all summer. Crowds were excellent. Money flowed. But Jimmy was still depressed, bellyaching about how "it don't smell right."

Now, as I passed through the crowd, I noted that my derby was half full with ones and fives. Excellent! A man emerged from the throng, pushed a couple bills into my derby and thrust out his hand.

"Pretzel Boy!" he said. I looked up. It was Monty Dweck, the real estate man. He was wearing a white tee shirt with "HERS" printed in big letters on the front.

"How are you?" I asked, taking his meaty palm in mine and shaking it warmly. "Where've you been? I haven't seen you around this summer."

"We moved to Ocean City," he said. Now I saw that he wasn't alone. To his right was a pudgy, smiley woman wearing a tee shirt with "HIS" printed on it. And to his left, two little kids wearing "THEIRS" tee shirts.

"Did you guys like the show?" I asked.

"Yes!" the kids shouted in unison, bobbing up and down.

"I'm gonna do another in about five minutes. If you stand up front, when I ask for volunteers from the audience you can come up and we'll do some fun stuff together."

The Dweck kids did a good job tossing me items that audience members handed to them—swimming trunks, shoes, beach balls, cotton candy, stuffed animals they'd won at the Wheel of Fortune. Everyone liked when I juggled the odd-sized assortment of common and not-so-common boardwalk items. Through the lopsided cascade I could see Monty and Mrs. Dweck, proud and happy, looking on.

That night, when I got back to the house, I sat down at the kitchen table and wrote Sarah in Cape Cod. I told her about the Dweck family and how we should probably have children while we were still young.

Two weeks went by before I heard back from her. She wrote nothing about us having kids. Instead, she filled me in on the usual: The pool, the restaurants. The Bonnie Raitt concert her aunt and uncle had taken her to. How great it was to be away from her mom.

As the summer went on, Madam Diane never arrived. She skipped out on her rent and left a bunch of furniture behind. One afternoon, two men in black suits stopped by the bakery and asked Dad and me if we knew of Diane Bano's whereabouts.

"Who the hell's Diane *Bano*?" Dad asked, shaking his head.

"Fortune-teller," said one of the men. "Had a shop across from Million Dollar Pier." The other man stood back, cracking his jaw and eyeing a batch of pretzels on the counter.

"Want a pretzel?" I asked. "On the house." The man in the background held up his hand and wiped a bead of perspiration off his forehead.

"You guys must be super hot," I said. I'd never seen anyone wearing a black suit on the boardwalk in the middle of the summer. They looked like a couple of lost pallbearers.

"We haven't seen Diane all summer," Dad told them.

"You know where we can reach her?" asked the first man.

Dad shook his head. "No idea. I didn't even know her last name until now."

The man squinted like he was sizing Dad up. Dad looked him in the eye. He was better at lying than Lita was, even though he'd answered the man's first question with a question. I was glad he was sticking up for Madam Diane. "My wife died four years ago," Dad told the man. "I didn't know how to reach Diane to give her the news. And I sure as hell don't know how to reach her now."

One of them handed Dad a business card. "If you hear from Mrs. Bano, will you let us know?"

Dad promised he would, and he slipped the card into the cash register.

After the men were gone, Dad told me to give the card to Jimmy when I saw him. I opened the register and took out the card. "**FBI**," it said in big block letters. The men were special agents.

"Something interstate," Dad said. "Otherwise the FBI doesn't get involved." He opened the oven door and peeked at the pretzels inside.

I had never known what Jimmy and Madam Diane did during the off-season other than visit the Gypsy King at his trailer park. Jimmy was a good friend, but he was secretive.

For the final two weeks of the summer, Lita had a steady boyfriend—a brooding, pockmarked eleventh grader from South Philadelphia. Tony didn't seem to like me very much (Lita probably told him she and I "used to go out" or something). He draped himself all over Lita, basically keeping her in a headlock as he paraded her up and down the boardwalk like a prize catch.

The last night of the season, we went to the same Italian restaurant we'd been going to since my first summer. When I asked Jimmy what was up with Madam Diane, he said the FBI wanted to frame her for stealing fifty thousand dollars from a widow in Miami.

"That's insane," I said, picking at a plate of roasted peppers. "How could anyone accuse her of that?"

Jimmy shook his head and took a long gulp of red wine. "I'm with you. *Preposterous.*" But I caught Dad and Norman exchanging a suspicious glance. Did they think Madam Diane was a thief? She was our friend, one of us.

On our way home from the restaurant I told Dad there had to be a logical explanation for why the FBI was after her. "You're a loyal friend, son," he said.

"And you're not?" I asked facetiously. "You could've told those FBI guys more than you did."

Dad rolled his eyes toward the sky. It was the first week of September. Autumn was in the air, but it hung back for one last warm, mosquitoey summer night. Dad seemed a little tipsy from the wine.

"Now wait a sec—" I stopped in my tracks in front of a small surfboard shop on Atlantic.

"Let's keep moving," Dad said. "I have to go to bed. I'm exhausted."

I clasped his elbow and held him with my eyes. "Do you actually believe she ripped some lady off for fifty grand?"

He frowned and shook his head. "No idea. But if she didn't do it she ought to come forward and clear things up. Seventy-five-year-old widows don't ordinarily accuse fortune-tellers of robbing them. Why would she go after Diane for no reason?"

We walked on, past more stores, most of which had already closed for the day. Dad gazed absently into the storefront windows. "Don't get me wrong," he said. "Diane's a friend, and if I can help her, I will. But on the other hand, first she tells the lady that the money was cursed. Then she casts a spell and wraps the cash in burlap, tells her not to open it for ninety days. Two weeks later the lady's son opens it—and there's nothing but newspaper. How do you explain that?"

I looked at Dad helplessly. "The son opened it too early?"

"If she has nothing to hide, she should talk to the FBI."

If the woman in Florida had waited the full ninety days, I wondered, would she have gotten her money back? Maybe the whole trick is that Madam Diane puts the money in a bank for ninety days, earns a little interest and then returns the money to her client. No harm done.

We arrived at the house on Virginia Avenue. "I'm beat," said Dad, slipping off his blue canvas deck shoes and heading for the stairs. "We'll talk in the morning."

I wasn't tired, so I stayed up for another couple of hours, trying to forget about Madam Diane's legal troubles, watching TV and daydreaming about holding Sarah in my arms—smelling her hair and tasting her breath, sweet as saltwater taffy.

21

EILEEN, RUTH AND I are close to the inlet. We've hit a noncommercial stretch—a few mustard-colored apartment buildings but no casinos or shops. No loudspeakers blaring casino promotions. I can hear the ocean lapping the shore.

Ruth asks, "What happened to Skip?"

"Remember a few years ago, I got a letter in the mail? And when I read it, I cried? We were in the front hallway."

Eileen looks up. "You said an old friend had died and you didn't want to talk about it."

"He'd been living with his father all those years, dealing pot to the neighborhood kids and spending most of his days getting high and watching TV in his bedroom. I'd almost forgotten about him. I was on the road for years, and then I met you in New York. Somewhere along the way I packed my juggling stuff and my derby and my old pal Floppy, and I stuffed them in a box, in a closet."

"Did Skip overdose?" asks Ruth.

"Painkillers. But get this. When he died, he wasn't at his dad's house. He was house-sitting for a neighbor of theirs."

Ruth regards me with curiosity, her brows arched. "So?"

"He died in a foreign country . . . or something like it."

Now she smirks. "Madam Diane. Woo-woo."

"Poor Skip," I say. "We joke about 'Mother's Little Helper,' but it wasn't funny. His mom was his role model for all the wrong things. She was clean and sober for her first two sons, but then she got depressed or something, and she got on those pills. Speed to wake up, Valium to chill out and a sleeping pill to knock her out. And she just couldn't give Skip what he needed, you know? Plus with his dyslexia, his self-esteem was shot. But I had my juggling, and my dad believed in me. Even though I let him down in the end."

I'm saving the worst for last: the circumstances of my departure. I'm working myself up to tell it.

But there's one story I won't tell today—not in front of Ruth. The story of Jennifer, my accuser. Just last week her complaint went away. I suspect Allen spoke with her, told her I was in therapy, assured her it would not happen again, and she agreed to drop the charges. I promise myself to tell Eileen about it as soon as we have some time alone. Now that she understands the context, and especially because she knows me, I think she'll be okay with it. I resolve also to write an apology to Jennifer, which I'll send in care of Allen.

"THE PROM?" I winced at Sarah's suggestion. "You're kidding. Right?"

We were behind the school on a bright blue autumn afternoon, sitting on the bleachers overlooking the football field. Thick, muscle-bound guys clad in gym shorts and tank tops circled the track, grunting and sweating, while their coach bellowed at them from a shady spot under the grandstand.

"It's our senior year," she said. "We should do something extracurricular, don't you think?"

I shrugged. "I don't know. We've made it this far."

Sarah was still bristling over the *Inherit the Wind* audition last year. Ever since the semester began, she'd kept telling me I should go and talk to Miss Smith, whose feelings I'd "really hurt." And now this: prom talk. "Proms are romantic," she said, clasping my knee.

I reclined against the metal grandstand. "They're silly. I don't do tuxedos, and proms are expensive. We need to conserve our money now that we're homeowners."

Sarah fidgeted whenever I brought up the house. She was nervous about The Move, so I seldom mentioned it.

A pack of four or five runners tromped past us, their feet sounding like horse hoofs on the clay track.

"You don't even like to dance," I said.

"I want to go," said Sarah, firmly. "But we could leave early . . ." She tilted her head and bit her lower lip seductively. Senior year was like junior year: Mrs. Gilquist allowed Sarah out on Saturday nights only, from seven forty-five until eleven o'clock sharp, when she wasn't grounded for arriving home fifteen minutes late.

"You could come down and see the house," I said.

She took her hand off my leg and sat up straight. "We . . . could do that."

"Senior prom, here we come!" I clasped Sarah tight, drawing her close and ignoring the tension in her neck. How bad could a prom be? We'd show up, have our picture taken, eat dinner and leave for Atlantic City. At long last, we'd make love in our own bed.

"And I think you should talk to Miss Smith," said Sarah.

"Don't start this again."

"You hurt her feelings."

"She hurt mine first."

The coach barked at a trio of runners straggling past him. Sarah rested her hand on my knee again. "You should apologize."

It occurred to me that there were quite a few subjects we struggled with. But maybe I could do something about this one. The next day I went to see Miss Smith. She was in her classroom, puttering around with her bookshelves and a huge, dusty pile of old hardback volumes stacked on the floor. I stuck my head in the door and cleared my throat. Miss Smith turned, peered up over her wire-rim glasses and shot a cold glance at me.

"May I come in?" I asked.

She stopped working and faced me. "What can I do for you?" She looked at her watch.

I stepped into the classroom. "I want to talk to you about that thing last year."

"Was there something you left out?"

"I'm sorry, I really am. I was angry that you told Sarah to go to Greywood College. I thought you knew . . ." I hadn't come to apologize, just to talk. But I saw the indignation in Miss Smith's eyes.

"Knew what?" she asked testily. "Knew that you're a couple? Everyone knows that. Jason, I did nothing wrong. And I assure you, your hostility was ill-placed."

"I felt like you purposely tried to come between us." I walked across the classroom to a window, leaned on the radiator and looked out over the football field. "It's like you were trying to break up a marriage."

"Who are you really angry at?" Miss Smith asked. "Sometimes when we're hurt and we have no way of getting back at the person who hurt us, we take our anger out on other people."

She sounded like Rabbi Greenblatt. "I'm not angry," I said.

She returned to the stack of books she was sorting. "I don't know if I believe that. You have good reason to be angry. Your mother died when you were thirteen, right? Aren't you angry about that?"

"No. Not really." It wasn't like Mom died to punish me. She got sick. Why would I be mad at her for being dead? "Why'd you give Sarah that catalog?" I asked.

"Young people fall in love," she said. "And sometimes they go their separate ways. If you and Sarah have something strong enough, it will last. You can't tell me that a simple suggestion by one's English teacher can have that much influence, can you?"

"No. I guess not. But . . ."

Miss Smith raised an index finger to silence me. "I suggested Greywood to Sarah for the same reason I suggested Carnegie Mellon's theater program to you. I thought it was a good fit. Sarah is an exemplary student; Greywood has an excellent liberal arts program. I wasn't thinking about the two of you when I gave Sarah the catalog. I was thinking about *her*."

I scratched my head and stared at my feet. "Sorry."

Miss Smith held up her hand. "Not everything is about Jason Benson." She turned around, picked a book up from the pile, ran a finger over the front cover and slid it onto the shelf among the other volumes.

"I am *really* sorry," I said feebly.

She faced me. Her eyes were damp. I wanted to hug her. I began to move toward her, but she warded me off. "It gave me tremendous pleasure to watch you develop your creativity these past years. You are a young man of exceptional talent and great potential, but if you are not careful you will alienate yourself from the people who love you."

"Why would I do that?" I asked.

Miss Smith pursed her lips and took a deep breath. "Because you are so goddamned self-centered."

The back of my neck prickled. I blinked back the gush of tears that swelled behind my eyes.

She took a step toward me. "All those notes I gave you about sending and receiving? That's what I was talking about. No matter how many people you're on stage with, you never see anyone but yourself."

I gulped at the air and sucked in my gut. "Sorry."

"You can't see past yourself. You have to get out of your own head. I once heard you say you never learned to juggle with a partner . . . you never learned to . . ."

"Pass."

"You only juggle solo. I think you should learn to pass."

"Okay," I promised.

"In your adult life, your biggest enemy will be bitterness," she said, turning toward her books. "Watch out for that."

I wobbled out of the classroom, down the corridor to study hall, where I practiced twirling two lacrosse balls in my palm until the bell rang for lunch.

22

I<small>T WAS MID</small>-M<small>ARCH</small>, with the prom in six weeks. Senior year was moving at a good clip. If school were a juggling routine, I'd be preparing the finale where I bounce-juggled five balls in a two-story-high arc. Graduation and our big move were three months away.

Saturday nights, Sarah and I played house at Dad's: After making certain that his car was neither in the garage nor parked in front of the house, we'd fumble through the front door, giggling and groping, grappling up the stairs—pulling off our clothes and lavishing each other with sloppy kisses. Once in my room, we'd flop naked across the bed and copulate, grinding and grunting like bears.

Over winter break I'd spent four days and nights in our house on Virginia Avenue. I bought a few cans of white paint at a hardware store on Ventnor, borrowed a roller and brushes from Norman and spread a couple of coats in the kitchen and bathroom, where the yellowy walls were cracked and stained. Each time I visited the house, I brought along more of my stuff—summer clothing, a clock radio, boxes of books. Eventually my bedroom in Dad's house was almost empty.

Over the course of the year, Miss Smith had warmed up to me. By winter break she smiled cordially when we saw each other in the halls. When it came time for spring play tryouts at the end of February, I decided to skip them because I didn't want to be stuck in Philadelphia over three weekends in the spring. I secretly hoped Miss Smith would summon me to her room to find out why I hadn't auditioned. But she didn't.

The tuxedo fitting was ludicrous. I had to stand around the cramped, stuffy shop for nearly half an afternoon, when I could have been juggling on Chestnut Street, just to rent what felt like a navy-blue body cast. Standing in my stocking feet—an old man with a mouth full of straight pins kneeling before me, tugging at my trousers—brought back bar mitzvah/wedding/funeral memories. If Mom were alive, she'd be going bonkers over the prom. Even Mrs. Gilquist was getting into it. She allowed Sarah to go downtown after school with me one day before my tuxedo fitting to pick out a dress at a fancy shop on Walnut Street.

"Your mom knows I'm going with you?" I asked while we rode the bus into the city. I'd brought my suitcase of juggling gear along in case I had time to squeeze in a show on Chestnut Street.

"Of course," she said, cheerfully. "You didn't think she'd let me go by myself, did you?"

I puffed my chest. "She's letting you go downtown be*cause* I'm with you? Nice!" The bus turned off the Schuylkill Expressway onto Market Street near a row of porn shops and the King of Pizza storefront. "So," I said, trying to sound casual, "while she's in a good mood and feeling like I'm okay and all, you should probably tell her we're moving in together in a few months, right? And about the house?"

Sarah turned toward the bus window. I couldn't tell whether she was avoiding eye contact or staring at the used furniture store we were passing.

"Come on," I said. "You need to tell her."

Sarah started to say something, but then she stopped and turned her head to look out the window again.

"What's the matter?" I asked.

"Nothing," she said, her breath fogging a small spot on the window. "I'm going to tell her, but not until after prom."

Frustrated, I gazed at the blur of cars and shops. "We'll get off at City Hall," I said. "Then it's just a three-block walk to Walnut."

It was a crisp, clear afternoon, one of the first days all year when you didn't need to wear a coat. Men and women bustled along the street, dodging in and out of office buildings and shops, lining up at the vendors' carts.

Sarah turned toward me—a lilting smile on her pale face. "My mother said you can come for me extra early on prom night." It was good news, but it felt like she was throwing me a bone.

"What's the big deal about prom anyway?" I asked her.

"It's the senior prom," she said matter-of-factly, as if that were the only explanation necessary. I waited for more. "Look, you and I aren't totally alike," she said.

"Yes we are," I told her.

"No we're not," she said. "You don't like school. And I do."

"No you don't. Nobody likes school. Some kids are just better at it. Some fit in easier."

"You're wrong," she said. "I like school and you have no right to tell me otherwise."

Yes, I do, I thought, *because you only think you like school, but wait until you get to Atlantic City. Then you'll know what liking stuff is all about.*

Out on Market Street, bus brakes squeaked and car horns honked.

In what other ways did she think we were not alike? I recalled a couple things she'd mentioned about the school newspaper and the philosophy club.

"Sorry, I didn't know," I said. "I thought you joined the clubs because it kept you from having to go home after school."

Sarah shook her head and chuckled under her breath. "You are really something."

I reached up and pulled the plastic cord to signal the driver. "Our stop's next."

Wrapped in each other's arms, we climbed off the bus and headed to the dress shop on Walnut.

Inside the shop, I sat on a metal chair, my juggling suitcase on my lap, next to a rack of dresses, while Sarah picked out a long blue gown. The dress-shop ladies stood her on a pedestal. They buzzed around her, pinning and hemming, twittering like birds. Although I'd have preferred her in cut-off jeans, a bikini top and flip-flop sandals, I had to admit she looked amazing in her formal dress, holding her hair up with her hands, turning this way and that while one of the ladies tucked at the material around her long neck and stepped back to assess the effect from a distance. I flipped open my suitcase, took my derby out and inspected its brim.

"Nice hat," said one of the dress ladies, coming over for a closer look. I handed it to her. She studied it inside and out. "Hand stitched," she said, running her finger over the fine, even thread. "I've never seen stitching quite like this." She took it over to the other two dress ladies. Sarah winked at me from her pedestal as the ladies skittered around my derby like a flock of pigeons.

"You don't wear this all the time, do you, son?" one of the ladies asked.

"No," I said, grabbing the lacrosse balls from my suitcase. "Only when I juggle."

"You know how old this is?" asked the first lady, bringing it back to me.

I put the balls back in my suitcase and held the derby between my fingertips. "Funny you should ask." I flipped the derby into the air and caught it on my head. "It's either two and a half years old or almost ten."

"It's at least a hundred years old," the dress lady assured me, her hand on her heart, like I'd just tossed an infant into the air.

A chill raced from the back of my head down my spine. "No way. A friend of mine in Atlantic City made it for me. I get one about every three years. It's a Gift for Life."

She shook her head. "It's an antique."

"No, it's not," I said. "My friend made it. She lives in Miami and she used to sew the costumes at her husband's marionette theater in Atlantic City." I knew if I told her about how the old one disappeared when the new one came, she'd think I was nuts.

She dismissed my explanation with a wave of her hand. "You just take care of it. Don't be tossing it up and down, and you ever wanna sell it, bring it back here. I'll get you a price."

"Not for sale," I told her. "But thanks."

ON PROM NIGHT, corsage in hand, I waited outside Sarah's big front door. It swung open, revealing Sarah's mother. "How are you, Mrs. Gilquist? It's nice to see you."

In two and a half years of Jasonansarah, I'd laid my eyes on Mrs. Gilquist about half a dozen times. These viewings came mostly as total surprises: Sarah would call fifteen minutes before our date and request that I come to the door for her and say hello to her mother, instead of waiting in my car out front. A short time later, I'd find myself standing nervously before the big door. "Hello, Mrs. Gilquist," I'd say when we were face to face.

Sometimes she'd respond haltingly. "Good evening, Jason. . . . How are *we* tonight?" Other times, she'd stare at me blankly until Sarah came to the door, reminded her mom to take her medication at ten o'clock and ushered me down the front path to the car.

On prom night, Mrs. Gilquist eyed me up and down, smiled and extended her hand to invite my tuxedo and me inside.

After a few minutes, Sarah appeared at the top of the stairs, announcing herself with a gentle clearing of her throat. She glided downstairs like a runway model. I stood up and kissed her cheek (right in front of her mom!).

"We'd better hit the road," I said. Sarah took my arm and we walked down the flagstone path to my car.

"Be good," said Sarah's mother—sounding like a real mom for the first time since I'd met her.

The prom was at a fancy downtown hotel that reminded me of the Warwick where Mom and Dad had put on my bar mitzvah five years earlier. As we approached the brass-rimmed front doors I had a momentary flashback to the grand ballroom packed with a miscellany of relatives. Once or twice a year we still talked on the phone to Aunt Harriet from Cleveland, her disembodied voice crackling over the lines about her grown children and other relatives I'd never met. And once every few months we talked to Mom's parents in California. The first time I'd told them about Sarah, my grandmother immediately asked if she was Jewish. "Uh, yeah," I lied, knowing that Dad would back me up.

"Good boy," said my grandmother, like she was rewarding a dog. "Stick with your own kind."

"That's a will-do," I said, rolling my eyes and handing the receiver to Dad. I decided not to invite Mom's parents to the wedding. Big deal. They'd been to my first one.

Now, at the prom, I soon found that I was having a good time, to my surprise, and I forgot about the relatives and the bar mitzvah/funeral.

First we danced to a rock band called Petrified Grapefruit, comprised of three hippies playing three sloppy chords over and over. It was the first time Sarah and I had ever danced together. In eleventh grade we'd been to a couple of cast parties where kids were dancing, but we spent most of our time huddled in a corner, making out. Now, on the eve of our long-awaited move, here we were, ducking and twisting, clapping our hands, dipping our heads, stomping, laughing and flailing our arms.

After two or three songs a bunch of kids formed two lines; then one couple at a time danced down the floor in between the lines. Everyone on the dance floor gravitated that way, and one by one, couples faced off and took a turn, shuffling and shimmying through the gauntlet. When it was almost our turn, a redheaded boy I didn't recognize tossed me three apples from a fruit bowl on one of the tables. When Sarah and I hit the tip of the gauntlet, I launched into a three-apple cascade. Everyone clapped. Next, while Sarah twisted and shimmied toward the end of the line, I circled her, juggling the apples erratically, mixing high and low throws, tossing one behind my back and over Sarah's head and quickly circling her just in time to make the catch. As we reached the end of the line, a bunch of kids shouted, "Encore!" and applauded. Good, hearty applause. Boardwalk applause. I looked at the crowd that had formed around me. Sarah moved off to the side. At the back of the crowd, I saw Miss Smith, who was chaperoning the prom.

I held the apples in the air. The crowd grew silent. Petrified Grapefruit stopped playing. At that instant I did something I'd never done before—neither as a juggler nor as an actor: I paused to look at the audience. Not scan the crowd for familiar faces, easy laughers or drunks—I'd been doing that for years. This time, I looked into the eyes of the people who were watching me, inviting them to look into my eyes.

That's when I smelled Atlantic City. Salt air and melting caramel. Seaweed. French fries.

I juggled, but not my standard routine—none of the usual patter, no jokes. I worked silently, reaching out to the audience with my heart, with the subtle expectation of a swift catch, the risk of a near miss, the shift of a gaze, the arch of an eyebrow. I communicated in a language that seemed at once old and new, familiar and foreign. Briefly gazing through my pattern, watching Miss Smith watching me, I knew she understood. I was sending her something: an acknowledgement, a confession, a message beyond words.

I ended the show by tossing all three apples aloft, doing a fast three-hundred-and-sixty-degree spin on my heels, dropping to my knees and snatching the apples out of the air a split second before they hit the floor. Everyone clapped and whistled.

Guided by an invisible hand, I walked directly to Miss Smith, stopping along the way to drop off the apples at a table. The band had begun playing a slow song. "May I have this dance?" I asked the English teacher, enunciating slowly so she could read my lips over the thunderous guitars.

She offered me her hand. We stepped onto the floor. First with her eyes, then with her hips and her feet, she led me through a series of steps. Left. Right. Forward. Back. Left. Right. Forward. Back. It felt awkward at first, but Miss Smith led me using the same silent language I'd just discovered in my juggling. With the slightest crook of her head, she signaled a turn or twirl. With her breath, she suggested a glide to my right followed by a sudden change in direction.

Word had gotten around about last year's *Inherit the Wind* incident, and some kids were curious about us dancing together. But I spotted Sarah standing at the edge of the dance floor watching Miss Smith and me dance—a gorgeous smile plastered on her face, one hand on her heart.

Suddenly Miss Smith threw her arms around me and hugged me tightly. When she pulled back I saw tears in her eyes. We weren't dancing anymore. "You're a remarkable young man," she said. I stared right back at her, sending her my emotions.

"And you're the best teacher I've ever had."

"You'd better get back to Sarah," she said playfully. "Before people start talking about us."

I planted a kiss on her cheek. "Let 'em talk. Thank you so much for everything you taught me. You and your plays were the only good things about high school. Except for Sarah and the high ceilings in the student lounge. Will you visit us in Atlantic City? I mean, now that we're graduating, we could be friends."

Miss Smith smiled. "Thank you. I'd love to." Then, curiously, she said, "We'll see."

The band took a break. The dance floor cleared as people returned to their tables for the first course of the evening's meal. Waiters in black pants and white dress shirts came around with salad and rolls, filling everyone's water glass and asking whether we wanted chicken or beef.

"You and Miss Smith were wonderful out there," Sarah said, munching happily on a buttered roll. I'd never seen her this animated. Dinner was being served so slowly and so late, I began to doubt whether we'd make it to Atlantic City. But I didn't care; I was having a great time. Even the tuxedo felt good.

A bunch of jocks must have snuck some alcohol into the hotel, because they were wobbling around with their eyes glazed. Miss Smith watched them stumble across the ballroom. She crossed her arms and shook her head indignantly when three of them launched into a raucous chorus of whoops and hollers.

I leaned across the table toward Sarah. "Are you having a good time?" She nodded eagerly, sliding a forkful of lettuce into her mouth. "I thought this would suck," I said, swiping a knife full of sweet butter on a sesame seed roll. "But it's cool. That was the best I've ever juggled, and I was thinking, would you rather stay here tonight instead of making a run to Atlantic City? I mean, I want you to see the house, but it'll be dark and the season hasn't started yet, so you may as well wait."

Sarah looked so relieved, I thought she'd leap across the table and hug me.

Waiters came around and refilled our water glasses. Kids approached our table to talk with Sarah and me. This was new. Four years of high school and three years of Jasonansarah, and no one had said boo, basically. Now, suddenly, we were popular. I'd starred in four plays; these kids had seen me juggling in the hallways, the lounge and the gym. But I'd never felt connected to them until tonight.

The waiters served our meals—stuffed chicken breasts swimming in a brown mushroom sauce. Sarah ate my glazed carrots. Actually I fed them to her, marveling the entire time at how cute she looked nibbling the shiny orange chunks off my fork.

At eleven o'clock Petrified Grapefruit kicked up again. Instead of trying to read each other's lips, Sarah and I danced some more. At midnight a gangly, frizzy-haired guy walked up to the bandstand and took the microphone from the lead singer. Everyone applauded. "Who's he?" I asked Sarah as we made our way to our table.

"That's Steven Thomas. The class president."

"I didn't know we had a class president."

President Steven gave out awards to the king and the queen of the prom (a burly football player and his cute, blond cheerleader girlfriend) and to a bunch of other kids who'd helped to organize the evening. He gave a special thanks to Miss Smith and the other teacher-chaperones. And he thanked me for my juggling and said that my performance made the night special. When he said my name, the back of my neck grew warm and I bit my lower lip. Everyone applauded. I stood up very quickly and acknowledged President Steven.

After the award ceremony, we danced some more. Pretty soon it was one o'clock in the morning. The hall was thinning out. Girls scrounged around under their tables, found the shoes they'd abandoned and wearily slipped them back on their feet. Everyone headed to the lobby or to the street in front of the hotel to meet their rides, or, like Sarah and me, down to the underground parking lot.

"That was the best thing ever," Sarah said with a yawn as she climbed into the Dart, gathering up her gown. By the time we turned onto the Schuylkill Expressway, she was asleep, smiling contentedly, her head on my shoulder. The Schuylkill River, shimmering in the moonlight to my right, gave off an almost imperceptible fishy smell that wafted into the car, reminding me of the ocean.

When we reached Sarah's house at a quarter to two, the lamps out front were still on, but it looked as though the house was dark. I walked Sarah to the door and kissed her goodnight.

When I got to Dad's house, he was asleep. I went up to my room, climbed out of the tuxedo, crawled into bed and replayed the evening's events in my mind: Dancing with Sarah and Miss Smith; the impromptu juggling show; President Steven's kind acknowledgment; the friendliness of the other kids; the rambling, unrelenting, unsophisticated blare of Petrified Grapefruit.

Now there were just six weeks of school left—almost nothing, half a summer season. I could endure anything for six weeks, especially now, since when I closed my eyes and concentrated, I could smell Atlantic City.

23

I TOLD DAD, Sarah and Miss Smith that I planned to skip the graduation ceremony. The prom had been liberating—the perfect cap to my high school career. But I wanted to go straight to Atlantic City the day after school ended rather than sit around for a week until graduation day.

Sarah, on the other hand, had made National Honor Society and graduated with honors in math and French. I understood why she wanted to be at the graduation. After the ceremony, she promised me, she'd go directly home and tell her mother about our plan. Then she'd pack her bags and catch the first bus.

My first-ever one-way drive to the shore! I rolled down all the Dart's windows. Along the Black Horse Pike, I passed through sleepy Pine Barrens towns. I squeezed the gas pedal and sped toward my new life, where fat dragonflies buzzed over sun-drenched lawns, where the boardwalk nights pulsed with neon and adrenaline.

It was mid-morning when I pulled into my driveway. *Our* driveway. The sky was overcast, the air chillier than usual for the middle of June. But that didn't stop me from a quick dip in the ocean.

I walked down to the beach. It was cool and gusty, the sand almost empty. Over the next week the season would get rolling with "summer people" trickling in, pilgrims in station wagons. Before I knew it, our block would be a blooming summer scene: Families traipsing to the beach in their flip-flops, beach chairs and umbrellas in tow. Bare-chested boys dodging traffic and playing raucous games of street Wiffle ball. Moms and dads sticking their heads out second-floor windows, yelling, "We're goin' down the beach in five!"

Dropping my shirt and sneakers fifty feet from the shoreline, I skipped across the cold packed sand on the balls of my feet. When the first icy wave rippled over my toes, I plodded forward, eyes cast beyond the waves to the glassy green expanse of ocean. A wave caught me off guard, hitting me at my waistline, sending streams of freezing water down the front and sides of my cut-off jeans. "Yahhhhhhhh!" I yelled, sucking in my belly, bobbing up and down on my tiptoes and raising my arms above the water. Two seagulls circled overhead, mocking me with their caws. Holding my breath, I plunged beneath the next wave. Emerging, I shook my head and beat my chest with my fists.

I splashed and hopped, howled at the seagulls and lunged under the waves. I propelled myself in front of a smooth, looming swell, caught it just right and body-surfed all the way to the shore, my cheeks puffed. Breathless, I did a handspring on the wet sand and ran full speed toward the boardwalk, scooping up my sneakers and shirt.

Teeth chattering, I ran all the way home repeating, "V-r-r-r-! I live running distance from the ocean! V-r-r! I live running distance from the ocean!" I passed a mailman walking toward me on Virginia Avenue. When I arrived at the house, I scuttled up the driveway to the little shower spigot, pulled its chain and stood for about thirty seconds under the glacial jet.

At my door, I saw that a letter and a package had arrived. My first mail! How cool! Dripping, I rummaged through the boxes until I found a big blue towel. I yanked it out of the box, wrapped myself in it and snuggled into the sofa, feeling squeaky clean, pores tight, senses as sharp as ice water. I reached to the floor and picked up the package. I knew what it was. It always arrived on the eve of a change. When Mom got sick. Just before I met Sarah. And today.

Inside the box was an exact duplicate of the derby I'd been wearing for almost three years. Except, of course, it was a little larger. I examined the hand stitching and the slightly frayed brim. I put it on my head. As always, it was a perfect fit. I dashed out the front door and opened the trunk of the Dart. Inside, I'd packed my old yellow Jason the Magnificent suitcase that Mom had painted. I opened the latch and reached inside.

The old derby was gone. I stood in the driveway, suitcase in hand, derby on head, knowing it was useless to rummage through the trunk or call Dad in Philadelphia. I shook my head, closed the trunk, returned to the house and picked up the letter that had arrived. It was addressed to me; no return address, but the handwriting on the powder-blue envelope was unmistakable. I tore it open, but before I began reading, I adjusted the towel around my waist and turned on the radio. I worked the dial past the disco and top-forty stations until I found an FM station on the far left of the band that was playing a soft, sweet jazz number. With a tenor sax wailing plaintively in the background, I sat on the couch and read Sarah's letter.

Dear Jason,

This is about my twentieth start. I write a few lines then crumple the paper and throw it away. But now I promise myself that this is the letter I shall mail to you. I know how much this is going to hurt you, and I realize that you may never forgive me for what I am about to say.

I gasped for air. My throat constricted and my guts lurched.

I have felt so torn. I don't understand everything that happened. I know I promised you I'd live with you in Atlantic City. It's just that you put so much pressure on me. Even back in tenth grade, you made me promise you. As time went on, I felt like I was being pulled in deeper and deeper. The longer I went without telling you the truth, the harder it became to be honest with you. I know I am taking a cowardly approach by not telling you to your face. I'm so sorry.

It's not that I didn't love you. Please don't think that. I did love you. You opened my eyes to new and wonderful possibilities. For you, life is an adventure, and you are a truly original, creative and beautiful person. But we are both so young. And I have begun to feel that your love for me was a way for you to make up for something else, maybe for the loss of your mother. But I can't be what you want me to be. And mostly, I can't be responsible for your happiness. I want you to be happy, but I can't handle the pressure of having to live out your dream.

Finally, after four years of acting like there wasn't any problem, my aunt and uncle realized that something is wrong with my mother when I told them she wouldn't be attending my graduation. She will see a specialist who says he can make her well again. After a four-week treatment, she will come home and continue to visit her doctor a few times a week. I promised that when I return from Europe next month, I would stay at home for one year to help her get better. Then I plan to attend Middletown College in New Hampshire.

I need to be far away right now. Away from my mother and from my home. Away from you. Please don't contact me. Some day we will talk. But not now.

We had something that was beautiful. I will cherish it forever. But in my heart I know that it is over. I'm not ready to settle down and start a family. Maybe in five or ten years, but not now. You may not be ready, either. Sometimes I feel that you're in love with being in love, but in reality you are searching for something else. Something I cannot give you.

Please stay as special as you are. I know this will make you stronger. And I know you will meet the right girl one day.

I will always remember you juggling at prom. I will always remember what we had. Thank you for opening up your life to me.

Fondly,

Sarah

At first I didn't cry.

For over twelve hours I didn't even move; didn't get up; didn't piss; didn't eat or drink; just sat there, balled up on the couch, wrapped in the damp blue towel, twiddling its tiny strands of terry-cloth between my thumb and forefinger. A draft of ocean breeze floated in through the open window and the soft jazz played from the radio as I drifted in and out of a mournful delirium. Around two o'clock in the morning, I got up and made my way upstairs.

The next morning I woke early and stared blankly at the ceiling. Eventually I got dressed and stumbled over to Atlantic Avenue. I bought a steak sandwich and a couple cups of coffee at Jack's Subs. Greasy white bag in hand, I returned to the house and wolfed down the food while watching a dull TV show about a group of college professors on an arctic expedition. After I finished the coffee, I curled up on the couch and stared at the TV until the station went off the air at three in the morning.

Bright and early the next day, I heard a knock at my front door. Glassy-eyed, unshaven and unshowered, wearing only my underpants, I dragged myself off the couch and answered the door. It was Dad, his arms full of grocery bags. Having thought Sarah was going to be in the house, he had rented a hotel room for himself. The moment he saw me, his eyes opened wide. He set down the bags and extended his arms.

"What happened?" he asked as I hugged him, sobbing and sniffling.

"She . . . broke up." My voice was a whimper. "She's not coming down." I grasped his shoulder as he maneuvered me into the house and sat me on the sofa.

Dad didn't say anything. He just held me.

For a week I sat around the house in my underwear, staring vacantly at the television. I told Dad to tell Jimmy and Norman and Betty, and especially Lita, that I didn't want visitors.

"Are you practicing your new routine?" Dad asked whenever he called, or when he stopped by to drop off groceries. "I'm going to need you for July Fourth weekend. Can I count on you?"

"Huh? Yeah," I said drearily.

After a week I decided to get dressed and go out. I was ready to juggle. It was Saturday night, the last weekend in June. The boardwalk was more crowded than usual this early in the season. I strolled from Virginia Avenue up to North Carolina. The best crowd would probably be near the new casino. Besides, I ought to take a look inside, I thought, see what legalized gambling looks like.

The thick glass doors of Resorts International seemed to be held open perpetually by the visitors who filed like a bobbing line of ants into the elegant monolith. I got into line behind a middle-aged man in a thick plaid sports coat. He smoked a cigarette and nervously scratched numbers with a pencil on a small pad of paper. Before the line had moved very far, a half-dozen more people fell in behind me. In a few minutes I was inside the casino's lobby. Whistles, bells and raucous laughter called from the nearby gaming room.

I followed the flow of the crowd into the vast, noisy space. Roulette. Blackjack. Baccarat. Craps. Desperate-looking people with twisted smiles, puffing cigarettes, gulping booze and communicating with the dealers in a rapid patois. Who were these people? Where did they learn to talk like that?

I passed the gaming tables and made my way to the slot machines. Definitely less intimidating. It was pretty clear how to play them. I reached into my pocket, pulled out a quarter, slipped it into a machine and pulled the handle. Lights whirled while images of fruit whizzed around in a multicolored rush. When they slowed down and came to a stop, I had two oranges and a cherry. The machine emitted a friendly toot. I was surprised when it coughed up two quarters into its little change trough. I jutted my jaw, cocked my head and stared at the gleaming machine. I pocketed the change. "Fuck it, I'm ahead," I said to no one in particular. I spun on my heels, headed back through the lobby and out the doors.

On the boardwalk I thought, *So that's it, huh?* That's what all the fuss was about? Casinos. Big deal. Look at this boardwalk. Look at all these people. Jimmy had been wrong. I crossed the boards and set up shop near the railing, with my back to the ocean. First I took off my derby and dropped my casino winnings—well, my casino winning—into it. Next I took out my three juggling clubs and stood them up, balanced against one another, teepee-like.

"Ladies and gentlemen!" I cried, launching into a three-ball cascade. "Place your bets on Jason the Magnificent. How long can he juggle before he drops a ball? Which ball will he drop? Ladies and gentlemen," I intoned in a mock-serious voice, "these balls are numbered zero through two. All proceeds from Jason the Magnificent's Famous Juggling Lottery and Thrill Show will benefit Jason the Magnificent, thank you very much."

A crowd gathered. "Who came down on the bus?" I asked. Several hands went up. "Ladies and gentlemen, the Greyhound Juggle." I tossed one ball way up high; while it was in the air, I looked first at my watch, then in one direction down the boardwalk, then in the other direction. Meanwhile I purposely missed the ball. "Damn, missed it again."

Laughter. Soothing laughter. It was the best I'd felt in days.

"If you folks wouldn't mind, I'd really appreciate some appropriate oohing and ahhing as it will make my work a lot easier." I brought the pattern down until it became a blurred little cascade in my palms.

"Ooohhhh!" crowed the audience.

I made the pattern bigger, each throw flying fifteen feet into the air. "Here's something for you folks in the back of the crowd!"

"Ahhhhhh!" they cried. I threw my body into my work—half juggling and half dancing to the jazz tune playing in my head.

Next I juggled three clubs, then four balls, and then five. Soon I spotted a distinct wash of blue at the front of the crowd. Gazing through the five-ball pattern, I made out two policemen—a tall one and a short one. I stopped juggling and regarded the officers. "I know what you're thinking, ladies and gentlemen. You're thinking, 'Sure this guy's good, but can he juggle two nightsticks and a walkie-talkie?'"

I smiled and winked at the cops, hoping they'd give me a chance. They shook their heads. The tall one crossed his arms. "Show's over."

Why would a cop try to stop a guy from juggling—unless the guy was juggling something dangerous, like chain saws or babies?

"Show's over, son," the cop repeated, louder and more assertive. The crowd began shuffling away, turning their heads from time to time for a final glimpse while a few stragglers tossed coins into my derby.

"What time is my next show?" I asked.

The cop shook his head. "No soliciting on the boardwalk."

"I'm not soliciting," I said. "I'm performing. I'm Jason Benson. My dad owns the pretzel bakery at Texas Avenue. What's going on?"

"You're not allowed to put on shows on the boardwalk," said the tall cop.

"Since when?"

"Since now," he said, his voice rising. "I'm issuing you a warning . . ."

"You're warning me not to juggle? You're kidding, right? Did Jimmy put you guys up to this?"

The cops were not amused. "Yeah. I'm warning you not to juggle on the boardwalk," said the tall one. "And I'm warning you not to be a wiseass." He jabbed his fat finger at my face, nodding to his partner who pulled a little pad from his utility belt and wrote something on it.

"Just a warning," said the short cop, handing me the citation.

I stuffed it in my back pocket, packed my stuff and stormed up the boardwalk to the pretzel bakery. "Will you look at this?" I asked, slapping the citation on the counter. "Can you believe these bozos?"

Dad looked at the document, shaking his head. "Looks like they mean business."

"They can't stop me from doing shows. This is my livelihood. You can't just stop a guy from earning his livelihood!"

"Apparently they can stop you from doing shows on the boardwalk," he said. "It's always been technically illegal. But now they're enforcing it." He took off his glasses and whistled under his breath like a bomb dropping.

A couple of days later, Jimmy, Dad and I ate an early breakfast at a deli on Pacific Avenue.

I poured cream into my coffee and took a sip. "I may need to get away for a little while," I said as a young redheaded waitress brought us a plate of Danish pastries.

"Where to?" asked Dad.

"I was thinking maybe out west. Henry the Juggler told me about a bunch of places where street performers can do really well."

"New Orleans," said Jimmy, reaching across the table for a blueberry pastry. "Frisco."

"Don't worry, I won't just split," I said. "I'll stick around until we get somebody new trained. Couple weeks or whatever." Dad sat silently. Jimmy drained his coffee. The waitress came by and poured refills without asking.

Dad waved me off. "Go when you're ready. I've got enough help to get started; I'll hire another guy and we'll break him in before the season gets crazy."

The three of us made an awkward little toast with our coffee cups. Dad reached over the table and clasped my hand. "This is your home," he told me. "No matter where you go, no matter what you do, you always have a home."

I held back a swell of tears. "It's just so weird. Everything changed. I hate that."

Dad puffed his cheeks full of air and exhaled, hissing like a pressure cooker. He released my hand and mussed my hair. He finished his coffee and took a roll of bills out of his pocket, laying down a five for the waitress and handing me the rest. "Here's a couple hundred. If you need more, let me know."

I thanked him and pocketed the bills.

Dad stood up. "You guys take your time, but I've got to get a batch of dough mixed. Jason, will you be in by eight? I could use you today." Dad stepped out of the deli and disappeared around the corner.

I looked up at Jimmy. "I guess you were right about everything changing."

"It always does," he said.

"Let me ask you something." I could tell by his sly smile that Jimmy knew exactly what I was about to ask. I had little hope of a straight answer, but I plowed on. "How does it work?"

"How does what work?" he asked innocently.

"The derby."

Jimmy chuckled, exasperated. "That again?"

"Come on," I pleaded. "Tell me!"

"I swear I don't know." He finished his coffee and inspected the remaining pastry on the serving plate. "Wanna split it?"

I pouted. "You go ahead."

Jimmy licked at the filling, nibbled around the edge of the pastry and sank his teeth into the center. With his thumb he wiped a drop of blueberry from his bottom lip.

"If you don't know how," I asked, "can you tell me why?"

Jimmy looked up, a wide grin spreading across his face.

"What's so funny?" I asked.

"You never asked why before. You only asked how."

"Okay, now I'm asking why."

His grin faded. He looked me in the eye. "To protect you." He stuffed another hunk of pastry in his mouth and washed it down with a gulp of water.

"From what?"

Jimmy took his time to search for exactly the right word. "Bitterness," he said at last. That stung. *Bitterness* was exactly what Miss Smith had warned me against. "Happy now?" he asked. "It was so you won't grow up like the rest of the assholes out there, thinking, oh, you know everything. So no matter what, you'll always have a little mystery in your life, something you can't explain. Something not everybody's gonna believe."

"You're shitting me," I said.

He held up his hands and threw back his head. Jimmy meant business. He finished the pastry and patted his mouth with his napkin. "And maybe why you got taught to juggle was so you wouldn't end up like your friend."

Skip. I hadn't spoken with him in months—hadn't even told him I was leaving the neighborhood. I had no idea what he was doing next year, but I suspected whatever it was, he'd be doing it stoned out of his mind.

Jimmy leaned across the table, his gaze like a laser beam. "Listen to me. This is important."

I perked my ears.

"Stay the season. Your old man needs you."

"No, he doesn't. He can hire somebody else. He can replace me." I fingered the handle on the white porcelain coffee cup.

Jimmy pointed at me. "Nah, you're wrong. He needs ya this season."

I began to protest, but Jimmy talked right over me. "You seen him workin' in that heat? Hundred fuckin' degrees in there. You seen him sweatin' in that bakery like a coal miner? He *can't* replace you. He needs you, but he ain't gonna admit it. He don't trust nobody else to run the place. Gonna wear himself out, you understand?"

My mind was made up, but I knew better than to argue with Jimmy. You could ask him what he had for lunch and he wouldn't give you a straight answer. He actually believed he could read secret signs, like the smell of Atlantic City ending. But he was wrong. It wasn't ending—it was just changing.

"Do you understand?" Jimmy repeated, irritated. "Remember when Bobby had to leave? He still stayed the season."

I looked him square in the eye. "Okay."

ALL THE WAY at the south end of the boardwalk, there's an extra-wide ramp that the lifeguards use to drive their jeeps from the street to the beach. At the bottom of the incline, the ramp extends down the beach to where the sand's wet and hard. At three o'clock the next morning, in the pitch dark at low tide, I backed the Dart down the ramp so that its rear wheels touched the ocean itself. It was risky. Driving on the beach might or might not be as serious a crime as juggling on the boardwalk. I didn't want to get caught, and I didn't want to get stuck and look like an idiot, standing knee deep in the waves, trying to explain to a lifeguard why I was pushing my car out of the ocean.

It worked like a charm, though. I backed the Dart down the ramp, onto the hard sand in the pitch dark. The lolling waves grew louder, blotting out the grumbling engine—freshly oiled, fluids topped off, tuned up, with new tires and brakes.

It was my first trip anywhere outside of Philly or Atlantic City. A few hours earlier, I'd stopped by the arcade to say goodbye to Norman, Betty and Lita. I'd avoided Jimmy. Norman shook my hand and wished me well. Despite all the worry, he and Betty were having a decent season, and they planned on returning next year. He handed me a slip of paper.

"What's this?" I asked.

He pointed his thumb at the arcade's back office. "Phone number."

I stuffed the paper in my pocket. Betty hugged me and handed me a brown shopping bag full of cake and sandwiches. "A little something what to nosh on the road."

Lita kissed me on my cheek. "Be good," I told her.

"Take me with you?" she whispered desperately under her breath.

I shook my head no.

Now, as the water lapped at the tires, I stopped the car and cut the engine. I sat in the dark for several minutes, my throat and lungs seizing the ocean air. I rolled down the window, stuck my head out and cried, my tears adding extra salt to the wet sand.

Then I started the motor and eased the car out of the ocean, up the ramp, over the boardwalk, up to Ventnor Avenue, to Albany Avenue, to the causeway, to the mainland, to the highway, the turnpike, the interstate and another interstate, and another and another. I didn't know exactly where I was going, but I'd know when I arrived. I'd know by the smell.

A few days later, at ten o'clock on a Friday night, I pulled into the parking lot of a motor lodge in Boulder, Colorado. I paid cash for a room for a week, unloaded my stuff, took a hot shower, collapsed on the bed and slept for twelve hours. In the late morning I stepped out of my door and looked around. The Rocky Mountains loomed over this bright little town full of a curious mixture of men and women in cowboy hats, student types and hippies in drawstring pants and leather sandals. These people—so different, so much more colorful than the boardwalk crowd or the commuters on Chestnut Street—milled up and down the Pearl Street Mall, a four-block promenade tucked into the foothills. On this mall, people like me performed for crowds. There were jugglers, mimes, singers, a sword swallower; I watched a few of the acts, getting up close at the end to see what kind of tips they were making. Ten-dollar bills, even a couple of twenties. Better than Atlantic City. And shows in the daytime, not just at night. I quickly calculated: I could make a fortune here. I stopped and drew a deep breath through my nose. There it was: sea foam and salt air. I was home.

I spent a few hours walking around, checking out the people and the majestic mountains spread across the edge of the city. Finally I went back to my hotel room, grabbed my juggling stuff and headed back to the mall. After finding a good spot in front of the Mountain High ice cream shop, I studied the strolling crowd of tourists and hippies. I reached into my suitcase and pulled out my magic derby, set it lightly on my head and smoothed the rim with my fingers. I took out three lacrosse balls painted red, white and blue and began to juggle. Pretty soon a crowd gathered. At first they oohed and ahhed and laughed and applauded. But little by little, they realized they were watching something more than a clever juggling act. And they stood back and scratched their chins and scrunched their brows and grinned and watched.

I juggled better than the best night on the boardwalk. Better than the prom—my arms heaving the huge, wide cascade higher and higher, five balls arcing skyward and screaming to earth. "Come watch Mr. Boardwalk!" I shouted, my voice choked. "Direct from Atlantic City! Watch him hold the precious orbs in a delicate balance! Watch him throw what he's got! Watch him catch what comes. Please, hold your applause . . . but not your cash!" The sun went down and the rustic streetlamps on the mall blinked on. I kept juggling, drawing bigger and bigger crowds who gasped and clapped their hands and watched my patterns like they were looking at a meteor shower.

When the show was over, they wiped their eyes and stuffed money in my derby and told me I was magnificent.

24

THE END OF the boardwalk doesn't look the way I remember it. In my recollection, it widens at the island's northern tip, extending over the inlet, across which you can see the island of Brigantine. I recall fishermen lined against the railing, casting their lines into the ocean at high tide.

This afternoon it's windy and the tide is low. There are no fishermen. Captain Starn's is half demolished. The restaurant closed several years ago, and I cannot tell whether the marina is merely shuttered for the winter or permanently abandoned. I stand where Skip tried to feed a cigar to a sea lion. The sea lions are gone. The dry, gray cement pool sprawls like a discarded segment of a highway underpass. Nearby, waves roll up the beach, straining toward the boardwalk. Soon the tide will be high and the waves will wash against the pilings and rumble beneath the boards.

"This is it?" asks Ruth.

"It's different than I remember," I say.

Unmoved by the view, Ruth looks up at me. She wants me to continue my story. "I was in Boulder for four months," I say. "I had a hotel room, and I had money. I was making a good living juggling on the mall. In October we had a cold snap and I couldn't juggle. I was thinking about heading down to New Orleans. Jimmy had always told me that New Orleans was a good town for street performers. But I decided to stay in Boulder. I liked it. I holed up in my hotel room for three weeks and learned to juggle seven balls."

"*Seven?*" asks Ruth. "You can juggle seven balls?"

"It's been a while, but yeah, if I had a little practice, I'm pretty sure I still can. But juggling shouldn't be a numbers thing. I should have learned to pass, you know? I never learned to work with other jugglers.

"Anyway, I stayed in my room and practiced—you know, came out for meals and a cup of coffee once in a while. But for three weeks I was pretty much a hermit, until I could juggle seven, until I'd mastered a hundred throws a hundred times in a row. With seven balls, there are no real tricks, not a lot of variations; it's all you can do just to keep the cascade going. With seven balls, that *is* the trick.

"So, I come out of the hotel and I walk over to the mall, but before I do my show I go to a pay phone and call my dad. It's Saturday night. It's nine o'clock in Boulder and eleven o'clock in Philly. But he doesn't pick up. So I do my show. I juggle three balls with all the tricks and patter; and I juggle five, and I juggle my clubs; and then I go for the big finale, the seven-ball cascade, which went over well. The pattern was so high that people saw it from a block away. Big crowds. Good money.

"I did three shows that night and then I tried calling Dad again. By then it was one o'clock in the morning in Philly. No answer. I figured he was asleep already. But in the morning I still couldn't reach him. Now I'm a little worried, so I call Norman and Betty. And that's how I found out. He'd had a heart attack, two weeks before. Just like his dad. He was in his car. He was parked outside a warehouse. He'd been inside buying parts for an oven. He got in the car and he slumped over."

"You missed your dad's funeral," Ruth says, like she has solved a mystery.

"I missed my dad's funeral," I admit. "But worse. I abandoned him. Mid-season, when he needed me."

At last we've arrived at the truth. "If I'd stayed . . ."

But I didn't stay. I can't change that. And so far I haven't done too good a job of living with it. Would he have had his heart attack if I'd stayed around? Maybe. But I didn't ever want to face Jimmy and hear his opinion. So I crammed Atlantic City and my memories of it in the box in the closet—along with my juggling gear, my magic derby, my stuffed dog Floppy, Lita's conch shell and the deed to the house on Virginia Avenue.

Wincing, I fill in the details for Ruth and Eileen. "No one knew how to reach me. I used to check in every couple days, but when I was learning the seven balls I forgot to call. They waited as long as they could, and then they buried him. Later, I learned that Skip's dad had put up the money for the funeral. No one even knew how to reach Mom's parents."

Ruth nods. "You must have felt like a real shit."

"Jimmy warned me, but I blew him off."

Eileen raises her hand to her mouth. She gets it. She sees who I am: a man who pissed away his gift; who scapegoated his first love, his best friend, his favorite teacher and his family.

Incomprehensively, Eileen holds out her arms. I fall into them. I clasp Ruth and the three of us hold one another.

HALF A BLOCK off the boardwalk at the inlet is a small row of businesses—a barbershop, a pawnshop and a dollar store. Noticing the shops, Ruth slips from our embrace. Holding up one finger to signal that she'll be right back, she dashes down the ramp and slips into the dollar store. Eileen and I rest our hands on the boardwalk railing and watch the ocean.

"I was afraid of what you'd think if you found out I abandoned my dad and pretty much caused his death," I tell Eileen. "It's the worst thing I've ever done. I was afraid that if I told you about the house, I'd have to tell you everything. And I didn't want you to see me like that. Then the longer I didn't tell you, the more impossible it became." Tears sting my eyes. "I'm so sorry my mom and dad never got to know you and Ruth."

Eileen tugs at my collar, puts her hand to my chest. As she presses near my heart, I think about my soaring cholesterol level. "I don't want to die suddenly like my father and his father," I tell her. "I want to change. I'll exercise, I'll eat better, and there's a pill to lower the cholesterol. But if something is going to happen, I want things to be okay."

She rests her head on my shoulder, holds her face against mine. Her breath is warm and smells like fudge. I close my eyes and breathe with her until I cannot distinguish between her breathing and my own, or between us and the sound the waves make when they lap at the shore, or the thrum of the wind, or a teeming river running its course, or the fatty blood in my arteries.

A minute later, Ruth returns with a plastic shopping bag, holding it open so we can see inside. She has invested in nine apple-red rubber balls. "Teach us?" she asks.

I swallow hard. My daughter smiles, radiant and wise, like a woman who knows the right thing to say. I put one arm around her and I take Eileen's hand. Our fingers entwine. I think about seven balls—about a cascade so fast it's no longer seven objects but one single, blurred thing, a wild pattern you can't stop to think about or it will come apart.

An hour later, having caught a bus back to Virginia Avenue, we're at the house. The sun's still out, but the sky is flat gray. The temperature has dropped to the high thirties.

I find the key and we enter through the back door. Eileen and Ruth follow, like archeologists on a dig. The kitchen is unremarkable—pale yellow and moldy. On the outside of the refrigerator are last year's calendar and a menu for Al's Pizza on Ventnor Avenue.

But the living room looks different. There's the checkered sofa I saw earlier today through the window, and the rickety card table and the hutch loaded with snow globes and cheap commemorative plates. I know all of this is mine, but it's unfamiliar and random, like a bargain basement. Earlier today, I couldn't see the wall, but now I can. It's lined with framed paintings of fruit baskets, sailboats and flowers. They're my mom's. Skip's dad or Norman or Monty Dweck must have brought them from Philadelphia after Dad died.

Like visitors at a gallery, we study my mother's work.

I crank up the thermostat. We push the chairs aside. We kick off our shoes. The radiator hisses. I show Eileen and Ruth a simple three-ball cascade. I'm a little rusty, but it all comes back. My hips and shoulders relaxed, feet planted on the carpet, I work the balls effortlessly, throwing high, throwing low, tossing overhand, behind my back and under my legs. I return to a simple cascade, my throws wide and big. "See how there's a moment when the ball isn't going up and it isn't going down? That's called the *peak*. That's where the magic happens—at the peak. See? Right . . . *there*! That's when you make a throw—when the throw before it isn't going up and isn't coming down. If it's not going up and it's not coming down, just that split second, it's like the sun in the sky. Now . . . you try."

We throw. We catch. The balls bob in spiky, sloppy cascades—patterns we cannot fathom yet strive to maintain. They bounce and collide. We shuffle, we falter. We stoop to recover. We throw and catch, throw and catch.

It's the middle of March. By June I think we'll be passing.

Acknowledgments

The author would like to thank the following people and organizations, without whose assistance, support, feedback and encouragement this novel would never have seen the light of day: Mark Arost, Barry Greenstein and Catherine Greenstein; current and past members of the Working Writers Group of Philadelphia, including Robin Black, Eliza Callard, Ann de Forest, Bonnie Gordon, Doug Gordon, Neal Gordon, Larry Loebell, Mark Lyons, Ligia Ravé, David Sanders, Debra Leigh Scott, Miriam Seidel, and Martha Witte; Kate Ferber, Steve and Louie Asher, Barbara and Charles Blum, Larry Pitt, and David Bradley; Gap International and Maria Little from the Center for Operational Oceanographic Products and Services.

Finally, thanks to Dream Forge, Inc., which published an online, very different version of *Mr. Boardwalk* in serial installments in 1997–98.